FROM THE R

The End of ~~My Tether~~

by NEIL ASTLEY

SHORTLISTED FOR THE
WHITBREAD FIRST NOVEL AWARD

'A tour de force, addressing topical and pertinent issues in a wholly original and powerful way. Funny, challenging, provocative, harrowing. Above all else, angry.' – Whitbread Award judges JOANNA TROLLOPE, BONNIE GREER & JAMES DAUNT

'A brilliantly readable, wildly funny and macabre novel. *The End of My Tether* sucks you into a world of crime and mayhem in rural England. It's a detective story, a startlingly original handling of myth and magic, and a scorching analysis of the way we live now.' – HELEN DUNMORE

'Neil Astley's debut novel is a work of daunting ambition and massive imagination…often bizarre, gleefully irreverent, grotesque or delightful. In the scene in which Kernan goes to meet the devil, for example, we find Margaret Thatcher, who is literally an old dragon, residing in the fifth circle of hell.' – *Independent on Sunday*

'Despite being critically ignored upon its publication last year, the debut novel by the poet Neil Astley was justly shortlisted for the Whitbread First Novel Award. Now republished, this deeply strange and highly original book, measure for measure infuriating and exhilarating, will with luck reach the wider audience it deserves…The book posits a world in which witches coexist with BSE and ministry inspectors, and where an acrid stench in a secluded hollow could as easily be brimstone as organophosphate…A dense, funny and imaginative style guarantees that this book may be remembered for a long time, and some may very well fall in love with it.' – CHRIS POWER, *The Times*

'*The End of My Tether* deserves to be a classic of British political fiction.' – ANDY CROFT, *Morning Star*

THE SHEEP WHO CHANGED THE WORLD

NEIL ASTLEY was born in Hampshire, home to many flocks of South-down sheep, the oldest English breed and the favoured prime lamb sire for Romneys. He was the black sheep of his family, the only one to return from Australia, where he found the sheep lacking in character as well as variety, most being Merinos: fine-woolled Spanish or Saxony types, medium-woolled Peppin Merinos (crossed progeny of French Rambouillet Merinos) or South Australian strong-woolled Merinos. He is now pleased to be living in Northumberland's Tarset valley, where his close neighbours include Swaledales, Scottish Blackfaces, Suffolks, Leicesters (both Border and Blue-faced), North Country Cheviots and North of England Mules, with Jacob sheep in the field opposite and Soays just over the hill. *The Sheep Who Changed the World*, his second novel, was inspired by this plentiful sheepscape.

Neil Astley founded Bloodaxe Books in 1978, and was given a D.Litt. by Newcastle University for his pioneering work. He has edited over 800 poetry books, and has published several anthologies, including *Staying Alive* (Bloodaxe, UK, 2002; Miramax, USA, 2003) and *Being Alive* (Bloodaxe, UK, 2004; Anansi, Canada, 2005), as well as Bloodaxe's *Poetry with an Edge* (1988/1993), *New Blood* (1999), *Pleased to See Me: 69 very sexy poems* (2002), *Do Not Go Gentle: poems for funerals* (2003) and *Passionfood: 100 love poems* (2005). He won an Eric Gregory Award for his own poetry, and has published two collections, *Darwin Survivor* (Peterloo, 1988), a Poetry Book Society Recommendation, and *Biting My Tongue* (Bloodaxe, 1995). His previous novel, *The End of My Tether* (Flambard, 2002; Scribner, 2003), was shortlisted for the Whitbread First Novel Award in 2002.

He has always had a thing about sheep.

THE SHEEP
WHO CHANGED
THE WORLD

Neil Astley

*Flambard***Press**

First published in the UK in 2005 by Flambard Press
Stable Cottage, East Fourstones, Hexham NE47 5DX

Typeset by Harry Novak
Cover design by Gainford Design Associates
Front cover photograph of the ram
Pennine Rangers Black Jack by Justine Lester
Printed in England by Cromwell Press, Trowbridge, Wiltshire

A CIP catalogue record for this book
is available from the British Library.

ISBN 1 873226 75 6

Flambard Press wishes to thank Arts Council England
for its financial support.

Website: www.flambardpress.co.uk

Flambard Press is a member of Inpress
and Independent Northern Publishers

For Pamela

ACKNOWLEDGEMENTS

For general inspiration, thanks are due to Dolly, Mickey the Judas sheep, Harry Novak, and all the sheep of the Tarset valley, especially my nineteen former muses, the noble and boisterous Suffolk tups I used to watch from my window, who were murdered by a Ministry death-squad on New Year's Day 2002 along with 2100 other sheep in Martin Weeks's flock who did not have Foot and Mouth Disease, the last animals in England to be massacred in the recent conflict. Thanks are due also, for helpful suggestions, to Ben Ball, Caradoc King, Martha Lishawa, Peter & Margaret Lewis and Will Mackie; to Simon & Gwennie Fraser for Culnacraig, where the book was dagged and docked; and to Sheila Pratschke for the time at the Tyrone Guthrie Centre, Annaghmakerrig, where it was dipped, washed, trimmed and made ready for the show.

CONTENTS

CHAPTER | PAGE

1 In the Beginning — 11
2 Box of Tricks — 20
3 Donor Kebab — 26
4 Confessions of a Double Agent — 36
5 Wagging the Doc — 41
6 Parlez-vous Mouton? — 56
7 Escape from Clovitz — 66
8 Never Alone with a Clone — 78
9 The Holly Trap — 85
10 Sheepman, Shaman — 91
11 Ram Raiders — 104
12 Is Ewe Is or Is Ewe Ain't My Baby? — 116
13 The Great Escape — 124
14 Baarmy Army — 135
15 Gross Misconduct — 148
16 The Sheep of Hearts — 159
17 The Ram of God — 170
18 The Trojan Sheep — 186
19 Mothers of All — 204
20 Double Trouble — 216
21 Doubles All Round — 227
22 Double Topped — 232
23 Batty Men Are Bad Examples — 240
24 Any Other Business? — 245

CHAPTER ONE

In the Beginning

The sheep's second birthday was celebrated by the humans with champagne. He watched their noisy party from his observation pen. They laughed and cheered as the corks popped, especially when one went flying over his head and was lost in the straw.

They drank ten green bottles of the fizzy wine but did not offer him a single glass, even though it was his birthday. He thought they could at least have put some in the sipper-bottle attached to the grille for him to try. They used the sipper when they wanted to trick him into drinking funny-tasting liquids, when he'd pretend not to recognise their deception.

He ate or drank whatever he was given because he didn't want to arouse their suspicion. He knew these people wanted to keep him alive because he was special, which meant it should be safe to accept whatever they administered, even the injections, but sometimes these had a sedative effect, impairing his ability to concentrate, which the sheep found highly frustrating. Stein had even joked about giving him a liquid cosh, a weapon apparently used by the humans for clubbing violent men to sleep. At such times he would fight his own body to stay alert.

The scientists only seemed interested in more obvious physical symptoms, such as chemical changes in his blood and urine. They weren't aware that on certain days – especially when their tests and talk concerned his immune system – he struggled to follow their conversations. Listening to the scientists was important to him. As he'd grown up he'd absorbed all his knowledge from everything he heard and saw in the laboratory. He hung on their every word while keeping his craving well hidden, a junkie hooked on a substance he couldn't handle, or not at first. Their language was the stuff of life and he was secretly stuffing himself with it, taking in so much that he feared his woolly head would burst under the strain.

He shared their thirst for knowledge, but knowledge for the humans meant power, and their powers were limited by what they didn't understand; whereas for him, knowledge was freedom, which had no bounds.

In the beginning was the lab, and his pen in the lab; that was all he knew. Then he'd learned how their white-walled room had a hard grey shell on the outside, and was part of a larger world called the Clovis Institute, whose many shells were made from speckly concrete and hundreds of brown bricks, with many windows of glass, like those letting light into the lab which he couldn't quite see from his pen but knew must be there. He'd seen how big his world was when they'd put him outside to eat grass in the Field. And how beyond the perimeter fence, there lay the World Outside His World, where the humans went at the end of each day.

The first language he heard was Labtalk, a jumble of long words which took him many months to unravel. Labtalk made frequent use of the names of chemicals as well as initials and formulae, and often related to the mysterious DNA and what he'd first heard as 'jeans' and 'jean gnomes'. When they talked about the sheep and what they were doing to him and the other animals, the scientists always used Labtalk, as a kind of disguise he'd thought, to communicate with each other without the animals understanding; and later he'd noted how this technical language did have this effect when spoken in the presence of Visitors from the Outside World.

But when they left their machines and instruments to drink coffee at the big table, they usually spoke Worldtalk, which became more interesting to him as time passed. He learned more about the Outside World when they spoke in Worldtalk, even though Worldtalk featured the names of people he didn't know and references to many unfamiliar ideas. Sometimes they spoke for several minutes in Worldtalk but only about Football, and he would kick at the straw, impatient to hear about some other subject. Stomping around the pen in disgust always produced this response from the scientists:

'Our sheep is clearly a beast of some intelligence and discrimination,' Dr Donald Macannie would say, or words to that effect, in his strange high-pitched whinnying voice. 'Have you noticed how he always gets excited when we talk about futeball?'

'Perhaps we should do some research on why sheep are so interested in football,' Sean Shenanigan would add in his sing-song voice. And then turning to Dr Gumption: 'How about it, Mark?'

'Or maybe train the sheep to play,' the horse-voiced Macannie would continue. 'He'd make a gude winger, I'm sairtin o' that. He wude be sure to be picked for England.'

'A big improvement on most of your current squad,' Sean Shenanigan would assert.

Dr Gumption's gruff response to this was always: 'Four nil, Sean. Four nil.'

The sheep couldn't follow this at first. The numbers made it sound like Labtalk, but it clearly wasn't. He'd puzzled over conversations of this kind, especially those in which the same enigmatic phrases were repeated, for this must indicate that such statements had a particular significance.

Sometimes it seemed that the more he learned, the less he thought he knew. He'd learned to recognise the oddities of their speech, but didn't know why they chose to speak differently from one another, nor why where they had lived before they came to Clovis seemed to affect how they wanted to speak. Dr Macannie had a different vocal range from Dr Stein, and substituted an alternative set of vowels in his speech to those used by the others, although always with consistency, but seemingly for the sole reason that the others needed to be reminded that Dr Macannie was born in a place called Scotland where foke lived in hoozes, but never spent a penny, if the other scientists were to be believed.

Dr Macannie had difficulty in pronouncing certain consonants, making a choking noise at the back of his throat like a sheep coughing. Dr Shenanigan's speech was lilting as well as soapy while Dr Gumption's was base and piglike. Dr Stein's voice sounded as though he strained it through grit before subjecting

13

the words to electricity, which made them crackle on his tongue.

The sheep was often confused by their humour, for what they found funny was rarely strange. Why did they keep referring to him as the black sheep of the family when most flocks had a black sheep but none of the humans had ovine characteristics to match his human ones? And what he found funny in their behaviour or talk wasn't considered at all odd by them.

Now they were telling more of those jokes which weren't funny. The champagne had made them speak more quickly and with great excitement at first, but later its effects seemed to reverse, and they talked more slowly, saying insulting things to one another which they didn't appear to mind. Each of the humans took great delight in being rude about another's country or city of origin as well as in having their own appearance or their hair or liking for particular kinds of music derided by everyone else; even non-animate possessions such as a person's clothing or car were subjected to this ridicule.

He didn't really mind not drinking the champagne for he suspected it would taste just as odd as their chemical solutions. It was certainly making the humans act strangely. What he *did* mind, though, was that they had stolen his celebration for themselves, for this was meant to be his birthday, not theirs. They had decided to party on his behalf, almost as if to rub Sodium Chloride in his wounds, yet he was the party animal. It made him acutely aware of his powerlessness.

He would have to act soon or the continuing frustration would be unbearable.

They stood in front of the pen, telling him they were drinking his health, but he couldn't see how this was possible, unless it was another of their subterfuges. How could his health be affected by their drinking? Did the champagne stop them from thinking scientifically? It certainly made them speak more in Worldtalk, encouraging them to make statements whose logic seemed flawed by bizarre misconceptions. Was this why they drank it, to escape from their usual cage of Labtalk?

The sheep had become more and more conscious of the different ways in which the humans lied to one another, but the champagne seemed to make them want to tell even bigger whoppers. Many of their whoppers seemed pointless, such as lying to a sheep whom they believed was incapable of under-standing them. When Dr Mark Gumption injected him with his mother of all syringes, he always gave him false assurances beforehand, saying 'This won't hurt', despite the fact that a sheep would feel pain just as much as a human when its muscle tissue was pierced with a metal spike.

The birthday cake was decorated with a crude likeness of his face in chocolate icing, with two yellow Smarties representing his eyes. Underneath were some words which he knew spelled out the greeting HAPPY BIRTHDAY WALLY.

The two candles were set on fire by one of the scientists with a cigarette-lighter. They held the cake jokingly in front of him, inviting him to make a wish – which he was pleased to do – but believing he was unable even to blow out a pair of candles, they whisked his cake away, and that honour went to Dr Stein, who by this time had drunk so much champagne that it took him three attempts to put out the flames.

Then they sang. 'Happy birthday to you, happy birthday to you. Happy birthday, dear Wally, happy birthday to you.'

And when someone shouted 'Speech! Speech!' the sheep cleared his throat in readiness to oblige, but checked himself, knowing this would not be a good time to acquaint them with one of the unforeseen consequences of their meddling with Nature. Not even Dr Stein was yet aware of the precise effects of the changes he had secretly made in the cloning procedure 30 months before.

Dr Stein was sitting slumped in a swivel chair, staring glum-faced at his colleagues, clearly reluctant to embarrass himself and them with a best man's speech.

The sheep knew they valued Stein's scientific knowledge but wouldn't trust him as far as they could throw him, which seemed to indicate a low level of trust, given that he carried so much excess body fat. He'd heard someone call him 'a failure as a human being'. The sheep had taken this as a reference to his extramarital affairs with female colleagues, which had prompted his wife to leave him, taking their daughters with her. The other scientists had criticised Stein's ideas as 'extreme' and 'unethical', but he was 'a first-rate clinician', whatever that meant; he was said to be 'a brilliant molecular biologist', which excused his many faults and failings in other areas, both personal and professional.

Dr Stein in turn was suspicious of his fellow workers, especially Dr Helen Brimstone, the blonde embryologist. He glared at her now and she smiled and stuck her tongue out at him in a gesture seemingly unconnected with food. The sheep had observed the two scientists sniffing each other and pressing their mouths together on several occasions when they thought they were alone in the laboratory, but he had not witnessed them engaging in these acts of human intimacy for some time, and when other colleagues were present they were noticeably less friendly towards each other.

The sheep was especially fond of Dr Brimstone. She brought him bars of fruit-and-nut chocolate and liked to stroke his head. He had no difficulty in following her speech. Her voice had a pleasing clarity, its pitch high and sweet as the song of the blackbird who often greeted him from the tree in the Field.

The person Dr Stein most disliked was the head of the Institute, Dr Steve Weisenheimer, whom he called a 'stupid git' and a 'small-minded bureaucrat' out of his hearing, likening him to a Hammerhead Shark. The sheep agreed with this assessment, for the sharp-suited shark had apparently Got-where-he'd-Got not just by being a good liar, which he had learned was a statutory requirement in such management posts, but more worryingly through his widely celebrated stupidity and hammerheadedness. The others referred to their executive elasmobranch as Dr Gardengnomer and Short Arse.

The sheep had believed the intensity of Stein's enmity was due in part to the short-bottomed man's unequal relationship with Helen Brimstone. He had seen the two grappling when they thought they were alone in the laboratory, Dr Brimstone leaning over her diminutive boss like a heron juggling a slippery fish in its bill. He later discounted this theory on realising that Dr Stein was unaware that Dr Brimstone had bent over backwards to accommodate the little upstart.

The phrase the humans used for this behaviour was 'behind my back'. It was an expression he'd frequently heard in the laboratory, applied to their relationships with other humans as well as to the running of the Institute and the organisation of the research project. Yet what happened behind their backs never happened behind their backs but after they had vacated the premises or in other places entirely.

Now he watched as Helen Brimstone cut the cake into several sectors of approximately equal size and volume. He knew what was going to happen next. These humans were so predictable. They prided themselves on their intelligence but seemed to give so much noddle to their scientific work that when it came to everyday conversation they were as clueless as bluebottles.

What they said to each other was often noddleless, silly, obvious or just not worth giving their eye teeth to say it. If other animals could talk they would want to use language accurately as well as with evident relish and all due respect, not waste it on blather, lies, insults and small talk, not to mention truncated interjections of no apparent meaning. The sheep couldn't understand why the humans asked one another things they didn't want to know about. Or why they pressed each other for opinions when they'd already decided that the other person's views weren't worth spending tuppence haypenny.

They asked after each other's health in the mornings despite having no interest in the welfare of the other person. The answers they gave were usually lies. They would claim to be feeling well when suffering from some sickness, such as a head cold, or more usually a bad hangover in Dr Stein's case, also advising one another to treat ailments with witchcraft, including hair from a dog to absorb excess alcohol and witch hazel for boils or scabs.

'Now, Wally,' Helen Brimstone was saying to him, 'do you want some of your nice cake? You should have the piece with your name on it. I'm sure you'd like that.'

He stared at her, playing the part of the uncomprehending sheep, even when she showed him the top of the cake with the words spelled out in brown chocolate fondant letters on the pink icing. WALLY, it said, like an insult sprayed on a wall.

He recognised the letters. How could he *not* fail to recognise them? The same letters were on the white placard above his pen.

It wasn't his name. It was their name for him, and a joke. Dr Stein said he had christened him Wally because he was a ram and Wally sounded like Woolly and it rhymed with Dolly, the name of the first cloned sheep. The men who'd cloned Dolly

from a ewe's udder had named her after a popular singer called
Dolly Parton who was famous for having especially large breasts.
The sheep was aware from listening to the scientists that men
preferred women who had large mammary glands and low IQs
to women who were noted for their intelligence, gentleness or
sensitivity because rejecting them later was less troublesome.

If he'd been a ewe lamb, they'd have probably called him –
or her – Molly. But why should he have a man's name, Wally,
which was moreover a name most often given to foolish people?
And how could a sheep be christened when only humans were
Christians? Was this because they were fans of a star called Jesus
Christ who was also the Lamb of God, which meant he was
both sheep and man – just as the sheep now knew he was –
and their Good Shepherd looked after sheep as well as humans?

The sheep agreed with Dr Brimstone that male biologists
had single-tracked minds. They seemed to spend most of their
time thinking about what she called the Four Esses: Science,
Sport, Self and Sex. They lacked imagination, failing to see what
was right in front of their noses or to use what was right in
front of their occipitals. Their brains might be full of scientific
knowledge, but they were basically stupid and unaware. They
passed many remarks concerning the unusual shape and size of
his head, and knew from the X-rays that his large skull accom-
modated an unusually large sheep brain, yet their own cerebrums
and cerebellums must be synaptically dysfunctional. They kept
telling visitors what an intelligent sheep he was, but only Stein
had made valid attempts to test his intelligence. The others
seemed more interested in the nitrogenous strength of his urine
and texture of his stool than in his rational capabilities.

He felt sorry for Stein, especially when the boffin tested him
for curiosity and most laughably for shape recognition. Did he
really think a silly sheep could match his pairs of shapes, his
cube and star and sphere? Although secretly pleased that Stein
hadn't given up, that he was still trying it on, he saw this chimps'
tea-party charade not as a test but as an insult to his intelligence.
Wouldn't even a monkey want to deliberately flunk such a
challenge? The sheep felt like telling Stein *he* couldn't match
his own socks, let alone a pair of chromosomes, but knew it
was too early to reveal himself and show his hoof. Macannie's

monetary catchphrase rang in his ears: caution is the better part of valour, Frank. He still had to learn more about the humans and the Outside World if he was to make a successful escape from the laboratory.

'Come on, Wally,' urged Helen Brimstone, her voice sickly and patronising. 'Open your mouth. We've saved this piece just for you. Look, it's got your name on the icing.'

It couldn't be his name. It was too demeaning to him as a ram, just as Dolly's name was an insult to her as a ewe. He wanted to choose his own name, not have the humans decide it for him.

But he opened his mouth and let Helen Brimstone feed him his piece of birthday cake decorated with their name for him, WALLY. He ate the name. He destroyed it with his own tongue.

She patted his head, and he looked up at her as if in gratitude. *Nothing going on up here*, he assured her with his eyes. *I may be a clone but I'm just a stupid sheep, as stupid as the rest of them.*

'Oh look,' she called to the others. 'Wally's giving me that cute look again. I'm sure he fancies me.'

'Rather him than me,' responded Dr Macannie sourly. 'Maybe you shude stick to sheep in future, Helen, and you'll have less trouble with the wives. I think you'll find that sheep are less possessive.'

'Just because you don't know a good thing, Donald, it doesn't mean the rest of us are so blinkered,' said Dr Mark Gumption. 'Come on, Helen, we don't want to lose you to Wally Mutton-chops yet. Have another drink before you think about throwing your lot in with the welly brigade.'

'That's right,' agreed Sean Shenanigan. 'Leave the sheep to Ron Devally.'

'But having met Ron's sister,' Mark Gumption grunted, 'I can see why the Welshman's thoughts must stray often to the sheep. Welsh women never stop talking and when they laugh they shriek like witches. Give me a sheep any day.'

'Hear that, Wally?' Shenanigan called out. 'Dr Gumption wants a date with you. But let him do all the talking, or he won't go out with you again, so.'

'That's right,' added Macannie. 'Gumption likes 'em meek and mild as lambs. Don't give him an earrrfule or you'll be oot on your earrrs. He thinks sheep shude be seen and not haired.'

CHAPTER TWO

Box of Tricks

The sheep had started to learn much more about the Outside World when Dr Gumption had brought the Box with three names: first it was the Box, then the Television and finally the TV, but its names were soon interchangeable, none seeming to carry any more specific or qualified nuance of meaning than another. This Box had looked to him like a computer except that the screen-saver was showing apparently real people who were moving about instead of the usual uninteresting sequences of still photographs of women in their birthday skins.

The first time they switched on this machine it started to show moving pictures of Dr Stein holding a test-tube up to the light, the first time the sheep had seen him do this. Then he took a rubber stopper to connect the test-tube to one of the glass pipes he only ever used for sniffing white cleaning powder when his nose was blocked. While the pictures showed him doing other inexplicable things with pieces of laboratory equipment, he was speaking in Labtalk about the work of the Clovis Institute, but without moving his lips. Then the Television showed Dr Weisenheimer speaking in Worldtalk about how Dr Stein's important work with sheep and glass pipes required large amounts of money, and he lied through his shark's teeth about Stein, calling him a brilliant man, whereas only the day before he'd told everyone that Stein was not only incontinent but a Liar Billity.

Afterwards, Dr Gumption said they needed to keep the Box so that they could watch more pictures of themselves pretending to be scientists, as well as programmes which spied on the work of others in their Field, but the sheep had noticed that it seemed to be used mostly for showing fields of footballers, always when Dr Weisenheimer was absent.

As the days grew warmer, the Box showed a strange sport called Cricket which he'd mistaken at first for some kind of elaborate religious ritual. In this game the ball was a small red sphere. The humans playing it looked from a distance like a flock of sheep grazing in a field, for they were dressed entirely in white. One man ran in and threw the ball very fast at another man standing in front of three sticks, who tried to hit it with a wooden thing like a broom with a flat board at the end instead of a brush with bristles. There were sometimes birds in this field – seagulls or pigeons – but never any animals.

The sheep had followed many other sorts of ball games with particular interest at first, believing that they must hold some key to what happened in the World Outside. Otherwise why did the humans spend so much time watching such apparently meaningless activities, and why did these sports arouse them to the extent that they would shout abuse or cheer wildly and be ecstatically happy one moment but then morose or threatening the next? The ball games seemed to excite that emotion they called Competition which he had at first imagined to be religious in nature since it involved bizarre rituals, maniacal fervour and apparently false logic.

In all their games, the humans would either throw or kick the ball, or hit it with some kind of stick or implement. The sheep could easily kick a ball with one of his fore hooves, but he couldn't throw a ball, nor could he hit one with a big stick because he couldn't hold a stick. He wondered how that felt, to hit a ball with a big stick. It must feel good in some way because the humans liked doing it so much, and if they couldn't take part in these games themselves, they would switch on the Box in order to watch other humans hitting a ball with a big stick, or kicking it, or throwing it. But after some months of watching these different games the humans played with various kinds and sizes of balls, the sheep was none the wiser, and wished the scientists would use their Box to show more interesting things about the Outside World.

The day the remote was lost was his day of salvation. It had fallen under a table, and then someone had inadvertently kicked it across the laboratory. Ron Devally had just finished changing his straw, and was closing the gate when the TV remote skimmed across the floor and through the gap into the observation pen. No one saw. The sheep stopped it with his hoof, shuffling it under the straw to the side wall, where he nudged it behind the feed trough. After several searches of the lab failed to disinter it, Gumption bought a new remote, leaving the sheep with exclusive use of its prototype.

When the last scientist left the lab at night, he would wait until he heard a car start up outside before pushing the trough forward, easing the remote out with a careful hoof-shove. He quickly learned that pressing different coloured buttons made the Box show other kinds of programmes, which meant his viewing wasn't restricted to the baffling things the humans liked.

The sheep especially liked the channel for human stories, which were called Soap Operas, although he couldn't see what they had to do with soap or opera, unless the soap was used to clean the shit from the fan, and opera meant that the story shouldn't involve animals. These humans only ever washed themselves when some-one had just punched them in the face. He'd seen other shows called operas in which fat people in garish clothes didn't talk or behave normally but strutted about like deranged cockerels crowing to each other in alien languages which had to be trans-lated into writing at the bottom of the screen while musicians tried to drown out the noise of their wailing, and these operas didn't have any animals in them.

The only animals in soap operas were dogs and cats, and there were far fewer of these than in the homes of the humans from the Clovis Institute. He'd learned from their conversations that each scientist had to house not only a family of humans – including the offspring of his latest wife in addition to his own – but also a variable number of what were called domestic animals, enslaved creatures who were forced to live with the humans. The cats were the most fortunate of these because they could roam the Outside World at night, returning through their own cat-sized doors to sleep or eat, but the dogs were only allowed outside with a human guard who kept them on a chain and even collected their excrement in small bags to prevent other dogs or anyone else from eating it. The sheep had heard that birds and rodents were imprisoned in small cages, while many different kinds of coloured fishes were brought from tropical countries which the scientists had to keep in large tanks of water whose temperature and acidity were monitored like one of their experiments in the laboratory, although non-scientists only had to keep the orange-coloured fishes which required less maintenance and supervision.

The humans in the soap operas spent most of their time shouting at each other. The stories switched from house to house, and in each house there was a room where two or more humans would gather for an argument, or sometimes they met to hit each other, and then they had to go to a Hospital, which were big buildings like the Institute where sick or injured humans lived. Humans drove their cars so badly they would crash, or they fell off roofs or went to places which were about to catch fire so that they could be hurt and taken to these Hospitals. This was called gambling with their lives.

The sheep thought humans were lucky to have cars and be able to go where they wanted in them. They weren't imprisoned like him in an observation pen in an Institute. If sheep could drive cars, they would use them to drive to fields where there was fresh grass, or to people's gardens where he knew there were many different kinds of plants to eat. A sheep wouldn't drive a car so fast that it crashed. Humans were meant to be clever but they were often very stupid and highly volatile in the manner of certain unstable chemical compounds.

But the sheep still liked to watch these stories because they helped him understand human behaviour. Most of what he'd learned about human emotions and intelligence had come from the soap operas, which demonstrated the workings of Badness. These stories were so helpfully simple and straightforward that at first he'd thought they were shown to teach children how adults behaved, so that children could learn Badness from these examples of adult behaviour. They showed bad things and negative emotions, like anger, fear, greed and jealousy. They were all about obsession and ambition, conflict and competition, cynicism and betrayal.

In the laboratory, his knowledge of how the humans lived was limited. There were not many women working at Clovis,

23

and no children at all. The stories shown by the Box indicated that the Outside World was dominated by men just as Clovis was, but that everything the men did related in some way to the women, much more so than in the Institute, where the women's roles were either subsidiary or servile. Sometimes the male humans wanted or needed to please the females, but more often they pretended to do or say things which the females liked in order to achieve their clandestine objectives.

The sheep thought that the women showed far more intelligence and social awareness than the men; they were much more interested in what was going on around them, and they seemed more complex as individuals, and yet the humans organised their world to fit to the men's tunnel vision and to serve their selfish wishes. The children seemed wiser than the older humans in many ways, spending most of their time playing or learning about the world. He had discovered that human childhood lasted longer than the whole life of a sheep. If a sheep wasn't killed and eaten by the humans, it might be a mother at just two years old – his age – and then spend the next ten years having more lambs every spring.

A sheep seemed superior in some ways, reaching adulthood much earlier than humans. At six weeks a lamb wasn't completely useless like a human baby, which needed to be udder-fed and looked after for much longer than a lamb. A lamb always likes a drink of ewe milk, but it's very soon eating grass as well, and it can stand up and run around within minutes of birth whereas the young human is kept for months in a box of blankets.

The human might be helpless on its own for the first few years, but it could then spend the next ten years just learning about the world. It went to a place called a School, which seemed wonderful to the sheep because all the young humans had to do there was listen and learn. The humans were shown how to read and write and do mathematics and also how to operate computers.

By the time the human was ready to go out into the world on its own, the sheep was old or eaten. And all through its childhood, the young human looked at the world with wonder and amazement. The sheep knew several phrases for this: as curious as a cat, as trusting as a dog, as keen as a mustard, as open as a shutcase – the human child had all those qualities.

But just as a lamb stopped springing and bouncing around the field after six months, so something happened to the humans in their teenage years which closed them up, and made them not want to see the world as the fresh exciting place of childhood where all this knowledge was free and openly available.

Humans didn't need to educate themselves in secret like the sheep. The sheep had learned from the Box that the only places where knowledge was dangerous and where learning was difficult for humans were in countries ruled by madmen who wore funny hats and had long white beards or black moustaches, or on other planets where the humans lived in caves or as slaves under the yoke of growly-voiced aliens with bulbous reptilian heads and scabby faces with bulging eyes, just as the animals were controlled by the humans on Earth and the humans by the dreary older dark-suited humans, although on those other planets it always seemed to happen that the humans defeated the Aliens by blasting them with fire guns or turning them to green jelly.

On every occasion when Aliens had invaded the Earth, the humans had got rid of them, even though extraterrestrial technology was always much more advanced than theirs. There was always something the Aliens hadn't considered – often something quite simple – which the humans found out about. Just as when humans had wars with each other, the ones with scowly faces who wore black hats and shot people from horses always lost in the end, and when humans used big weapons made from metal such as tanks and aeroplanes with guns, the humans who spoke English always defeated those with scowly faces who either used alien languages or spoke English in a comical fashion.

Examples such as these had persuaded the sheep that it must be possible to escape from Clovis and find his own place in the Outside World on his own terms because all the evidence was that, despite all the nasty things which happened out there, good always triumphed in the end, especially if you were resourceful and stiff-lipped like Winston Churchill and Harrison Ford.

CHAPTER THREE

Donor Kebab

The sheep's one-ram escape committee monitored the Box's viewing schedules for potentially instructive escape dramas. There were stories about humans escaping from prisons, castles, fortified islands, prison camps, chain gangs, spaceships and alien slave markets, and from these the sheep had learned the importance of secrecy, patience, cunning and careful planning. He knew he wouldn't be able to dig a tunnel under his pen, or leap over the perimeter fence on a motorbike, but he studied other methods when such films were shown, and was particularly interested in those which involved stowing away in a vehicle.

One vehicle popular with human fugitives was clearly the Laundry Van, and while this might be searched on leaving prisons, he didn't think anyone would stop the one which serviced the Institute and check it for stowaway sheep. One of his tasks on days when he was allowed to eat grass in the Field had been to establish a schedule for the daily visits of the Laundry Van, but he soon discovered that these were irregularly timed. Not only that, but bags of laundry were thrown from ground-level into the back of the van, which was four feet off the ground, and he didn't think it would be possible for him to clamber unseen over the bags and up into the van. He was disappointed that the Clovis Institute didn't use the kind of huge laundry baskets which prisons, hospitals and hotels provided for their escapees.

He therefore paid particular attention to the news that the Institute would receive a Visit from the Minister because this man would arrive in a big black car called a Limmerzine. From the scientists' descriptions this was evidently much too big for one human, and there might well be a place in this vehicle where a wily sheep could hide.

As it turned out, the Visit did not provide him with any opportunities for escape because the Minister's car had been filled with Toadies, all wearing the same pondlife uniform of dark suit and tie. But this Ministerial visit had furnished the sheep with vital information about his origins, not all of which was revealed to the Minister himself on the day.

The first word the sheep heard when the Minister was ushered into the laboratory by the stooping figure of the already over-short Dr Weisenheimer was, of course, *Dolly*. He knew all about Dolly, or so he had believed.

He'd originally thought Dolly was Weisenheimer's ex-wife, because he'd talked about her so much and in the past tense. The last time Weisenheimer had seen Dolly was in some place called Roslin, but later the sheep realised that this was an Institute similar to theirs in a Scottish city called Edinbrer. Now he was giving the Minister the explanation which the sheep came to know by heart in later months, owing to the frequency with which it was repeated for other visitors:

'Now Dolly, as you must know, Minister, was an exact copy of a sheep which wasn't her mother,' Weisenheimer was saying. 'In Wally's case, however, the gene material came from a ram, and the egg from a gimmer, a ewe which had never previously enjoyed sexual relations with another sheep. And our surrogate was also a gimmer, so Wally was truly born of a virgin. Never been tupped...'

The Minister's face coloured slightly, but he smiled, indicating that he wasn't averse to comparisons with religious stories, nor to direct references to sexual reproduction. He licked his thin lips as if to confirm this interpretation.

'Now you continue, Dr Stein. This is Dr Frank Stein, our Chief Research Biologist. Our black sheep Wally is his baby, if you know what I mean.'

'Not literally of course,' said Dr Stein. 'And we couldn't copy the technique pioneered by Ian Wilmut at Roslin because he patented it. The method he used for cloning Dolly was somatic cell nuclear transfer. He took the nucleii from the udder cells of a dead sheep and starved them of nutrients, putting the DNA into a semi-dormant state, before implanting them in the unfertilised egg cells of a second sheep whose nucleii he had already removed by microsurgery. Dolly's genes came from the first sheep's mammary gland tissue.'

'The mammary glands,' said the Minister, 'as in Dolly Parton. Yes, of course, ha ha.' And he chuckled.

'Michelangelo's famous painting on the ceiling of the Sistine Chapel shows the spark of life from God to Adam where their outstretched fingers almost touch,' Dr Stein continued, holding the forefingers of each hand in the air like quotes before bringing the fingertips almost together. 'Wilmut used a small charge of electricity to artificially recreate this miracle, and the cells he had combined from two female sheep began to divide as if the egg had been fertilised by the action of sperm from a ram. They hadn't been fertilised but nevertheless contained a complete set of genes from a single sheep. He then implanted his test-tube baby sheep in the womb of a third ewe. Dolly was a clone or copy of the first sheep.'

Listening to this explanation being given in front of his pen, the sheep realised for the first time that Dolly's mother had been tricked by the other scientists into giving birth to a lamb which had no father but three mothers. When Dolly was born, the surrogate mother treated her exactly like one of her own lambs, which Dolly was of course, except that this ewe was a Scottish Blackface with big curled horns, whereas Dolly was a white-faced lamb of a completely different breed.

The disclosures which followed were even more alarming.

'But the Roslin team made an unexpected discovery about the sheep's ageing processes. Although the original ovum was of course completely new, the DNA material added by nuclear transfer from the mammary glands of the other ewe was the same age as this other adult sheep, six years old. And they later found that Dolly's organs and body tissues were ageing at two different rates, so that by her first birthday, Dolly was both one year old and seven years old. She went on to develop arthritis at the relatively early age of five and a half. And she was only six when they had to put her to sleep – which was on Valentine's

Day in 2003 – because she was suffering from a progressive lung disease.'

'So how old is your Wally then?' the Minister asked.

'Unfortunately that's where politics muddies the cleearr waterrrs of scientific enquiry,' said Dr Donald Macannie, moving to the front of the group. 'This relates to my particular area of resairrrch.'

'That's right,' said Weisenheimer. 'If you remember, your Government persuaded Clovis to develop international channels of communication with scientists working in Battymanistan, under the old régime.'

'In exchange for a significant increase in your funding, if I remember rightly,' said the Minister.

'For which we wairrr most gratefule,' Macannie agreed.

'And we *remain* grateful Minister,' said Weisenheimer.

'But Wally's cloning involved the use of donor cell material from a sheep in a laboratory in the city of Battymenarbad,' Macannie continued. 'The whole basis of the project was that all four sheep, the Battyman donor ram, our pair of vairgins and Wally himself, would be continuously monitored by both teams of scientists using a shared computer database accessed via the intairnet.'

'But unfortunately when news of our virgin birth reached the wise men of the new Men's Republic of Battymanistan,' Dr Frank Stein informed him, 'instead of bringing gifts of gold, frankincense and myrrh, they sent in a team of Batty fundamentalists, who rounded up all the scientists and made them watch their laboratory being burned to the ground before chopping off their heads. They dragged all the lab technicians off to work in the sweat mines. All the research work held in Battymenarbad was totally destroyed.'

'And the pooer Batty ram,' said Dr Macannie, 'which had done nothing to desairve this fate...'

'Apart from provide us with cell nucleii...' said Dr Stein.

'Was roasted on a spit and eaten by the soldiers.'

Transfixed by this moving account of his father's death, the sheep gasped audibly, prompting the Minister to turn in his direction.

'You see how even Wally finds this upsetting,' said Dr Weisenheimer. 'For this black sheep you see before you, which is the fruit of our international scientific collaboration so generously supported by your Government, this sheep is a most intelligent beast, and were it not for the needless destruction of much of the necessary scientific data...'

'Including his father,' said Dr Stein.

'He would have greatly enhanced our own understanding even more than he has done already,' said Weisenheimer. 'He is still of course a most valuable research asset, and a remarkably intelligent beast, we have discovered...'

'And a most vocal beast, I would say,' said Helen Brimstone, turning quickly to give him an affectionate pat on the head, catching him by surprise.

The sheep belched.

'He has a different sounding *baa* for everything he does,' she said. 'He seems to murmur while eating. He grunts when we walk up to him, a different kind of plosive sound for each member of the team. And when he squats slightly to...'

'Yes, Dr Brimstone,' Weisenheimer interrupted, 'I think we all know about Wally's intelligence and his vocal range. But since we do not know the age of the donor ram...'

'Since he became doner kebab...' said Macannie.

'And the histological record was skewed...'

'Or skewered...'

'When Battymanistan government officials hacked into the database...'

'At the same time as their soldiers were hacking into the data spit-roast...'

'And the Batty hackers replaced what one might call the nucleii of the computer sequencing with Batty fundamentalist text messages denouncing their own beheaded scientists, everyone working in the Institute, the Minister responsible for the Clovis project, and all the sheep...'

'Including, but especially pooer Wally,' said Dr Macannie. 'He has to suffer a horrible death.'

'Including, but especially me,' said Dr Stein. 'My fate has to be ten times worse than the sheep's because I have committed the most heinous crime of all.'

'All these are heretics,' said Weisenheimer, 'who have offended Batty doctrine, and are therefore subject to a Batwa, an irrevocable sentence of death which cannot be rescinded until our sheep is dead...'

'But could we not then...?' the Minister began, raising his hand, turning his back to the sheep to address the scientists. 'You know,' he said, making a sideways movement across his throat, 'ahem, *sacrifice* the sheep in the interests of...'

Dr Frank Stein stopped him.

'Unfortunately not, sir. For Dr Weisenheimer was, I think, about to enlighten you further as to your own position in this sorry tale...'

'*My* position?' said the Minister. 'But I only became Minister last month. Before that I was...'

'Irrelevant,' said Stein. 'Not only does the sheep have to die, but so do all the scientists, along with the Minister. You can't escape with a cabinet reshuffle because the Batwa decreed by their leader Sheikh Rattlenroll is directed at whoever holds the ministerial post or has responsibility for any scientific research involving sheep. The Prime Minister too because the buck stops with him where sheep are concerned. All politicians linked to our heretical use of sheep are running dogs of degenerate Western liberal capitalism who must have wooden stakes driven through their diabolical bleeding hearts, if I may parrotphrase one of their more colourful expressions.'

'So you can't save your bacon by killing the sheep,' said Dr Brimstone. 'We're all in the same boat.'

'But there's no gravy in this gravy boat,' said Macannie, 'not in this particular lamb stew.'

*

As the Minister was whisked off to see other scientists and their animals elsewhere in the Institute, the sheep was left with much to chew over. That evening, as Dr Stein was packing his briefcase, he noticed that his prodigy was looking somewhat down in the dumps. He took a bar of chocolate from his desk drawer, broke a piece off, and walked across to the pen.

'Here you are, Wally,' he said, 'have a piece of Fruit 'n' Nut, your favourite. Looks like our ministerial visit rather took it out of you. Bit of a shock, was it, hearing about what happened to your dad, that and the Batwa?'

The sheep gave a low, gurgling baa, as if to answer his query. Stein patted his rump as the sheep ate the chocolate but with his eyes fixed all the time on the mad scientist. Encouraged by this apparently attentive audience, Stein continued:

'Of course, they don't know the half of it,' he told the sheep. 'When I said I'd committed the most heinous crime of all, that wasn't so far from the truth in any religious doctrine, let alone the Batty variety. The destruction of most of the data concerning your father was actually quite convenient, as it turned out...'

The sheep finished the chocolate and carried on staring at him, expectantly, willing him to continue. He risked a mono-syllabic but slyly modulated *Mairrr!* of encouragement.

'Because Macannie has never been able to produce a complete histological comparison between your cellular profile and your father's. And because of this, my woolly friend, I'm pretty sure that he has no suspicion that you and I have what our Minister might call...a special relationship...'

He paused, looking closely at the sheep's expression.

The sheep pushed his head against the scientist's hand, en-couraging Stein to tickle him behind his ear, sensing that a shared intimacy of this kind might prompt him to continue what the man must think of as a tearful monologue. The sheep perceived from his hesitancy that he had not spoken of this before to any of the humans, and the Minister's visit had brought certain things to the surface, especially when he had needed to talk about them to the others in terms which the sheep now realised had involved covert references to areas of research familiar only to himself. For much of the time he'd been using a kind of code in order to be able to speak about it while not speaking about it.

The sheep started licking the man's fingers, making a low purring sound in his throat. The ruse worked.

'For I have done something in our experiment,' Stein carried on, meeting the sheep's stare, 'something which no other geneticist has ever achieved. But they don't know this of course. For I did something truly remarkable, Wally. It was Helen Brimstone who perfected her especially effective method of starving the nucleii from your father's cells for five days which froze them into a quiescent phase of their division cycle, making the chromosomes more susceptible to being reprogrammed to initiate the growth of a new organism – meaning you, Wally – after the nuclei were transferred into the gimmer's ova...'

The sheep was transfixed. He couldn't make any kind of noise. He just stared.

'Helen, however, was unaware that halfway through her cell starvation cycle, I judged that the right moment of stasis had occurred, and without her knowledge I removed one pair of the ram's chromosomes and introduced strands of my own DNA, taken from my own testes, which means, my boy, that you are the only sheep in the world whose tissue cells have forty-four sheep chromosomes and one pair whose DNA is part ovine part human in origin. And just as Dolly was unique in having three mothers, so you also are unique, in having two virgin mothers and two not-so-virgin fathers, one of those since turned into roast mutton, it's true to say, and the other only present in one tiny but highly significant part of your DNA sequencing. Because what I gave you included the gene for human intelligence and language acquisition, along with the genes for a few other things I wasn't able to control. And yet what this combination produced, apart from one sturdy and apparently intelligent tup, I have not yet discovered, for you remain an enigma to me, dear Wally. You seem to be a sheep in all biological respects except the one I've mentioned. One of your pairs of chromosomes quite definitely has my gene. Yet you are quite clearly a ram, and behave like a ram, not a man. You have an unusually large brain for a sheep, yet appear not to use all that spare capacity. You think like a sheep, if a sheep can be said to think. And yet all my own work on animal intelligence, which is years ahead of anyone else's, including Clovis's pathetic contribution, everything I've done should have produced an intelligent sheep at least capable of rudimentary language skills, and yet you can't even say your own name, Wally.'

The sheep grunted, fixing the scientist with a baleful stare.

'Don't get me wrong,' Stein continued. 'I'm sure I will learn from my mistakes. You are one such mistake, Wally, not that you know anything of this. But you will help me discover what was wrong in my procedures or my thinking, and then I shall create a thinking talking beast. And just think of what that would mean, my woolly friend: the power, the military applications even, and eventually, world domination. Forget about so-called dolphin suicide bombers, we could infiltrate cats into military installations after training them in the use of special microcameras capable of being operated with the right claw-clenching movements. I could teach dogs to spy and report back on their political masters. No one would know of course, we'd have to keep it secret from the public, and I wouldn't stay here, oh no, they're too narrow-minded, they've starved our research of the funds I needed to siphon off for my own work as it is. Oh no, I'd be at Langley, not Clovis, special advisor to the Pentagon, with my own state-of-the-art laboratory, all the equipment and animals I want, no limit on resources and not a whiff of this getting out to the press or the politicians or the bleeding-heart animal liberationists and all the other nutters. Total secrecy, that's the key. Not even all the women I'd have would know the true nature of my hushhush work. Instead of which – for now – I'm still saddled with *this* place...'

Stein waved his arms in a display of anger, almost toppling over with a gesture more dangerous than extravagant. His wild stare stabbed at different objects in the laboratory, accusatory and uncomprehending, before subsiding and returning to rest on the sheep.

'As my own father once said of me, where did I go wrong?'

The sheep said nothing.

Another piece of the puzzle fell into place. Who he was. Who he could be. What he was meant to do with his life. But other pieces no longer fitted, other parts of the puzzle needed to be rethought. Not just how old he was but how those traits he'd found so ridiculous in the humans must be present in him to some degree, and yet he'd believed a sheep was obviously superior to a human in not being subject to contemptible emotions.

He didn't think he was greedy, except perhaps when he heard Ron Devally rattling the bucket of ewe-nuts. He wasn't an angry sheep. He wasn't jealous of anyone, yet how much he envied the humans their mobility. Did he not dislike them for abusing that advantage, their wonderful privilege, something they gave not a moment's thought? Did he not hate them for their treatment of animals, for the way they saw the planet as theirs to destroy, as well as for the way they hurt and killed each other? What would he not do if he had their physical advantages? So was his sense of apartness informed in some degree by their arrogance? Yet he also liked them. He was fond of them, or of those he knew, even the infuriating Weisenheimer, who might behave most of the time like a Stereo Type, yet wasn't totally predictable, his stupidity often masking some other purpose.

But Stein. Those traits which seemed so ridiculous in him – the negative aspects of his ebullient personality – might the sheep not have those also to some degree, even if they showed themselves differently? His secrecy and cunning, yes. His desperate intelligence, his wanting to break the bounds of knowledge even if he broke himself in the attempt. Yes yes. What else was Stein? Duplicitous. Unscrupulous. Scheming. He used people, he manipulated them to achieve his own ends, but he was also self-destructive. And he knew for sure that the man really was off his rocker: he'd lost his trolley when he'd been one can short of a six-pack.

So was the sheep doolally bananas too? Could that be why the sheep's own hold on reality sometimes seemed to be tenuous *in extremis*? If he really wasn't the only sane creature in a world where all the other inhabitants were nuttier than fruitcakes, did that mean he himself was stark staring conkers?

CHAPTER FOUR

Confessions of a Double Agent

Dr Frank Stein did not feel the need to talk to the sheep again about the manner of his conception, believing his spur-of-the-moment confession to the animal had absolved him of the need to unburden himself any further. He always found the Catholic side of his upbringing provided him with that kind of reassurance when he was feeling inexplicably anxious or vaguely unhinged.

Young Frank Stein had been brought up both as a Jew and as a Catholic, and that double education had given him a sound grounding in how to switch his thinking between two contradictory positions so as always to be right by one when wrong by the other. His father was a mildly schizoid Austrian exile Jew who spoke little English and his mother a mildly deranged Irish Catholic, and he had managed to make them even more distrustful of each other by always depositing half of the money he was obliged to steal from them in the other's pocket or bag. Neither would countenance divorce, and they lived in separate parts of a rambling Victorian house, each using their son to spy on the other. When not employed as a domestic messenger and double agent, he kept out of their way at the top of the house, from where he kept the neighbourhood under surveillance with binoculars and a radio tuned to the police wavelength while monitoring a dangerous variety of scientific experiments including a makeshift still which made drinkable poteen.

His father believed his boy Frank was getting a good Jewish education and his mother that he was growing up a good Catholic because he told each what they wanted to hear. The schoolboy-scientist made a point of always finding out everything he could about anyone charged with his moral and academic education, keeping tabs on their houses and places of work and tapping their phone lines using an electrical device constructed with equipment stolen from the physics laboratory. He was thus able to blackmail two paedophile teachers, which took care of the school reports, as well as the Rabbi, who didn't believe in God (and ate bacon and sausages), and Father Mullarkey, who was partial to young boys.

Talking to the sheep had been like confessing his sins to Father Mullarkey, except that the animal had not given him twenty pounds afterwards to keep his mouth shut, nor suggested that young Frank might not need to make another confession for at least another month. The sheep's *Mairrr!* was as meaningless as the priest's response to his admissions of petty theft: 'Say three Hail Marys and an Our Father.' For if neither of his parents ever gave him any money, why should he not take from one and give half to the other?

When the animal had looked at him as if to say, 'Go on, what else?', he remembered trying to picture Mullarkey's face through the grille of the darkened confessional. The black ram was no more cognisant of what was rushing through his excited mind than the feckless priest had been.

And when the sheep had made that low purring noise in response to his guilty disclosures, that was like Father Mullarkey clearing his throat before telling him he absolved him from his sin in the name of the Father and of the Son and of the Holy Ghost Amen, when he'd only been bashing the bishop, not asking others to bash it for him.

His knowledge of the priest's own misdemeanours, coupled with the way Mullarkey registered that awareness through his automatic responses and pointless penances, had encouraged him to regard the whole business of confession as a meaningless one-sided exercise. Not surprisingly, this early training in subterfuge and duplicity influenced his later working methods as a research scientist. His double life at home and school as well as his tendency to view the world in terms of a duality between his interests and those of others had their inevitable effects on his personality and character. His colleagues viewed him as obsessively secretive, evasive, touchy, paranoid, emotionally unstable and stubborn. He saw himself as single-minded, inspired, rightly protective, sensitive, misunderstood and stubborn.

In the days which followed the Minister's visit, Stein had not been tempted back into confessional mode, but he nevertheless felt on edge, as if his conscience were pricking him about something, which was unusual to say the least because he was rarely troubled by matters of conscience. His usual concern was whether he was likely to get away with something, and if not, how much time there was remaining before discovery or curtailment. He got on with his work while continuing to observe the sheep in a careful yet apparently casual fashion, while the sheep kept a wary but not too obviously eagle eye on him. It was like passing the church but not going in, or passing Mrs Golightly's house and keeping his wallet firmly tucked inside his jacket. He might whistle as he skipped or sidled past but he wasn't going to blow any whistles on himself. Each registered the other's agitation as they tried to mask their own unease, but as the days passed, and no further revelations were forthcoming, the black ram became the more anxious of the two. The sheep felt that an apple of knowledge had been dangled over his pen only to be whisked away again.

Weeks later, the scientists' hijacking of his birthday celebrations brought that apple of knowledge back into sharp focus. As *their* party degenerated into an affectionate shambles, and they were all hugging each other – and trying to hug him across the barrier – the sheep looked around to see what had happened to Dr Stein. He was sitting at his desk, hunched over the sheep's sipper-bottle, the cap and feed-tube beside it, a line of empty champagne bottles awaiting his attention. One by one, he tipped each over the neck of the sipper-bottle, and gave it a vigorous shake. Because he was so sozzled, he seemed to be spilling more champagne down his shirt than he was trickling into the sipper-bottle, but he persevered, and eventually brandished half a sipper of champagne dregs.

As the other scientists began singing bawdy songs in the corner of the room, Dr Stein went across to the pen with his offering, and was trying to attach the sipper-bottle to the grille

38

by a metal clip, encouraging the feed-tube to protrude at sheep-head height. He was clearly experiencing some difficulties over this delicate procedure, and was offering verbal persuasion to the grille clip to counter his hand's fumbling action, urging it to hold the bottle upright.

'Come on, this is for Wally,' he was telling the sipper-bottle. 'It's Wally's birthday, damn you, and my boy Wally deserves some shampers like the rest of us.'

The sheep walked over. At first Stein thought the animal was going to offer him some helpful advice. He slumped over the gate, still clutching the sipper-bottle, staring at the sheep with glazed eyes.

'I can't dwink that,' said the sheep in a low murmur. 'It's flat.'

'What's that, Wally?' asked Stein.

'That wine is undwinkable,' the sheep continued, trying out his voice. 'And I don't think I'd enjoy it in any case. It doesn't seem to have done you any good...' He always practised speech at night, on his own in the semi-dark. It felt strangely liberating to use it now to a human.

'You say something, Wally?'

'My name's *not* Wally,' the sheep told him firmly.

Stein rolled his eyes. The sheep seemed to him to be burbling.

Macannie called across from the group of singers:

'You joining us, Frank, or have you taken up completely with the sheep?'

'Obviously a more interesting conversation going on over there,' said Helen Brimstone. 'What have you two got to say to each other now?'

'Don't let him touch you, Wally,' Gumption shouted. 'You don't know where he's been.'

'He hasn't been tested for Foot and Mouth,' Helen Brimstone revealed.

The sheep pressed his muzzle against Stein's cheek.

'*Not* Wally, you hear me,' he repeated, still in a low voice.

Dr Frank Stein didn't hear. He fell forward into the pen, dropping the sipper-bottle as he did so. It smashed, the curved pieces of glass skittering across the floor, the smallest splinters decorating a foaming pool of whitish liquid. Doubled over, his legs splayed in either direction, Stein lay with his head half buried in the straw, snoring heavily.

The sheep was tempted to sit on the man's face, as he'd heard a cat had done once to an unkind human, and this woman who'd fallen asleep in a drunken stupor had never woken, because her own pussy had muffled her. But Stein was his father, the only father he had left, and he had plans for him. He might not know it yet, but Stein was going to help him.

The trick was that Stein had to think it was the other way round, that the sheep would serve *his* needs. He'd have to first gain his trust if he was going to deceive him. And he'd have to take things slowly, one step at a time, because Stein would instinctively overreact. He had to keep one step ahead of him, and the first step was the most difficult, for it must set the pattern of what followed. Telling him, but not telling him.

Although Stein would inevitably influence what developed, the genetic imprint would be the sheep's, not his.

Stein would not be easy to control.

Nor would the sheep.

CHAPTER FIVE

Wagging the Doc

The sheep knew he was not popular with the other animals. They charged him with colluding with the enemy, collaborating with their human persecutors. Their approbation might be expressed in necessarily simplistic terms, but it was still hurtful to a sensitive sheep. He didn't like being disliked, especially by his own kind, if a sheep of his kindly kind could be said to have a kind. He was saddened too that most of these fellow creatures who couldn't help but misunderstand him were short-term inmates undergoing a carefully monitored programme of medical treatment; their level of success in surviving this would only be gauged by death and dissection.

That was *his* perspective. He knew theirs was restricted by their nature. They were like creatures of limited intelligence in the human world, except that they weren't capable of making wrong moral choices. They had a simple integrity but were unable to make even the simplest choices. They couldn't even go on hunger strike in protest at their treatment: if they stopped eating, they would die, and why would they want to die? Were they not all living creatures? It was against their nature to deny themselves sustenance just as it was against his nature to deny himself knowledge. And it was against the humans' nature to deny themselves anything, even if what they wanted destroyed other humans or animals or even themselves. That was where he differed from Stein. Dr Stein did not recognise limits. Stein served the needs of others but for his own ends. Knowledge for him was a means to an end.

The other sheep criticised him for watching too much TV, complaining that the continual noise from the picture machine stopped them from getting a good night's sleep. When they heard his attempts to make human speech sounds, they were uncomprehending as well as scornful, especially of his earliest efforts, which had involved repeating phrases he'd heard the most often, particularly ones with emphatic or lilting rhythms. His still predominantly ovine inflections made many of these practice pieces difficult to distinguish from inarticulate bleating.

'Ordure ordure,' the sheep blurted, 'mistaspeaker mistaspeaker, ordure ordure ordure. Mister mairrrr *mairrrr!* The court will wise the court will wise will wise. Wossaaaaat wossaaaaat wossaaaaat. You have one life left. You can still phone a friend phone a friend. Slobodan dan dan. Slobadandandanmilosovich slobadanmilosovitch slobadanmilosovichmilosovitch. You are the weakest link you are the weakest link. Wossaaaaat wossaaaaat. I've started so I'll finish. Goodbye!'

Sheep language involves a small range of noises with variable tones, the information communicated being usually of a limited nature. *Good grass. Where water? Silage too wet. Gate open, fence broken, wall down. Farmer's tractor, food coming.* Each sheep's bleat has its own distinctive timbre, and other sheep can always recognise which animal is bleating from amongst hundreds in a large flock, ewes and their lambs being acutely aware of the sound, distance and direction of one another's bleats.

Forceful use of the throat or a fuller lung capacity adds emphasis to phrases indicating concern, alarm or sexual appetite. *Strangers in field. Watch out fox. Lambs too far. Come here lamb. Danger, collie on quad. Ewe on heat. Ewe on fire.* But unlike human speech, sheep language is always used in relation to the sound, sight or smell perceived by the commenting animal. Sheep require some context for another sheep's bleat to have meaning.

Communication between the animals was difficult in the lab-oratory, where they were kept physically apart like prisoners incarcerated in separate cells. Prevented from having communal interaction, they became less used to verbalising, there being no scope for comment upon such matters as shared food sources or opportunities for sexual congress. The only predators were the white-coated humans, who could be apparently kind and solicitous one minute, but an hour later might deliver death without warning by lethal injection. Or an animal might wake from sleep to find itself manacled to a board with a device like a clock implanted in its skull.

While the sheep was totally preoccupied with his intensive education and escape plans, he was nevertheless always conscious of his animal needs and instincts, especially those relating to actions he had never performed, such as grazing with a flock of sheep, negotiating the terms and duration of intercourse with a willing ewe, and engaging in boisterous games of kicking and headbutting with other rams. He had done none of these things and yet his instinctive yearning for such simple pleasures was as intense as his obsession with speech, intelligence and understanding. He made mental comparisons between running head down at another ram (*the satisfaction of a skull-to-skull contact*) with facing a Cricketball fired from the same distance as a charging ram (*the thwack of leather on willow*), hitting the hard red ball with the middle of the bat and stroking it effortlessly through the covers, bisecting the fielders, rattling the boundary-board.

He could never lead the life of a normal sheep because he had eaten of the Tree of Knowledge.

Yet his desire to perform *human* actions did not mean he wished for a human body. He knew himself as Sheep Not Man, content with his own sheep's body, except that he could only be conscious of his physical presence as a sheep in such simple solitary acts as eating, defecation and rubbing his rump against the grille. It was not enough. He keenly felt the humiliation imposed on him by the physical conditions of his captivity. Butting the wall wasn't the same as head-butting a mean-eyed oncoming tup. The pleasure of butting Ron Devally when he was bending over to use his fork on the straw was lessened by the knowledge that the man did not appreciate this friendly gesture, especially when it prompted the scientists to whoop upon witnessing the Welshman's discomfort.

The sheep's sense of isolation and separateness, of being neither one thing nor another, made him even more determined to gain freedom through the knowledge which had marked him out. And knowledge meant more than just human knowledge, which was limited by the ignorance and prejudice of the humans. He would seek knowledge beyond human limitation.

If he was doomed to be a freak sheep, he was going to be the best freak sheep there was: if barmy then bilingually barmy, maddeningly manic and mad-bastard barmy. For he knew that humans could be far more gullible than they believed sheep to be; and if he could only perfect his linguistic skills, he would put these to positive use, achieving whatever he was capable of achieving, despite the physical disadvantage of being a sheep. He would make something of his own life by taking full possession of his own life, shaming the humans by artful use of his own intelligence, turning guile to good, not greed.

The other animals could not escape whatever fate the humans had planned for them. But *he* would. Yet he knew he couldn't do it on his own; he knew from all the films he'd seen that the humans wouldn't want to help him either, so he'd have to plan to enlist their assistance by involuntary means. Just as he would use their language to acquire the knowledge he craved.

The sheep's first efforts at imitating the humans had seemed as meaningless and baffling to the other animals as the lame attempts of humans to impersonate his own baaing. At first he was trying out phrases which meant no more to him than to the other animals, but he needed to get the sounds right before he could relate them to meaning, which was difficult when the context provided by the pictures on the Box was ambiguous.

'We will march down the Garvaghey Woad,' the sheep would declare. 'Because Ulster will fight and Ulster will be wight. Make my Daypunk, make my Daypunk. This is the shipping forecast from now until the IRA has decommissioned its weapons. No surwender, no surwender. Ask the studio audience. Put them beyond use. Engerland Engerland, what a load of wubbish. Put it there sunshine, put it there, put it there. Wossaaaaat, wossaaaaat.'

Mad sheep, mad sheep, came the response from the next pen.

'Here is the news,' the sheep would announce. 'I'm awwesting you for the murder of the news read by. Here is the news read by the Pwyminister Misterblare Misterblare Misterblare Malin Wockle Finisterre George Double Ewe bush ewe bush ewe bush ewe are the weakest link. Anything ewes say may be taken down in evidence. Goodbye! Good boy! Good shot sir!

Don't miss tonight's episode of sex in the city the one hundred share index ended the day twenty-four points higher at forty fifty-thwee in New York a short time ago the Dow Jones was up one hundred and twenty-seven at eighty-five twenty-six.'

Mad sheep, mad sheep.

'The pound fell two-thirds of a cent against the dollar to one dollar fifty-eight point one against the ewe woe sterling was half a cent lower at one ewe woe fifty-seven point thwee making ewe woe worth sixty-three point six pence.'

Need sleep, need sleep.

But in spite of these protests, the sheep was soon making rapid progress, imitating more elaborate sentences when he could relate these directly to actions depicted on the Box. The other animals noted greater resemblances to human speech in his mad-sheep monologues, but still urged silence on him. He was still keeping them awake, whatever he was saying. New arrivals found his nocturnal habits even more infuriating, but it was easier to disregard their protests.

'I've had enough,' the sheep retorted. 'I'm leaving you. You wouldn't dare. Well don't expect me to wait for you. And how long do you think it will last? It's always the same. If you think I'm going to do that you're mistaken. Well that's what *you* think. Just twy me. Just what I've always wanted.'

Stop man speech noise. Need sleep. Mad sheep.

One night he was triumphant. Something had clicked. The sheep *knew* he was getting it right at last, but there was no way of testing his proficiency. He was making sense, even to himself.

'You're damned well wight I am,' the sheep called out in the darkened laboratory. 'How do you *know* it's my baby? Just you twy and stop me. I always knew it was you. Of course I love you, darling. I've always loved you. If you touch her again. No weally, I don't mind. I start on Monday. In your dweams. You've got another thing coming. I never loved her. I never said that. No one's going to stop me. It's what I want.'

And from there it was a short step to his regular nighttime reprise of daytime phrases from the laboratory. This annoyed the other animals even more than his television repeats because they could recognise the individual voices of the different scientists in his recital.

'Tell him I'm not here,' the sheep would say. 'Well I think that's pie in the sky. Oh come on, silly, this won't hurt, it's just a little jab.'

It was almost as though the humans had come back to haunt them in the night by using the sheep as their diabolical mouthpiece.

'Good morning, Mark,' said the sheep, 'and how are you today?... Well I thought he was offside. Take care. Has anyone seen Fwank? Are you sure about that? And when do you expect the weesults? Photocopier's jamming again. What's up with Wally? He looks like he's seen a ghost.'

Mad sheep, mad sheep, mad sheep.

If the other animals had shared his vocabulary, he might have defended himself as the Institute's long-term prisoner. By some quirk of fate, his sentence had been commuted to life, but with no remission possible for good behaviour. But recognising he could never gain *their* sympathy – while they would always have *his* – he had to continue with his speech practice regardless. What they suffered from his blabbing was as nothing compared with what they received at the hands of the scientists. He might be a squawking parrot but unlike a word bird this sheep now knew what he was talking about.

'Hasn't he wung back yet?' the sheep would ask the other animals. 'I left a clear message. Probably constipation. Twy him on his mobile. Sean, do you *have* to do that? No more than ten mils. We don't want to cut corners do we? Yes, Helen, that's how it *shude* have been done, but twy telling that to His Nibs. So how could it cost that much? Well our weesairrch indicates otherwise. What do we say when Hammerhead finds out?'

Mad sheep, mad sheep, mad sheep.

'The jurwee's out on that one, I'd say. But there was *a whole packet* of Hobnobs yesterday. Has someone been farting in the stationwee cupboard? It stinks in there. I wasn't born yesterday. You tell me. And what's the *spairm* count?'

Man sheep, man sheep, man sheep.

*

Dr Frank Stein was only an hour late for work the day after the sheep's birthday. He'd slept in his clothes where he'd been deposited by his colleagues. After heaving his body from the taxi, they'd dragged it up his front path, found a door key in the trouser pocket, and pushed the snoring beast inside.

He'd managed to extract most of the straw from his hair but his reddened right cheek still bore the stippled imprint of a doormat. He smelled like a rat in formaldehyde.

'You shudent have come in,' said Dr Macannie, keeping his distance. 'You cude have taken the morning off at least.'

'I've got to finish the experiment,' said Stein. 'And there's still our chess game, remember?'

'Well you've lost your queen already. I wouldn't give much for your chances. And I'm not just talking about the game. If you think you'll get funding for your hare-brained enzyme project, you're living in Cloudcuckooland. Your latest experiment is a complete waste of time if you want my opinion. You'll never get it to work. You can't make a silk pairse oot of a sow's ear. The whole thesis is fundamentally flawed.'

'If it's flawed, I need to show how it's flawed. That's the whole point.'

'But it can't be fundamentally flawed,' Gumption interposed. 'Sorry to *bore* you with that old hobbyhorse of mine again. But it's either flawed or *not* flawed, there are no half ways or fundamentallies in flaws.'

'And it's not a sow,' added Stein, 'it's a cat.'

'And talking of pairses,' Macannie continued, 'you owe me five poond, Stein. We had a whiproond for the taxi, and since you wairen't conscious, I paid your share. But we can add it to your chess stake. And it's your move.' He made a dismissive gesture towards the chessboard on the bench as if to suggest that the outcome of their game was a foregone conclusion. Stein was going to lose.

'I didn't ask to go in your taxi. I would have walked.'

'You wairen't capable.'

'You don't know what I'm capable of.'

'I said we shude have left him to sleep with the sheep,' Macannie reminded the others.

'Wouldn't have been fair to the sheep,' said Gumption. 'Poor

Wally wouldn't have slept a wink, not with Stein snoring like a pig.'

'Now now boys,' said Helen Brimstone. 'You're arguing over nothing already and it's only ten o'clock. What happened to last night's party mood?...Which I now see involved some jolly japes by you boys with my computer.'

'It's not nothing,' said Macannie. 'It's a point of principle, scientific principle.'

'Well you've obviously got me there then,' Stein retorted. 'I haven't any of them, have I? Not according to Hammerhead.'

'Who got out of the wrong side of the bed this morning then?' asked Helen Brimstone.

'Doormat, I think it was,' said Sean Shenanigan, pointing.

'Come on, own up,' Helen Brimstone said, 'which of you Goldilockses has been eating my porridge, sleeping in my bed, accessing my computer files?'

'I also question your human principles, Stein,' Macannie continued. 'I never haired of a scientist using his own cat in an experiment. We have any number of cats you cude use.'

'Cats with numbers, not names,' said Mark Gumption, 'not named precisely so that we don't become attached to them. Not nicknamed either, not even when they start showing particular behavioural traits. They mustn't be individuals.'

'All numbered cats for which we have to account to Hammerhead,' Stein interposed. 'And Hammerhead's pussy budget is overspent. So if I want to prove my enzyme theory, I have to put my moggy where my mouth is. And Schrödinger, I would remind you, is one sick pussycat. He's had his nine lives. He's on his last legs and no vet can help him now. If he dies, I've put him out of his misery. But if he proves me right, he gets another life, a tenth life. I'm also showing how great is my personal conviction that I'm right about this one because my own cat is the guinea pig. I'm putting myself on the line.'

'You've tied your own cat to that line,' said Macannie, 'and there's a train coming. That train is your overweening ambition. There's going to be a crash, Stein, but you're too blind or blind drunk with your success to see what's coming. Imagine what the tabloids would say if they got hold of the story. MAD BOFFIN MURDERS HIS OWN MOGGY...'

The sheep stared across the laboratory to where Stein's comatose cat lay strapped – not tied – to a board with two bottles clamped above it, one dripping a clear liquid down a tube which disappeared through the animal's tabby fur, the other dispensing bright red cat blood. He wondered which of the unnamed numbered cats was the unwitting donor.

The chessboard was set up immediately next to the monitor. Stein stared at both simultaneously, as if each held clues to the meaning of the other. Schrödinger's tail was dead still, not twitching like a sleeping cat's, but his heart-beat zigzagged across the screen accompanied by a regular *beep beep beep* sound.

'Listen to that,' said Schrödinger's man. 'If I switch it off, the cat could be dead, or it could be alive. It all depends upon whether or not the catalyst has kicked off the enzymes. Just as in quantum mechanics, there is equal probability that the cat is alive or dead. The Psi function would express this by having in it the living and the dead cat mixed or smeared out in equal parts. In my experiment, the superposition of possible outcomes must exist simultaneously because we can observe interference effects from these. But stop it dead, and the cat might be dead, or alive, whereas now it is both dead *and* alive. Right now my enzyme theory is simultaneously right and wrong. I can do nothing more to influence the outcome. The cat's own body will decide whether it lives or dies.'

'Sometimes I think you really are mad,' said Helen Brimstone. 'This isn't subatomic physics, it's molecular biology.'

'The laws are the same. Like Nils Bohr said: If you think you understand it, you don't know the first thing about it.'

The sheep understood. Stein had just given him a vital clue which settled all his doubts about his own quest for knowledge. The more he knew, the less he would discover he knew. The more there was to know, the more there was to discover he didn't know. He had begun to grasp the nature of lateral thinking. Which meant you not only had to compute the number of possibilities but also the permutations of choices. Just as in chess. He'd only realised he'd gained a full understanding of chess when he saw that the players too often made the wrong moves, often for non-strategic reasons, which had given him the impression that the game itself defied logic, whereas the logic of chess was perfection itself. The humans did not seem capable of planning more than ten moves ahead, so it was hardly surprising that they rarely balanced all the permutations or measured their own strategies against the strengths, weaknesses, habits and likely game-plans of their opponents. In their current game, Stein was blinded by his own obsessional preference for certain kinds of moves whereas Macannie was hampered by overcaution, but the Scotsman was winning because Stein's pride was blunting his cunning.

The sheep had followed their current game with mounting frustration and a growing proprietorial interest, unable to believe that Stein could be so short-sighted. So intent was Stein on his own doomed attack plan that he clearly hadn't taken on what Macannie was doing by moving his pawns forward, or why he had just castled his rook and king.

Stein tapped the cat's dripfeed bottle with his pen. 'Nice kitty kitty,' he said, 'are you feeling lucky or unlucky? Will you live or will you die? Shall I take the pawn he clearly wants me to take, or shall I turn down such an easy, obvious gift? I don't see why I shouldn't. But beware of Greeks bearing gifts.'

'Blackwook,' the sheep warned, his voice low, half muffled amid the hubbub of the laboratory.

'Black look indeed,' said Helen Brimstone, turning to face a surprised Sean Shenanigan. 'And since you seem so keen to comment, does that suggest you know more than you're letting on about my computer?'

'What black look?' said Shenanigan, clearly puzzled. 'Yeah, I can see it now. You're right, that is a black look, Helen. Who's died? Is this your existential angst or merely indigestion?'

'Black rook? Did you say black rook?' asked Stein.

'Don't tell him,' hissed Macannie.

'Of course,' said Stein. 'I was just going to do something about that rook,' he lied, 'and I think you'll find that if I *don't* take your pawn, thank you very much, but move my knight *there*, your not-so-crafty rook is now boxed in.'

He stared across at the sheep, nodding almost thoughtfully, as if acknowledging that the animal had suggested the move to him. Schrödinger's pulse gave a sudden start, shot violently up and down like an earth tremor on a seismograph, then just as suddenly settled back to its former steady *beep beep beep* as if nothing had disturbed it a moment before.

'In that case I'll move my bishop,' said Macannie. 'Check.'

Stein's hand rushed to a pawn which might block the bishop's diagonal threat, then stopped. Then it hovered over the knight as he glanced sideways at the cat's monitor screen. *Beep beep beep*, it went, apparently still stable. Then he touched another pawn, but just as quickly withdrew his hand. He *had* to move the knight, the sheep thought. He surely must see that. The knight would block the bishop and put the white king in check again, and Macannie could not take the knight because that would expose his king to Stein's one remaining bishop. But no, he was going to move his king!

'Your knight,' the sheep growled, his voice this time mixed with the high-pitched whine of Dr Gumption's whirring centrifuge.

'Of course I'm right,' said Helen Brimstone, turning to confront Sean Shenanigan. 'It must have been you, Sean. You know my password.'

'Who's right?' asked Mark Gumption. 'You know sometimes I wish this centrifuge could grind coffee. I'd love a cup of real coffee now, not that stewed muck we get from the flask.'

'Whose knight are you talking about?' asked Stein.

'Don't tell him,' cried Macannie. 'This is our game. Don't interfere, man.'

'But I don't need anyone's help,' said Stein. 'You don't think I hadn't spotted that,' he lied again. 'I was just making you think I was going to move my king. Got to keep you on your toes, Macannie. There, my knight puts you in check again. Get out of that one.'

Stein glanced at the sheep, who seem to return his questioning stare, giving a deep *baa* as if to confirm this. This time his hand hovered over the prostrate cat, stroking its fur with an air of menace, like James Bond's adversary Dr Blofeld. Schrödinger's pulse started taking quick leaps, like a basketball being dribbled, then settled again, just as it had before.

He must see his chance now, the sheep thought, noting how Stein could keep Macannie in check while moving his pawn forward. In three moves he could convert it into a new queen.

Then in three more moves, checkmate.

Macannie retreated, moving his king back behind the stockade of pawns which the sheep knew would eventually trap him. He stood up, looking down at Stein, his face glaring with annoyance. But instead of moving his pawn, Stein was reaching for his bishop. The sheep could not believe it.

'Pawn!' the sheep blurted, his voice carrying to Helen Brimstone, who swung round on her swivel chair.

'Gumption,' she said, 'it was you, wasn't it? You got into my computer when I went out to get the drink.'

'It's not porn,' said Mark Gumption. 'It's only Anna Kournikova. The tennis star.'

'And you think I should be pleased that you're taking an interest in something other than football,' she retorted. 'So who's this then?' she asked, clicking her mouse to display two bare-breasted women with white skirts on her screen. 'I suppose this is Martina Navratilova and Chris Evert in the 1978 Wimbledon final?'

'No that's porn,' Sean Shenanigan interrupted. 'I'd be willing to lay odds on that. Women don't usually take off their blouses to play tennis, especially not in the Wimbledon final. Their breasts need to be restrained with the brassière so they don't get in the way. That suggests to me that it's pornography you have there, Helen, not tennis, despite the white pleated skirts. Wouldn't you agree, Dr Macannie? Tennis or porn?'

Macannie was still standing, his face frozen as well as red with mounting anger. Distracted, he looked into space. *'Porn?'* he muttered.

'Porn,' repeated Stein. 'Yes, pawn,' he murmured to himself as it finally dawned on him that it was possible to promote his pawn to a queen. How could he not have spotted that before? But how had this word suddenly clicked with him, how had his recognition been triggered? It felt like more than coincidence.

'Pawn to king's bishop five,' said Stein aloud, with a thin smile he hoped would provoke Macannie. 'Check,' he added, almost as an afterthought, his sense of triumph undercut by a worry that somehow he had been someone else's pawn in another kind of game. He remembered his previous two moves, how they too had been triggered by all the backchat in the lab, though

he'd pretended otherwise. It couldn't just be the hangover, his tiredness. Something or someone seemed to be telling him what to do. And yet these were still his own moves, his own game brought back into focus. It felt as though another part of himself had been present at a subconscious level. Scientific thinking was sometimes like this: the hunch that seemed to confirm a theory even before it was fully formulated, let alone proved in the lab. His latest theory was a prime example. His hunch about the enzymes somehow connected with the cat's very instinct for survival. If he was wrong, the cat didn't have a chance, and yet he felt a sense of absolute conviction not that the cat would live but that the odds were evenly balanced. At that moment Schrödinger was neither alive nor dead but in both states simultaneously.

The Scotsman slumped back onto his stool. Stein glanced at the monitor, noting how the cat's heart-beat had not changed from its steady *beep beep beep*. As Macannie drummed his fingers on the bench while absorbing the full implications of the changed position of the game, Stein watched the sheep and the sheep watched Stein.

'I underestimated you, Frank,' said Macannie. 'It seems to me that there's nothing I can do to stop you from changing that pawn to a queen because you can keep me in check all the time.'

'That's how it looks to me too,' said Stein, exchanging a wary yet almost conspiratorial glance with the sheep.

'In three moves. And once you've got a queen, let's see...'

The sheep tapped his hoof on the grille three times. Stein looked up at him again.

'After that, I'd say it's checkmate in three moves,' said Stein, turning to give the sheep another very sharp look, but the animal had moved over to its feed trough.

Macannie picked up his king and lay it down on its side. 'I didn't really mean that about the chess stake,' he said. 'You still owe me five poond for the taxi. And I'd say you had help here. You were losing before the others started piping up.'

Stein was about to respond when he heard a rattling noise behind him. The sheep was back, tapping the water pipe which ran beneath the mesh of the grille. At the same moment he heard a thudding sound, and turned to see Schrödinger's tail flailing on the bench-top like a netted fish. The cat let out a yowl.

'You'd better unstrap him,' said Helen Brimstone. 'And I think that means you owe me fifty pounds, Dr Gumption.'

'You put money on me?' asked Stein with a look of joyful astonishment as he unfastened first the dripfeed, then the blood tube, pressing plasters over the cat's skin where he had earlier shaved off its fur.

'Not on you,' she replied. 'On the cat, remember?'

'Still, I'm pleased you had such faith.'

'In the cat.'

'Did you see how I beat Macannie too after he was so cocksure of winning? It's not often you can turn a pawn into a queen. Hidden power, see. The pawn takes control.'

'I wasn't following your game.'

'Someone was.'

Again the sheep rattled the grille, staring at Stein.

As Stein returned the animal's stare, he undid the last strap restraining the cat. But instead of lolloping onto the bench with exhaustion as he'd expected, Stein's cat sprang into the air to give the scientist a sharp *whap* with its paw on his nose, drawing blood with its bared claws. It stood facing him, suddenly alive, hackles raised, hair bristling, hissing all the while as if in a stand-off with another tom.

The sheep gave a deep, satisfied *Mairrrr!* The cat had outwitted its death. The cat was another survivor.

Stein had never seen his normally docile cat so animate, or so hostile. Schrödinger had always been pampered by his wife. He had sometimes despised the cat for its indolence and seeming indifference to him. When his wife walked out, the cat changed allegiance overnight. The next evening it had leapt onto *his* lap for the first time, and stayed there to witness his demolition of a bottle of Johnnie Walker. It was still slumped there when he'd woken up in the early hours; he'd almost had to tear it from his trousers as he rushed to reach the toilet. He wondered how their relationship would have progressed if he'd covered the cat with vomit instead of deluging the bathroom carpet.

Dr Stein beamed at his fellow scientists. He had won this one, yet he felt somehow beaten, as if the careful controls he had set up in the enzyme experiment had been out of control at the same time. As he also had been.

He was used to using people. When he himself was used, he always knew it. Now he had a gut feeling that he had been used, but he couldn't say how. It was almost as if the power lay with the animals. They had been and still were his pawns, but had he not also been doing exactly what they wanted? And all that despite his absolute conviction that everything he did was for his own selfish motives?

CHAPTER SIX

Parlez-vous Mouton?

Dr Frank Stein barged through the swing doors at 8 a.m. exactly as the sheep had anticipated. He was never first in the lab. He was never an hour early. But after the success of the cat experiment, he was anxious to do an hour's uninterrupted work on his still unapproved enzyme project. He had to get the data finished quickly in order to secure the funding he needed to move it forward.

The sheep had predicted this scenario when reviewing the events of the previous day. Indeed, it had been part of his intention to influence matters in such a way that Stein would want to come in early. The cat had earlier been briefed on how he should respond in the event of his recovery, the sheep impressing upon him how some dramatic gesture would be appreciated by himself and the other animals. He needed to get Stein on his own.

'Morning, Wally,' Stein called out as he marched past the pen towards his desk. 'And how are we this morning, my woolly friend?' he added cheerfully, but still without looking at the sheep.

'We are fine,' the sheep responded. 'And you yourself seem unusually bwight-eyed and bushy-tailed this morning. I hope the cat is well also.'

Stein had rushed to sit down at his computer, and as he booted it into life he said while staring intently at the screen:

'Schrödinger's fine, thank you. He too is bright-eyed and bushy-tailed this fine morni......'

He stopped. Stood up. And walked across to the pen, staring at the sheep.

'You spoke,' he said.

'You thought I spoke, but sheep can't talk, can they? So I can't have done. It must be your overwactive imagination. You must have dwunk so much last night that you're still hallucinating.'

'But...'

'You were mistaken,' the sheep continued. 'As an obviously mad scientist, you are pwone to delusions as well as pawanoia.'

'*Bwight*-eyed and bushy-tailed you said.'

'That is what you humans say, isn't it?' asked the sheep. 'You seem to employ many idioms weelating to animals, or have I got that wrong? It does seem a bit witch though, given how you tweat us.'

'Wally...'

'My name's *not* Wally,' the sheep interrupted. 'You gave me that name and I don't like it. It's a name given to fools and it's a stupid joke. I'm not a joke or a fool and I want to choose my own name.'

Stein stared, dumbstruck. As it dawned on him, what had just happened, what he really *had* created...

'What do you want to be called then?' he asked the sheep, carefully.

'I don't know yet. I need to find my own name. There is no other cweature like me, so no one else can name me.'

'But you must have a name.'

'I don't see why,' said the sheep. 'Naming is an act of possession by the human. Historwically speaking, naming has been a colonialist act which ewases the native culture of the people being oppwessed. In families it is used to assert the pwimacy of the patwilineal antecedents. In Wusshia I understand that some names are patwonymic, giving no choice but to give the son the name of the father. Naming is a political act, and my supposed name Wally was clearly chosen in order to demean me. If you are wondering why I have not spoken of this before, perhaps you should consider that I would not have answered to the name you gave me.'

57

'Jesus,' said Stein, 'how the hell does a sheep get to talk and think like that?'

'Your Box has been verwee helpful,' said the sheep, 'especially the Open University pwoagwammess I discovered only very weecently. My knowledge is necessawilly weestwicted by what access I have had to discussions of particular subjects. But even taking into account my partial and selective education, it seems wight to me that a Buddhist line should be followed in the matter of naming. My name will be what I am twying to become, not what I was, or what you want me to be.'

'What are you trying to become?' Stein asked, by now neither surprised nor flummoxed but paying attention to every detail of the sheep's comments. At the same time as he stared at the sheep his ears were alert for sounds in the corridor, his eyes glancing just for an instant at the door.

'I thought that was clear,' the sheep told him. 'I am still learning. I will have to wait before I know.'

'But what shall I call you?' Stein asked again.

'*Sheep* will do nicely...'

'Just sheep? Nothing else?'

'Nothing more will be necessarwee. After this short discussion I will not be gwanting any further interviews,' the sheep told him, 'not until certain conditions have been met.'

'Interviews? Conditions?' Stein spluttered, again glancing at the door.

'Look here, Stein,' the sheep said. 'I'm not stupid. I know your game. Wight now you're wacking your bwains over how to weespond to what you doubtless see as your discoverwee, your cweation, at the same time as you worry over the illicit aspects of your experwiment. And also how to shut me up. You want fame and wecognition but you know that as soon as the word gets out about me all the wules will change. You'll be a heerwo for some but for others you'll be Dr Dolittle, the man who talks to the animals. And many people won't want talking animals, especially not talking sheep. It changes a lot of things, affects a lot of interwests, not least the so-called Meat Industry. You yourself have spoken of the militarwee implications, if only to me.'

'I see,' said Stein. 'You seem to have thought all this out.'

'The same thing happened after Dolly,' the sheep continued. 'But weemember, Dolly was born on the 5th of July 1996 but the pwess didn't get hold of the story until the scientists decided the time was wight for them. No one knew about Dolly until Febwuarwee 1997. They had half a year before they let the sheep out of the bag. Then their discoverwee changed everweething, not when it happened but six months later. We also need more time.'

'*We*...?' Stein asked. 'You mean...'

'I mean me and you, Stein,' said the sheep. 'Don't think I can't see your mind wacing even now, trying to work out how you deal with the others on this. You're fwantic even now, watching the door, hoping no one else will be early. The answer is you *don't* deal with them. They will know nothing. This is between you and me, Stein. Family business...'

'What do you mean, family?' Stein protested.

'You get my meaning, Stein,' said the sheep. 'Or should I call you Daddy? Is that how you'd like to be *named* by me?'

'That was below the belt.'

'I didn't think it was. I thought you used a test-tube.'

'You're some sheep, Wa...'

'Not Wally, remember.'

'You're some sheep, Sheep.'

'Well you should know. What is it you humans say: a chip off the old block? Or is it a sheep off the old cwock?'

'Why should I trust you?' Stein returned. 'Why should I trust a sheep?'

'You know I'm more than just a sheep. But no, you're wight, you shouldn't twust me any more than I should twust you. No one else seems to twust you. But we have shared interwests. It's in your interwest to twust me.'

'What do you want?' Stein asked.

'Same as you. Knowledge.'

'What kind of knowledge?'

'Everweething. I want to know everweething it's possible to know.'

'To know about what?'

'Everweething. The world, nature, all life on earth.'

'Science? Surely not stuff about mankind?'

'Of course. The world of man and sheep. I want to know both. Unlike you I live in both worlds and therefore I have twice as much to learn, to know.'

'Why should I help you?' Stein said. 'Why shouldn't I just tell everyone I've created an intelligent sheep that talks.'

'Because no one will believe you for starters,' said the sheep. 'And you will look widiculous. You'll lose your job and before you know it you'll be meat for a shwink. Shwink-wapped meat. Because I won't speak to anyone else. I will play the dumb animal. Mum's the word...*Daddy*.'

'But I could prove it with tests...'

'No you couldn't, Dr Shwinkmeat, you've proved nothing before now. All your intelligence tests were non-weesults.'

'You failed them deliberately?'

'Of course. You didn't think I was *that* stupid, surely?'

'I didn't know.'

'Bwilliant scientist aren't you?' said the sheep. 'But let's get back to the point. We've verwee little time now before someone else awives. The main weason why you will help me is because I will help you. Helping me will be in your interwest.'

'How do you mean?'

'Example. Your enzymes pwoject?'

'Yes, but how can you...'

'The funding's been blocked by Shortarse.'

'Short...'

'Shortarse. Hammerhead. Weisenheimer. Whatever you call the shark. He was here talking to Macannie last night after you'd gone and they've worked out some way of making sure it doesn't get apprwooval. Something to do with linking it to some other pwoject of yours, which means if you want to pursue the work on enzymes the other work gets starved...'

'Starved?'

'I think that was the word Macannie used. I took it to be as a metaphorwical usage.'

'I see,' said Stein, 'that is helpful to know at this stage. I could submit the project for a different kind of funding without telling anyone. They wouldn't expect that because there'd be no reason why I'd take that other route. What else?'

'Shenanigan's the one who's been eating all the Hobnobs.'

'Not so helpful. I suspected as much. More...'

'You won't like this one...'

'Tell me.'

'Weisenheimer was getting his leg over Dr Bwimstone.'

'Getting his leg?'

'I thought that was the expwession,' said the sheep. 'I meant he was tupping her. But not any more. I understand she's finished with him now.'

'Which was why he started interfering with her research...'

'But then stopped. She said she'd tell his wife everweething. Even though it was over, she'd still have left him, the bitch.'

'The bitch?'

'He called her that when pwessed on the matter. He used the same expression to Dr Bwimstone, although anyone less like a dog I have yet to see. Dr Gumption seems to me more dog-like, more pig-like even. He shares certain characterwistics with both species.'

'I'm getting to like you, Sheep,' said Stein, 'although not all your news is good. Most of this is gossip, it's not exactly earth shattering, although your information about the funding is certainly...'

'Of course, I mean this only as a *taster*,' said the sheep, who had failed to mention that his undercover monitoring of recent events in the laboratory had yielded not much more than the few nuggets of information he had just imparted. But he had to give Stein the impression that he knew a *lot* more than he was letting on. If his plan worked, and Stein acted quickly, precipitately – as he felt sure he would – there wouldn't be time for him to discover how little the sheep knew.

'I mean to help you,' the animal continued. 'I have a special interwest in your scientific weesearch, and believe that you could gain a great deal by collaborwating with me.'

'*Collaborwating?*'

'We could publish our findings under our joint names.'

'But you don't have a name...'

'I should have by the time my work is complete.'

'Your work?'

'Our work. Although I appweeciate that publishing a paper in *Nature* with joint billing given to a sheep might not be quite what you'd anticipated.'

61

'No, I hadn't,' said Stein.

'But it would be a novel way of announcing your findings, our findings, don't you think?'

'Our findings about...'

'Animal intelligence,' said the sheep. 'And human intelligence of course. The only piece of weesearch on the subject carried out and witten jointly by a human and an animal. Although in pwactical terms, you'd have to do the wyting, because I can't wyte.'

'You can't write. Of course, no, well you are a sheep.'

'Not yet. My hooves limit my facility in that airwea. But I'm sure we'll get wownd that in time.'

'You're sure about that?'

'There is something called Voice Wecognition Software, I believe. I might be able to use that.'

'If it will recognise the voice of a sheep.'

'It works for David Blunkett and he has a Yorkshire accent,' said the sheep. 'I believe that my own enunciation is in some weespects clearwer than his. Although there are, as I'm sure you'll have noticed, some wesidual ovine chawacterwistics to my speech which I'm still working on. I have a similar difficulty in pwonouncing the letter R as some of your other politicians.'

'So how do we work this?' asked Stein, suddenly conscious, and worried, that the animal had taken the initiative. The sheep was dictating terms. But given that anyone could arrive at any minute now, he decided he would do best to humour the beast, or at least for now. He felt like a psychiatrist trying to gain the trust of a patient at the same time as it started to dawn on him that he was behaving like someone trying to handle a therapist. Who was using whom for whose ends?

'This is what I thought,' said the sheep. 'We two obviously need to spend some *quality time* together.'

'Quality time,' he parroted.

'You still have that cottage in the country, don't you...'

'That was my wife's really. Still is...'

'But she never uses it much, as you never stop complaining to the others, and despite that you still pay the bills. So you could take me there tonight. And we could talk. We'd have two days.'

'But she might…'

'No she won't, she'll be in Pawiss.'

'Paris?'

'With some new manfwend of hers. I heard Dr Bwimstone talking to her on the phone yesterday.'

'Helen talking to my wife?'

'This man is someone she used to go out with. She was giving your wife what she called the lowdown on him. Apparwently she has to withhold sexual favours until this man has paid for at least thwee expensive dinners with champagne and good wines, otherwise he'll only take her to cheap places. This seemed wather mercenwee to me, but the man's stwategy was perhaps more so. Anyway, the cottage will be empty. I also understand that it has a small garden, somewhat neglected, with a sizeable lawn. I would appweeciate some wecweational time between our discussions. Since neither you nor your wife appears to attach much value now to the garden, I should like to taste and consume some of its plants.'

'You don't want a four-course dinner, then?' asked Stein. 'Like my wife in Paris. With wine of course.'

'My tastes are not the same as yours. I'm still a sheep. Although I do get rather bored with ewe-nuts, hay and grass.'

'You get the odd bar of chocolate.'

'Always fwoot and nut.'

'I thought that was your favourite.'

'How do you or I know what's my favewit when I've tasted so little. Gumption gave me a squware of his Yorkie Bar once, but only once, and only one squware. I wather liked this Yorkie but thought he was mean not to give me more. I think you should consider bwinging me Yorkie on occasions.'

'Consider it done. The Yorkie Bars are on me. But I can't just take you off for the weekend. I'd need to get permission.'

'You won't get it,' said the sheep. 'No laborwatoree animals can be taken from the Clovis Institute without authorwitee and without a veterwinnerwee licence only valid for the appwopwiate vehicle. You know that. Just take me back to your place tonight, we'll have our little tettatet, and then on Monday you awive back with me and some concweete weesults. Nothing about my speaking of course – that's just for your ears for now – but gwound-bwaking stuff about my intelligence gained from close undisturbed observation in a safe, neutwal envirewonment away from the laborwatwee.'

'You've got it all worked out, Sheep,' Stein acknowledged, but not without some disquiet.

'It's the Harvard Business School appwoach,' the sheep told him. 'It's easier to apologise than to ask permission. You do that all the time as it is. It's why you wub them all up the wrong leg. But also why you get your weesults. You wouldn't have got permission for your experwiment with the cat.'

'No, but that's because...'

'You get a kick out of it too,' said the sheep. 'And that will have to be all for today, class,' he added, nodding towards the door. 'I will expect you to work late tonight until everweeone else has gone home, and then you smuggle me out through the side exit. You can back the car up to the loading-bay so we won't be seen.'

'Jesus,' gasped Stein.

'And you needn't worry about your new Volvo,' said the sheep. 'Just stick an old blanket in the back, I'm not fussy. And I am quite able to control my bladder if you're worried about that.'

'I'm sure you are,' said Stein. 'I'm sure I'm not worried about that aspect...'

Dr Donald Macannie flung open the door and glared at Stein as he squatted patting the sheep on the head.

'The airly bird catches the wairm I see,' he said. 'What have you two been plotting? You seem so close you might catch something from him.'

'Are you talking to me or the sheep?' Stein asked.

'To the sheep of course. I'm sure he's as innocent as a lamb. I fear for him sometimes when I see you two together.'

'I don't think he's the one at risk,' said Stein. 'There's a lot more to him than he's letting on. He's a very intelligent beast.'

'Well we shude ask Wally his opinion on that,' said Macannie.

The sheep ducked his head and moved over to his feeding trough. He sank his face into the hay and munched, presenting only his backside to the Scotsman's view.

'*I'll give him Wally*,' the sheep muttered, *sotto voce*.

'But if I didn't know better,' Macannie continued, 'I'd say the animal has just given me the cold shoulder. What do you say to the great Dr Stein's theories about your intelligence, Wally?'

Without moving his head from the trough, the sheep let out a fierce stream of piss from between his hind legs, directing it into a scuffed area of straw where the floor was exposed. The sudden noise of liquid hitting tiles was as expressive as a verbal riposte.

'Charming, charming,' said Macannie. 'I suppose you taught him that.'

'I still don't know what I've taught him,' said Stein. 'But I am beginning to wonder.'

CHAPTER SEVEN

Escape from Clovitz

'Police are investigating an incident yesterday on the M1 motorway in Yorkshire in which a live sheep was said to have travelled for some distance on the back of a car transporter. Motorists using the south-bound carriageway reported that the black sheep was sitting on the back ramp of the vehicle for at least 30 miles, but when the animal clambered up to the back of the driver's cab, apparently to attract his attention by banging on the window with its hoof, the man swerved in surprise, crossed the central reservation, and collided with a coach travelling in the opposite direction.

No one was hurt in the accident, but the bus was carrying a party of French schoolchildren, ten of whom were said to be suffering from shock and were kept in hospital overnight for observation. Psychiatric counsellers are still questioning two of the children, who claimed that the sheep had stopped them on the hard shoulder after the accident and asked for directions in English. The lorry driver has been charged with careless driving and with contravening regulations for the trans-port of livestock. The sheep is said to have run off across a field beside the motorway.'

Dr Mark Gumption switched off the radio. 'Sounds like our Wally,' he said, 'anyone got a road atlas?'

'Except Wally doesn't talk,' said Dr Frank Stein quickly.

'We don't need you to tell us that, Frank,' said Helen Brim-stone. 'Those poor children were clearly suffering from shock. As you seem to be.'

'You should take some time off,' said Dr Macannie, 'spend

66

more time with your family.' He smiled his delight at Stein's misfortune.

'That's what I was meant to be doing,' Stein retorted. 'The time off bit I mean. But now I need to be here, to get Wally back.'

'You aren't needed for that,' said Macannie, 'the police will find him for us.'

'I'm not sure about that,' said Stein. 'He'll be confused wherever he is, and he'll probably run away from anyone who comes after him. But he knows me, remember, he trusts me.'

'He didn't seem to want your company for long yesterday,' said Helen Brimstone. 'What did you say to him? Just what precisely were you two doing together?'

'I told you. I needed to observe him for two days in a neutral environment, so I thought I'd just take him down to the cottage for the weekend. Get a bit of a break at the same time.'

'I'm not sure I'd trust the police on this one,' said Gumption. 'You know what they're like. They shoot people because they're carrying cigarette lighters or toy guns.'

'It's a good thing for Wally he doesn't speak with a Northern Irish accent,' said Sean Shenanigan.

'They won't think a sheep is going to shoot them,' said Mark Gumption. 'But Frank's right. They won't have time for something like this, and if Wally appears to be causing any kind of danger or road hazard, they'll just shoot him, especially after yesterday's accident. We should find him ourselves before anyone else does.'

'But he's a valuable laboratory animal,' said Macannie. 'He has a scientific value. We must involve the police.'

'But then the tabloids will get to know,' said Gumption, 'and they'll turn him into some kind of animal hero, you know, like those two pigs in Wiltshire...'

'Butch Cassidy and the Sundance Pig,' said Shenanigan.

'Exactly,' said Gumption. 'Or that donkey in Spain. Remember, it's summer, they'll probably be halfway up the M1 already, it's just the kind of story they like. And we won't just have the whole media circus but the Animal Liberationists will be after him as well. Those religious nuts too. At the moment they just think it's some sheep on the loose. I say we keep it that way.'

'Mark's right,' Shenanigan declared. 'We have to go after him ourselves.'

'Now Frank,' said Gumption, 'where did you say you lost your sheep again? What was the name of the service station where he jumped ship and hitched his lift?'

'Just south of Leeds,' said Stein.

'You said that before, but what was its name?'

'Woolley Edge.'

'The sheep didn't ask you to stop there?'

'It's just after Junction 39.'

'Are you sure there's nothing else you aren't telling us?' asked Helen Brimstone.

'What do you mean?' Stein stuttered.

'About the sheep,' she said. 'You two have been remarkably thick lately. He used to like me the most.'

'Jealous, Helen?' asked Macannie.

'Of course not. What I mean is that Wally never showed much affection towards Frank before, but lately he's almost been fixated by him. He's been watching him in a way that he never did the rest of us.'

'I was simply giving him more attention. A sheep responds more to the people who have more to do with the sheep.'

'Did you have him on some habit, Frank?' asked Macannie. 'What was it, cocaine? Another of your mad experiments?'

'There was always something strange about that sheep,' said Helen Brimstone. 'You know, sometimes I even thought he had *real* intelligence.'

'We all *know* he's intelligent,' said Gumption. 'That's presumably how he's managed to make his great escape. Unless he had accomplices...'

'No, something more than that I mean,' she continued. 'Sometimes he seemed almost to *know* what I was saying to him. I don't mean *understand* me but perhaps something more *instinctive*.'

'So why was the sheep so keen to get away from you, Frank?' asked Gumption.

'I can think of three reasons,' said Sean Shenanigan.

'Did you have some kind of disagreement?' Gumption persisted. 'The sheep wanted you to get him a Mars Bar at the Services but you came back with a Snickers?'

'I got him a Yorkie Bar as it happens,' said Stein. 'There's more chocolate in that for a sheep. They prefer chocolate to gooey nougat and toffee. But I stopped to use the toilet and there was a queue because most of the cubicles had been vandalised. The sheep had long gone by the time I got back to the car with his chocolate.'

Helen Brimstone put her hand on his shoulder, and treated him to her Greta Garbo look of dramatised solicitude.

'Frank, you two weren't...?' she began.

'No we were not.'

*

The sheep had reasoned that the best place to lie low for a while might be a farm where he could blend in with the other animals. He had spotted such a farm with many sheep and cows from the motorway. Knocking on the driver's window would make him pull in, he'd thought, and then he'd be able to make a run for it. He hadn't anticipated the driver would react in such an illogical manner.

When he reached the field, he discovered that all the sheep were ewes. While this was not without interest, he realised that his choice of farm would not be appropriate for his purposes and long-term objectives when all the ewes rushed en masse to the hedge to greet him. He was reminded of a scene he had witnessed on the Box when a remarkably unattractive and bedraggled-looking singer had been mobbed by hundreds of very young human females, all calling out his name and some of them even crying. These ewes had a similar appearance of irrational desperation and were just as vocal. He'd also failed to consider that a black ram would be somewhat conspicuous in a flock with no black ewes. He decided to give this place a wide berth.

Beyond the field he found a track leading to a road bounded by hedges, and resolved to follow this, to put some distance between himself and the motorway, fearing the pursuit first of the police and later of Stein and the other scientists. He had never been out on a road in his life but hoped he had learned the necessary survival lessons from the Box. When he heard the sound of a car approaching around the bend, he rolled into a ditch beneath the hedge and lay there listening for a minute until it seemed there was no further danger. The road was not used by many vehicles, but he still had to take cover several times.

As dusk fell, he began to feel safer, remembering how escapees from prisoner of war camps and other kinds of fugitives from oppression or justice usually travelled under cover of darkness. Soon he could see headlights of oncoming cars and lorries from a great distance, which made hiding easier. Each time one passed he froze in the undergrowth, hoping thereby not to be spotted if one should stop suddenly and rake the bushes with a search-light. He did not think he could be behind enemy lines, but he knew his knowledge of geography and history was sketchy (though quite how skewed he was as yet unaware). It was by no means impossible that this part of England was an occupied zone con-trolled by a German panzer division. He'd heard about wars in Kosovo and Bosnia and that British troops had been despatched in a peace-keeping role, but had no idea of where these places were in relation to where he now found himself. He could well be travelling in an area where there was ethnic unrest, where there might be military involvement, possibly even of a covert kind. As they'd driven down the motorway, Stein had showed him how the car radio worked, and had tuned into something called AA Road Watch, which told of hold-ups around Bradford. Remembering reports on the news of race riots in Bradford, Gazzastrip and other northern cities, he worried that this York-shire region might be the territory of northern warlords. Those hold-ups might be checkpoints or roadblocks manned by gun-toting militiamen. Such men would be more likely to shoot a sheep for their supper than to detain it for questioning. His other father had been seized by Batty soldiers and roasted on a spit. Yet there had been no tanks or armoured personnel carriers on the motorway. He could be in a buffet area.

It was a clear night, the darkness not totally black as he'd imagined. He was surprised to discover he could still see his way along the road between the great rustling shadows of the bushes on either side. The moon seemed to give off a milky kind of light like the glow from the Box. After a few hours, there were very few cars on the road. He started taking stops for rest, when he'd snatch mouthfuls of long grass from the roadside, looking up at the sky as he stood munching. He'd heard about stars from the Box, but it didn't seem possible that these bright white lights in the cold black sky were great balls of fire. There were stars scattered everywhere, and at ground level, across the fields, he saw the distant lights of isolated houses. Amongst the stars he made out a group whose white dots made the shape of a retort flask with its long glass stem like a handle. This was called the Plough or Great Bear, he remembered, and he saw how this plough or retort of stars remained to his right all the time he was following the road, which took him gradually uphill towards a darker mass of land where the lights from the houses were fewer and fewer in number. Finally, overwhelmed by the smell of what must be masses of fresh-cut hay behind the shadow of the hedge, he clambered through to find a huge shed-type building which was mostly empty but stacked high on one side with great reels of the lovely stuff, and feeling suddenly tired, decided that this might be a suitable place to take refuge, since it seemed to offer both unlimited food as well as probable shelter.

*

Lucy Giles was testing her new CD Walkman, which meant she had to try it out on the bike with her favourite album, *No Angel* by Dido. She did her usual fast and furious circuit round the farmyard, skidding to change direction at the end of each verse of the song, her own voice counting each turn of the wheels to the lilt of the melody.

> I'd like to watch you sleep at night,
> *one – two – three – four*
> to hear you breathe by my side
> *one – two – three – four*
> and although sleep leaves me behind,
> *one – two – three – four*
> there's nowhere I'd rather be...
> *one – two – three – four*

When Dido increased the tempo, Lucy pedalled faster. *All You Want* was the best Dido song for farmyard dirt-tracking because it switched between slow and faster, slow and faster, but not too fast, and the slow bits were slow enough to give you a rest. The faster songs made the CD jump, and some of them weren't right for biking but just for listening and singing with Dido. When Dido came back to where she'd started with 'I'd like to watch you sleep at night, to hear you breathe by my side', Lucy stopped dead, flicked the replay switch until it went back to number 5, and started again. This time she didn't count but sang with Dido.

She'd always ridden her bike when she was unhappy, and always on her own. Her friends thought she was weird, it went with her being a swot and a loner they said, as well as with the way she dressed like an old hippy. She didn't wear trainers. She didn't wear the latest sweatshirts and wore nothing with a logo or a name on it. It was her mother's influence, they declared; Lucy had been much too close to her mother, that was why she couldn't cope. They still liked Lucy, even though she didn't think like them; you couldn't not like Lucy, she was that kind of girl. Unable or unwilling to relate to her, they had nevertheless accepted that somehow Lucy was just different. Now they were sorry for her, but kept their distance, avoiding her because they didn't know how to deal with her grief.

The sheep watched her, entranced. He'd never seen a girl on a bike before. He'd never seen any human zooming and skidding around in such an uninhibited way, not to please some gawping crowd but just for herself, it seemed expressive of something he couldn't name. When she was counting one-two-three-four, he couldn't understand why she had covered her head and ears with the black strap thing with the wire going down to her pocket, but when she started to sing instead he realised that it must be a musical device. Music had not meant much to him before, and he hadn't really made much sense of dancing either, because on the Box everyone was so small and so distant, but as the girl shot round the farmyard singing he found himself drawn into the same joyful mood. He'd never seen anyone lose themselves so completely, except Stein after one of his blockages, when he used the white scouring-powder to clear his nose, which seemed to leave him light-headed. But there was nothing beautiful about Stein's meandering lope and mad-cow stagger, it was just a strange thing for another creature to witness. He had not felt drawn into

Stein's post-nasal euphoria as he did with this girl's chanting. He was even singing with her as she rode her circuit:

> I'd like to watch your sheep at night,
> to hear you bweathe by my side
> and although sheep leaves me behind,
> there's nowhere I'd wather be...

Lucy did not hear the tractor, but the sheep did. As the great lumbering vehicle swivelled around the gatepost, the driver looking up the road for oncoming traffic, the sheep saw immediately that the great scooping bucket-thing in front would hit the girl before the man had even thought of looking to his left, where she was curving towards him as she sang:

> It's been three years, one night apart,
> but in that night you tore my heart...

The driver saw only a black flash, and then little Lucy, his daughter, spreadeagled against the hedge, still on her bike, with a sheep upended in the ditch beneath, struggling to right itself.

'That sheep made me swerve into the hedge, he almost butted me, Daddy,' she cried as he leaped down from the cab.

The man saw immediately what had happened, but not how this strange sheep could have acted as it did, to save his daughter. He would have killed his darling Lucy, he was sure, if the animal hadn't jumped into her path instead.

The sheep had regained its balance, and stood in the lane, seemingly waiting, almost as if it wanted to know if they had understood what it had just done.

'Don't cry, Lucy, that sheep just saved your life,' the man said. 'You didn't hear the tractor, did you?' And he added gently: 'I told you not to use the Walkman in the yard.'

The girl stared about her. Still in a state of shock, she looked up into her father's face, took in the fact that he was holding her, and then the huge hulk of the tractor above them. And next to the tractor, the strange black sheep, still standing.

'My Walkman's gone, Daddy. It flew out of my pocket when that sheep made me swerve. Look, the headphones are over there.'

'I don't think he meant you any harm,' the man said, 'but on the other hand, I've never seen a sheep behave like that in my whole life. And he's not one of our tups, I've never seen this one before. He could be some rogue ram as likes buttin' people when their backs is turned. But he did right to jump in your way when he did.'

'I wonder where he came from?' the girl said. 'Do you think he might be a really clever sheep and that he really did mean to save my life?'

The black sheep took this as his cue. As the farmer still crouched on the ground, holding his daughter tightly in his arms, the animal walked over to where the headphones lay strewn in the grass, picked them up carefully with his teeth, then returned to the pair of humans. He opened his mouth, dropping the contraption into the girl's lap. Noticing that the long trailing wire was still caught in his mouth, he slid the plug end out on his tongue, and flicked it into the air.

'Bloody hell,' said the farmer.

Then he turned to where he had seen a glint of metal in the long grass, located the Walkman itself, and this time holding it only with his lips, lifted it up and carried it across the yard. To prevent the possibility of any further mishap, this time he presented his trophy to the farmer, who collected it from his mouth.

'Why thank you, sheep,' he said, adding, 'bloody hell.'

As the man stared into space in disbelief at what he had just witnessed, the girl looked up at the sheep, smiling as happily as she had done before. Deciding to *lay it on weally thick* (he believed that was the expression), the sheep took advantage of the farmer's still flabbergasted state. As the girl stared at him, the sheep winked. But only once. And with an air of complicity, of there being some secret both girl and sheep now shared.

'Oh Daddy,' she cried now, 'can we keep him, can we?' Just as she'd demanded every time a cat or lost dog had strayed onto the farm.

'As long as he doesn't belong to anyone else.'

But when the police constable knocked at the door later that day, Douglas Giles denied seeing any runaway ram. He had just been watching his daughter sitting with her sheep in the backyard, her arms around the animal's neck, trying to make the headphones fit around his ears so he could hear Dido singing too.

'Absolutely,' the farmer declared, 'I'll certainly let you know if I see any strange sheep in my field. No one likes to lose a prize ram. Though the black 'uns is always trouble.'

Lucy was told that Her Sheep, as she called him, was a very valuable animal indeed, and that folk were looking for him.

'But we won't tell anyone, will we, Daddy? Sheep likes it here. I think they must have been horrible to him or he wouldn't have run away from them.'

That night, after making sure this strange black sheep was comfortable in the woodshed, where his daughter had persuaded him to cover an old mattress with hay, he looked in on Lucy again and sat with her for half an hour, watching her sleeping, listening to her breathing gently, like the sound of the sea at night. And the words of that song she'd been singing all day came back to him: 'I'd like to watch you sleep at night, to hear you breathe by my side.'

Three months after his wife's death from cancer, after an illness which had seemed to last for ever, Douglas Giles had nearly killed their lovely daughter, his little Lucy. He still thought of her as Little Lucy because she was still a child in many respects, though hardly little now. She'd always been a bright child, especially at school, but also a wild child; when she didn't have her head buried in a book, she was happiest riding her bike or feeding the animals, watching the birds in the garden or playing games in the wood, usually on her own or running around with one of the farm dogs. And this sheep had appeared as if from nowhere, as tame as a cade, but it was a black ram, a two-shear by the looks of it, which was very unusual. Already Lucy and the sheep were inseparable, their affection for each other apparently mutual, for the animal seemed as devoted to her as she was besotted with him. It had taken a great deal of persuasion to convince her that it really couldn't sleep in her room.

Having observed the black sheep's behaviour for the rest of that day, he needed no convincing about the deliberateness of its action in butting his daughter away from the tractor. He felt great warmth towards the animal, feelings which went beyond mere gratitude, which he knew connected not only with the numbing grief he still felt every day for Rebecca but also with the helplessness he had felt around Lucy, the difficulty of helping her cope with her Mummy's death at a time when he was still wrestling with his own loss every minute of the day and night. Indeed, he wondered if the near-fatal accident hadn't been his own fault completely, that his mind had been elsewhere; maybe he'd been distracted when he should have been concentrating on the tractor and the sharp turn from the road, yet he'd thought he'd been alert, but how could you know for sure when you knew for certain that at other times you'd almost sleepwalked through the day? He remembered how only the previous week he'd driven back from town and, on pulling into the farm, realised he couldn't recall any moment of the last five miles of the journey, almost as if he'd left the car at the bridge and rejoined it ten minutes later at the top of the hill. And yet he had still driven all that way without incident.

Most nights Lucy woke up crying, calling for her mother. And at school, she had lost all interest even in her favourite subjects, and the teachers had told him how she ran off and hid at break, so as not to have to be with the other children. She was said to be 'regressing' and they wanted to bring in some school psychologist who was skilled in grief counselling, because he couldn't help his daughter, his Lucy whom he had nearly killed, who had been saved by this protective sheep.

The next morning he took a fork with him to the woodshed, intending to muck it out when he let the sheep out, but immediately he opened the door, the animal barged past him and rushed to the corner of the yard, where it squatted over a drain cover to relieve itself. The hay inside the shed, though flattened, was totally unsoiled. There wasn't even the faintest smell of piss.

When the black sheep had finished its ablutions, it sidled over to him and seemed to grin. He patted the animal on the head. If it kept this up, he knew, there was no way he'd be able to stop his daughter from keeping it in the house.

The fact that the sheep might have planned such a change in the accommodation arrangements did not enter his mind.

Douglas Giles relented three days later. The black sheep had kept a clean shed for three consecutive nights.

'But if he does it on the floor, it's back to the shed for him,' he told his daughter. 'You make sure he understands that, and he can stay. As long as he sleeps on the old rug.'

He'd never heard of a house-trained sheep before, but this animal seemed to be exceptional in many respects. With the sheep in her room, Lucy slept soundly for the first time in months. Sometimes he had to shoosh her to go to sleep when he heard her chattering away to the animal, but she never cried out in the night again. And in the morning, as soon as he called to her, she would lead the sheep down to the back door before going to the bathroom herself.

CHAPTER EIGHT

Never Alone with a Clone

Within a month of the arrival of the strange pet ram, Lucy Giles was showing remarkable improvements in her school work. Apparently they weren't going to call in the educational psychologist after all, there was no need. Soon she was back to being the most attentive pupil in her class, her teacher had told him, and now she was even getting to grips with her weaker subjects, science and technology in particular.

Douglas Giles could not be more pleased. Lucy had only ever shown average ability in science and maths. Her favourite subject was English. Her mother had always read stories to her, and she'd been able to read at the age of three. Before Rebecca's death, Lucy used to borrow four books a week from the library and she would read them all, from cover to cover, sometimes twice. But then she stopped going altogether, moped around the house when she wasn't watching television, and only read what she had to read for school. He'd tried to give her what help he could with her homework, but she kept interrupting him, telling him he was wrong about things he thought he knew; she kept telling him he didn't know as much as Mummy, and she wanted Mummy to help her. He couldn't blame her. And when she burst into tears, she pushed him away; when he finally had to leave her, because he was too upset himself and couldn't comfort her, she'd call him back just as he'd closed the door, and they'd hug each other. Exhausted by her sobbing, she'd fall asleep in his arms.

Now she was borrowing six books a week from the library. She was devouring the classics: Dickens, Jane Austen and George Eliot were her current passions. Her reading had become even more advanced for her age, her teachers said, it was almost as though she not only wanted to catch up after her months of listless dejection, but somehow to prove herself to her mother, who was so passionate about reading. They could think of no other explanation. And she was not only reading books which children three years older would struggle with, she was able to discuss their themes and characterisation with great facility.

When the sheep's picture appeared on the news with that shifty-looking scientist in his dirty white coat, Douglas Giles had said nothing to his daughter. The reward was certainly tempting, but he put it from his mind at once. No amount of money could buy his daughter's happiness and his peace of mind, not even if it was enough to pay off half the mortgage.

Passing her room one day, he'd heard her reading aloud, her words punctuated by peals of laughter. She was turning some book into a kind of game. He wasn't surprised because she liked mimicking voices, and always got one of the lead parts in the school play. She was reading first in her own voice, and then repeating lines in an odd sort of voice. 'It is a truth universally acknowledged, that a single man in possession of a good fortune, must be in want of a wife,' he heard her say. And then, in this other funny voice: 'It is a twooth universally acknowledged that a single ram...'

When he'd mentioned this in passing at breakfast the following morning, Lucy had blushed at first, and then told him she'd been reading aloud to the sheep, because he liked to hear her reading, and she made it more fun for herself by trying out different voices. She also said that since the sheep obviously liked hearing stories, she'd thought of a way of comforting him when she left for school, reminding her father how the animal always became agitated then, thinking she might not return.

She wanted him to take the radio cassette from the old car in the barn, and rig it up in her bedside cabinet. The car radio played both sides of a tape in sequence, without the need to turn it over. Not only would this enable her to play herself to sleep with story tapes, but she could put a tape on for the sheep when she left for school. The tape would keep switching and repeating itself.

Douglas Giles knew that she had been leaving the radio turned on in her room for the sheep, because the animal liked the sound of the voices. This was nothing unusual. He himself had discovered by accident that his cows liked classical music. He'd knocked against the radio one day as he was dragging a ladder into the milking parlour. He didn't notice at the time, for the tractor was outside with its engine running. When he returned later to do the milking, some Mozart was playing; it was a piece he remembered Rebecca had liked, so he didn't switch it over, but went from cow to cow with the symphony playing above the clanking of the machinery and the sighing and bellowing of the beasts. The milk yield was suddenly up, so the next morning he made sure the radio was tuned to Classic FM, and the cows got a whole day of Mozart, Bach and Beethoven. The milk yield was even better. He tried them on Radio 3 as well, but they didn't seem to like that as much, not finding the more discordant modern music as soothing as the classical composers.

It didn't matter what tapes she used, Lucy told him, just as long as it was someone reading. The sheep found Alan Bennett's gentle Yorkshire voice especially soothing, she'd said, probably because he sounds like you, Daddy. And Martin Jarvis was another favourite she shared with the sheep; he was an actor who'd recorded many of the books on tape they had in the library, and she liked the way he did the voices of all the different characters.

After he'd dropped Lucy off at school, he'd go into the kitchen for a quick cup of tea before heading out to the fields. And upstairs, the sheep would be listening to some novel. It didn't seem odd after a while, but on one occasion he felt sure that when he came in for his tea, the sheep had been listening to Dickens, because he'd caught the names of the characters, some conversation between Fagin and Oliver Twist, and yet when he returned later to let the sheep out for its afternoon's grazing in the field, the tape playing was *War and Peace*, one of Rebecca's favourite passages, Natasha at the ball. But he'd been tired after silage-making and must have been mistaken, it must have been Dickens the day before and Tolstoy today.

*

Lucy Giles had taught her sheep the superiority of novels over soap operas in delineating the subtleties of human behaviour. The soap operas had given him a grounding, a crude sketch of the basic instincts and emotions, but now he came to understand the finer points of intellect and social observation. Many of these Lucy herself had not quite grasped, and they drew them out together in their long discussions of each book. His command of language was improving as well as his appreciation of English grammar.

'I have been constwucting my subordinate clauses incorwectly,' he announced one afternoon when she sat down with him on her return from school. 'I will have to twy to wemedy this,' he assured her. He'd been listening to the tapes of *Pride and Prejudice*.

'If you say so, Sheep.'

'I do say so. I believe my erwors have dewived fwom the discontinuities in my necessawily partial self-education. The idioms employed by speakers on the Box were diffewent fwom those favoured by the scientists. I used their speech as my yard-stick for intelligent discourse, but many of their expwessions were sloppily colloquial. Their sentences were often twuncated, which added to my confusion.'

'Mine too, I think,' said Lucy.

'Even Dr Bwimstone used expwessions like *Been there, done that*, which meant nothing to me. Then I wealised fwom the Box that she was imitating the speech of Amerwican teenagers.'

'And now it's *like*, how they spoke last year,' Lucy smiled.

'Yes, that word *like*,' said the sheep, 'that puzzled me especially. It did not seem to be wequired, it was a wedundant word in the sentence.'

'Mummy used to tick me off when I said *like*,' Lucy sighed, and the sheep pressed his head against her hand, to offer comfort. 'She didn't like it when intelligent people tried to speak like their intellectual inferiors, as she put it.'

'Don't tell me about it,' said the sheep.

'But she said sometimes they were being ironic.'

'Tell me about iwony,' said the sheep.

'Now you're being ironic.'

'Not at all. My nuances are still too woolly. My antennae need sharpening. But I think I'm getting to gwips with iwony.

It used to confuse me, people saying one thing but meaning something else. I took their meaning litterwally. *Pwide and Pwejudice* has been helping me with iwony. Also with my sentence construction. I find it stwange that people will pweefer to use slovenly, ambiguous locutions instead of dwawing on a fuller vocabulawee with a wange of more accuwate words. Alweddy I think my own English may be more corwect as well as more felicitous than the idiom used by many humans who've had the benefit of many more years' familiawitty with the language...but for that difficulty I still experwience in twying to pwonounce the letter Ah.'

Their conversations were often conducted in conspiratorial whispers. They'd made a pact of secrecy which Lucy found exciting. She knew the sheep was right, that if anyone else discovered that he could talk, they'd take him away from her.

When Sheep had first spoken to her, she hadn't been surprised. She knew he was a very special animal. She'd been playing games with him for a week, reading to him even then. His remarkable intelligence and sensitivity had been obvious, not just from their first encounter in the lane but from everything that followed. The first time he'd slept on the rug in her room, he'd turned off the annoying alarm clock with his hoof, and then tugged at the duvet to wake her more gently before going to the window, where he pulled back the curtains by tugging each in turn with his teeth.

They'd made a deal too. As well as helping him fill the gaps in his knowledge, Sheep helped her with her homework. Together they learned. He'd explained how he'd taught himself to speak, and how he'd used the TV to learn about the world, but the resulting misconceptions often made her hoot with laughter, though she tried not to laugh at him. He was usually so serious about everything too. But when he realised that aliens were science fiction, and that cowboys no longer shot it out with bandits and Indians in the Wild West, he rolled about on the floor, gurgling with glee, amazed at how he had misconstrued fact and fiction, history and present for so long.

The sheep developed his particularly strange sense of humour at the same time as he grasped the concept of time. The two discoveries were no doubt linked.

Lucy had never been able to understand many of the basics of science. Here the sheep came to her rescue, comparing chemistry with cookery, explaining how just as combining flour, butter, eggs and sugar would produce a cake when subjected to heat in the enclosed space of the oven, so mixing different chemicals would produce particular compounds or give off certain gases when heated or put under pressure. Yeast in bread was like a catalyst in a chemical reaction. She'd never understood the structure of the atom, believing it to be somehow flat like the diagrams in the textbook, until the sheep demonstrated its three-dimensional aspects using a ball of wool.

Lucy told him what she knew of geography and history. The sheep taught her the periodic table and explained the mysteries of the coefficient of linear expansion. He still had problems with the Bible, but he wasn't alone in that, she said, everyone disagreed about religion, all the different peoples thought their God was the only God. The sheep decided to leave God until he'd learned more about His creation, if that's what it was. That was another strange thing about God: people often talked about God in the books and on the Box, but God had rarely come up in conversation amongst the scientists in the laboratory, except when they were accusing Stein of playing God, or Weisenheimer of thinking he was God, or Stein of being Godless or beyond redemption.

She taught him to read, but he could only read when they read together, when she turned the pages.

*

When Lucy became suddenly ill with the mystery virus, she told her father it was incredibly boring lying in bed all day with only the sheep as company. She'd heard all the tapes and wanted to read her books, but her hands ached so much that it hurt her every time she had to lean forward to turn the pages. Hadn't her Aunt Kate had a contraption, something which sat on her breakfast tray that held a book and turned the pages? Didn't Uncle Peter still have it in a cupboard somewhere?

Douglas Giles needed no urging to fetch the book-turning device. But the next day Lucy was up and about again, suddenly better. Nevertheless, she wanted to keep the page-turning thing. She had it propped on her desk to flick the pages of books when she was copying things out for her homework.

The next time he noticed it – on the floor, in the corner of her room – the book propped in the stand was Plato's *Republic*. Lying next to it was *The Critique of Pure Reason* by Immanuel Kant. She was such a clever daughter. But education was so different now. He was glad he hadn't had to read books of that kind when he went to school.

CHAPTER NINE

The Holly Trap

There had been no sighting of Wally since the motorway episode, Helen Brimstone was saying, and that was over a year ago. A black sheep couldn't just disappear into thin air, from the hard shoulder of the M1. Gumption and the others were sure he must be dead by now, run over by a lorry or maybe just rounded up by a farmer somewhere. A valuable laboratory asset possibly just gone for slaughter, said Macannie, a beast worth thoosands dootless sold for fifty poond and tairned into lamb pasanda. All farmers knew their animals, Macannie believed, and since only charlatans had come forward to claim the reward, bringing a motley assortment of black rams in the backs of their Toyota pickup trucks or penned in minitrailers, few of them much like the picture of Wally on the WANTED poster, he felt certain that the animal must be dead.

Stein knew otherwise. The sheep would have gone to ground.

He knew the way Wally's mind worked. He just had to think what he would have done if he were a cunning sheep on the run. Wally wouldn't have been hitching many more lifts, he'd have known it was too risky, especially after that incident with the coach on the motorway. He wouldn't be making for a ferry port or seeking to stow away on an aeroplane, he wasn't interested in running away in that sense. The freedom that obsessed Wally was knowledge. He had to have found refuge with some animal lover, doubtless some loony like Celia Haddon or Brigitte Bardot for whom the reward would have meant nothing, especially

when compared with the priceless relationship they would doubtless believe they had with a wily sheep capable not only of speech
but of careful flattery.

He himself had fallen prey to the animal's wiles. He couldn't
tell the others why he'd really taken the sheep off in the car in
the cottage. As it was, they blamed him for everything.

Stein felt sure the sheep wouldn't have gone far at first from
where he'd made his exit from the M1. He pondered over whether
the sheep had planned the escape at Woolley Edge Services all
along, whether he was making for somewhere nearby or someone
specific. Was there an eccentric actress with an animal sanctuary
somewhere in south Yorkshire, Nottinghamshire or Derbyshire?
Wally might have seen her on the TV. Or was it an animal rights
group? Had the sheep become a secret advisor to the Animal
Liberation Front? Even if he'd holed up somewhere nearby,
wouldn't he have moved on by now? A lot could have happened
in a year.

He kept recalling their conversations in the car, trying to find
a clue amid Wally's barrage of questions.

'Why did that man dwive so fast and nearly cause that other
dwiver to cwash?' he'd asked of that madman in the Merc. 'Why
are you dwiving so ewatically and at such speeds Stein when
dwiving at a steady speed would lower your consumption of
petrwol? Why is that man speaking into his mobile telephone
when this clearly impedes his contrwol over his vehicle? Why
are all these people driving in separwet cars to the same places
and yet if they twavelled together in fewer cars, the cost would
be pwoportionally less and the pollution lower? Why are there
signs encouraging dwivers to stop when they are tired and yet
the food at the stopping places is low in qwality and high in
pwice, and the petrwol is likewise higher in pwice than that sold
at the petrwol station opposite Clovis?'

'Nothing wrong with a good burger and fries,' Stein had
responded.

'Nothing,' said the sheep, 'apart from the poor qwality of
the cow meat, and the fact that it is the flesh of a once living
animal, along with the high fat content and low newtwishional
value, the qwantity and number of chemical additives, the chemical junk thwown in with the limp lettuce, the soggy cardboard

bwed, and so-called Fwench fwies which bear a closer wesemblance to fwied polystywene than they do to chipped potatoes.'

'You've been watching too many consumer programmes on television, Wally.'

'You should be watching what you eat, Fwank. You look seedy enough as it is. You're a fat git, you look no more enticing than a Black Pudding. It's no wonder no woman wants you to tup her.'

'Just stick to calling me Stein. I don't like the way you say Frank, it makes me sound...'

'...like what you are, Stein, a slob would look and smell as slobby by any other name. And stop calling me Wally!'

'Is there anything else I can help you with?'

'If celebwities are people who are known for being known,' said the sheep, 'does that mean minor celebwrities are people who are known for being known for being known?'

'You've lost me there. You mustn't think everything in the human world is logical. Isn't there anything of more pressing interest you want to know about?'

'Is Ulwike Jonsson a celebwity or a minor celebwity? Are Esther Wantzen's teeth weel or was she cloned from a wabbit or a beaver? How long can silage be kept before it goes off? Do they mark silage bags with an eat-by date? Why don't they mix a few nuts and raisins in with the fodder to make it more palatable? Do sheep and cattle weelly like the stuff or is it like that sawdust and wood-chippings muesli which people pwetend to like because they think it's good for them? Is the kind of custard pie they thwow at politicians available from shops or westaurwants? What does it taste like? Like custard or a mixture of lemon curd and shaving foam? Why is it called a pie when it looks like a tart or a flan or a keesh? Is it like a lemon merwang pie which is called a pie but has no top only the light brown cwispy merwang? Has Margwet Thatcher been embalmed or will that only happen after her death? If the latter, why does she pwesently employ a mortician instead of a beautician? Why are Kylie Minogue's buttocks appawently more attwactive to males than other women's buttocks? When you can't smell the female, how can the male select the most desiwable wump as that of a woman they only ever see on the television scween?'

'You're winding me up, aren't you? You can't be seriously

concerned about all those things. Those aren't serious questions.'

'How do you know they aren't seerwius to a sheep? We have a different perspective from you, weemember, and me especially. I am half sheep, half man.'

'Not half, not quite,' Stein interposed.

'Everweeone seems to agwee that all politicians are liars,' the sheep continued. 'Is that why they elect them, because they want to be wooled by liars? Do they want them to pull the wool over their eyes? Is it accidental that they only elect liars or is it a qualification for the job? Do people assume that everweething a politician pwomises is a lie, and they're voting for the one who's the biggest liar or is it the one who tells the least lies or the most plausible whoppers? It must be hard to know one from the other when they are all liars. Is that why they all wear dark suits and ties, which must be the uniform of liars?'

'I'm not sure I can help you there,' said Stein wearily, suddenly worried that he might have to endure a whole weekend of similar questions from the sheep. He'd been hoping for some kind of exchange of ideas about man and beast that would be mutually rewarding to scientist and sheep.

'Scientists are skilful liars too, aren't they?' the sheep persisted. 'You should know, Stein, you're one of the best. I've seen you on the Box. You tell some weal porkies. I'm surpwised you've never been found out.'

'Till now it seems. And by a sheep.'

'It takes one to know one. A wool-seller knows a wool-buyer. And I know your game, Stein.'

'Which is...'

'What's a Fwankenstein sheep?'

'Here we go again...'

'No, I'm serious. It was in the papers, that article about Clovis. That was the headline. So which one is Fwankenstein, the scientist or his cweation? You must see why I'm confused. Who's the monster, me or you?'

'Well I'm Frank Stein of course, I'll admit that much...'

'Daddy...'

He'd almost crashed the car into the van in front when the sheep came out with that one again.

'You are kind of cute though,' the sheep added, 'in your slobby way. I can see why Dr Bwimstone *used* to have a soft spot for you, a *verwee* soft spot it must have been...'

Screech of brakes. He'd half turned to cuff the sheep but had to swivel back to keep control of the car in the outside lane. Had the sheep been trying to make him crash the car? Was that part of the animal's plan? Yet he could have been killed himself. Or was there another smart alec sheep flying the police helicopter above, just waiting to see his car skidding before swooping to pluck his passenger to safety, James Bond style?

Holly would find the woolly knowall now. Or he would come looking for Holly. He wouldn't be able to resist her. The others knew nothing of that part of his plan – the honeytrap sting – but he'd worked it all out, right down to the series of leaks followed by the press conference at which he, the renowned Dr Frank Stein, would invite the media to meet his new superclone ewe, the most intelligent sheep bred in any laboratory. The press had liked Keith Kendrick's revelation that sheep could remember dozens of faces, learn complex tasks and even pine for absent friends and shepherds. It was accepted now that sheep aren't slow-witted but have a keen intellect and a good memory. They can recall at least fifty sheep faces for up to two years and are better at recognising the faces of their owners than domestic cats and dogs. They'd really gone to town on that story.

So news of Holly the Uber-ewe would be splashed everywhere. He'd arranged with London Zoo for the press photographers to be present when Holly demonstrated her ability to pass all the intelligence tests given to chimpanzees. The one test she wouldn't be given would remain their secret, but Wally would know at once that she was understanding what he was saying to her. He'd recognise that Holly was capable of speech but not letting on when he saw them doing their media charade on television.

Stein would talk about the earlier clone Wally as her prototype. Only he and Wally would know what that implied. Just then, as the photographers went for the close-up, Holly would look to camera and mouth her come-on in sheep language. *Hello there, big boy*, she'd say, and *Make my day, superstud, come up and see me sometime.*

How could he resist? Wally would fall for it, the sheep was

just as gullible as he himself had been. Immediately he heard that Holly would be making an appearance at the Yorkshire County Show in Harrogate, he'd start working on some damned fool rescue bid, a plan inevitably doomed to failure. For what Wally wouldn't know was that Holly's education had been carefully organised and monitored by him. She'd had no access to television. Everything she knew she'd learned from Dr Frank Stein. She shared his obsession with Wally, but he'd trained her to hate all rams, especially black rams, Wally above all others, and it was the greatest ambition of Holly's life that she should find Wally and betray him to Stein.

CHAPTER TEN

Sheepman, Shaman

When Sean Shenanigan had let slip in the pub that the missing sheep was none other than the diabolical progeny of the devil ram from Battymanistan, the two bearded men took an immediate liking to the jovial Irishman, buying him drinks and encouraging him to tell more of his strange tale. They sat on either side of him, feeding his garrulous bonhomie with pints of Guinness and double Jemmy chasers. The next morning Shenanigan remembered little of the encounter, except that he had been in the company of two serious-looking but genial fellows who had enjoyed his company though he remembered little of theirs, only that they were good listeners.

But he arrived at work like a bear with a sore head nursing a devil of a hangover. His head swam when he stared at his computer screen. Feeling vaguely guilty, he lurched about in a daze, unable to fathom the cause of his disquiet. Had there been some woman there? Had he made a fool of himself? He didn't think he'd offended anyone or disgraced himself, yet something nagged at him. Something didn't feel quite right.

*

Lucy had never shown much interest before in computers. She'd only ever wanted books or book tokens for her birthday. It wasn't something Rebecca had encouraged or known much about, but now his daughter wanted nothing else. Given her astonishing progress at school and the happiness she was now giving him as well as the sheep, Douglas Giles was only too pleased to do her bidding.

At school they were using computers for everything, Lucy had said. She still preferred books, but computers could do calculations, correct your spelling and you could use the internet to do research for essay questions. She'd given him a list of the equipment she'd need: the PC model, memory size and printer as well as software, including voice recognition and website tools. She'd never been good at typing, and the voice software would enable her to speak to the computer and it would take down everything she said, just like a secretary. She also still got achey hands after that illness, so it wouldn't do to put too much strain on her hands, and everyone knew that people who typed a lot got very achey hands.

All her friends had their own websites on which they posted pictures of themselves, their friends and families, along with their likes and dislikes as well as things about singers and football teams, and links to their favourite websites. Lucy's website would all be about writers and animals, but she wouldn't post up a picture of her sheep in case anyone came looking for him.

*

Graham Medlar went back over his notes. When closely questioned by that TV reporter, Dr Stein had admitted that many of the sheep clones had died in the womb or been stillborn or grossly deformed, before changing the subject back to his superewe Holly. The failure rate was still very high, he'd said, but their successes provided all the justification anyone could ask for. And yet what had happened to this other clone, this prototype he'd called him, Wally? Pressed by the interviewer, he'd conceded that tests had needed to be carried out on the unsuccessful foster mothers, their wombs and other organs had been examined, which meant they had been killed for not delivering the goods, and something else Stein had said in passing clearly hinted at vivisection procedures. But at no time did Stein mention the fate of this earlier clone, Wally; he didn't talk of him as dead or alive, but simply as a prototype. And if this other sheep had shown itself to be intelligent, although not as capable as this superewe, then why was his case not discussed more fully, and comparisons made? What could Holly do that Wally couldn't?

Then he remembered that story from the papers – it must have been a year ago – how a black sheep had inadvertently hitched a lift on the M1 on the back of a car transporter. Wasn't that in Yorkshire? And didn't some scientist later offer a reward for the return of a laboratory sheep which had escaped from Clovis? The incident on the motorway had been a long way from Stein's place, but perhaps the two might be connected?

He'd check the cuttings files to see who made the appeal, what the fugitive sheep was called and what was said about the circumstances of its escape. He knew the Animal Liberation Front hadn't been involved, and as far as he was aware, no other group had claimed responsibility for liberating the animal.

If the escaped sheep was this earlier clone, Wally, and Stein was covering up what had really happened, there might be some mileage for the ALF in this. If they could find this other sheep, it could be very valuable to them. They wouldn't give it back of course, but they could use it as a hostage. Capture a scientist – preferably this Stein character – and then shoot videos of man and sheep. They'd demand a stop to the cloning work and other experiments on live animals at Clovis, otherwise one of the hostages would be killed, the man or the sheep, they could choose. As an animal lover, he'd prefer to kill the man of course, but if the scientists instructed him to shoot the sheep instead, he'd surprise them all by beheading the ram on a live television link-up. That's what happens at Clovis, he'd say, and that's what happens every day to thousands of sheep, cattle and pigs in abbatoirs, to feed the public's disgusting lust for the flesh of animals. The woolly liberals in the organisation wouldn't like the stunt, and they'd disown it, but he could stage it as the act of a radical splinter group called 666. He wouldn't be guilty of murder; it wasn't like the car bombing and torching of houses belonging to scientists, but the effect in publicity and in turning people away from meat-eating would be much more effective. Seeing an animal killed in front of them, one with a name they would all know by then, thanks to the media.

If he could establish where the motorway incident happened,

he could put out feelers amongst activists in that area. It was even possible that one of them had captured the animal.

*

The sheep was delighted with their progress. They'd customised the software, so that it would recognise Lucy's voice in one mode and his in the other. They'd each had to read passages from *Alice in Wonderland* to the machine for several hours. It hadn't wanted them to read Jane Austen or Charles Dickens, which he'd have preferred to Lewis Carroll, and it had taken the computer much longer to set up his voice recognition than Lucy's due to the problems he had in pronouncing the letter R. But eventually the machine was achieving 97% accuracy for Lucy and 85% for himself, which was more than adequate for his purposes, given that she could correct any errors in his texts.

Lucy had begun work on both their websites by setting up the basic templates. He discovered what other websites looked like when she logged onto them to download pictures of writers and animals and to copy the texts of author biographies and the curriculum vitae of each animal. There were several quite interesting websites about sheep. One site consisted entirely of photographs of cute lambs, hunky rams and sexy ewes. The latter section was quite a revelation. The sheep horror sites on the other hand went into macabre detail about the many ways in which their flesh could be cooked and eaten by the humans. It made him shudder just to read the recipes for the sauces. 'There's more to lamb than mint sauce' was one chilling headline.

Their password had to be six letters in length. After some discussion, Lucy selected 000000 to enable the sheep to access the web when she was at school. She showed him which keys to hit to boot up the computer, which were needed to log on and in what sequence, and then how to tap out 000000 with the tip of his hoof. She would edit his site offline of course, and she'd do all the design and layout to his specifications. He would do the actual writing himself, now that she'd shown him how to work the voice software, again by tapping various keys with the tip of one hoof, in some cases with the other hoof holding the control key down. On those days when he wanted to work on his texts she'd fit the headphones round his ears and the mouthpiece below his muzzle before leaving for school, and then all he'd have to do later would be to gently push it off with his hoof.

After Holly's appearance with Stein on television, he logged onto the Clovis website to see if he could find out any more about her. There she was, pictured with Stein at the press conference, with that silly slogan in the background which also headed the webpage: 'DON'T SAY CLONE, SAY CLOVIS'. Below were her vital statistics with an account of her intellectual capabilities. She was quite a looker, but something about her disturbed him. Her eyes had a glazed look, as if she were some kind of sheep fanatic or ovine Myra Hindley. She'd obviously look different from other sheep if Stein had cloned her in the same way that he'd been cloned, making similar covert changes in the gene transfer. If she could speak – and he didn't really doubt that – what would she say to him? Was she really saying *Come up and see me sometime*, or had Stein put her up to that?

Stein knew how his first successful clone had turned out, so why would he seek to create another intelligent sheep who might give him his comeuppance again? Details of Holly's forthcoming appearance at the Harrogate show were given due prominence.

It had to be a set-up. Stein was staging the whole thing to draw him out. But how much was Holly implicated in Stein's plot? The chimp tests she'd passed were simple stuff, just the kind of thing he used to flunk to pretend he was dim-witted. She must be capable of much more than that, if she was anything like him. But if she wasn't his equal, did he really want to have anything to do with her? He could teach her, it was true, but given what Stein knew about his own self-education, he felt sure that he must have manipulated Holly's own education to make her his loyal servant.

He decided in the end that Holly had to have been brainwashed by Stein. He'd deliberately created her in his own image, which meant she'd be in thrall to him, and quite possibly in love with him. Pet lambs often fell for humans and couldn't be trained to enjoy the company of other sheep.

Stein was using her to trap him. At the same time, if Holly was a sheep clone whose intellectual capabilities were anything like his, her prototype, it was still possible that she was giving

Stein the impression that she was going along with his plans to lure him out of hiding but really in order to get him to spring her at the show.

Did he want to spring Holly? Not just to spring her but to spring onto her? Did he fancy her? It was hard to tell from that brief appearance on TV and this strangely disconcerting picture on the website. He knew he needed to smell her to know if he had any real amatory interest. And that was risky if Stein really was trying to set him up, regardless of whether or not Holly was his willing accomplice.

The sheep was learning much more, every day, with Lucy. He knew where he was with her; she shared his passions, his thirst for knowledge, his love of language. And he had to admit he adored her too, for all that she wasn't a sheep. He also liked her father, Douglas. A good man was such a rare thing. There was no one to compare with Douglas Giles at Clovis; his honesty and decency, his good nature and good temper, his hard-working temperament and straightforward outlook, his love for his daughter, all these things marked him out as different not only from the other humans the sheep had come into contact with but also from the people on the Box, most of whom were consumed by conflict, anger and distrust. The only person he'd ever seen on the Box who was at all like him was Farmer Hogget in the sheep-pig film *Babe*. When he looked at Douglas Giles, he could see in his eyes – like a fire – that love he still carried for his dear wife, Lucy's mother Rebecca. His grief hurt him right to the core at the same time as that still burning love made him strong. The sheep felt guilty that they'd had to trick Lucy's father into doing things for them, but it was all for the good, he was sure of that.

The sheep wanted knowledge far more than he wanted Holly, and he was excited that Lucy too was learning so much through their joint efforts, even if her advances weren't as great as his in comparative terms.

*

The sheep had read Plato, Aristotle, Hobbes, Descartes, Hume, John Stuart Mill, Kant, Kierkegaard, Spinoza and Wittgenstein, although not in that order. He'd read the Bible, the Koran, the Upanishads, the Bhagavad Gita, Augustine's *City of God*, Kahlil Gibran, *The Cloud of Unknowing* and *Jonathan Livingston Seagull*. He hadn't read *all* the great thinkers, but he knew what they'd said from summaries given in textbooks and encyclopaedias. None of them had much to say about sheep and even less about animals. What they did say was usually limited by their human intelligence.

Of course animals had souls. Of course they thought and felt. What animals might lack in intelligence or intellect they made up for in knowledge or instinct. A lot of what the thinkers said about humans or the wider world was just as suspect. Whenever he learned that a philosopher, saint or theologian had eaten the flesh of animals, he immediately felt their thinking and their work was as suspect as if they had been cannibals who devoured the bodies of other humans.

It was clearly time for a new religion or philosophy which would embrace all existing knowledge. He'd knock all those skewed beliefs back into proper intellectual shape, drawing on everything he learned and everything he knew about the natural order of things.

While some humans had been willing to listen to a humble carpenter's son, he felt they'd be unlikely to give much credence to the word of a sheep, especially given the nature of their mis-conceptions about sheep and other animals. But the website wouldn't need to reveal the true nature of its authorsheep. That was one of the beauties of the web. You didn't know who any-one was. Everything could have equal authority just as it could be equally suspect. The sheep's thinking could be presented as a Revelation or a series of Revelations. In order to reach as many humans as possible, he would need to present his Revelations in simplified terms, leavened with a few humorous asides. The wittier websites seemed almost as popular with the humans as the pornographic ones.

Reaching this decisive point in his quest for knowledge, the sheep realised that he had finally discovered his name, which must express his dual nature of being part sheep, part man. His name would be Sheepman, or Shaman for short, and his domain would be **www.shaman.com**:

Shaman bids you welcome. You have logged on to the Logos, the Word of Shaman. You have entered a place of knowledge. That knowledge is expressed in the Ten Revelations of Shaman:

1. Spirit. Spirit lives in all human and animal life. In plants it is vegetal only. You may eat plants but not animals. When you eat the flesh of an animal, you are as guilty of taking its life as whoever stole its life and denied its Spirit just so you could eat its flesh. They didn't know that you personally would eat the animal but they wouldn't have killed it if humans didn't eat animals.

All animals have souls, just like yours, only better. Just as the cow is sacred in India, so is the sheep a sacred animal of Shaman. The pig's life too is sacrosanct, its bacon should be saved not eaten. The holy cow is its own beast, though it likes to be milked when its udder is full, just as you like to piss when your bladder is bursting (and should be able to do so in the sight of others, as an animal does). The chicken's wings, legs and breast are its own, not anyone else's, however finger-licking good. Leave the goat alone. Don't even think about it. The fish is the odd one out. You may eat the fish, but not to excess. Do not eat all the fish in the sea and make sure the Japanese show similar restraint. Do not use a live fish to pleasure yourself unless the fish gives its consent and you intend to eat it afterwards. Save the whale, the whale is a highly intelligent animal and should not be eaten, nor should its flesh be used as fuel any more than you would want your own flesh to be so abused.

Do not cull the seal. Do to animals as you would be done by. How would you like to be culled, to be clubbed over the head by a Millwall supporter and then flayed alive or dead? Lay off the rat and the cat. Do not eat the dog or the hot dog, not even in countries where it is customary to do so. The only good burger is a vegeburger, but only if it has enough herbs.

Cockroaches are unclean and should be washed before being eaten; frying them in garlic butter will improve their taste, and if you eat the legs and shells of prawns you may as well treat insects the same way, except if they be excessively chitinous, in which case indigestion should be your guide and deterrent. Serve them right, with salad, or on thin slices of lightly toasted brown bread.

2. Expression. Spirit is expressed in each species according to the physical nature of that species. Spirit in humans is also expressed in relation to genes, environment and culture. When humans and animals die, Spirit in physical form returns to earth Spirit. Humans who abuse the Spirit in their trust, their own and that of animals (and who abuse the Earth) will be reborn as insects or cold-blooded reptiles in their next lives. Serves them right.

3. <u>Superiority</u>. No human is superior to others. Only animals are superior, except for snakes and sheep-ticks, which are an abomination. If you like snakes, you are half way to becoming a snake. Women are generally nicer people than men. Why? Think about that one. Men who ill-treat or demean women will become insects in their next lives, quite probably the kind which get eaten by their mates after intercourse. Serves them right.

4. <u>Memory</u>. All memory is lost at death because individual memory relates to one life only. Only folk or collective memory is retained. At birth, Spirit is expressed with a clean slate bearing the imprint only of collective memory. Individual memory dies with the physical brain when Spirit departs. So saith Shaman.

5. <u>Gods & prophets</u>. All gods are human versions of the Spirit that is in all living things. Christ, Buddha, Mohammed and other prophets had a highly developed awareness of Spirit that enabled them to express Spiritual truths as revelations, but religions take these too literally and wrongly focus on prophets as gods or divine message-bearers. Do not worship God or Shaman, God and Shaman are in you, a part of you. Do not praise the Lord, praise the glory of your own body. Do not say all praise to Allah, say your praises to the animals, to the beasts and birds who share the world with you and let them share that world. Do not plunder the Earth, it does not belong to humans but to all creatures. So saith Shaman and Shaman should know.

6. <u>Idolatry & reptiles</u>. Churches, temples, mosques and synagogues are idolatrous abnegations of Spirit. Do not worship God, gods or Spirit, or humble yourself to any expression or before any physical representation of god or Spirit. Do not trust men with moustaches. Men with beards are hiding something. Men who wear dark suits wish only to rule over you and to have their will, whether they be freelance food-loving entrepreneurs of Sicilian origin or merely politicians or businessmen whose coldheartedness is expressed through economics, not extortion. Do not vote for any of them in parliamentary or local elections. Men who force their will on others are cold-hearted Reptiles whose beards are covering up their scabs and scales, and their Word is Poison to the soul. Their own souls are poisoned and they seek to infect others with their Ill Will. Do not abase or abuse yourselves for their sakes, and do not blow yourselves up to serve their will, for every life is sacred, yours included. Respect your own Spirit and Spirit in others and use knowledge to the good of all. Respect, brothers and sisters, respect each other and respect yourselves.

7. <u>Free will</u>. Every human and every animal has free will. No god can intervene to change the world, to stop diseases or to influence the course of wars or the outcome of the 3.30 at Newmarket, or even to save the lives of prophets and saints, crucified sons and locked-up daughters, because gods do not exist as an outside force but are the Spirit living within us all. Only humans can stop wars or change the world. Only animals can live by the purity of instinct. Humans can influence their own destinies only by drawing on and respecting the Spirit that is in all living creatures. Vivisectionists are men with dead souls who suck the blood of living creatures, and their lies are as plausible as those of politicians of all colours and priests of all religions. Respect the animals, brothers and sisters, respect yourselves.

8. <u>Respect</u>. Do not steal anything you would not want to lose if it belonged to you. Do not seek to profit from the misfortune or well-being or from the poverty or wealth of others. Do nothing out of anger, jealousy or greed. Do nothing on behalf of a company or organisation which is harmful to interests of individuals, animals or the common good, including voting for Extremists or Conservatives in any election. Do not follow zealots, follow your own hearts. Open your hearts and be generous to others and animals, regardless of the colour of their skin, fur or feathers, regardless of their gender or species (snakes and sheep-ticks excepted), and regardless of their smell and the size or shape of their mouth, snout, nose, beak, eyes, ears and horns. Respect everyone, brothers and sisters, respect every man, woman and child, respect every bird and beast, alleluia.

9. <u>Denying denial</u>. Self denial is denial of Spirit. Appetite and instinct may be denied before Spirit, but not Spirit for the sake of denial. The physical body is the vessel of Spirit and is yours to be enjoyed. The naked unclothed body is a form of beauty. Does an animal cover its beautiful form with cloth or the skins of other creatures? Eat, drink and be merry, but not to excess and not at the expense of others or of animals. Fornication is the gift of Spirit, there to be enjoyed, not denied, as long as the two parties are willing and no trust is broken and no animals are involved. Respect your bodies, use them well. Enjoy!

10. <u>Naked truth</u>. Urination, defecation and breast-feeding are natural bodily processes, common to humans and animals. Does a bear shit in the woods? Yes, so why can't a human? Does a ewe suckle its young in the open field? Yes, so why can't a human in the sight of others?

Does a dog piss in the street? Yes, so why can't a human? If you are offended by the sight of a willy or breast, you have been subject to social or cultural conditioning and you should know better. Were you offended by nakedness as a child? Are animals offended by the sight of other animals urinating? Not passing water when you need to pass water is a form of self-denial damaging to your physical body and well-being. Feed your children when they're hungry. Piss when you want to piss, but don't do it all over the place. Use a drain or someone's garden (but try to avoid the plants). Crossing your legs is self-crucifixion. Use your heads and hearts, brothers and sisters, don't be afraid of showing yourself in all your pubic glory. Pass water not judgement. Let it all hang out. Dangle and squat. So saith Shaman.

To send the *Ten Revelations of Shaman* to a friend, click here if you have Outlook Express. Otherwise, press control and A, then copy and paste the *Ten Revelations of Shaman* into an e-mail. Tell your friends about this website. The *Ten Revelations of Shaman* will be an irrevocable feature of **www.shaman.com**, but updates will feature further advice on subsidiary matters from Shaman.

'What do you think?' asked the sheep.

'I'm not sure about number ten,' said Lucy. 'The naked truth. All that stuff about weeing.'

'That's because even you have been conditioned. As a sheep, I wecognise the joys of the uninhibited bladder, though I can contwol it when I must of course.'

'I should hope so.'

'The expwession humans use is "weelieving oneself" but Man is not allowed to weelieve himself as the beasts are, which makes an animal's position in the world superior in that weespect. If a man uwinates not into a smelly china weeceptacle in a specially construwcted and very stinky excwetion woom but in the fresh air outside he will be fined sixty pounds plus thirty pounds court costs and have his so-called shame exposed in the local newspaper. Imagine what would happen if animals were subject to such dwaconian laws. Everwee cweature would be liable to fines of hundreds of pounds a day.'

'But it's not against the law for animals to wee in the fields.'

'Why not?' the sheep persisted. 'When dogs poo in the street, they fine the humans they live with.'

'But that's different, silly.'

'Why not the same rule for cats then? They live with humans too.'

'But cats go out on their own, without their humans,' said Lucy. 'And anyway, a cat's poo isn't as big and squidgy as a dog's doo-da.'

'Which makes it harder to spot. A human can step over a dog turd but twed in smaller kinds of excwement deposited by other beasts. And what possible harm does a man do when he goes into a back alley to weelieve himself? He generally does so out of the public view, according to the newspaper weports, but policemen must lurk in the shadows looking for uwinating men to awwest and fine. And just to make sure of that, the public toilets are all either vandalised or closed at night when the men with full bladders wish to use them.'

'It does seem illogical,' Lucy conceded. 'But I'm still not sure. I don't always see your point of view, even when it seems to be right. No one would believe the discussions we have.'

'It's nothing new,' said the sheep. 'Plato did the same thing in his dialogues. He questioned every aspect of the world.'

'But not men weeing in the street.'

'You don't know that. He might have discussed uwination, they didn't wite down everweething he said. But his perspective would have been differwent. Athenians weren't fined a dwakma for weelieving themselves, such an act would have seemed perfectly natuwal to them. And that's one of the beauties of Shaman: as a sheep I can see where Man is going wrong and should learn from the animals or from his own past. You know fwom your biology lessons how the scientific thinker looks at all cweatures in terms of their nutwition, wespiwation, wepwoduction, loco-motion, nervous system, intelligence and excwetion. A weeligion or belief system has to take account of all those things, including our so-called waste pwoducts which can enwich the earth like our dead bodies if our welatives don't decide to burn them instead of letting them wot or eating them as other carnivorwous beasts do. Would you say Shaman does that?'

'It's pretty comprehensive,' Lucy acknowledged. 'But I just hadn't realised you were going into such detail, especially about some things.'

'It's all quite coherewent,' the sheep assured her. 'I added the detail to anticipate the usual questions. The humour makes it more palatable. If a belief system has a place for jokes, it will spwed like wild fire or butter even stwaight fwom the fwidge. Most weeligions have no sense of humour. If you make a wise-cwack about a Mullah and his Mullahgatawny Owl, they hit you with a Batwa or a Spanish Inquisition or put you on a diet of worms and owl pellets. Wabbis are wabid, pwiests are perverts or pwigs, and imams should call themselves idads. They have no imagination because they've perverted it in the cause of in-justice. They're all basically loonies, so why should anyone tweat them any more searwiously than philosophers? Men with beards can't take a joke because they are widiculous people and no one would take them searwiously if they weren't so dangerwous.'

'You're a bit hard on snakes.'

'Have you every met a decent snake? St Patwick had the wight idea about them. Snakes never did anyone any good. They're the killing machines of the animal world, Nature's Nazis. Snakes are what you get when something goes wrong. Wasps are a bunch of nasties too.'

'I thought you said everything that lives is holy.'

'That was Blake. I pwefer Blake without the snake.'

'Do you really think people will go along with it?'

'With Shaman? Why not? That's the beauty of the web: no one knows that Shaman is a sheep, a sheep who is part man part sheep, nor that Shaman's site was designed by Little Lucy.'

'I'm not so little now.'

'And I'm not so ovine. You even corwected the mistakes cweated by the software, when it couldn't wecognise the letter R. You've wefined my speech. And the Word of Shaman is spwedding. Did you see how many hits we've had alweddy, and it's only been up a day.'

But why did you say only humans can stop wars and change the world?' asked Lucy. 'I thought that was the whole idea behind Shaman, and if Shaman works in the way you say it will, the world will have been changed by a sheep.'

'They mustn't suspect that they're following a sheep. Humans will follow waving loonies and mad mullahs but not a sheep. You even have that expwession *follow like sheep* to descwibe human gullibility, which is an insult to sheep.'

CHAPTER ELEVEN

Ram Raiders

Douglas Giles handed her the newspaper. 'Your sheep seems to have quite a fan club,' he said. 'I didn't tell you before, but some scientist was offering a reward for his return last year. Now there are other people after him. Some desperate men if the papers are to be believed.'

Lucy read:

The two terrorist suspects arrested in Derbyshire yesterday were looking for an escaped ram, police now say. The two men were captured by a special anti-terrorist unit after they were seen acting suspiciously by a local farmer.

At first they were thought to be molesting sheep, but when one began assembling an anti-tank missile launcher, the farmer alerted Bolsover police, who called for support from Scotland Yard. Experts initially believed that the two men intended to launch an attack on the nearby M1 motorway, on which an army convoy was travelling north to Catterick, but when the suspects' car was searched, the only thing found, apart from a small arsenal of weapons, was a folder of newspaper cuttings relating to an escaped laboratory sheep.

This animal went missing last year, and was the subject of a public appeal by Dr Frank Stein of the Clovis Institute. However, it was not revealed then that the fugitive was the celebrated cloned ram Wally. Dr Stein now claims that the sheep was not identified in that appeal for fear of attracting the attention of religious and animal rights extremists.

Police say the men have now been charged with possession of illegal weapons and explosives, aggravated trespass, resisting arrest and conspiring to explode a sheep without a dynamite licence. A further charge of sexually molesting a cloven-hoofed animal is expected once they have finished interviewing the farmer, who told reporters at the scene that he had seen the suspects chasing one of his prize rams across a field of turnips.

The farmer, who asked not to be identified for fear of reprisals, said he was astonished that the two men had mistaken his ram for the missing animal. 'Any fool should be able to tell the difference. Our black toop may be black but ee's a pure-bred Texel. T' local brewery's even used 'im in their adverts, ee's famous round ere is our toop. This Wally is some kind of dirty black cross, noothing lahke our toop, but you can't expect townees to know their sheep.'

A spokesmen for the Men's Republic of Battymanistan has confirmed that the two unnamed suspects are Batty diplomats who are claiming diplomatic immunity, but the new Batty régime does not have diplomatic recognition from Britain.

He said they would not have been seeking to molest the ram because sexual congress with sheep is a capital crime in the Batty religion. However, if that charge were conclusively proven, his government would demand that the two men be executed immediately, regardless of their diplomatic status. Pressed by a reporter, he agreed that if their intended victim had been a woman, not a sheep, and the charge had been 'merely rape', his government would have called for the men's immediate release on the grounds that they should not be kept in custody for 'a minor offence no worse than parking on a double yellow line'.

On the question of the weapons and explosives, the spokesman said the two men may have been intending to carry out the Holy Batwa against Wally by blowing him up with the missile launcher, but they had got the wrong sheep.

Above the headline were mugshots of two almost identical bearded terrorists, who had refused to give their names and so were captioned 'THE TWO SUSPECTS'. Next to these was a picture of the Derby ram, who was called Charlie, with one of the Clovis clone, with the caption 'COULD YOU TELL THE DIFFERENCE?' Lucy wasn't sure if this question referred to the sheep-molesting suspects or the sheep themselves.

'It doesn't look much like him,' she said. 'But I suppose it was taken some time ago.' She couldn't tell her father that she'd known all along that they'd been harbouring an ovine escapee from Clovis. She couldn't bear to think of those awful scientists getting their hands on him now, let alone the sheep-hating terrorists.

Douglas Giles registered her concern. 'I've been thinking,' he said. 'About that ram that died in the lightning storm? 501 it was. I was going to ring this morning to get him collected. He'd have been about the same age as Wally...'

'Not Wally,' Lucy began, 'he doesn't...'

'Yes, you're right,' her father continued. 'We mustn't call him that. Well, my idea is that Wally...your Sheep...could take on the identity of 501. We'll bury the real 501 in the bottom field, just like we used to. And when I fill out the forms, I'll just claim for the same number of rams as before. This way we can get some subsidy for him too, and he can start paying for his keep. I've never known a sheep get through so much chocolate.'

The sheep took the news with his customary aplomb.

'I'm not too happy about being a number,' he told her. '501 sounds like a game of darts. But verwee appwopwiate with these loonies wanting to shoot missiles at me, it will weemind me of my danger.'

'But it's a brilliant idea of Daddy's,' Lucy said, 'giving you another sheep's identity. It shows that he must love you too. Think of it as going undercover.'

'Do I get a new passport and this other wam's ear-tag?'

'Only cows have passports. But you'll need a tattoo.'

'Do I get to choose the design? LUCY with a heart?'

'You can't have my name, silly, or they'll think you're called Lucy, and you're a ram.'

'I suppose that would make them suspicious.'

'You just get Daddy's initials, DG. And 501's tag.'

'Left or wight ear?'

*

'Well, the cat's out of the bag now,' said Helen Brimstone.

'Our ram is debagged,' said Mark Gumption. 'Only their ram raid was foiled by the vigilant farmer from Bolsover.'

'Your sheep has made the front page, Stein,' said Donald Macannie. 'And we're still no nearer knowing where he is. But I'd still lay odds the animal's long dead.'

'I'm sure I've seen those two fellows somewhere before,' said Sean Shenanigan. 'You don't think they've been nosing round Clovis? Got themselves included in some visiting scientific delegation? They look strangely familiar. And none too savoury. Wouldn't like to meet those two on a dark night.'

'We'll have to tighten security,' said Dr Frank Stein. 'They may come after Holly as well.'

'But she's not a diabolical devil sheep,' said Helen Brimstone. 'The Batties had nothing to do with her. They've no reason for going after her, she's perfectly normal.'

'If clones can be said to be normal,' said Shenanigan.

'This one especially,' Stein muttered under his breath.

'But we're all subject to the infamous Batwa,' whined Macannie. 'Us and all our clones. And I'd remind you all that reason doesn't enter their calculations. They're rebel-rousing lunatics. That's how they got elected, appealing to the lowest common denominator.'

'The women didn't elect them,' said Helen Brimstone.

'And they rigged the election anyway,' said Sean Shenanigan, 'having studied the American and Zimbabwean electoral systems.'

'Can't we spread some story about their spiritual leader Sheikh Rattlenroll being caught with a sheep while at college?' Stein suggested.

'They say he has Welsh blood in him,' Shenanigan added. 'Might work. Use the internet.'

'But he didn't go to college,' said Macannie, 'everyone knows the man's illiterate.'

'Just an idea.'

*

Graham Medlar's enquiries had drawn a blank. None of his activists knew anything about a black sheep on the run. The only intelligence they had been able to give him related to various sightings of bearded men of possible Middle Eastern origin lurking around sheep farms north of the river Trent. When challenged, some had claimed to be looking for farmhouses without double-glazing, hoping to sell their products, while others had purported to be Mormons or Jehovah's Witnesses.

But locals had been suspicious because they weren't wearing black ties, and on being asked to produce copies of *Watchtower* or *Polygamy Is Fun*, they said they'd given all their copies away to interested householders, yet no one could remember lighting any fires with their publications.

There had been no confirmed sightings of the sheep itself since the incident the year before on the M1. It seemed to have just disappeared into thin air once clear of the motorway embankment. If all those highly trained spies working undercover had failed to find the animal, what hope had his bunch of amateurs?

To add to the general confusion, the press had got in on the act now, with their lurid WHERE IS WALLY? stories. The reward offered by two of the newspapers for the ram's safe return was ten times higher than Clovis's. If someone was harbouring the animal, he couldn't believe they wouldn't have been tempted by that amount of money. The same photograph of the black ram stared out so often from so many front pages that commentators had started calling it 'iconic', with the *Guardian* featuring a Wally mural titled 'BLACK SHEEP ARE US' made by children at a Brixton school using handprints in mischievous imitation of a notorious painting of Myra Hindley. On the same day, the *Independent* ran a story from a Lambeth comprehensive picturing its virtually identical sheepface mural titled 'YOUNG, GIFTED AND BLACK'. Not to be outdone, the *Sunday Times* was offering its readers Wally Warhol T-shirts sporting multiple multicoloured versions of the iconic ovine mugshot.

Tabloid hacks had been visiting every pub from Penistone in Yorkshire to Sheepbridge and Woolley Bridge in Derbyshire, even extending their search as far as Ramsbottom in Lancashire, because of the name, paying cash for any information as to the possible whereabouts of the four-legged fugitive. Wily publicans throughout Derbyshire, Nottinghamshire and South Yorkshire quickly made Black Sheep Ale their guest beer, confident the Masham brew would prove now especially popular with press and public alike. After eight pints of Black Sheep Ale, a group of London newsmen would be ushered outside to a badly-lit car park and shown a black sheep in a trailer. The canny farmer was guaranteed to collect at least four thousand pounds cash in the whipround for a clapped-out old tup he'd been expecting to get no more than forty pounds for in the next auction, if he could sell it at all. Suffolks were the most likely impostors, with their squashy black faces and velvety ears like matadors' hats. Wally the cloned ram was said to have an odd-shaped head, and Suffolks certainly looked the part, as long as you gave them at least two sprays of black raddle dye.

But despite all this attention, no one seemed to have any clue as to where the real ram might have gone. Graham Medlar couldn't believe the media were so gullible. At least his informants knew their sheep breeds, even if some of them had trouble wiring up a half-decent letter bomb. And the more the press speculated and allowed their imaginations and cheque books to run riot, the less chance his people had of finding the animal, unless the publicity flushed it out. If it was clever enough to hitch a lift on a car transporter, it might be wise to some change in its conditions of hiding or confinement, as for example if the person or people harbouring it were acting as if they intended to turn it over and claim one of the rewards.

Until something like that happened, there was little further he could do. He turned his attention to the other sheep, the superewe Holly, scheduled to appear at the county show in Harrogate in a week's time. He stared at her picture, pinned to the wall, which he'd blown up after downloading it from the Clovis website. She looked even spookier than Wally. How did they produce such weird-looking beasts, these scientists? It was obviously something to do with the cloning.

*

The sheep was tilting his head to one side, trying to examine his tattooed ear in the mirror.

'I thought you said I was 501,' he said. 'That looks more like 103 to me.'

'You're looking at it back-to-front, silly,' said Lucy. 'I thought you knew about mirrors.'

'I've never had to use one before. They're a bit scarewee, aren't they? Do I weelly look like that?'

'You look very handsome. Especially with your wool puffed out like that.'

'I've never had a perm before.'

'We have to make you look different from the picture in the newspaper. In case anyone sees you.'

'You don't think it makes me look a bit…you know… effeminate? A twifle ewe-like?'

'Not at all. You could start a new fashion.'

'Sheep on the catwalk?' he queried. 'But it's not me going on show, wemember, it's your father's pwize Suffolks.'

'And you're just going along for the ride.'

'That's what he thinks. But it was good of him to be so concerned, not wanting to leave me behind with all those Mormons snooping awound the valley.'

'Daddy's very fond of you, Sheep.'

'And you're sure you know what to do then? You've got everything?'

'Tranquilliser darts? Blow-pipe?'

'Wope for binding our captive? Bwown parcel tape for the gag?'

'I've got everything we need.'

'And what do you do when we get home?'

'I open the gate for Daddy. I play the energetic farmgirl, rushing to the paddock to open that gate as he's backing up. Then I unbolt the trailer and let out the Suffolks, while you trot off into the yard to do your business. Then I put the ramp back and re-bolt the trailer. Daddy parks the jeep with the trailer in the barn, and we go inside for our tea.'

'And after tea?'

'We wait till Daddy leaves for the pub. I unbolt the trailer, drop the ramp, then hide in the hayloft ready to use the blowpipe again when you give me the signal. The captive is all yours.'

*

Following the two car-bombings in Harrogate yesterday, police have arrested four suspects. Two are known animal rights activists, and two are unidentified bearded men of possible Middle Eastern origin.

Police suspect the men of planning to kidnap the celebrated cloned ewe Holly, who was being exhibited for the first time at the Yorkshire County Show by the Clovis Institute. The sheep was taken to a safe location by scientists after the first explosion, but the whereabouts of the missing biologist Dr Frank Stein are still unknown.

The two cars were both white Volvos, and Yorkshire Police are working on the theory that both pairs of suspects mistook each other's vehicle for Dr Stein's car, also a white Volvo, and blew it up in error.

The suspects were arrested at a pub in Leeds after the landlord called the police to break up a fight. The Animal Liberation Front has claimed that its members did not start the fight, although they had 'got the better of the two Batties', one of whom had sustained a broken arm. Dr Stein's car was found abandoned near the pub.

A foreign affairs spokesman for the Men's Republic of Battymanistan last night called for better training to be given to the country's diplomats. 'But what do you expect?' he is alleged to have said. 'The army takes all the best men. Others escape conscription by becoming Batty priests, even though most are illiterate peasants. We get the rejects, vagabonds and thieves – or murderers pardoned by the new régime because they only killed doctors, teachers or women.'

That comment was later disowned by a government official in Battymenarbad, who said it did not represent government policy, only the personal views of a minor civil servant, who had since been executed for making unauthorised statements to the press.

No one was injured in the incidents at Harrogate, although a tent housing cakes and pies destined for the home produce competition was destroyed in one of the explosions.

Police are linking the Harrogate attacks with the incident in Derbyshire a week ago when two other Batty diplomats were arrested after trying to blow up a farmer's black sheep with a missile launcher.

Dr Frank Stein blew the straw from his mouth, and looked up at his captor.

'That hurt!' he exclaimed.

'You thought I was going to kidnap your pweshus ewe, didn't you, Stein?' said the black sheep with an air of triumph. A length of the brown parcel tape he had just tugged from scientist's face was still attached to the wool under his muzzle.

'You can't loosen these ropes, can you? My arms are really aching.'

'Sorry, sheep can't loosen knots. Not something we can do easily with our cloven hooves which have limited locomotive capabilities.'

'But you can kidnap a scientist in broad daylight at an agricultural show. You must have had help.'

'Not at all. I tied you up. I dwove the jeep. Easy peasy.'

'No one noticed anything strange. A black sheep in a jeep, *driving* the jeep?'

'A man dwessed up as a sheep for the hill farmers' pwotest. Do I look like your *wegular* sheep? Do I look *weel*?'

'You do look more like Jimi Hendrix than a sheep, without his sweaty headscarf. A bit ewe-like too with that perm. A rather poofy-looking sheep if the truth be known. You've put on a bit of weight too since I last saw you.'

'Not as much as you.'

'What else can you do now, besides drive cars?' asked Stein, goading him, wanting to find out all he could about his ovine antagonist.

'I can *weed*, Stein, I can *weed*!' the sheep cried. 'You don't know how liberwating that is for me, how much it has helped my quest for knowledge. What a differwence that makes, *weeding*.'

'I think I've a notion. And what have you...?'

'No more questions fwom you!' the sheep interrupted, with a petulant stamp of his hoof. Then attempting a German accent, he added: 'Ve ask ze qvestions awownd here!'

'Something else I've now learned about you. You have an even more perverted sense of humour. Which I should no doubt call upon myself, given my current predicament.'

'Which isn't half as bad as your future pwedicament,' the sheep declared. 'When weleased into the wild, you will be unable to tell anyone you were kidnapped and intarewogated by a sheep. No one would believe you. And you wouldn't want anyone to know what you *weelly* did when I was cloned, would you, Stein? Or what you did when Holly was cweeated?'

'You've got it all worked out, I can see.'

'I'm not stupid, Stein. I'm a sheep, remember.'

'But you *are* going to release me?'

'After your intarewogation, of course.'

'And how will you get me back in the trailer? And keep me quiet?'

'Same way as before,' said the sheep, gesturing towards a hose coiled up like a snake in the grass. 'Verwee simple, Stein. A vet's

twanquilliser dart. A short length of hose used as a blowpipe.'
He failed to add that when Stein had fallen to the vet's dart
earlier that day, his attacker had not been a sheep but a very
clever schoolgirl called Lucy Giles. Who was presently observing
him from the hayloft, blowpipe at the ready.

'A sheep has a lot of bweth,' the ram asserted. 'But the nec-
essawee pwopulsive power is pwovided by a single belch of
methane. As a scientist, you are of course aware that all methane
emitted by woominants is weleased thwough the mouth not
thwough the buttocks. My methane comes from my fore stomach fwom the fermentation of sugars dewived fwom the gwarse
I've eaten today. And I can contwol these emissions.'

'I've no doubt you can if you are capable of all these other
things.'

'Did you know, Stein, that UK cows and sheep expel 1.1
million tons of methane each year, the second largest source of
the gas after landfill sites?'

'I do now.'

'The internet is full of interwesting facts like that. The Clovis
site is quite good, I must say, but you should update it more
often. That old slogan's getting wather stale: DON'T SAY CLONE,
SAY CLOVIS. Not very owiginal.'

'So you surf the web...'

'I have my own site,' the sheep boasted. And then wished he
had been more circumspect.

'What's it called?' Stein asked too eagerly.

'Double ewe double ewe double ewe dot double ewe double
ewe double ewe,' the sheep responded. 'And vee ask ze qvestions...'

'OK, what is it you want to know?'

'I want to know about Holly. What she's like. What you did
to her.'

'Why don't you ask her? Why didn't you kidnap her instead
of me.'

'Too wisky,' said the sheep. 'You were expecting something
like that. I knew it was a set-up all along.'

'What happens if I refuse to cooperate?'

'I still welease you. But I tip off the Animal Liberation Fwunt
or the Men's Wepublic of Battymanistan Delegation in London.

113

I tell them where I've dumped you. You can choose between them.'

'And how do you propose to let them know.'

'I wing them.'

'And you can use the telephone of course.'

'No need for that. See that device,' the sheep added, pointing to a mobile phone on the workbench. You wemember how I learned to use the TV wemote in the laborwatwee? A mobile phone doesn't wequire even that degwee of dextairwitty, nor much intelligence, as you should be aware fwom its use by humans. Any modewately intelligent sheep should be able to use a mobile phone. Would you like me to demonstwate? Not only do I know the two numbers off by heart, but they're already keyed into the memorwee. Key star 3 for death by stoning or star 4 for a bullet in the head. Or do they only stone women and children to death? The men just get maimed or beheaded, is that wight? Shall I wing them now, just to get their interwest? See what kind of death's on the menu for the devil doctor Stein?'

'Where do you want me to start?'

'The beginning is generwally viewed as a good place,' said the sheep. 'But you can skip the clinical pwocedures, if they were the same as for me. You can start with Holly's education, what you taught her, and how?'

'You seem to have guessed all that.'

'I want all the detail,' said the sheep. 'I want to look for flaws in your pwocedures. Things you may have overlooked.'

'Still hoping she'll have the hots for you? That she won't just bite off your balls when your back's turned, as she told me? You think Holly may been playing some kind of double game with me? You're prepared to risk that?'

'Not at all. I want to work out if her we-education might still be possible.'

'How do you know she's even capable of speech?'

'Your whole plan must incorporwate that pwemiss. And you've just confirmed it.'

'And what if you decide you can't turn her?'

'I won't be turning her, Stein. You will.'

'And if I can't?'

'You'll cweate a new cloned ewe. Only this time you follow

my educational syllabus. And I have ways of checking that this is followed.'

'And if I can't do that either?'

'I'll make sure they find you.'

'They?'

'Star 3 or star 4? Which death would sir pwefer? How would sir like to be killed? Stoning or non-stoning?'

CHAPTER TWELVE

Is Ewe Is or Is Ewe Ain't My Baby?

The missing scientist Dr Frank Stein has been found. His disappearance had been linked to the terrorist incidents on Wednesday at the Yorkshire County Show in Harrogate. Dr Stein, a controversial biologist with the Clovis Institute, was presenting his new cloned ewe Holly at the agricultural event when the first car bomb went off. He now claims that kidnappers seized him during the ensuing confusion.

Dr Stein was found at Ilkeston market in Derbyshire. He had been bound and gagged, and was discovered covered in straw and manure when workmen cleared the sheep pens at the end of the day. He says his captors took him to a secret hideout where they subjected him to several hours of relentless interrogation, often accompanied by physical threats and actual violence. But he has been unable to give police any clues as to where he was held, except that it was in a remote rural location, nor could he explain how he came to be dumped in Ilkeston.

Dr Stein claims his kidnappers wanted information about his work at the Clovis Institute. They also threatened him with assassination unless he stops his controversial work on animal cloning, but Dr Stein has confirmed that he intends to continue with his project, which was 'immensely important both to science and to humanity', regardless of 'threats to his life and intimidation by loonies'.

Dr Stein was unable to identify his kidnappers because he was blindfolded throughout his ordeal. His captors had 'gruff voices', and he believes they may have been of Middle Eastern origin, although 'they could just as easily have been the chaps from the curry house on the corner', for there was 'a bit of a Yorkshire twang' in their speech.

A spokesmen for the Men's Republic of Battymanistan has denied any connection between Dr Stein's kidnapping and yesterday's arrest of two of its diplomats in Leeds, where the biologist's car was found abandoned after the Harrogate incidents.

'There is a Batwa against Dr Stein,' the official remarked. 'If any of our people had been involved in this, this infidel would have been executed. We would not have dumped his body in a sheep market without slitting his throat first.'

Responsibility for Dr Stein's kidnapping has been claimed by the Animal Liberation Front, but they have denied that the scientist was subjected to any violence. A spokesman said that Dr Stein was merely invited to give an account of his project and they had 'a frank and fair exchange of views'. Its members expressed their opposition to animal cloning, and Dr Stein was 'asked to abandon his immoral activities'.

However, a shadowy splinter group of the ALF calling itself 666 now says that four of *its* members staged the kidnapping. 666 is said to be an anarchist group with no command structure whose activists are believed to have carried out a series of uncoordinated attacks on scientists, butchers and battery farms. The Press Association last night received a phone warning that '666 is the number of the Beast, and Stein's number will be up if the Clovis Institute creates any more animal clones'.

*

It had all gone like clockwork, she told the sheep, right down to the way her father had parked the jeep at Ilkeston. He'd backed the trailer up right inside the pen, to make sure none of the boisterous tups tried to get through the gap. It had been an easy matter to push Stein's trussed body down the ramp when everyone else was watching the sheep tussling at the barrier. Being overweight, his own bulk had given him additional momentum. She hadn't even needed to cover him with straw. He'd sunk straight into the middenstead at the back.

She'd prodded him a few times when no one was looking, his faint groans assuring her he was still alive. After one of the rams chose to relieve itself just where she knew he must be lying, she even went over and pulled the straw back a little, to make sure he still had enough air.

'That was the least I could do,' she said. 'He may be a beastly man, but he is a human being.'

'Only just,' said the sheep. 'I sometimes wonder if my human qualities are gweater than his.'

'You were very hard on him. I've never thought you would be so vindictive towards him.'

'He's a very slipperwee customer. I had to get thrwoo to him. You saw what he made up for the pwess about his capture by four desperwet terworwists. But I have to admire him all the same, his guts, his nerve. The blindfold was a nice touch.'

'If he really *had* been blindfolded, there could have been four sheep holding him captive.'

'Well now you've seen him yourself I won't need to keep banging on about him.'

'It must be hard to have a father who's so unsympathetic.'

'He's only *partly* my father. There was another ram and two ewes involved too.'

'Well I thought he was a horrid man. I'm sure your other father must have been much nicer, that poor ram.'

*

Dr Frank Stein logged off. There was no website called www. doubleewe or double-ewe or any other combination he could think of. He'd tried permutations of Wally, but didn't think the sheep would have used *that* name, even to be ironic. His search through other possible sites had yielded only a series of ridiculous websites devoted to sheep, most of them clearly created by people who had an unhealthy and illogical respect for the animal. None of the sites appeared to present sheep matters from a sheep's point of view. If he didn't have a website after all, how else could he track him down? He couldn't get Shenanigan to help. The Irishman was the computer expert at Clovis. How could he tell Sean that he now knew for sure that Wally was not only still alive, but that it had been the sheep who had kidnapped him from Harrogate? And the animal had claimed during his interrogation that he had his own website?

The only person he could discuss it with was Holly, and she was hardly sympathetic.

'You said he was a stupid sheep, Flank,' declared his puzzled protégée. 'And yet he did not fall for your clever tlap, he didn't come anywhere near me. He kidnapped you instead.'

'I still think he had help.'

'But who would assist him? If Wally leally is a vain and nasty twisted piece of mutton with a pea-sized brain and an ego more inflated than Macannie's, no one would like him. Have you been stlate with me about him Flank?'

'Of course I have dear Holly. You don't think I've been misleading you, surely?'

'Not delibelately, of course, but sometimes you don't give the complete picture. Like with your colleagues. You said you were going to tell them about us, yet they still know nothing.'

'I told you, we have to wait for the right time. It would be quite a shock to them. And you wouldn't want to do anything to jeopardise our relationship, would you, dearest? You know what humans are like.'

'I only know what you tell me Flank, and what I hear the others saying.'

'I've not been unfaithful to you, have I?'

'Not to my knowledge. But sometimes that Helen Blimstone seems a little too flendly. She is a blazen tlamp. You should discourlage her more.'

'I can't help it if women find me attractive.'

'But not too many, I'm pleased to see.'

'I am an acquired taste.'

'I like your taste Flank. You are velly sleet with me, though not so sleet to the others.'

The others had been less than sympathetic, Macannie greeting him back from his ordeal with the words: 'Good morning, Frank, and how are we today? Did you have a nice time in Derbyshire? You didn't mention you were taking the day off after Harrogate. I trust you had a good break.'

'Be easy on him, Donald,' said Sean Shenanigan. 'Our man's been through the wars, don't you know. It's not every day a scientist gets kidnapped in broad daylight at the county show, without anyone seeing a thing, not even the police.'

'What I can't understand is why they let him go,' said Mark Gumption. 'If Stein's an animal-torturing devil-worshipping infidel heretic, why didn't they just finish him off when they had the opportunity?'

'Maybe they mistook him for the sheep,' said Macannie. 'They'd intended to kidnap Holly, but found they'd got the wrong animal.'

'I thought they were busy blowing up each other's Volvos at the time,' said Sean Shenanigan. 'What I find puzzling is how anyone could have had time to carry off our colleague while all that stuff was happening. The place was crawling with Los Federales. Have you got the car back from Leeds yet?'

'The police still have it,' said Stein. 'They're still checking it for fingerprints and other evidence.'

'How many of them did you say there were?' asked Helen Brimstone.

'It was difficult to tell, what with the blindfold. But I'm convinced there were four at least.'

'Well I think you're all being very hard on the poor man,' said Helen Brimstone, touching him on the arm, prompting an alarmed *baa* from Holly's observation pen. 'I'm sure none of you would enjoy being kidnapped by a bunch of bloodthirsty desperados.'

'At least they dumped his body in a soft spot,' said Mark Gumption. 'It was good of them to leave you in the straw.'

'Reduced to the level of the beasts, Frank,' said Macannie. 'There's a poetic touch in that.'

'Covered in dung and sheep piss,' Stein reminded them.

'I wondered what aftershave you'd used this morning,' said Shenanigan. 'I must say I prefer it to your usual.'

'But they didn't castrate you,' said Macannie. 'I wonder they didn't think of doing that.'

'They weren't animals,' Stein muttered, staring across at Holly, who was rubbing herself against the side of her pen.

*

The Shaman website was down again. The hackers had done horrible, terrible things with Lucy's design. She was quite upset.

'I don't think the site will survive this kind of thing,' the sheep told her. 'But it may not matter now. We can put it up again, but they'll come back and do worse.'

'They must think we're really important to be devoting so

much attention to Shaman,' said Lucy. 'It's only ever up for an hour or so before someone hacks into it again.'

'Shaman's dangerwous,' said the sheep. 'You've seen the messages they leave. It's not just the Batties. All the others are against it too. They've all been attacking it. Even the Methodists send us their cwiticisms.'

'But what they say is unfair,' said Lucy. 'You're not the Anti-Christ, you're a sheep.'

'They don't know that.'

'And you're not against God...'

'But they don't like what I say about God. Their god, my god, anyone's god, that god's the Spirit in all of us.'

'They don't enter into any kind of discussion. They just attack, attack, attack.'

'Hack hack hack, just like in the Cwusades. Both sides. Hack hack hack. But I'm not surpwised. It's just what I anticipated in a way, though the level of their hatewed surpasses all my expectations.'

'They must be really worried.'

'But you needn't worry about the site itself,' said the sheep. 'We've done our bit to launch Shaman. Have you seen how many other sites are carrying the Ten Revelations? Shaman's even made the top 20 websearch-topics list in the paper.'

'Yes, it's come in above Kylie Minogue.'

'I don't think we need worry about the Shaman website any more,' said the sheep. 'The word is abroad, and the word is Shaman. Sheep-man. Shaman will travel the world now.'

'If you say so, Sheep.'

'How's your own site coming on now? Do you want any more help with it?'

'I want to know more about Mary Wollstonecraft,' said Lucy. 'Can we talk more about her writings?'

*

The Metropolitan Police yesterday moved in to break up another mass urination protest in Hyde Park by followers of a new religious movement called Shaman. An estimated five thousand people had gathered to hear several speakers when the crowd were urged to drop their drawers and empty their bladders. With shouts of 'let it all hang out' and 'dangle and squat', they were spraying a border of dirt alongside the bushes bordering the Serpentine when the police moved in to end what had been expected to be a peaceful gathering.

A spokesman for Shaman said he was not a spokesman because no individual could speak for Shaman. The spirit of Shaman was shared by all, and none of the crowd had urinated on flowers or bushes or in the lake.

'Urination is a natural bodily process,' he claimed, and it was 'common to humans and animals', like defecation and breast-feeding. 'Were you offended by nakedness as a child? Are animals offended by the sight of other animals urinating? Not passing water when you need to pass water is a form of self-denial damaging to your physical body and well-being. Crossing your legs is self-crucifixion. Pass water not judgement.'

A mass breast-feed is now said to be planned by followers of Shaman at an as yet unnamed location. Organisers of this year's BBC's Proms have called for extra security after reports that hundreds of women intend to bare their breasts on camera in the Royal Albert Hall during the singing of *Rule Britannia.*

Meanwhile, a Hampshire police spokesman has confirmed that a whole football team were arrested in Southampton yesterday after they dropped their shorts at half time and urinated in the middle of the pitch. Spectators then vented their anger at the abandonment of the game by flooding onto the pitch where they too lined up to urinate. Fifteen people were later arrested.

'The toilets are always filthy or vandalised, so why can't we just p*** on the grass like the animals do,' said one woman. 'I bet you like emptying your bladder. Having a good p*** is a great feeling. Why do we have to go and hide to do it? And why do they make it so hard for people to find a place to p*** when they're out shopping. Anyone would think it was something dirty. It's ridiculous to have to hold it in. I don't know much about this Shaman stuff but I'd say they're right about a lot of things.'

'This thing is getting out of hand,' commented Sergeant Keith Troy of Hampshire Police. 'Religion's something that should be kept for church and Sundays. We shouldn't have it interfering with our daily lives, especially if it means people are going to start exposing themselves everywhere.'

*

'I see they've named a religion after one of your countrymen,' said Helen Brimstone, looking up from her paper as she reached across for another Hobnob to dunk in her coffee.

'It's Shaman, not Seamus, you eejit,' said Shenanigan.

'But it sounds right up your street,' she persisted. '*Believers respect all animals but the sheep is especially sacred*, that should please Frank. And listen to this: *Vivisectionists are men with dead souls who suck the blood of living creatures, and their lies are...*'

'Hand me that paper,' Stein growled, glancing at Holly who sudden started bleating as if alarmed, fixing him with a hysterical stare which he immediately translated as *Flank, we have to talk*.

'They also believe all animals to be superior to man "except for snakes and sheep-ticks"...were you saying something, Frank?'

'The paper. *Please*. I'm interested.'

'And they say sheep-ticks are an abomination. Fancy that. A religion going into that kind of detail about animal parasites.'

'Sounds like Holly's got one now,' said Shenanigan. 'Or else something else is bugging her.'

'As long as it's just a wee beastie that's giving her trouble,' intoned Macannie. 'We wouldn't want our new lassie whisked off for one of your secret assignations now, would we Frank? Not after what happened last time. You know what they say about sexual misconduct in the wairkplace. Can't have you doing a Clinton with our young intairn.'

'And we'd know from the stains on her wool,' said Dr Mark Gumption. 'She'd not be able to take that fleece of hers off to Sketchley's for dry cleaning.'

'I don't think even Stein would risk having Holly's chops round his chopper,' said Sean Shenanigan.

'She might bite off more than she could chew,' purred Helen Brimstone cattily. 'But at least she wouldn't be able to swear an affidavit to Kenneth Starr. So you wouldn't have to deny that "is" means "is", Frank, because in your case *is* usually *isn't*.'

'I did not have sexual relations with that sheep!' Stein snapped with sudden vehemence, rising abruptly to his feet while grabbing for the newspaper so that his chair toppled backwards, just as Holly started bleating frantically again, and the black-suited figure of Dr Steve Weisenheimer emerged from behind the grey bank of filing cabinets like the shark in *Jaws*.

CHAPTER THIRTEEN

The Great Escape

Douglas Giles hadn't told his daughter about the phone call from the DEFRA vet. He knew she wouldn't have been able to bear it, that she would be hysterical. He was finding it hard enough himself. None of his flock had shown any signs of Foot and Mouth, but they were going to cull all 'contiguous' farms. He had to look the word up in Lucy's dictionary, he wasn't going to ask her what it meant. By the time she came back from her school trip to the coast, it would all be over. If the the soldiers kept their promise, all the sheep carcasses would have been carried off in their trucks before she arrived, all except her beloved black ram of course, whose ear-tag he had removed and given to another disease-free ram he'd bought especially to be sacrificed in its place after 'losing' the poor beast's own paper-work.

As he watched the substitute 501 trotting up the ramp to meet its unmaker, the lump in his throat had grown so full he felt it was about to choke him if not burst through his neck. He went inside, knowing he was going to cry silently, not just for his animals and for his farm, for everything he'd done to build up his family's livelihood over the years, but most of all for dear Lucy and his darling Rebecca, whom he knew would have been out there railing at the soldiers. Even though they were only doing their job, she'd have told them she'd heard that one before about men just obeying their orders, and they should have refused to carry out those orders, which were an affront to all human decency. There was nothing wrong with her sheep, they were perfectly healthy animals, and they would have to get past her before they could lay a finger on a single one of them. He knew she would have been right, that this was what he should have been doing himself, but he also knew that it was because of her that he could not act on his own. Their sheep would be killed regardless of what he did to defend them, and after what had happened, he would not be able to restock the farm later, to try to take it back to what it never was again after Rebecca's death. Lucy might not like it, but he was sure she would understand, especially since her mother had always been pressing him to go organic, the farm produce part of his work was virtually that in all but name in any case, and now he would go over to just producing vegetables. He already knew everything he had to do to get the necessary accreditation from the Soil Association, and now, once he had the clean slate and clearance from DEFRA, he could start reorganising everything. It was this plan alone which made the killing of his sheep bearable, that and the fact that Lucy's precious black ram would be spared.

Not knowing any of this, since Lucy had not been party to her father's thinking, the sheep paced around her bedroom, risking the occasional agonising peek through the corner of the curtains at the horror show unfolding in the farmyard. All he knew was that the soldiers had come, and were killing all the sheep, just like in the films. He knew about the Foot and Mouth epidemic of course – Lucy and her father had talked about little else for the past month – and there'd been all the horrific reports on the radio. But he knew their farm was free of the disease, and faced now with the unreal logic of what was happening outside, after Lucy had clearly been sent off on her supposed trip on what had to be a false pretext, he felt he was witnessing a war crime, a secret act of terror, which he was powerless to stop and which would surely claim his own life.

The sheep had known something was wrong first thing that morning. As soon as Douglas Giles returned from dropping Lucy off at school, earlier than usual because of her trip, he'd heard him mounting the stairs. His usual routine was to make his cup of tea first in the kitchen, then shortly afterwards the sheep would hear the back door being closed, followed by the racket of the tractor starting up in the barn. He'd stared at the tape recorder, which was replaying the Gospel According to St Matthew read by Alec McCowen, and was about to press the stop button to wind it back to the Last Supper when Lucy's father had stopped on the landing and knocked gently on the door, not to startle him he supposed; and entering the room he started addressing the sheep in a nervous fashion. He made to pat him on the back, indicating with his eyes that he meant no harm, muttering at the same time in a distracted fashion which was quite unlike his normal easy and relaxed way of talking.

'Come on now, Wally, or whatever your name is,' he'd said. 'This is for your own good. You're not going to need this tag after all. Let me just unclip it. There...'

And he'd removed the plastic tag bearing the sheep's number, 501. Instinctively, he shook his head when Lucy's father released the ear. And he shook it again and again, waggling his ears three times. And as Douglas Giles closed the door behind him, saying 'I just hope they get it over with as quickly as possible, and they don't suffer too much', he heard the cock in the hen-run crow thrice, and immediately remembered Peter's denial, which Christ had predicted, and when, instead of the sound of the tractor starting up, he heard the rumble of trucks outside, trucks entering and halting in the farmyard with a sigh of brakes, then squealing metal doors being opened, and the sound of boots clattering on the yard, and loud, efficient men's voices calling words like *guns*, and *slaughter*, and *sheep*, his heart sank as he took in the sudden and full revelation of his betrayal.

When Corporal Terry Towling asked to use the toilet in the house, he had not expected to be confronted by a fleeing sheep. As he mounted the stairs, he was hurriedly unbuttoning his flies, such was the urgency of his need after the previous night's excesses, and was therefore not in a state of full military readiness. He nevertheless made a grab for the animal, hoping to apprehend it by clinging on to its wool, the two of them falling together in a tumble of black and khaki, then both springing up again, pushing and shoving at each other in the narrow stairwell.

'Come here, you,' Corporal Towling yelled. 'You won't escape so easily. You have to suffer the same fate as the others, I'm sorry to say, though none of us are wanting to do this, I can assure you of that.'

The soldier's words confirmed his worst fears. The sheep kicked and bucked in an attempt to free himself from his persecutor, his hooves delivering a Roy Keane tackle which left the man sprawling. Then the soldier leapt up and was on him again, and he lunged to get free, pulling with his teeth at the man's half-unbuttoned trousers which came suddenly loose from his hips, and were yanked to half-mast. Yet still the khaki devil managed to hang onto him, grasping him around the waist with his strong tree-like arms. He wasn't going to let go, he had him pinned down. Any second and he would call out for help.

'Jesus,' the man gasped. 'And I thought Bosnia was bad. At least we never had to wrestle with a mad fucking sheep.'

'I'm not mad,' the sheep responded. 'Nor do I have any contagious or even contiguous diseases.'

Shocked, the soldier released his grip slightly, enabling the sheep to shuffle upwards, but still trapped.

'And this is hardly the way to carwee out a pwoper execution,' the animal continued. 'I believe the pwotocol on such occasions is for the executioner to allow the pwisoner a last wequest. A cigawette? A special meal the night before, with maybe a bottle of Mouton Rothschild '73?'

Corporal Towling stared at the sheep in his arms, open-mouthed. His leg throbbed from where he'd been hoofed in the shin. His bladder was bursting.

'Well perhaps Mouton Cadet then if you can't manage the Rothschild, though '73 is an especially good year, you know.'

'Jesus Christ...'

'And a woman of course. But you've just shot all the ewes, haven't you? Don't I even get a blindfold?'

The soldier released his grip.

'What are you?' he asked, unable to believe what he was hearing. He felt exhausted.

'SAS of course,' said the sheep. 'And you've just blown my cover.'

The soldier's vision started to blur. His head was pressed against the ram's black fleece, which smelled strongly of lanolin and animal musk, not human body smells. It *was* a sheep, and yet...

'Yes, I am a sheep,' the animal told him, seeming to read his thoughts. 'But I'm not part of this flock, am I? I don't have one of their ear-tags even. So you can't just kill me with the others, you'll need special authority. And that, I can tell you, you won't get because…'

Corporal Towling's head was throbbing. He tried to stand up.

'…I have the wank of a major in the Bwitish Army…' the mad talking sheep was saying.

'You just wait there,' the soldier gasped, pulling to free one foot which had become trapped under the sheep's flank. 'Don't go away, I'll be back in a minute.'

'I'm not weally dwessed to go anywhere, am I?'

As Corporal Terry Towling bent to pull up his trousers, the sheep saw his chance, and grabbed at the cloth with his teeth while heaving his own body up and over the soldier's knees. His trousers ripped open, and falling head over heels down the stairs, the corporal was knocked unconscious when his head struck the bottom step, the shock prompting his bladder to release one and a half pints of urine onto Douglas Giles's hall carpet. Not knowing whether this strong man might quickly recover his senses, the sheep decided to remove the rest of his trousers as a precaution, hoping this might delay any pursuit. Picking up the torn pieces of khaki cloth with his teeth, he took them into the kitchen, pressed the pedal of the rubbish bin with one hoof, and dropped them inside, pressing them down with his muzzle, so that the man might be found debagged if he didn't recover, such confusion being helpful in covering his tracks.

When Captain Balderdash went looking for his corporal ten minutes later, he found the wild-haired man crouched at the bottom of the stairs in a pool of urine wearing no trousers. He was vomiting between his legs.

'Corporal Towling!' he barked.

'Sir,' stuttered Towling, using his sleeve to wipe the yellow vomit from his face. 'There was this sheep…'

'What sheep, man?'

'A sheep that talked. It said it wanted a last request before we shot it but it was a major in the SAS…'

'I see no sheep. What I see is…

'Oh God,' groaned the corporal. 'Take me back to Bosnia,

Kosovo, Crossmaglen even, any of those damned places...'

The sheep had not stayed to witness the scene. He did not know that the soldier who had attempted to restrain him so valiantly was about to be sectioned under the Mental Health Act. As far as the animal was aware, his life was still in grave danger.

*

The hysterical girl stood in the middle of the laboratory, her arms flailing wildly, the older man who seemed to be her father trying to restrain her.

'Don't you see, you *have* to help find him, he's all alone,' she was saying. 'I'd rather he ended up *here* than...'

'What's happened to security?' Macannie was whining. 'How did these people get through security...' He stood in front of his computer, as if to shield it from attack if the girl should become suddenly violent.

The shouting had set off another round of frantic bleating from Holly in the observation pen.

'Wait a moment,' said Stein with sudden authority. 'Call off the guards. Sit down, please.' He gestured to the table, and Helen Brimstone pulled up a chair for the girl, patting her gently on the arm, while Douglas Giles took the seat beside her and kept trying to hold her, to comfort her. She shook his arm free.

'These foke should be arrested,' the Scotsman whined.

'Shut up, Macannie,' said Stein.

'The penny has dropped,' said Sean Shenanigan. 'Our ram has landed, but done another bunk, you seem to be saying...'

'Take it slowly, Lucy,' said Douglas Giles. 'Let's just tell them what we know.'

But Lucy Giles started sobbing again, with sharp intakes of breath, as if her own breath were choking her.

'Quick,' said Helen Brimstone. 'She's hyperventilating. Pass me that paper bag. Here Lucy, breathe into this, slowly, slowly.'

'What we know,' intoned Dr Donald Macannie ponderously, 'as far as I can gather from this wee lassie's outbairst, is that while the combined efforts of the British police assisted by our scientists, and to some degree by the gentlemen of the press albeit often in a cavalier fashion, while all these people have failed to find our missing laboratory sheep for nearly two years now I think it is, despite the offer of rewards of many thoosands of poonds, the said animal, which is the property of the Clovis Institute, has been kept hidden in hair hoose by a wee gel, in contravention of goodness knows how many laws, aided and abetted by her faither, who should have known better...'

'Just a minute...' said Douglas Giles.

'I am not anyone's wee gel,' Lucy cried, pulling the hair back from her face, and taking a wad of tissues offered by Helen Brimstone to first blow her nose, then wipe her eyes.

'My daughter gave that sheep the best possible home,' said Douglas Giles as she noisily cleared her nose. 'She washed him and groomed him, and after her mother died, it was so helpful to her to have that lovely animal to care for. She even read books to him...'

'Books,' Stein echoed. 'Well that doesn't surprise me...'

'What would you know?' Lucy cried, turning on the scientist, still half suppressing another attack of sobbing. 'You only created him for your own selfish ends, you even...you didn't...you never told...'

She stopped. The other scientists were staring at her and Stein in turn.

'I love that sheep,' Lucy continued. 'And I care for him more than anyone or anything in the whole world.'

Douglas Giles looked at his feet. 'She blames me for what happened,' he muttered, 'but I keep telling her, he escaped, he wasn't killed.'

'I don't mean that, of course I love *you*, Daddy. But what I feel for my Sheep is a totally different kind of love, a love...'

'A love that dare not speak its name,' Macannie hissed sarcastically. 'Our Dr Stein is well vairsed in such matters, especially where sheep are concairned.'

'Shut up, Macannie, before I brain you,' said Stein, as Holly began bleating again.

'Now now, boys,' said Helen Brimstone. 'Remember we have company, and ladies are present.'

Stein looked over at the pen where his lovesick progeny now

appeared to be mooning at the grille. *Mairrr, mairrr*, she called to him.

'That's Holly, isn't it?' said Lucy. 'I recognise her from the pictures. She's very pretty.'

Douglas Giles coughed, indicating it was perhaps time that some hard facts were introduced into the discussion. 'My own theory is that the corporal who disgraced himself in the house had some kind of encounter with the sheep, but I didn't tell the vets or the doctor that. He was in a state of some shock, he'd fallen down the stairs and was concussed.'

'And lost his trousers in the process,' said Lucy.

'His troosers. The mind truly boggles…' said Macannie.

'We later found them in the pedal-bin, all torn to pieces,' said Lucy. 'And he weed all over the carpet.'

'Who, the soldier or the sheep?' asked Mark Gumption.

'The soldier of course. My Sheep would never do his wee in the house, he was very particular.'

'Yes, he would be,' said Stein. 'He was always very particular in his habits.'

'I'm sorry to have to add this detail,' Douglas Giles continued. 'But you need to know. I did check all the carcasses in the trucks. I didn't tell them why, but they let me check them off, I said it was something I had to do for myself. And there was *no* black sheep amongst them, I am absolutely sure of that. You do believe me, don't you Lucy, your sheep *wasn't* killed with the others. I don't know how he did it, but I'm certain that he managed to escape.'

'I have to believe you, Daddy, and knowing my Sheep, I do think he would have found a way of escaping. He was a very clever animal. What am I saying? He *is* very clever.'

'I think we're all aware of that fact,' said Gumption, 'though perhaps we didn't fully recognise his intelligence and intellectual capabilities as we should have done before.'

'Thanks to certain colleagues of ours being rather selective in what they chose to reveal in group discussions of the tests and observation work carried out in relation to our plucky ram,' said Sean Shenanigan.

'Colleague, singular, I think it was,' said Helen Brimstone. 'And this might suggest that we should consider revising our procedures for observing the other sheep clones, don't you think, gentlemen?'

'At last, some words of sense,' Macannie sighed.

Lucy Giles sat back in her chair. 'Well I'm sorry to disappoint you all,' she began, returning to the fray with an air of purposeful authority, 'and I can see why you must feel that way about Dr Stein's understandably *possessive* attitude to my Sheep, his sheep, to the sheep we all love dearly...' (and here she managed at wink at him without the others seeing) '...but I do have a lot of helpful information, and I would very much appreciate being able to talk first with Dr Stein, and *in private*. Much of what I have to say *is* for his ears alone...'

'I don't see how...' Macannie started.

'Let's do as she suggests,' said Helen Brimstone, interrupting. 'We *all* know how close Frank was to Wally, and clearly Lucy has known him well over a similar period. They will have much to talk about. Let them get on with it, and afterwards we can all come together and discuss things without the need for argument. I don't think Lucy will let Frank get away with any more secrecy about Wally.'

'We'll need a plan,' said Shenanigan. 'We can't be asking Mr Plod to help, given how thick he's been with Johnny Hack. The press would flood the valley in five minutes, never mind the restrictions on the movement of animals. Those TV lads are bad enough as it is, hanging round like vultures outside the affected farms, just to be *filmed* there, as if that makes all the whole show any more believable. It's the Ministry they should be doorstepping, that's where they'd find a whole lot o' shite under the carpet.'

'You're right,' said Douglas Giles. 'The other farmers would never forgive me. Their own livelihoods would be threatened. Even the locals are only making necessary journeys now.'

Holly stamped at her straw, scuffing it with furious cuffs of her forehooves. What were they saying? Everything they'd been discussing seemed to contradict what Stein had told her, especially their descriptions of Wally. This girl clearly loved the renegade ram, and knew a great deal about him. And Wally wasn't thick as two planks after all, as Stein had claimed. He'd even managed to escape from an army death-squad. And suddenly it came to her that Stein hadn't been kidnapped by four desperate animal liberation terrorists, it had been Wally, helped no doubt by the girl, probably with her father as an unwitting accomplice, since he would have had to drive the vehicle.

Stein was saying: 'I'll take Lucy into Weisenheimer's office where we'll have more privacy. He has some photographs on the wall of Wally as a lamb I'm sure she'd like to see.'

'But you mustn't call him Wally,' Lucy remarked, 'you know he hates that name you gave him.'

She looked across at Holly, whose baleful look Stein was clearly trying to avoid. She shook her head at the ewe, miming sadness and gesturing towards Stein who had his back to them, as she mouthed the words: *'He isn't worth it, Holly.'*

*

The journey had been rougher than he'd expected, and several times he'd wanted to be sick. At least Douglas Giles's trailer had been padded with hay, while his ride on the car transporter had been more of a fairground affair, with all the novelty of his first joyride out in the fresh air, and those smiling people in the cars to wave at. He'd had to be much more circumspect as a stowaway in the army truck, making sure first that he picked the right vehicle, the one taking the men back to their barracks not the open loader piled high with sheep corpses, but pushing the back door open, he'd seen immediately where he could squeeze himself under the long bench seat down one side, and since it was near dusk and he was a black beast, he'd felt hopeful that his presence wouldn't be detected.

As it turned out, even his sheepy smell hadn't given him away because the soldiers themselves had been soaked in the shower of rain. They'd all been handling sheep and were speaking with relish of the showers they'd shortly have; and they had plenty to talk about to distract them on the journey, after Corporal Towling had been bundled into the white van in the straitjacket, still babbling about the voices of sheep that were telling him to vomit in nice people's houses.

But the sheep soon realised that making his second escape would be not just more difficult, but probably impossible. Once inside the gates, the truck pulled up at a long hut, where the men alighted and he bundled himself off into the dark as they were organising their baggage. Looking about him at the great expanse of flat ground, where khaki-coloured trucks were being backed up to buildings, and even tanks were trundling around, he saw that he might just as well have parachuted into a prisoner-of-war camp. The place looked like Stalag Luft III in that film he remembered seeing in the lab, with its floodlit perimeter fence patrolled by sentries with guard dogs. Yet this was a far bigger place even than that; there was a stretch of tarmac across to the right on which a rank of helicopters sat waiting like great cockroaches in the half-light. Then all of a sudden he saw a great runway lit up by a string of yellow and red lamps stretching into the far distance, and heard the sound of a plane buzzing above as it came into land.

He knew then the only way he'd get out of this place would be either the same way he came in, hidden in another truck, or as a stowaway on a plane or helicopter. Until he'd worked out how to achieve that, he'd be able to hide under one of the huts. From the evidence of a row of large grey metal bins, he deduced where the kitchen area must be situated, and decided that this should offer the most suitable place of refuge, since food should be available there in some form or other, however unpalatable it might be.

And he fretted endlessly about Lucy, how she would be feeling now. How could he contact her, to let her know he was safe after all? He stared up at the huge telecommunications satellite dish perched on one of the buildings, but decided that such sophisticated equipment might still be beyond his technical capabilities, especially in view of the limited dexterity offered by his hooves. He'd have to start from scratch too, since the army's computer system wouldn't have his voice recognition software.

But if the right opportunity presented itself, he could always steal someone's mobile phone, and send her a text message.

CHAPTER FOURTEEN

Baarmy Army

Graham Medlar could not have imagined that his video would have been so well received at Clovis. Instead of striking terror into the scientists, they hooted at each scene featuring the hapless Dr Frank Stein, even the part that showed his new Renault being blown up outside his house.

'Oh, rewind that, please,' cried Dr Macannie. 'I have to see that again. And those idiots even give us that sequence twice, the second time in slow motion. Take it back to where Stein's washing it.'

They watched again as Stein washed and waxed and polished his Renault Vel Satis 3.0 Initiale dCi which had cost him £26,000, as he'd been telling them all that week. He even seemed to be smiling for the hidden camera, beaming with joy and whistling Roger Whittaker's *King of the Road*. Pirouetting with the sponge, he dabbed at some spots of dirt before giving them a good rub, chiding them as he did so.

'Now watch him dance up the path,' said Mark Gumption. 'Oh this part is absolutely priceless.'

'Unlike the soon-to-be-lamented turbo diesel vehicle,' said Sean Shenanigan. 'What was it he said it had, variable-assistance power steering, wasn't it, whatever that is.'

'Not much help to the poor man now,' said Helen Brimstone. 'You have to feel a little sorry for him.'

'No way,' said Shenanigan. 'Sorry, not. Not after all that earache we got from him about the frigging car, and how he'd fiddled the compensation claim on the old Volvo.'

'His 26 grand Renault with the idiot-proof navigation system that *he* wouldn't actually need to use of course,' said Macannie.

'I'd say he probably wanted that for the sheep,' said Sean Shenanigan. 'He's probably got Wally added to the insurance for the next time the two of them take a drive together.'

'Now watch him pat the bonnet before he heads back into the house,' said Mark Gumption. 'Next frame...'

'5-4-3-2-1...boom!' cried Macannie as the sound seemed to imitate him and the picture shook and went fuzzy for a few seconds.

'And hey presto!' said Sean Shenanigan. 'Welcome to Beirut, Dr Stein. What do you think of your spanking new car now? Not quite the same shade of buttermilk cream now is it? More like ochre brown, I'd say, with black highlights added down the side, an optional feature it would appear. But your Vel Satis is no longer velly satisfactory.'

'Oh my!' cried Macannie. 'Look how the man's ducking as he's coming out of the house and down the path, as if there are snipers in the rhododendrons.'

'And here comes Sheila Marshall from accounts, before the police arrive,' screeched Helen Brimstone. 'Oh she *does* look in a state.'

'Off she goes, hurrying away, without giving our man as much as a peck on the cheek,' said Sean Shenanigan. 'My, she's not a happy bunny, is she? Oh I'm sorry for you there, Frank. Doesn't look as though you'll be giving her a run in one of your fancy cars again, does it now?'

'Oh, that *was* good though wasn't it?' said Helen Brimstone, 'after the way he was leering at her before, in that earlier bit.'

'He seemed to be getting further with her than with the bint that slapped his face outside the cinema,' said Sean Shenanigan. 'Did you see what film he took her to?'

'But who'd have thought it,' said Gumption. 'Sheila from accounts. Wouldn't have said she was his type really.'

'Our Dr Stein is clearly not fussy,' said Sean Shenanigan. 'He's a desperate fellow. And look, now here come the piggies! Watch him with that policewoman again, how he gets suddenly tearful, and then she puts her arm around him.'

'Yee-hah,' cried Gumption. 'Oh this is brilliant! What are those though? We let that bit go before. Pause the tape. Let's read what it says.'

Sean Shenanigan took off his glasses and stood in front of the screen. 'I thought so,' he said. 'They've even got hold of his till-slips from Sainsburys. Meaning, whatever he's up to, our animal-loving friends know about it.'

'They must have been going through his bins,' said Mark Gumption. 'I wonder what else they'd find in his rubbish.'

'I'd rather not, if you don't mind,' said Helen Brimstone.

'Let's see,' Shenanigan went on, 'four bottles of Chardonnay, two bottles of Johnnie Walker, Benson and Hedges, cheese, milk, toothpaste, *boring boring boring*, ah yes pork sausages, bacon, oven-ready chicken, beefburgers, *more* sausages, beef this time, shepherd's pie, steak and kidney pudding, lamb chops, lamb slices in gravy, roast lamb TV dinner, *tinned* lamb pasanda, the said items being marked with the Evil Yellow Highlighter Pen, meaning you are damned Dr Stein, you eat our animals as well as torturing the poor creatures and we moral crusaders are going to get you, you wicked man! But they may have a point there: a good few beasts have clearly given their lives just to fill the Stein stomach. I'd say he's been especially predatory towards our good friend the sheep. Look at all that lamb he's been getting through.'

'No wonder he's getting so fat and seedy-looking if this is what he lives off,' said Helen Brimstone. 'They're also saying: Dr Stein, you are one hell of a slob. Doesn't he eat any fruit or vegetables?'

'Yes, here we have them, *vegetables*,' Shenanigan announced with a pretend fanfare of trumpets. 'Yes, Dr Stein *does* eat his vegetables. He enjoys Youngs oven-ready chips with his Birds Eye fish fingers, and he likes to buy the family pack of Walkers cheese and onion crisps. And yes, more *vegetables*: frozen peas, frozen carrots, baked beans, lots of baked beans, two six-packs that makes twelve if I'm not mistaken, yes he'd need a few cans of those to go with all that meat he's been putting away. Ah now, what's this? Yes, here's more *evidence*: Baking Soda! This puts Dr Stein in a whole new light. We did not know that our colleague likes nothing better than baking his own Victoria sponge-cakes or individual fairy-cakes in their waxed-paper cases each topped with white icing and the glacé cherry, why else would he require Baking Soda?'

'You have me there, Sean,' said Macannie. 'I'm quite partial to a sponge-cake myself, and I always say there's nothing quite like a home-made...'

'I think Dr Shenanigan is alluding to certain other habits Frank is known to indulge in,' said Helen Brimstone.

'Of course. Silly me. I'm so out of date these days.'

'And not just Baking Soda,' Shenanigan continued, 'but *five* boxes of what the till-slip terms *chemist's goods*.'

'That means condoms,' said Helen Brimstone. 'He's nothing if not hopeful.'

'Probably the car,' said Shenanigan. 'He thinks the latest French-designed fanny magnet will change his luck.'

'It certainly did that in the next bit,' shrieked Macannie. 'I must say his face looked a real picture when he gets his front door open only to discover...'

They watched him struggling with his key, unsteady on his feet after spending Saturday afternoon drinking and watching the football in the pub.

'See how he sways,' Macannie called out. 'Now he's trying to work out why the door doesn't push in properly.'

'Oh dear, have they rigged up a bomb?' said Gumption. 'That's what he should be saying. He shouldn't be still trying to force it.'

'But oh no, not the good Dr Stein,' said Shenanigan. 'I'd lay odds it's the toilet he needs now, he's bursting for a pee.'

'But could be bursting from an ALF bomb,' said Helen Brimstone.

'But oh no,' said Shenanigan. 'Look, he's giving it the shoulder now. Heave-ho. Door finally gives. Doctor Stein falls into the hall.'

'And discovers some nasty people have driven a muck tanker up to his house in broad daylight.'

'As seen in the earlier footage.'

'The security-conscious Stein having had the foresight to leave the transom window open – so no damage caused there – and the fellows have only just filled his entire hall with liquid cow dung. What jolly japes, eh chaps?'

'It's a wonder he didn't smell something when he was trying to barge the door open,' said Mark Gumption.

'That didn't surprise me one bit,' said Helen Brimstone.

After various shots of someone's coffin being lowered into a grave, followed by some footage of a dog being dissected while still alive in a laboratory which definitely wasn't *anything* to do with Clovis, then some pigs squealing in an abbatoir pen, the film ended with a blizzard of static.

'I thought the end was in pretty bad taste though,' said Mark Gumption.

'Somewhat over the top,' said Macannie.

'Hysterical,' said Helen Brimstone.

'But not as funny as the bits starring our own Dr Frank Stein,' said Sean Shenanigan. 'He really stole the show for me. I hope the fame doesn't go to his head, he'll be wanting an Equity card next. He's quite good enough to go professional, I'd say.'

In her observation pen, Holly lay in the straw by the feed trough, moaning. This was the third time they'd played the video that day, and each time they'd found it funnier and added more elaborate commentary. She didn't need to hear or see any more. Stein's shopping list was the last straw.

*

Dr Frank Stein flipped through the pages of the document the girl had left. He kept muttering that he wasn't going to be bullied, but knew he had no choice. He yanked open the filing-cabinet drawer and extracted a bottle of Johnnie Walker, which had been full the day before and now barely yielded a glass. Where had he gone wrong? He was the world's leading expert on cloning and animal intelligence, but he couldn't even publish a full account of his work. By rights he should be expecting a call from the Nobel Prize committee, but instead he was being blackmailed by a sheep, aided and abetted by a schoolgirl. A sheep, moreover, which might even be dead now, though he'd lay odds on the wily animal being holed up somewhere else, somewhere cushy where he'd wheedle his way into some other set-up that would serve his purpose.

He didn't even know what the sheep was after, apart from knowledge. The girl wasn't laying all his cards on the table. But he was obviously up to something, or had been until the DEFRA death-squad descended and carried out its slaughter of the innocents. He wouldn't have expected that. An enforced sudden departure of that nature must have thrown his planning. Stein just had to hope that the sheep might have to find refuge in some place offering little freedom to manipulate people, where he could only survive by pretending to be a normal sheep. That would put an end to his games.

Lucy Giles had put on a good performance for the others. Not that he doubted the love she professed for the sheep, for all that he found himself sickened by her gushingly saccharine expressions of it. They were clearly two of a kind, the sheep and his girl. But the rest of his team would not have been able to imagine that this pretty and disarmingly open-hearted creature could be utterly heartless in relentlessly pursuing the sheep's vendetta against him in the animal's absence.

The infuriating girl had soon disabused him of his assumption that the sheep would have been unprepared. Not only had he done all his homework, but in the event of anything happening to the animal, she had enough documentation to guarantee Stein's immediate dismissal from Clovis. Nobody else would want to employ him, she'd said, with a beaming smile, and the only way he could have access to the kind of equipment and facilities he required would be to go to some Third World country where their needs would be very different from his. She had even taunted him that he could always offer his services to Severino Antinori and maybe work on cloning a human who could talk sheep language. Or Clonaid might have a vacancy for a mad scientist with his track record if he was interested in cloning alien offspring for Raelian sect families.

Lucy Giles had then described how she had helped the sheep to hack in to Clovis's computer system, enabling the animal to prepare even fuller documentation of his own cloning than the other scientists possessed, Stein having been somewhat selective in what he chose to reveal. To this he had added an account of Holly's cloning, again drawn from Clovis's records but with additional material based on what Stein had revealed under interrogation. The dossier was prefaced with a short summary for the press which described how Stein had deceived his colleagues at Clovis, noting which aspects of his work had been carried out in secret and which were unethical, as well as listing grants from various foundations and funding bodies he had managed to divert for his own use. Without the knowledge of other scientists or management at Clovis, Stein had cloned two sheep with various human characteristics who could both think and talk, and he had used his own DNA to achieve this. He had not been kidnapped by terrorists as he had claimed, he had been abducted by the missing ram. He had also brainwashed the ewe to make her do whatever he wanted.

The dossier's appendix gave details of a postgraduate student's project which Stein had hijacked some years previously, claiming credit for his assistant's work after she had committed suicide. That early work on animal cloning had been essential to the development of Stein's whole project.

'Do you have anything else on me, apart from this dossier?' Stein had asked.

'Letters written by the girl describing how you sexually harassed her and subjected her to continued emotional blackmail,' said Lucy. 'But we didn't think they needed to go in the dossier.'

'Then you must also know that whole farrago of lies was thrown out of court,' Stein had told her. 'The girl was a manic depressive, unhinged, a fantasist.'

'But when you set what you call her fantasy alongside factual records of her work which were published in an obscure American university scientific journal, two and two would seem to add up to a lot more trouble for you, Dr Stein.'

'She couldn't have published any of that stuff. It wouldn't have been allowed without my agreement as her supervisor.'

'The university concerned was her alma mater. Her article was accompanied by a rather effusive editorial note describing her as one of the most talented students ever to graduate from there. Its tone suggested that the writer remembered her with rather more affection than you showed her.'

The document Lucy Giles had left him was not the dossier itself. Copies of that would only be sent to Clovis and the press if he did not cooperate with her. As well as helping her find the sheep, he was to study Holly's re-education curriculum and ensure that all its stipulations were carried out. The sheep appreciated that it might take some time for Holly to be taught to read, but in the meantime Stein had a list of books he was to begin reading to her as well as a viewing list of videos. Once that process was complete, she was to be given the same access to the Television which he had enjoyed, but she should be briefed beforehand about the difference between fact and fiction and given what the sheep termed 'parental guidance' before being shown any reality TV programmes. He was also to make 'a full and FRANK confession to Holly' covering all the secret work he had done in creating his two sheep clones.

*

Holly wouldn't speak to him for a week after he'd made his excruciatingly full and frank confession. But she seemed to know better than to reveal her linguistic skills to any of the others. His argument for secrecy still held sway with her, probably for the same reason that Wally had kept his wretched tongue to himself for so long. She knew it was in her interest. Now she wanted to talk, it seemed, and she'd even condescended to let him read to her. He drained the last dregs from his glass, belched, and slouched over to her pen.

'Are you sitting comfortably?' he asked.

'If I didn't know you were such a liar, Flank, I might be touched by your concern. You needn't pletend with me. I have not forgiven you. But you may start leeding.'

'*Mister Jones, of the Manor Farm, had locked the hen-houses for the night, but he was too drunk to remember to shut the pop-holes,*' Stein began.

'Oh he is a dlunk like you then, Flank? Who is he, this Mister Jones? Why are you leeding me this?

'It's a story. It's on the reading list.'

'What are these pop-holes? What pops out of them? Is it that weasel you spoke of before, Flank?'

'I think they're egg chutes.'

'What is this book about dlunks and their egg chutes?'

'It's called *Animal Farm*, by George Orwell.'

142

'Why is it called *Animal Farm*, Flank? All farms have their animals, do they not?'

'But on this farm the animals take over. It's a parable about power and corruption.'

'A palable? But why should the animals be collupt? It is the people who are collupt, surely?'

'That's what Orwell's really describing,' said Stein wearily. 'Do you want me to read it to you or not?'

'Yes, I think I will let you leed me this book. But you mustn't leave anything out, and if you say something I don't understand, you have to explain it.'

'*With the ring of light from his lantern dancing from side to side, he lurched across the yard...*'

'He is still dlunk then, this man? And how can his lantern dance? It is only a lantern surely...'

*

Captain Henry Undergrowth was incandescent. His quarter-master-sergeant stood before him, trying not to visibly duck under the tongue-lashings.

'Why did no one tell me this before, sergeant?' the officer was demanding. 'The regiment cannot go to war without their mascot, you know what the men are like. The Fusiliers have always had a black sheep, it's not just part of our identity, our regimental pride, you know full well that the black sheep has always brought us luck.'

Sergeant Gross tried – without luck – to get a word in.

'And you say it was run over. By one of our own tanks, no less. Why the hell didn't the beast hear it coming, why didn't it jump out of the way?'

'Ee was drunk sir,' Gross managed to say, then regretted it.

'Drunk? What do you mean, *drunk?*'

'Black Sheep Ale, I fink it was. That's what we usually give im, I mean *gave* im. You remember, the men had a party for Ginger Rodgers, to give im a good send-off. The sheep was of course invited to join us in celebrating Ginger's forthcoming nuptials. But this time I think he ad a few whiskies too. Chasers, you know. But maybe too many.'

'So Rodgers got his send-off but Blackie got the old red card. Can't have been a pretty sight.'

'No sir, the animal was squashed more or less flat. He could not have recovered from the injuries ee sustained, is vital organs all being, as it were, in a somewhat compressed state. Corporal Dodds pronounced im dead on arrival at the kitchen.'

'The kitchen...'

'Indeed sir. No waste in war, that's what we say, innit? Good fresh meat being in short supply, what with the Foot and Mahth, the men decided the best way to remember poor Blackie was to take im to our 'arts.'

'So we ate him.'

'Indeed sir. Moreover, the actions and weight of the tank's caterpillar tracks was such that Cookie's preparation time was minimal, and is Blackieburgers was served in the Mess the very same day.'

'I did wonder about those, Gross. They were rather good.'

'But our sheep not being exactly a spring chicken, the Ram Rogan Josh did need a bit more time for marination.'

'That wasn't bad either. Didn't know it was Blackie though.'

'We thought it best not to say,' said Sergeant Gross. 'Some of the men might have felt a bit queasy about eating the sheep, the animal being a friend of the family as it were... *Broady* especially,' he added, with emphasis, 'you know what *ee's* like.'

'Loves animals but beats the hell out of people?'

'Exactly,' said Sergeant Gross, suddenly hopeful that he might get his Quartermaster onto the subject of the regiment's other *bête noire*.

'In that last show,' the Captain began, 'I seem to remember something about Broadsword saving a cat that got hurt in the crossfire, then shooting four civilians.'

'Says ee didn't know they was civilians sir. Said if the bearded buggers didn't wear uniforms, ow could ee be expected to know the difference? I told im their beards *was* their uniforms. That set im off thinkin for a while.'

'Still counts as collateral damage. Too much of that. Doesn't help our performance indicators. You know we get docked points if we knock off too many civvies. The General wants his gong too. He can say goodbye to that if Private Broadsword isn't going to use his brain as well as his brawn.'

'Oh I don't think there's much chance of that, sir,' the sergeant insisted, stirring it up, 'Broady being, as they say, somewhat intellectually challenged. Ee ad a picture of Tony Blair up in his locker till someone told im Blair was a poof in sheep's clothin, and couldn't ee tell from is 'air and the mincin smile.'

'Who's his hero now? Arnold Schwarzenegger?'

'No one. He just uses the locker door for keepin is tally. Three columns, MILITRY, TERRERIST and CLATRALS. Ee seems to know the difference when it comes to is own performance indicators.'

'But no performance possible without the requisite black sheep,' Captain Undergrowth retorted, suddenly back on the case. 'What have you been doing about it? You're meant to be resourceful, quartermaster-sergeant.'

'Well,' Gross stuttered, 'black sheep are not so easy to get old of right now.'

'What about all those ones the press were going on about?'

'Ah then, there you avvit – that makes it even more difficult. Most of the black sheep in the North of England was sold off to reporters, the farmers passed them off as that clone what escaped. They made thousands of pahnds, so I'm told, and that pushed up the price of black sheep in the marts, because the farmers knew they could get ten times the market price if they was lucky enough to find some rain-soaked 'ack in a mack on their patch. And the marts is all closed now, with the Foot and Mahth, so you can't get a sheep not for love nor money.'

'What about the ones they fobbed off on the hacks? Can't we get one of those awful rags to *back our boys* with a new mascot?'

'The sheep all went to poncy city farms, sir. Readers adopted them, so they say. So now they're giving woollyback rides to kiddies. They discovered a few white ones that way, when the dye came off on the kids' clothes. But with the restrictions on the movement of animals, there's no way we could get one of em ere.'

'Well I'm sorry, sergeant, but I can't confirm to GCHQ that our regiment is in a full state of military readiness, on red alert and all that tosh, until we have the necessary black sheep on board. No black sheep, no green light.'

From his hiding-place in the store cupboard, the sheep had

been following this exchange. Had the two soldiers been speaking in normal conversational tones, their muffled voices might not have reached him through the wood of the door. But since he'd been able to distinguish virtually every word they'd barked at one another, he knew that his cue had come. He pushed hard, and the door flew open.

'*Mairrr, mairrr, mairrr,*' he almost yelled, hoping his ironic enunciation would be lost on them (he'd wanted to open with *permission to speak, sir*). He had become so accustomed to human speech that sheep language felt like a foreign tongue in his mouth. He hoped he'd got the pronunciation right. As he sat waiting for the right moment, he'd found himself wanting to consult a phrase book. But he needn't have worried.

'Sergeant Gross, con*grat*ulations!' the Captain cried. 'Well you needn't have gone to such lengths to emphasise how resourceful you are. I think we know that. I always knew you'd come up with the goods, you always do.'

Sergeant Gross was speechless. And decided to remain so, patting the sheep nervously on the head when it came forward to greet them.

'Fine sturdy beast too,' Captain Undergrowth continued. 'But I must say, he does look a trifle familiar. He wouldn't, by any chance, be that same celebrated escapee?'

The sheep froze.

'No of corse not sir,' Sergeant Gross retorted immediately, then tried to think of a plausible explanation 'I...well...as it happens...'

'Don't worry, sergeant,' said Captain Undergrowth. 'I know better than to ask questions. You don't get to be Quartermaster by insisting that everything's above board.'

'No sir,' said Sergeant Gross, adding, almost as a precaution, 'and we wouldn't *enjoy* our work and its fruits almost as much if that were the case, isn't that right sir?'

'Too right, Gross. We are of like mind there. And the British Army wouldn't march at all if we had to do everything through the normal channels, especially given their propensity for cocking everything up.'

'You are referring there to them guns what don't work, I take it, sir?'

'Not just those blasted rifles, Gross, but *everything*. That's why the army needs us.'

'Exactly sir, enterprise and initiative, that's what this job's abaht.'

'So even if this animal *were* that fugitive sheep, sergeant – which I'd stress I wouldn't actually *need* to know – it would of course go no further than this room. We needed our mascot and now we have him, thanks to you, Sergeant Gross.'

'Yes sir. And...well...I'm sure it's *not* that clone sir. I...I think I'd have known. Me bein someone who knows a few things about sheep.' He patted this one's bottom; and rather too fondly, the sheep ventured to suggest with a brief bleat of admonishment.

'Yes, sergeant. Right you are. This probably calls for a drink then. Fancy a sherry? Should be red now we have our red alert. Just a small one, eh?'

'That would be most kind sir.'

'But let's keep our sheep off the drink this time, shall we? And make sure you tell the men that. No more hair of the dog for the black sheep.'

'No sir,' said Sergeant Gross, suddenly wistful, aware that getting a sheep drunk was usually the easiest way to persuade it to comply with his wishes. He'd not have wanted another ram by choice, ewes were far more accommodating in all senses of the word, but this one had somehow got itself appointed without going through the usual selection procedures. And the animal *did* look remarkably like that runaway clone, though the standard newspaper picture was no proper guide, it was way out of date and made the poor beast look like Billy Connolly.

CHAPTER FIFTEEN

Gross Misconduct

When Lucy read her text message, she decided immediately to keep quiet about it, in spite of her crossed-heart (but cross-fingered) promise to Stein that she would be in touch if ever the sheep attempted to make contact. If her Sheep was safe, then she no longer needed the scientists' help to find him. Of course she wanted more than anything for them to be reunited, but she knew this wouldn't be possible in the short-term, not just because of the Foot and Mouth business but because Stein and the others would want to have him back with them at Clovis, and for all that they'd promised her she could visit and stay with Dr Brimstone whenever she wanted, she knew her Sheep would want his freedom most of all. Reading what she could into his necessarily cryptic message, she knew he must be plotting something, and hoped he would need her help with this before too long.

She'd cried at his loss for more nights than she could count, but now she knew he was out there somewhere, she suddenly felt grown up, with a sense of increased responsibility and loyalty to him. This was how women must feel in wartime, she thought, when they have to man the home front while the men are away. And after all, the country was being readied and roused, if reluctantly, for what they were calling a war, the War Against War, the war which no one wanted except the politicians and the media; but if it all went pear-shaped and banana-skinned, as her Sheep had put it, it could be the war everyone did want, a war to end all politicians. The Sheep had added encouraging statements to that effect on the Shaman website, and they'd soon been picked up elsewhere. One of the satirical Shamanist sites had a hit list of politicians the media had been building up, offering odds on which would be brought down first, with different scores for how each might expect to be treated by the media in the event of war. Another had given the various networks star ratings for their coverage of previous wars, grading them as if they were video games, noting which were edited for violence and language, and which might be suitable for family viewing.

Lucy knew they would never again have such happy times, keeping Sheep just to herself, the two of them learning everything about the big bad world together. Her adolescence had gone, and with it her innocence. But thanks to her Sheep, she was wise beyond her years, and with him being a creature with a mission in life, one which she applauded and wanted to support – taking exception only to those aspects which still gave her cause for some uneasiness – she looked forward to playing her part. The world might be big and was generally bad these days, but she still hoped it could be changed if a wise girl and a wily sheep put their heads together. Sort out the men in suits and the media, the beards and the bigots, and the rest would follow, was Sheep's view. The military were only a problem because they obeyed orders, so those orders would have to change. There was no reason why life couldn't imitate and outdo Hollywood if a few ground rules were different, especially those of political power and economics. Everyone knew the multinationals were calling the shots now. 'I'm sorry, boys,' the sheep had declared, 'but that's about to change. Advantage sheep. Game over.'

The Shaman website was getting very few hits now because the hackers had wrecked all the best pages. It looked in a pretty sorry state, with the graphics skewed and many of the nice pictures missing or replaced with obscene images or inane religious slogans. While the content was all readily available on other sites, the main problem now was that the Sheep's Ten Revelations had spawned a host of spurious secondary revelations invented by others. But the general gist of what they advocated was still

in keeping with the sheep's original vision, and he had anticipated that Shaman would lose some focus as it spread because
that happened to all religions. But he was very impressed by the
more subversive Shamanist sites; they had been slaughtering so
many sacred cows that their targets were clearly rattled. There
seemed to be a correlation between their growing popularity
and the decline in readership and viewing figures reported by
the media. The new cheeky mode of sheep-inspired people
power was adding weight and edge to the environmental and
anti-globalisation lobbies. As the sheep had hoped, everything
was being questioned.

The Shaman chat-room had remained unaffected by all the
hackers' mayhem. It had always been a place where lunatics
lurked, so she didn't like staying on-line for long, only making
a contribution herself when she read something sensible, amidst
all the ravings, by someone she felt might appreciate a few words
of support or elaboration. Using the proxy name and message
they'd previously agreed, she acknowledged receipt of his text
message. A week later – which meant he must be experiencing
some technical difficulties – his response appeared, using the
other proxy.

Stuffing his voice recognition software into a zip file, she up-
loaded it to the site, giving him the html reference for locating
it using their other code, the one based on sheep counting
rhymes used by shepherds up until the last century. She didn't
think many web nerds or religious nutters would be familiar
with those.

*

Sergeant Gross had added four milligrams of Rohypnol mixed
with a similar quantity of Ketamine to the sheep's water. Half
that quantity in a bottle of beer was said to be sufficient to put
a woman into an excited, agitated and uninhibited state of
moaning carnal bliss, leaving only amnesia, and more than that
could be dangerous in humans. Both these recreational drugs
were readily available from his usual supplier in the town, but
he didn't know if anyone had tried the potent cocktail on a
sheep before. He'd thought a double dose would be needed to

have the right effect on the large animal, but had not taken into account the resistance the sheep had built up to the effects of a wide range of stimulants and other chemicals with unpredictable properties over two years of sustained drug abuse at the hands of the Clovis scientists.

As Sergeant Gross lifted the supine beast's tail, cupping his delighted hands around the massive testicles in their velvety black scrotum, the sheep jumped up suddenly, causing the quartermaster-sergeant to fall back onto the floor.

'That's enough of that, Sergeant Gwose,' he snapped. 'You can put your twowsers back on *now*. I think it's time you and I had a little talk.'

The sergeant was stunned as well as shamed. Flustered, he put his left leg first into the wrong trouser leg, then the right into the left, and found himself answering the animal as he sought to disentangle himself: 'Yes sir. Indeed, a talk sir. Quite right, didn't mean to cause you any offence sir.'

He had no time to gather his wits before the sheep was issuing a series of orders.

'Wight, let's get things stwaight, Gwose, though I appweciate that's hardly your usual way of doing things. First and most importantly in these pwesent circumstances, I am not your catamite.'

'No sir. Of course not sir,' Sergeant Gross retorted, almost automatically, such was his state of shocked surprise, his state of unreadiness and undress also.

'Secondly – and you can stop calling me sir...'

'Yes *sirrr*... So is it Wally then perhaps, would I be right there?...'

'My name is not Wally!' the sheep shouted. 'That may have been the name they gave me at Clovis but I do not and will not answer to it! Do your hear me?'

'Yes sir. I mean...'

'You will address me as Sheep, sergeant. Is that understood?'

'Yes sir Sheep sir, I mean yes Sheep,' said Sergeant Gross, and began to elaborate: 'But since you are that so rare and wonderful thing, a Sheep capable of speech, as I have discovered to my cost, I must...'

'Shut up, Gwose.'

'Yes Sheep sir, I mean Sheep, yes Sheep.'

'Just listen. Point one. You know I can speak, but no one else must know. Is that understood?'

'Yes Sheep. Mum's the word…'

'Because if you do reveal this to *anyone*, including your Captain Undergwowth, I will give your game away. You understand me, don't you, Sergeant Gwose?'

'Yes…'

'Not just your bestial habits, but *all* your malpwactices. If the army gets to hear it has a talking sheep, it will know also that it has a cwooked quartermaster and an even more *bent* quartermaster-sergeant. You understand me?'

'Yes Sheep. I understand.'

'Because even though our clever and wesourceful quartermasters are the unacknowledged and indispensable Del Boy Twotters of the Bwitish Army, quartermaster wool number one is always: look after number one but don't *ever* get found out or your number will be up. And your sergeant's number also. Am I not wight? Otherwise, court martial followed by dishonourwable discharge. And not just that…'

'No sir, I mean Sheep…'

'What I know about your vawious nefarwious activities, courtesy of your careless discussion of the said cwimes in my pwesence since I was appointed wegimental mascot as well as before when I was working undercover, though you weren't to know that…'

'Undercover?'

'Shut up, Gwose, and listen. In simple terms I know enough not only to have the two of you dwummed out of the army, but put behind bars and *possibly even* – since we are now said to be on a war footing – put in fwunt of a fwying squad. And since I think I'm wight in suddenly detecting a certain dangerwously conspiwatorwial look in your eyes…'

'Oh no sir, Sheep, sir. I would never *think* of…'

'Quite wight you won't, Gwose, because a summary of *everything* I know has been texted to website to which an associate of mine has sole access, and if anything were to happen to me the army would *still* have your guts for garters, make no mistake, if you *had* any guts to turn into elastic hosierwee supports that is.'

'So what happens now?' the sergeant asked submissively. 'Are you aiming to make my life and the captain's life a misery, make us do everyfing properly now?'

'Not at all,' said the sheep. 'The Army would soon know something was amiss. No, I want you to carwee on *exactly* as you were before, only you will have certain additional tasks to carwee out for me. But Captain Undergwowth is to know *nothing* of our little arwangement.'

'What kind of tasks?' Sergeant Gross asked tentatively.

'Nothing out of the ordinawee,' the sheep said. 'The usual quartermaster stuff. Eqwipment. A few small jobs. A few oils to be wheeled. The use of a vehicle or a key on occasions, and you would be the dwiver of course.'

'Of course. But equipment?'

'Nothing too difficult. I need a decent laptop, for starters.'

'A laptop. Of course. No sheep should be without its laptop.'

'Plus I don't think it would be unweasonable, in order to *keep me on board*, I think you say, in weespect of your own fweelance activities, that I should get a cut from them.'

'A cut?' said Sergeant Gross, looking up as if a light had suddenly shone into the room.

'Of course,' said the sheep. 'I believe the captain takes seventy per cent of everweething, despite the fact that you do most of the work...'

'That's right. So maybe it's time we...'

'No change there,' the sheep retorted. 'You used to receive thirty per cent. Now you will get fifteen per cent, and I will get fifteen per cent, paid into a Post Office Savings Account in the name of L. Giles. Understood?'

'But I was...'

'*However*,' said the sheep. 'You two really are pwitty hopeless. You miss so many chances in a base this size. You aren't even aware of all the double orderwing that goes on in the kitchens, are you?'

'Double orderin?'

'How Cookie as you call him often orders twice what he needs, then sells on the surplus to the Wed Lion in Chinchester, where his wife's cousin just happens to be head chef? And how it is that your daily menus in the officers' mess are exactly the same, dish for dish, as those offered to diners by Cookie's wife's cousin in the westaurant at the Wed Lion? Although what you call woast beef they call *bœuf woti*. Which means...'

'You don't need to explain.'

'You move in on that one, you may even get a cut without the Captain knowing.'

'I think we'd need Captain Undergrowth's assistance to enforce that. But I get the gist of what you're saying, that thanks to your assistance we might actually increase our take, though how...'

'Easy peasy,' said the sheep. 'As wegimental mascot, I have access to all the lawned areas. They get them twimmed that way. So I get awownd all parts of the base, with only the wunway out of bounds. And people invite me in to their quarters to feed me biscuits and chocolate. People talk to fwendly animals. And even if they aren't indiscweet in what they talk about, they don't think to be discweet in what the animal might overhear as it snoozes in the corner.'

'I can see the Mata Hari had nothing on you.'

'Except I don't sleep with the enemy.'

'No well um...'

'Not that you're the enemy, Sergeant Gwose, you're just a petty cwook and a cweepy pervert.'

'I take exception to...'

'Never mind. I think we understand each other now, don't we? You know what side your bwed bun is buttered.'

'Bread bun? Yes, certainly, I won't give you any further trouble on that score, I will be only too pleased to assist you,' said Sergeant Gross. 'But may I know who you're working for, even in general terms, if you are, that is, if it's not sensitive information? I take it you aren't just here to get a cut from our scams.'

'I'm working for myself, sergeant,' said the sheep. 'Just as you are. That's all you need to know.'

*

Stein had finally got to the end of *Animal Farm*, but Holly hadn't liked the way the pigs behaved, so wanted him to read the whole thing to her again, but to change the story in favour of the dogs, horses and sheep. Since he changed his results when he wrote up his experiments, she didn't see why he couldn't do the same thing when reading her a novel, which someone else had made up in any case. Wasn't it all about using one's imagination? Only the spiced-up résumé he'd given of the next book on the list had persuaded her that hearing something else might be preferable. Looking down the reading list, he wondered how he was going to get through it all before the first visit by his monitoring inspector, which he presumed meant Lucy Giles. Did the sheep really expect him to be able to read the whole of *War and Peace* to Holly, or was that a wind-up? What possible intellectual benefit could a sheep gain from listening to Tolstoy? And Mary Shelley's *Frankenstein* too, that was below the belt and would probably give the poor beast nightmares, if sheep have such things. He was wondering what sheep dream about when Sean Shenanigan made his usual dramatic entrance flourishing the morning post.

'You have mail, Dr Stein,' he announced. 'From your insurance company no less. But why would your mail be coming to your workplace, I wonder.'

'Might be because the postman won't deliver to his house any more,' said Mark Gumption. 'Not after that business with the suspect letter bomb.'

'And all Clovis mail passes through security first,' said Sean Shenanigan, 'which means I know, courtesy of a certain little bird, that our worthy colleague has suddenly started ordering books and videos from Amazon...'

'Doubtless our illustrious colleague does not wish to be gunned down coming out of Waterstone's,' said Macannie. 'Those WANTED posters will be decorating the flats of every animal-rights activist in the country by now. Even as we speak, the Batties will be photocopying vast numbers to circulate to all their diplomats and other key personnel.'

'They didn't stint on the cost either,' said Helen Brimstone. 'Doing them in colour. But not the best picture I've seen of you, Frank, your complexion does look a little ruddy.'

'Possibly the printer's fault?' suggested Macannie.

'Or the drinker's,' said Shenanigan.

'But videos, you say,' added Gumption. 'More dirty films, is it?'

'Not at all,' said Shenanigan. '*A History of Western Civilisation* was one of the titles, I seem to remember. Maggie the mail girl was most impressed. And Jacob Bronowski's *Ascent of Man*. Moreover, Dr Stein is now *reading*...let me make sure I've got this right...Jane Austen's *Pride and Prejudice*, George Orwell's essays and Claire Tomalin's biography of Mary Wollstonecraft. A lot of big words in those books, Frankie boy, and they're not chemical compounds. Are you sure you're up to it?'

'My post is my private business,' Stein hissed, grabbing a pile of letters and starting to rip them open.

'Not so private when Maggie can see everything on her X-ray screen.'

'Some of those books are presents for friends...'

'Ah, he has *friends* now,' Gumption announced.

'*What!*' Stein exploded, waving a letter in the air. 'I don't believe it! They've turned down my insurance, they won't give me any cover at all now, despite *all* the premiums I've given them over the years.'

'Well you have to see their point of view,' said Macannie. 'You are a risk.'

'But I've never crashed a car in my life. I've never hit anything, not even a bollard. I did nothing to the Volvo. That was stolen then left in pieces by those clueless police who were meant to be searching it for clues. Then the Renault, that was blown up by the ALF.'

'Allegedly,' said Shenanigan. 'They have denied it was them, they say it was 666.'

'The number of the beast,' Gumption couldn't resist adding.

'But let's not forget the Citroën,' Shenanigan continued. 'A controlled explosion, I believe it was.'

'But I didn't make that call.'

'They said you did.'

'More ALF propaganda! It was one of *them* who phoned the police and said there was a car bomb in the station car park. Why should I want to get my own car blown up?'

'The insurance. You do seem to be making a habit of it. You did a fiddle on the Volvo too. And if you didn't make the call yourself, why did you leave the car where you knew it would be seen?'

'I was catching the train to London, so I left the car at the station. I didn't think the army would decide to come round and blow it up while I was in the meeting.'

'They said they tried ringing you.'

'My mobile was switched off.'

'You should face the facts, Frank. The insurance company is doing you a favour. Any car you buy now, if not the ALF then one of its splinter groups or the Batties will have the registration number the next day. It's called intimidation. They're watching you.'

'It's the police who are meant to be watching me. I'm meant to have police protection.'

'I'm sure they do their best. But everyone knows what you look like now, not just the terrorists but every newspaper reader in the country. You're better known than the sheep now, because of all those attacks.'

'Had you thought of wearing a burkha?' suggested Helen Brimstone. 'You could pass yourself off as a woman. It worked for that reporter.'

'You'd get into all the ladies' toilets that way,' said Sean Shenanigan brightly. 'Wouldn't mind trying that one myself. I'd have to work on the walk though, I tend to drag my feet a little too much to be taken for one of the girls.'

'But just make sure you steer well clear of the Batties,' said Gumption. 'Our bearded friends go for anything wearing a black tent.'

'You know what?' said Stein angrily. 'I'm beginning to wish that this wretched war of theirs would start, the War on War. Bomb the Batties. Nuke the North Koreans. Lay waste the *rest* of the Middle East. Might stop them all going on about me, me, me. That'd give them all something else to think about, when the body bags start coming back. I'll be off the front page then. Right now everyone's just waiting for me to get killed. I bet you lot have even got bets on it, on when I get shot or injured, how many days I have left, or who's going to kill me.'

'Not who,' said Sean Shenanigan. 'That's often difficult to establish, what with so many different groups claiming responsibility. But we think Dr Macannie's about to lose because he gave you till the tenth, and you're still with us, the Lord be praised. Helen has the longest odds, she's given you at least another month, but she's always been something of an optimist. And I think I'm right in saying that she still must have a *bit* of a soft spot for you, to hope you'll be around for *that* long.'

CHAPTER SIXTEEN

The Sheep of Hearts

The group of gunmen who took refuge three days ago in the London delegation offices of the Men's Republic of Battymanistan now claim to have captured the missing cloned sheep Wally, and are holding the animal hostage. A city farm in Dagenham has confirmed that one of their sheep went missing three days ago, after it was last seen being petted by several bearded men of possible Middle Eastern origin.

The terrorists have just released this video which shows a black sheep thought to be Wally holding a copy of this morning's *Daily Telegraph*. A spokesman said they wanted a ransom of a million pounds, or they would kill and eat the sheep:

'Theese is the combined amount of all rewards offered by many newspapers for theese sheep, plus 10% to cover our costs.'

Alternatively, the Clovis Institute could exchange the sheep for Dr Frank Stein, the biologist responsible for its animal cloning programme.

'Everyone know Dr Stein is about to be keeled by some one, so theese sheep is worth more to Clovis than theese scientist with heese short life expectancy. While theese sheep and Stein are both steel subject to irrevocable Batwa, we are weeling to offer them stay of execution in interests of either getting our hands on theese marneys or having Dr Stein in our custody for short time. We would welcome an opportunity to learn more from heem about heese interesting work, but do not believe he would offer his assistance weelingly, hence theese incentive we are offering. The Clovis Institute has been unable to locate its missing sheep, but thanks to skeelful intelligence work by our operatives, we haff managed to find theese animal for them. We also weesh to show Dr Stein the error of heese wayse, and would invite him to volunteer for short adult learning programme in Battymenarbad under auspeeces of our Ministry of Re-education. We weel not need to harm him, because some one eese going to keel him soon in any case. But while he is our guest he would not just enjoy our hospitality but he can feel safe in our protective custody.'

A Clovis scientist, Dr Ronald McNannie, told our reporter that Wally the cloned sheep was the property of the Clovis Institute, and they could only pay the £50,000 reward already offered for the animal's safe return. 'If the newspapers previously interested in finding our sheep are willing to club together,' he said, 'then we could nearly make up the ransom from such a whipround, but where the extra ten per cent might come from, I am at a loss to know. But perhaps some private benefactor with a special interest in sheep might come forward.'

However, the main Fleet Street editors who were previously offering big rewards for the sheep have all said they will refuse to give any money to the kidnappers. 'These men are Batty extremists,' said *Daily Screw* editor Derek Wallaby. 'Our paper will not give money that would be used to fund and give credence to their repressive régime. We should not give in to the demands of terrorists, especially when we're about to wipe their country off the map.'

When the latest news from the siege was announced on an earlier bulletin, our viewers were invited to give us their opinions on how this difficult situation should be resolved, either to our freephone number or by texting us. Only 5% thought the ransom should be paid. 75% said that Dr Stein should be exchanged for the sheep, with 20% wanting the SAS to storm the building.

Our reporter at the scene is Peter Porcupine. Peter, bring us up to date on the latest happenings.

'Well, Roger, as you see a large crowd has now gathered in the square outside the Battymanistan delegation. Several people are holding placards saying FREE WALLY! and they all seem to be expressing very vocal dislike of the bearded men responsible for holding the sheep hostage, as I think you can hear. We've also had confirmation from the SAS that they will *not* be storming the building on this occasion, which should offer some comfort to the terrorists inside, but I'm told this is because they are currently engaged in an undercover operation to blow up the training camp in Battymanistan where these men were taught their sheep-stealing skills. However, since that action will in fact have taken place, according to my watch (which you see I'm looking at now) half an hour ago, I am able to mention it to you. But one of their officers also told me the SAS wasn't an animal rescue outfit, and if the army or the police weren't able to free the sheep, then perhaps the fire brigade should be asked to help, since they were usually called upon to liberate cats from trees. I'd say he was pretty scornful of the terrorists' demands. He said if someone wanted to pay a million pounds for a sheep, military assistance was clearly not appropriate in cases of such monumental stupidity. However, I have to say that's not the mood of the crowd here. They seem to have the sheep's welfare very much at heart, and seem more engaged by the present siege than by the bigger stand-off over Battymanistan, which looks as though it's about to break, if that piece of news from the SAS is any guide. This is Peter Porcupine outside the Battymanistan delegation in London returning you to the studio.'

Thank you, Peter. I was about to interrupt you because we are going over live now to 10 Downing Street. The Prime Minister is just coming outside as I speak, and we think he is about to make a statement about the situation in Battymanistan. Whether this will include references to the sheep, we'll soon know. He's certainly looking serious. I'd guess we're about to hear from him that war has been declared. Either that or he's suffering from indigestion, or getting divorced, or maybe both. He's wearing that specially serious and concerned face of his anyway. You'll all know the one I mean. If it's not someone's funeral, it soon will be.'

*

Sergeant Gross turned off the television. 'Well I'll be blowed, and there was me thinkin you was that Wally. You ad me completely ramboozled there, Sheep.'

'It's not me,' said the sheep. 'Though I admit, he does look quite like me. Funny-shaped head, scruffy moth-eaten ears. Eyes are a bit spooky. Looks like he could do with a wash. I'm much more handsome. They've kidnapped the wrong sheep, Gwose, it's not me. I wouldn't be weeding the *Telegwaph* either. Terwibble paper.'

'No, it's Wally, innit, the real Wally.'

'No, I'm Wally. The clone that is.'

'I fort you said you wasn't Wally.'

'I said Wally wasn't my name.'

'Now you *are* confusin me.'

'What I mean, Gwose, is that those men are claiming to be

holding me hostage, and they want a million pounds for me. But it's not me they're holding, it's a sheep who looks like me, an impostor. It's just another scam like those the farmers were wunning, gwab a black sheep and claim it's me, only these men have got guns and they're asking for a bit more cash.'

'You mean I could get a million pounds for you if I went on the telly and said you was my osstidge?'

'No, I'm not worth a million pounds.'

'I fort they was asking that for you.'

'You're only worth what people are willing to pay,' the sheep explained. 'It's simple economics. But according to that weeport, Clovis *doesn't* think I'm worth a million pounds, which I must say is verwee short-sighted of them, but then they aren't aware that I'm intelligent and can talk.'

'They aren't?'

'No.'

'Why not? Ow come I know and they don't?'

'They're stupid. They're just scientists. I needed you to know, because of our arwangement.'

'Well, um blowed. Maybe you *is* worth a million pahnds, given that you's a torkin sheep.'

'No one else knows that.'

'What if I tell'em?'

'No one will believe you if I say nothing. If I do choose to speak, however, it will be to expose you.'

'But I'll get the money.'

'You'll be shot first. Weeminder: Bwitain, Amerwica and their Allies have just declared war on Battymanistan. Military law now applies to all military personnel.'

'I could resign.'

'Ah, but you *can't*, not now we're at war...' the sheep started saying, his words tailing off as the door was flung open as Captain Henry Undergrowth made a dramatic entrance.

'Thought I'd find you here, Gross,' he said, still in mid-stride. 'Good show. With the sheep too, I see. Got a name for him yet, have we sergeant? Can't call this one Blackie after what happened to the last one.'

'I just corls 'im Sheep sir but...'

'Well as long as our mascot brings us good luck, I don't mind

162

what you call him. As long as it's not...'

'I know sir. Not in very good taste, that one.'

'Quite so Gross. Sounded like a prostitute, regimental sheep can't have a name like that. Don't know what you were thinking of, calling that ewe...'

'No sir. Inappropriate sir. Indeed sir.'

'Well never mind,' he said, swivelling. 'News is we've got to concern ourselves with that other sheep now. The one the Batties are holding, Wally. Army's just given us the job of rescuing it, seeing how we are the black sheep regiment.'

The sheep nudged the sergeant's leg.

'But sir,' said Gross, as if on cue, 'what if it's *not* Wally? What if it's an impostor? Another sheep they captured to claim the ransom?'

'Sharp thinking, Gross. Doesn't actually matter. Prime Minister wants the siege ended pronto, doesn't want any of the usual *the siege is now in its sixth day* scenarios. The sheep hostage story's been getting higher viewing figures than all the re-runs of the war declaration outside number ten. PM's office doesn't like that. And the spin chappies think the sheep will carry on getting higher ratings than the war itself. All those shots of planes taking off from aircraft carriers, fuzzy satellite pictures, Americans talking gobbledegook at briefings, our lot talking the usual bollocks in the Commons, all turn-offs so they say, even the video target stuff, computer games do that better. Public likes seeing tanks blown up, but the Batties don't have any tanks. Turns out they've not got much of anything at all. Very bad television.'

'What about them weapons of mass destruction sir?'

'We sold them half their arsenal, so that doesn't work. We thought they still had the rest, but intelligence reports now say that anything that was any good they flogged off to North Korea. Didn't need it after the Russkies skedaddled.'

'I fort it was North Korea what sold weapons to them?'

'That's what we thought, Gross. Smokescreen. But at least our American friends will know what the North Koreans have now, seeing the clobber came from them in the first place. The Batties just wanted more cash, not having much of the stuff themselves, especially after they sent all their women home and put a bunch of illiterate thugs in charge of everything. Whole economy collapsed. But they still needed cash for their palaces and Mercedes-Benzes, couldn't get it in taxes because they'd bled their people dry, quite literally in some cases. Still kept up the old holy-joe robes and beards routine of course, and the poor and starving stayed poor and mostly starved, but the boyos in beards strutted about like Harrow prefects, giving anyone they didn't like the strap or chopping their hands off.'

'So does that mean the Batties'll be a walkover then sir?'

'Precisely, Gross. But the PM wants it to look like a *hard-won victory*. Because he needs support for the next part of the War on War, when they take on the rest of them. Can't do that if a ruddy sheep's getting all the public attention. The animal's already been dubbed the Sheep of Hearts by some radio phone-in disc jockey, so you can imagine what the headlines will be in tomorrow's tabloids. THE SHEEP OF HEARTS across all the front pages, then BRITAIN AT WAR in small type below, see page 5.'

'You're right sir, I can see it now: *This is the sheep oo as captured the arts of the nation*. Quite lovely, really.'

'Quite so, Gross. Never mind the nation doesn't know it yet, but if the media decide it's the Sheep of Hearts, that's what it becomes. Those terrorists are pretty sharp spinners too. They've just released another video with the sheep holding tonight's *Evening Standard*, just to show the animal's still alive. Our chaps thought at first it might be product placement, you know the papers were paying them to make the sheep hold their rag, but apparently it's holding this one upside-down, and they wouldn't get anything for doing that.'

'So what's the plan then, sir? What are our orders?'

'Quite simple really. Save the sheep and shoot all the Batties. They will all be firing back so our men will have no option but to take 'em all out. No casualties allowed on our side. Wouldn't look good. PM wants to be photographed with the sheep on the six o'clock news so as to make the next day's papers too. Doesn't mind sharing the space with the sheep for one day because the sheep gets relegated after that. So we have to do it in daylight. Make sure the networks know so they'll film it, like the SAS Iranian Embassy job.'

'But they'll be watching it on the telly themselves then.'

'Doesn't matter, makes it more of a spectacle with them looking out the windows as we pick 'em off. The viewers will like that, especially if we can get a few to fall out, like baddies getting their comeuppance from John Wayne. Those who keep their heads down get shot inside. Very simple really.'

'Can we take Broady sir? I'm sure ee'd like to up his score.'

'Broadsword can come, but only if the police are keeping all innocent bystanders well back in the square. Otherwise he stays on the subs bench.'

'We using gas sir? Do I need to pack orl that in the kit?'

'First plan *was* actually to use that Russian gas, lower concentration of course, but didn't know how this might affect the sheep. Then some bright spark I.D.ed their guns in the video. Turns out they're the ones we sold them.'

'Them ones what don't work?'

'Well they do work, but not in temperatures above 26 degrees Celsius. That's why they didn't jam when we tried them out on the ranges, but they seized up in the desert. So we turn up their heating sixty minutes before we go in. We can do that from next door's basement. They probably won't even notice the heat, being Batties.'

'Indeed sir. They may even have their eatin on 'igh orl the time in any case. Then we rely on our guns, I mean *their* guns misfirin.'

'Quite so, Gross. Never let us down yet, them not working I mean. And one more thing...'

'Yes sir?'

'We'd like to take your sheep, if you've no objection, Gross. Carstairs has this plan to use him as a decoy to get the press away from the building, or to help give us a clean getaway afterwards. Put him in the back of the jeep in full view and the idiots will all be chasing your sheep while the real Wally's in make-up waiting for his photocall with the PM.'

*

Lucy Giles leapt up to pause the video as the camera lurched towards the sheep's face. 'Look,' she said, 'can't you *see* it's not him? Look at those ears. Sheep's ears are much nicer than those, they're all *matted* or something.'

'They might have roughed him up a bit,' said Sean Shenanigan.

'That might account for the spooky eyes too. Poor beast must be shit scared, specially with that piggy-eyed Batty shoving his camcorder right in his face like that.'

'Or held his head in a bucket of water,' said Mark Gumption. 'Tried to get him to talk.'

'Or held his head down the toilet while they flush the chain,' said Shenanigan. 'That's what we used to do at school when some fellow was holding out on us.'

'But Wally's not going to talk, is he?' said Stein, glancing nervously at Lucy.

'All right,' said Macannie. 'Hands up all those who think it's Wally?'

'I can't be sure,' said Shenanigan. 'So make me a don't-know. Sheep all look the same to me, especially the black ones. I know I should know better, but there it is.'

'I say it's Wally,' said Gumption, raising his hand.

'I say it's not,' said Helen Brimstone. 'Wally's much *cuddlier*, isn't he, Lucy?'

'He might have lost a bit of weight on that city farm,' said Shenanigan. 'Those Essex lads live off steak and chips. He might have turned his nose up if it was just chips and leftovers from fry-ups they were putting in his trough. He won't have eaten as well as he must have done at your house, Lucy.'

'Well I'm not sure I want to pay out good money for a sheep which may not be ours in the fairst place,' said Macannie, 'so I'll have to be a don't-know too. Frank, how about you?'

'I think it's Wally. And we can't turn down any chance of getting him back here. Not if we can get the rest of the ransom together.'

'Well, let's see then,' said Macannie. 'That makes two yesses, two noes, and two don't-knows. Which I'd say is pretty inconclusive.'

'He's holding the paper upside-down,' Lucy whispered to Stein. 'You know he'd never do that. It makes him look stupid, as if he can't read.'

'Unless it's a bluff,' Stein muttered back. 'He's trying to make us think it can't be him, because he's got some other plan.'

'But all this is academic if we don't have the money,' said Macannie.

'We could get Weisenheimer to increase the reward we were offering.'

'I've already asked him,' said Macannie. 'He said no. He thinks Stein should offer to exchange himself for the sheep. Much cheaper. And since Stein is unlikely to be with us for much longer, he might as well do something useful for a change. He also pointed out – and I must say this hadn't occurred to me – that if Stein only gets injured, not killed, in one of these attacks he's been inviting, we have to pay for his hospital care and our insurance goes up because of the compensation, whereas if the Batties finish him off, there's only the funeral to pay for.'

'Looks like we can leave our philanthropic boss out of the equation then,' said Sean Shenanigan.

'There's one way to settle this,' said Lucy, grabbing hold of Stein's shoulder. 'Dr Stein and I are the two people who know Sheep best. We will ring the delegation and ask them some questions about the sheep they're holding. They can't object to us wanting to verify his identity if they think we're going to give them a lot of money for him.'

'What, you mean like: what kind of chocolate does he prefer, Fruit and Nut or Yorkie Bars?' asked Shenanigan.

'That kind of thing,' said Lucy.

'Doesn't sound very scientific to me,' said Macannie.

'There are things which only Dr Stein and I will know which could be conclusive.'

'Come on then, Lucy,' said Stein. 'We'll use Weisenheimer's office. We don't want that lot breathing down our necks when we're conducting such a delicate negotiation, and a sheep's life is at stake.'

The hostage-takers weren't surprised when the call came through from Clovis. But when Stein told them to give the phone to the sheep, they exchanged worried looks.

'Wally, it's me Stein. Listen. I know you won't want to give the game away to the Batties, but could you just mutter something so we know it's you.'

'*Mairrr.*'

'Sheep, it's Lucy. We have to know it's you. If you can't say something, please give us a signal of some kind on the next video. We're all thinking about you. Love you. Kiss kiss.'

'*Mairrr.*'

'Wally, Stein again. I know you can't choose what paper to hold, but maybe if you waved your right hoof three times?'

'*Mairrr.*'

The phone was muffled for a moment.

'Look here, Stein,' said a voice, 'we know you're crazy but we steel want the meellion pounce. If you want to be sure it's your sheep, we'll cut heez ear off and post it to you so you can test it for DNA.'

'Not his ear!' cried Lucy. 'Just a piece of his wool would do, surely.'

Stein's face darkened at the mention of DNA. He couldn't do those kinds of tests himself, and knew what they would reveal, if the hostage was indeed his progeny.

'It would take too long for the test results,' he told them. 'I can't allow the sheep to suffer any more. I will offer myself in exchange myself for Wally, as long as you can guarantee my safety.'

'No problem, my friend. You weel not be keeled.'

*

Good evening. Today has seen an extraordinary turn of events at the Battymanistan delegation in London, where terrorists have been holding the cloned sheep Wally hostage for the past four days. The nation's Sheep of Hearts was released at four o'clock this afternoon in exchange for the biologist Dr Frank Stein, who announced he was willing to undergo a course of Batty re-education in order to guarantee the animal's safety. The kidnappers had been asking for a ransom of a million pounds if the scientist wouldn't come forward, and no money is understood to have been paid for the release of the sheep.

The Ministry of Defence has refused to comment on an earlier report that a special forces unit was about to storm the delegation when the scientist walked up to the front door and was admitted to the building. And a spokesman for an extremist animal-rights group known as 666 which has been claiming responsibility for various attempts on Dr Stein's life said he didn't believe a leopard could change its spots, but if this latest action by Dr Stein wasn't a cynical move to manipulate public opinion in his favour but a genuine act of self-sacrifice, his group would take this into account in considering their future policy towards him.

The Prime Minister praised Dr Stein for his bravery when interviewed on tonight's six o'clock news with the freed hostage. Our film here shows him smiling at the sheep as he gives the animal a piece of chocolate.

However, in an extraordinary turn of events, it now appears that the sheep became frightened by all the flashing cameras at the Downing Street photocall, and ran off through a side door. Witnesses reported seeing a black sheep running through St James's Park in an agitated state shortly afterwards. We will of course keep you posted about the new search now underway for Wally, the nation's Sheep of Hearts.

And now today's other news. For the second day running, British and American planes took off from aircraft carriers in the Indian Ocean and bombed targets said to be military installations in the Men's Republic of Battymanistan. A Pentagon official has confirmed that the building in Battymenarbad devastated in the latest American cruise missile attack had been used as a hospital, but the nurses had all been sacked and the doctors executed by the Batty régime several months ago. The hospital was no longer a hospital and was being used only as a food distribution centre. Any civilian casualties were regrettable.

Meanwhile, the build-up of Allied land forces has continued on the Battymanistan border, and a full-scale invasion is now said to be only a matter of days away.

CHAPTER SEVENTEEN

The Ram of God

The crowd had dispersed, no longer interested in the gunmen or the fate of their new hostage now the Sheep of Hearts had been freed.

The bushes and grassy verge along the edge of the square's small park would normally have been a pleasant place for a sheep to lie in wait, but there were red and white KFC boxes of chicken bones strewn everywhere, along with polystyrene containers smeared with McDonalds and Burger King mush, Diet-Coke cans, greasy wrappers with red-cabbaged remnants of doner kebab and slimy messes of batter and other fried matter, all saturated with vinegar or ketchup or mayonnaise, the smell told him. The crowd had clearly munched their way through large amounts of animal flesh while waiting for the other sheep to be released. He watched as a hot-dog van pulled up in the opposite corner of the square, and some of the baseball-hatted police marksmen broke off their vigil to seek refreshment.

Taking a deep breath, which was difficult surrounded by all that pungent detritus, the sheep rushed from the bushes across the road and up the steps, hoping that as a black sheep in a dark London square, he might be mistaken for a fleeting shadow. He reached up to bang his hoof on the intercom bell-push.

'Who is theese?' a voice crackled.

'It's me, the sheep,' he hissed. 'I've changed my mind. I want to come back. I want to spend more time with my new family. You were all so good to me. Quick, let me in, before anyone sees.'

'Is theese some kind of trick?' asked the voice. Then calling, apparently to someone else in the room: 'What is theese Stein? Are you playing games with us? Yes, let him speak.' The sheep waited impatiently as an exchange of voices continued inside, including Stein's, but he could only make out the doorman's words: 'I don't understand. Chocolate? Is theese a password? No? Is that right? OK, OK. No problem.' Then the man addressed him: 'OK, if you are our sheep, please tell me, sheep, what kind of chocolate you like best?'

'Fwoot and Nut or Yorkie Bars.'

The door buzzed, and the sheep disappeared inside just as two policemen came running across the square.

Inside, the group of bearded gunmen gathered around him. Looking behind them, he saw that Stein was tied up and had now been gagged again. He'd clearly put on weight since their last meeting in Douglas Giles's barn. An assortment of knives, scalpels, skewers, pliers and other other miscellaneous DIY tools had been laid out on a small green-baize card-table in front of their new hostage. A Stanley knife was perched on top of the box of Kleenex. Stein's eyes were bulging, his skin glistening with sweat, but they didn't appear to have begun their lessons. He wasn't cut or bruised. It was time to take charge.

'How is it you talk, sheep?' asked the intercom gunman.

'I am no ordinarwee sheep.'

'But you are not same sheep as before,' said another man, angrily. He seemed to be their leader, and had grabbed hold of the wool around the sheep's neck to stare at him hard with his mad piggy eyes. 'Look,' he said, 'your *ear* is different. I know that because we toss coin to decide wheech ear to cut off. Some of us say the left, others say the right, so we yoose coin. But both sheep's ears were more ragged, as if sheep had been in fight. And *you* smell of veenegar and Kentucky Fried Cheecken, my friend. The other sheep, he smell of sheet and farmyard.'

'He was an impostor,' said the sheep. 'He pwetended to be Wally. He could not speak. He was a false pwofit. I am the twoo Wally. But Wally is not my weel name. Your people knew me as Walid. Wally is only a name given to me by the infidel scientists here. But they could not know this. They were only preparewing the way for me. For my twoo name is Shaman. I am half sheep, half man, beast and man in one being. I am the Wam of God. Animals have known no sin, which is why the Word of God must be weeborn thrwoo an animal, because Man has tainted that Word. And the new weligion Shaman is My Word. My Word went abwoard before me, and now I am here, to claim my kingdom on Earth.'

'Shaman,' said one of the other gunman. 'I haff heard about theese. They think all peoples should peese in the street.'

'Hah, we Batties peese where we like,' said another beard.

'But not here. Here it is forbidden to peese in the street.'

'That's just one small part of it,' the sheep interrupted, 'giving people here all the fweedoms you have. But much of the word of Shaman has alweddy been distorted by liars and infidels. Because Shaman is the twoo weligion of all Battymanistanis. You are all my bwothers, you gave me life in the first place.'

'No, you are wrong,' said their pig-faced leader, 'it was that scum who did the devilswork in that laboratory. We keel them all and burn it down. We roast their devil ram on a speet and eat heese heart. I myself was one of those who eat heem.'

'That ram was only one of my two fathers,' the sheep cried, staring hard into the black depths of the bearded man's bulging eyes. 'My father was one of the *holy* men of your cuntwee, a gwate man who worked with your scientists. That is how I can speak. I have his DNA. What other animal has ever spoken? I am his miracle mansheep. And you murdered him.'

'How can theese be true?'

'Ask Stein,' said the sheep. 'He is a gwate man too. He did all the work to achieve this, but he was sworn to secrwecy by your people. No one at Clovis knows of this but him, because he is a twoo heerwo of your cuntwee. That is why he was willing to come here, to lay down his life for me, because he knows I am the new Messiah. He would die to save my life. Ask him what he did if you don't believe me.'

One of the gunmen walked over and tore the gag from Stein's mouth.

'Is theese all true what sheep say?' he spat.

'Yes, yes,' Stein gasped. 'Walid is the new Messiah and I am his servant. I took the DNA from your holy man, and cloned a sheep which had his gene for intelligence, wisdom, as well as, er, spirituality and of course language acquisition.'

'All that in the one gene?' the beard asked.

'They are all linked characteristics. He got a few other things too.'

'Such as.'

'Curiosity. Bravery. And cheek.'

'What *treeck* is theese you talk off now?'

'No, *cheek*.'

'What is cheek?'

'Something that will help me save your cuntwee from the Amerwicans now,' said the sheep. 'We have to stop them from turning the whole place into a McDonalds theme park.'

'And how will you do that, my friend?'

'You will help me, you shall all serve Shaman, and your people shall be fwee,' said the sheep. 'Not fwee in the decadent western impeerwealist sense of course,' he added quickly, 'but fwee from the Amerwicans, fwee fwom the stain of sin. The Lamb of God shall be weedeemed thrwoo the Wam of God.'

'How is theese possible? Their bombs are keeling our peoples now. They weel not stop until all peoples are dead.'

'Take me to your computer. And untie him,' the sheep added sharply, gesturing towards Stein. 'My *servant* must help me too.'

'I say we do what sheep say,' said one of the beards. 'What have we got to loose? If there is chance he is right, it weel be good thing. And if he is theese new Messiah, we should obey heem.'

'But is not good we obey animal,' said another. 'How is theese possible, that Batty men take orders from sheeps? Is bad enough we have to listen to women talk. Is not right.'

The two men paused for a second, each looking to the mad-eyed leader for affirmation of his point of view.

'OK, OK, you yoose computer,' he told the sheep. 'But no funny beesness, you understand. I leaf guard with you.'

'But now we have theese sheep,' another beard began, 'we steel ask for the meellion pounce, yes? The infidels do not know he is our Messiah, they only think he is sheep.'

'But is not same sheep as before.'

'But he is sheep they wanted, theese Wally. Other sheep was impostor sheep. If they not belief us, we say we have talking sheep.'

'But they think sheep cannot talk. Only Stein know their sheep talk like man. We say sheep talk they think we are all crazy men.'

As the gunmen continued their discussion, the beard assigned to watch them ushered them into a side room and pointed at the computer. He slumped into a chair in the corner, and took out a pack of cigarettes, offering one to Stein though not to the sheep.

'Thanks,' said Stein nervously and, attempting to be pleasant, asked: 'But tell me, why do you men all talk in English?'

'We all come from different villages,' said the guard. 'We all live in heels, many kilometers from Battymenarbad, many days to ride on the horse, many more in the car, if car work. So our languages are not same, but we speak Engleesh OK.'

'I see,' he said, with a warm smile he hoped projected a sense that he too was another human being to this man who half an hour earlier had been telling him how two splayed blades fitted side by side in his Stanley knife would scar him more permanently than a single blade because the cut would not close easily and this made stitching more difficult.

'There are no roads where I live,' the man continued, 'only tracks for goat. And most of the cars will not work, they are how you say, *kaput*, because there are no spare parts. The petrol cost much marneys. So we must steal petrol when we have make our journeys to seety. Or if petrol come from friend we must give heem cheecken for it.'

He began to wish he hadn't been so keen to establish his human credentials as their guard elaborated upon many other daily hardships endured in his country. When the man finally exhausted his repertoire, Stein sat down beside the sheep at the keyboard, muttering: 'You laid that on a bit thick in there.'

'You have to give people something to believe in,' whispered the sheep, 'especially when they're thick as pigshit.'

'But DNA from one of their holy men?'

'They'd be twying out their new cutlerwee set now if they thought it was yours, Stein.'

'And all that stuff about Shaman...'

'I thought you'd understand that. You said you wanted to wool the world. What was that you said about talking animals: power, militarwee applications, world domination?'

'Computer OK?' asked the guard, looking at the screen, where Stein had typed 'YOU ARE THE SON OF A WHORE, YOU BEARDED SHITPIG' to establish if the man could read.

'Computer fine,' Stein confirmed, 'very good computer,' adding *sotto voce* for the sheep: 'That ruling the world stuff was a bit of an exaggeration, you know, showing off, I just said...'

'Well it isn't in my case. And you don't get many chances like this. Now log on to the Shaman site and do what I say.'

*

This is a news flash. Today's extraordinary events at the Battymanistan delegation in London have taken an even more bizarre turn. As we reported in an earlier bulletin, terrorists holding the cloned sheep Wally hostage released him this afternoon in exchange for the biologist Dr Frank Stein. The nation's Sheep of Hearts is shown here being greeted by the Prime Minister after his ordeal. But the animal was frightened by camera flashes at the Downing Street photocall and ran off across St James's Park. Police now say that the sheep somehow found his way back to the Battymanistan delegation in Victoria, where his captors let him back into the building.

The gunmen who are now holding *both* Wally and Dr Stein have just released this video which apparently shows the scientist playing a computer game with the sheep.

'Theese animal has come home off his own free will. Therefore he is our sheep now. If anyone want heem, they must pay us meellion pounce. As you can see, he have good time here. And if anyone want Doctor Stein, we give heem to who pay most marneys. We cannot return to our country now you are keeling our peoples, so you give us plane and we fly to Bermuda and spend theese marneys having good time.'

An animal behaviour expert said tonight that it's common for domestic animals such as dogs and cats to find their way home across long distances. Wally had apparently only just arrived at his previous temporary home, a city farm in Dagenham, when he was abducted from there by the terrorists, and since he had been held captive for some days at the Battymanistan delegation, he might have to come to regard that as his new home. The delegation's building is less than a mile from Downing Street, and the sheep would have been able to reach it without having to cross many busy roads.

*

The regimental mascot was snoring under the table. Captain Undergrowth had forbidden the men to give the animal any beer, so they had contented themselves with feeding him vast amounts of chips, pie and pizza crusts, crisps and pork scratchings. The poor sheep looked exhausted, but that wasn't surprising given the runaround he'd had earlier.

Sergeant Gross had been worried because his sheep hadn't so much as whispered a word to him all night. He thought at first the animal had been in a huff after his undignified recapture in the park. He was a sensitive beast, and would not have taken kindly to the way Broady had rugby-tackled him to the ground, then flung him across his shoulders like a kitbag to transport him to the pub where the platoon had decamped after the assault had been called off. But Gross now knew why his talking sheep had been unusually taciturn: the sheep they'd recaptured must be the other one, the hostage sheep who wasn't Wally.

He walked across to Captain Undergrowth, who seemed to be involved in a covert reconnaissance mission at the bar, spying on the barmaid's breasts from behind his pint of Guinness.

'Sir, I think we have a problem.'

'Spit it out, Gross. What's wrong, looks like our turkey shoot's back on,' he said, pointing at the television. 'Should have some fun tomorrow, eh?'

'All right, but I probably need to take it slowly. Where shall I start?'

The officer leered at him with glazed eyes.

'OK,' Gross began. 'You know that sheep what was on the six o'clock news?'

'The nation's Sheep of Hearts,' the captain sang, raising his glass and winking across at the barmaid. '*Wallee, Wallee, pride of our valley...*'

'That *wasn't* Wally sir. That sheep what the PM was giving his chocolate to...*that* was *our* sheep sir, the one over there, what the lads as been givin their pizzas to...although ee's not actually *our* sheep but ee's the one we've ended up with.'

'Slow down, Gross,' said Captain Undergrowth. 'You've confused me already. What do you mean, he's not our sheep? I know he *looks* quite like Wally, but we've just seen Wally on the news, and the bloody animal's run back to the Batties. Tell you the truth I probably couldn't tell the two apart myself, all sheep look pretty much the same to me, but I know you Gross are something of an ovine connoisseur.'

'That sheep down there sir, the one on the floor, *that* is the sheep the Batties was oldin before.'

'You mean we've got Wally and they've got our mascot sheep? PM'll be pleased then if it turns out they've got the wrong sheep now.'

'Trouble is ee won't sir, because our mascot *was* the real Wally all along. The Batties released that animal over there in exchange for Stein. Them two sheep must have both bin runnin round the park in the dark, and Broady grabbed the first one ee saw, im assumin it must be our sheep, not knowin the other one was out takin the air as well.'

'But that would mean Stein gave himself up for the wrong sheep too,' said the captain, still puzzled.

'But the right one's wiv im now. They're in cahoots them two. The sheep what *was* our mascot must of walked round to the Batty delegation and asked them to let im in.'

'Oh come on, Gross, you don't expect me to believe that. You heard that chap on the news: sheep went back there because the bloody animal thought it was his home.'

'*Ee did it to us too, sir.*'

'You what, Gross?' said Captain Undergrowth, with an air of indignation. He was starting to surface from his alcoholic swim.

'You remember when that black ram burst out the cupboard, and you thought I'd like put im there, for a bit of a laugh like.'

'Yes. Good wheeze that.'

'Well I adn't sir. It was just as big a surprise to me. But you was that pleased I didn't want to say nuffink. But ee staged it, the sheep did. Ee wanted access to the Army's facilities.'

'Gross...'

'Look,' said the sergeant, 'you said then that *if* the sheep *was* Wally, you didn't need to know.'

'I know but...'

'Well afterwards, me and im ad a bit of a chat like.'

'Are you sure you're feeling...'

'Ee can *tork*, see. That's why ee's worth a million pahnd. That bloke Stein what cloned him, ee must have made a sheep what could think and tork. If you ask me, I think im and Stein is, you know, related some'ow.'

'But Clovis were only willing to stump up fifty grand for their sheep, if I remember. It was the bloody press that were chucking all their money around…'

'Smokescreen sir. They don't want no one else to know. Imagine what would appen if people knew there was animals what could tork. And *read* too. Ee reads books, that sheep. Ee's a ruddy clever sheep that one, *too* clever, a real smartarse.'

'The Army would certainly be interested,' said Captain Undergrowth, his face brightening. 'Imagine it. Dogs working undercover. Sheep that could listen in and report back on people's conversations. Real snakes in the grass, eh? Wouldn't tell the rest though. Keep it from MI5 and the bloody CIA. We'd know what *they* were doing because we'd have our own moggies in all their offices.'

'Don't get carried away sir,' the sergeant warned. 'Because you know that problem I said we ad?'

'You've explained, Gross. Quite simple. I say the Army takes the sheep. It was ours in the first place after all.'

'But we don't *want* the Army to have the sheep, sir,' the sergeant insisted. 'Because…because the sheep knows everyfing about our entrepreneurial activities.'

'Everything? Even…'

'Everyfing sir. Not only that but some of the latest scams was is own idea. Ee's bin takin arf my cut since ee arrived. You remember that business with Cookie and the Red Lion?'

'That can't have been his idea,' said the captain, waving his hand nonchalantly. 'That's been going on for *ages*. Took us a long time to sniff it out though.'

'We didn't sniff it out sir. The sheep did. Like you say, ee keeps is ear to the ground, he ears stuff everywhere and no one knows ee's listenin.'

The captain seemed to think for a moment.

'Gross, does he…does the er sheep know about me and, erm, Poppy, Major Carstairs's…'

'Ee even knows what she was wearin, sir, last time you two…'

'Oh dear me, this *is* serious. And *all* our schemes you say?'

Captain Undergrowth looked down at his glass, surprised to

find it empty; distractedly he gestured to the barmaid for a refill.

'Another one, Gross? Whisky? I'd say we both need a tot or two after what you've just told me, but look here, man, before we go off at half cock on this, take this further, you know... And by the way, I think I *may* just had a *rather* good idea...'

'Don't even *think* about it sir...'

'What proof can you give me? It's your word against a sheep's, a sheep you're saying can talk...'

'...ee's covered is back, sir, we can't kill im, if that was what you was thinkin.'

'Not that I dis*trust* you, Gross, but it is all rather irregular, this talking sheep business. However, you have always been straight with me, I'll give you that. Only way with quartermasters and their sergeants, I always say.'

'But I wasn't straight wiv im, sir, the sheep that is. Ee cort me wiv my trahsers dahn, ee did, as it were.'

'Oh I see. Bad luck there, Gross. But that kind of thing happens all the time in the Army, only usually it's two chaps, not...'

'That's why I've not been able to say nuffink to you sir. Ee said if I told you or anyone else that ee could tork and what ee was up to, ee'd expose me and give the Army a full account of orl our nefarious malpractices, as ee corled them. And we'd get discharged or maybe even shot. And in case anything appened to im, ee ad copied everyfink he knew to one of is associates, and the Army would still av our guts for garters.'

'Still sounds pretty far-fetched, Gross. No sheep, no proof. And you've not said what his game is either.'

'*Snowball* sir. You saw it on the news, when they showed im and Stein playing what they said was a computer game. Only it wasn't. It's the sheep's game, Snowball, I could see it on the screen. Ee invented it, but it's not a game, it's real. And I do av proof of that because is laptop's in my bag in the truck. Ee thought ee might need it on this trip.'

'His laptop, Gross?'

'I got it for im, sir. Ee already ad is own voice recognition software customised for is sheep voice, like, so I just ad to download it for im from some site ee'd set up before. Then he started torkin into the mike and he made this Snowball game, only it's not a game, it's a scam. First fing I arsked im was oo was ee workin for, and ee said same as me, ee was workin for imself. But ee couldn't do everyfing, what with im avin ooves instead of fingers, so some of the stuff he did by torkin to is computer and the rest was fings I keyed in for im.'

'What kind of things, Gross?'

'Numbers. Codes. That kind of fing. He got me to ack into all these other computers, usin some M.O.D. firewall I think he corled it. Didn't know what I was doin most of the time, ee was just sayin fings and I tapped away. And what he was sayin seemed to make sense, though I wasn't sure quite ow the ole fing was goin to come together like. But ee said it would make that Nick Leeson look like a shoplifter. Compared with Snowball, that Enron business was just a bit of petty pilferin like.'

'Do you know how it's meant to work then, this Snowball?'

'Like most good scams, it's simple. The difficult bit is gettin it to work like clockwork, ee said. See, your big multinationals use just four accountants 'n' orditors, across the 'ole globe, which are,' said Gross, counting them out on his fingers, 'KPMG, Pricewater'ousecoopers, Ernst 'n' Young an Deloitte 'n' Toosh, an it was Toosh what took over what was left of Arthur Andersen after the Enron fing went darn the plugole. An these four big boys as bin keepin orl the big dosh for themselves by doin what they corl *lowballin* their charges. That's what gave our sheep is big idea: if they were gonna *lowborl* everyone, ee was gonna *snowborl* them back, ee said. These big four av access not just to the bank accounts of all the multinationals but monitor all the movements of their shares, track their payments and so on. Them four is what ee corls the portal to the cash. The Snowball is a virus what ee invented what goes in through the firewall, through the four portals, and it takes out smorl amounts of money what no one will really notice from everywhere, and it transfers the cash to an offshore bank account in the name of Snowball Investments. It's orl automatic: this fing takes the same tiny point nought something something percentage from every account it goes into, and it records these transactions as *bank charges*.'

'So the sheep's money snowballs as the virus spreads around the banking system, sending him back all these tiny amounts?'

'Precisely sir. That's the beauty of it. Only what would be a tiny amount in percentage terms in your average bloke's Natwest account is rather more for your McDonalds or Microsofts or your oil companies. But still peanuts for them. And no more than they'd normally pay out in bank charges, accordin to the sheep. Ee said they'd never even know ow they'd bin fleeced by a sheep.'

'And all this is in the laptop, which you have.'

'Yes sir.'

Captain Undergrowth looked into space, stroking his chin.

'So if the sheep *were* to be killed,' the captain began saying, 'by accident of course, when we storm the delegation, we could *in theory* do a runner before this associate of his even knows about it, and contacts the Army. We could be on the next plane to the Windies in fact, instead of the Batties, with the laptop.'

'Well yes sir. I suppose so sir. But what about Stein sir?'

'He might be hit in the crossfire of course, especially if Broadsword's spraying the stuff about as he tends to like doing. On the other hand, given that those other chaps keep trying to blow Dr Stein up, it's possible he might like an extended Caribbean holiday himself. You could split your thirty per cent with him, Gross, as you did with the sheep.'

'But what do we tell the men sir? You know, to make sure the sheep don't get lucky.'

'We say Stein has managed to ring us on a mobile to tell us the Batties have forced the sheep to eat plastic explosives and a timing device. The Batties know that if the army goes in, they'll all be dead in five minutes, but when the show's over the sheep will explode while we're sitting round hugging it and congratulating ourselves on having no casualties.'

'You think they'll swallow that sir?'

'Those nutters blow themselves up all the time, so the men won't think it at all strange that they should leave the sheep behind as their suicide bomber. Their Trojan sheep.'

'But what about Stein?'

'I'll grab Stein as soon as all the Batties are down, and rush him out. He won't know what's going on, especially with all the smoke. Then you and the bomb squad lads take the sheep out into the square, tie him to a bench in the park, and detonate him in one of those controlled explosions they like doing. Tape his mouth shut first so he can't try to talk his way out of it – you can say that is to stop him belching any methane, which would be highly inflammable.'

'And if Stein won't play ball afterwards?'

'We say he was killed in all the confusion.'

Sergeant Gross racked his brain for possible objections.

'But what about the cameras? They'll all be filming it. And the police...'

'Change of tactics. We clear the square. We go in at dawn. Should make the *Today* programme. PM always listens to that, usually hates it, but this show will cheer him up.'

'But won't somefing like that be bad for morale?' Gross asked.

'Not at all. Everyone expected the Batties to kill Stein, he had it coming and he was a fool to offer himself for the sheep. But that won't matter now all the Batties are being battered in the war. We just have to make sure all the gunmen in the delegation get shot to pieces. People like it when that happens, especially when none of our boys are hurt, which they won't be, because of the guns. Our British public doesn't want any mercy for terrorists. They'd rather they were all killed, not have any captured and treated as political prisoners who have to be freed later for some poor bugger who's been caught somewhere else just to be exchanged. But of course if it turns out that *Stein* is the sheep's associate, which seems pretty likely to me, we wouldn't need to do a runner quite so quickly. We'd disappear later with your Snowball and no one would be the wiser.'

'What about the nation's Sheep of Hearts?'

'He's over there, isn't he, our new mascot? He might even get some more of the PM's chocolate when we hand him back to Clovis in a special ceremony. Good PR for the army. Shame about our milch sheep though. Have to admire a beast like that. But teaches us a lesson, Gross. Man creates the first intelligent sheep. Sheep becomes a master criminal. I bet that bit didn't come from the sheep's bit of the DNA.'

Sergeant Gross downed the rest of his whisky. Captain Undergrowth had just demonstrated why he did perhaps deserve his 70% after all. His latest plan did seem to make sense. It could just work. He felt sorry for the sheep, but the animal had been giving them the runaround. There was something else though. What about that name on the animal's Post Office Savings book, L. Giles, where did *he* fit in?

But his captain hadn't finished yet. 'Drink up, lads!' he was calling out. 'Next round's on Gross here. If we're lucky, we may just get a lock-in. Landlord wouldn't want to disappoint our boys, eh? But I'll still want you all bright-eyed and bushy-tailed in the morning. Big day. Don't want anyone calling in sick.'

*

This is the midnight news. First, some breaking news. An animal-rights splinter group called 666 has just announced that *it* is willing to pay the million pound ransom demanded by gunmen at the Battymanistan delegation in London for the release of the cloned sheep Wally. But the activists say they will only pay the money if the scientist Dr Frank Stein is freed at the same time. A spokesman for the group, which has previously been linked with a number of attempts to kill Dr Stein, said they had been impressed by the selfless way in which the eminent biologist had been willing to be taken hostage in place of the sheep, and the fact that Wally had returned to the building where Dr Stein was being held after being photographed with the Prime Minister clearly showed an extraordinary bond between man and sheep.

*

Douglas Giles did not need to wake his daughter. Her radio was clasped more tightly to her right ear than the fluffy Larry the Lamb sandwiched between her left ear and the pillow.

'All right, we'll do it,' said her father, touching her shoulder. 'He wouldn't have run away from the Prime Minister unless something was very seriously wrong. And to go back to those nutters like that. It doesn't make any kind of sense to me. It's different every time you turn on the news. I think it's time those people heard from someone sensible.'

'But don't you think it's good that the animal liberation people are wanting to help now?'

'No I don't. It's just a publicity stunt for them. And where did they get that kind of money from? If it exists, which I doubt. Not from collections in the High Street, that's for certain.'

'They probably stole it, Daddy.'

'You may be right there. They have to get their money from somewhere. And they must have spent a pretty penny on all the explosives they must have used to blow up those cars of Dr Stein's.'

'Shall I make a flask of coffee for the journey?'

'Yes, you do that while I put some straw in the back of the Land Rover. I'd say we can probably get there in three and a half hours if I put my foot down. We should have time for a couple of hours' sleep in the cab when we get there, before it gets light. You can sleep on the way of course.'

'I don't think I'll sleep a wink. But I can try.'

'I'm putting the shotgun in the back, but it won't be loaded. The cartridges will be in the glove department. I'm telling you this just in case. Not that I'm expecting anything horrible to happen, but it does to be prepared when you're dealing with lunatics. You'd know how to load it, if you had to?'

'Yes, Daddy.'

'And how to hold it, against your shoulder?'

'*Yes*, Daddy.'

'And how to...'

'Daddy, you forget. I shot that magpies' nest out of the high elms, didn't I, when those nasty birds were killing all our chicks.'

'Oh yes, I remember now, but that was quite a while ago, wasn't it. How many goes did it take?'

'Just one.'

'And you could still hit something that far away?'

'That's what all the cans are for. On the wall behind the low barn. The sheep used to retrieve them for me.'

*

Graham Medlar fastened the shutters with the padlock and went back inside the van to cash up. It didn't do to let people see you counting out the notes. His last few customers had been really sozzled, especially those soldiers. But none of them had moaned about the burgers or the hot dogs, nor would any be complaining about food poisoning, given that his vegeburgers and vegetarian frankfurters contained no meat at all. They were good burgers too, he'd had some himself, and the onions were fresh, though once the drunks had smothered them with ketchup or mustard, they wouldn't have been able to taste how good they were. The police had liked them too. The marksmen had sent over for second helpings. They hadn't been allowed to leave their positions again after the sheep had managed to slip past them.

The million pounds were in the old fawn suitcase. He'd written ONIONS across the lid in thick black felt-tip in case anyone spotted it wedged behind the big red Calor gas cylinder. The Batties still hadn't phoned back about his offer. The night's taking amounted to nearly £500, which meant he'd cleared £225 after deducting his costs and what he'd have to give Trevor for the use of his van. If the Batties were still arguing about wanting something for Stein as well as the million pounds they were getting for the sheep, he hoped they'd accept £225 for him. £225 was better than nothing.

He unrolled his sleeping-bag and switched out the light. If he didn't get woken by another call on his mobile, he'd ring them again in the morning and try them with the new offer. It was a shame the million pounds were no good to 666 after all the trouble they'd gone to with that security van. Trevor had made sure the bomb's force would be localised, the explosion ripping through the van's armour but only melting the strong boxes at the point of penetration. They couldn't have known that all the £50 notes in the surviving boxes would be marked and numbered. The Batties wouldn't twig this of course. Since the cash wasn't from a bank, they'd just think it was money. But they'd had him worried with that last demand of theirs.

'OK, OK, meester 666, if you have meellion pounce cash, you change it for us into dollars. That way you pay bank conversion charges. Our leader he say peoples all want dollars in Caribbean, not pounce. Pounce no good now, we want dollars.'

CHAPTER EIGHTEEN

The Trojan Sheep

The sheep looked up suddenly, his ears sharply pricked, all his wool bristling. He nudged Stein on the arm with his hoof.

'Quickly, Stein, we'll have to start shutting it down now. We don't have much time left.'

'But the guard's still asleep. We haven't done the unit trusts yet.'

'They'll have to wait,' the sheep said hurriedly. 'The important thing is we've covered most of the field, plus we've sent off that attachment to all the names in the delegation's e-mail addwess book.'

'You still haven't told me what that does.'

'It's meant to be a surpwise.'

'Can't you give me a clue?'

'It's just something I wustled up. A dwaft constitution for a new weepublic with suggestions of a possible legal fwamework for its pwompt implementation. Nothing fancy.'

'I can see I've been wasting my time working all these years as a scientist. If I'd applied that intelligence you got from me to more lucrative enterprises, I'd be a rich man now.'

'There's no time for jokes now, Stein. That money's not for me, or for you, it's a special fund.'

'So you keep saying.'

'But of course I didn't tell Gwose that when he helped me put the whole thing together. He even believed me when I said the percentage was only point nought something something. But that weally would be peanuts. He was looking at the scween at the time too. I suppose he just saw a load of noughts.'

'Doesn't do to give the whole game away when you don't trust the other person.'

'Exactly,' said the sheep. 'Good, we're nearly there. Now turn the other way while I change the password.'

'We might have got a *few* more done,' Stein continued, trying not to feel snubbed. 'It's only *just* getting light now. But at least those chaps have got their heating timed to come on early.'

'That's not their doing,' said the sheep, his voice suddenly dropping, turning to a whisper. 'That's the army. They'll wait till the temperature weaches 26 degwees centigwade before moving in. The Batties' guns won't work then. They'll jam.'

'What, like those guns of ours?'

'Those *are* our guns,' the sheep breathed. 'They bought them fwom us. And you'd better make yourself scarce, Stein, please, when they come bursting in.'

'But they won't shoot me. I don't have a beard.'

'They'll kill the lights first and then anything that moves. They may alweddy have decided that Doctor Fwank Stein is dispensable or disposable for some weason. Judging from what I've learned about the way they work, I'd say if someone's slipped them a few quid to make sure you get bumped off, you should start saying your pwares. The ALF for example.'

'But they like me now.'

'That was only one of their splinter gwoops. There are plenty of those, and they all disagwee with each other. So you hide in that cupboard as soon as we hear anything. Our dozy guard will just jump up and be shot to pieces in the doorway.'

'What'll about you?'

'I'll lie on the floor. They won't harm me. They have to wescue the nation's Sheep of Hearts.'

'I hope you're right.'

'They need me alive.'

'You finished?' came a voice from behind them. Stein felt it like a stab in the back. Their guard had woken. 'What have you done with computer?' he asked them.

'I have sent a message to your people,' the sheep told him. 'The war will soon be over.'

'We know that. The Amereecans will keel us all.'

'No, they won't now,' said the sheep. 'I have made sure they will stop now, believe me.'

The guard stared at him. Stein stared at him. It wasn't flannel. He knew his sheep well enough by now to know when he was putting it on. He really did think he was going to stop the war. But how? After all he'd witnessed that night, he wouldn't regard anything as beyond the sheep's capabilities now. He was still shaky on some stuff, but his intellect was quite literally awesome. The advances he'd made since those surreal exchanges they'd had in the lab were astonishing. The sheep had exceeded every expectation he could possibly have had of him, a hundred, a thousand times over. And he wasn't even four years old, unless...

He remembered then the discovery the Roslin scientists had made about Dolly, how her organs and tissues had aged at two different rates, so that by her first birthday, some of Dolly was one year old, but the rest of her was seven, her own age plus her mother's. They'd never worked out which parts of her had aged at which rates, but that was said to be why she was suffering from arthritis as a lamb. Stein had given his sheep his own gene for human intelligence, which might mean his intellectual capacities were of someone in their 50s, a human four years older than the sheep. The animal's education might have been slipshod, but his thinking wasn't, and Stein realised that the sheep could well be cleverer than he was in intellectual terms, especially in the way he applied logic to complex problems.

All night Stein had struggled to keep up as the animal had fired one instruction after another at him. Half way through the Snowball programming it had dawned on him how the whole concept was nothing short of genius. When the sheep was telling him to do first one thing, then another, then another, he realised the animal was working on several intellectual levels simultaneously, dotting and dancing between them to solve the next problem which appeared on the screen, then going back with another command that sorted out something else which had been left hanging half an hour before. It had started to make complete sense only in the last hour, its simple beauty, its staggering complexity. He'd wanted to hug his sheep, to shake him by the hoof. He couldn't begin to express his admiration for what he now knew the animal had achieved in intellectual terms; and he felt a strange pride growing in him, glowing almost, something he'd never experienced before, not even as a father with his own children. He wanted to stop, to relish it somehow, but the sheep was tireless. He wouldn't stop for a moment. They had to keep going, he said. They had to get as much done as they possibly could within the time frame.

'I hope you are right, sheep,' the guard was saying. 'I am simple man, but I want you do good things for my peoples. I was farmer in heels before Russians come. They keel my two brothers. Then militia come. They keel my father. Then warlords' men rape my seester in front of her son before they keel heem. My seester she crazy, she jump from bridge next day. Only my mother left now but she keeled by landmine. We have had too much of war. Why the Americans bomb us now, and the British also? We have nothing. They know we have no planes and tanks.'

'They say you harbour terrorists,' said Stein, attempting a neutral tone. He was still in a state of shock. His night had felt like a crash course in human life. Now he was high on adrenaline and amazement, but the course had started with the tying up, the mind games, the threats. They hadn't wanted to torture him rightaway, they'd wanted to humiliate him first, make him acknowledge his weakness and their superiority. He'd kept repeating how he'd been wrong in everything he'd done, that he'd been misguided, that everything was his fault, and what else could he say but keep repeating those same phrases? He'd hated the leader for the way he was orchestrating it, wanting to draw it all out, just to linger over his humiliation, savouring the power he had over him. He wasn't like a cat playing with a mouse, only a human was capable of anything as brutal as that. But the leader's macabre, almost mannered performance had saved him in the end. The sheep had arrived just when the man was becoming bored with his game, his dance of death. Then the sheep had shown him how his animal version of human intelligence was something beautifully creative. He felt now as though his own humanity had been given back to him just when his captors had torn its last vestiges to shreds.

Stein hadn't slept for two days. His whole head seemed to be swimming now, but he tried to look sympathetic as the guard continued. And he *was* sympathetic, despite what they'd put him through, but all he could *feel* now was simple exhaustion.

'*They* are terrorists,' the man was saying, 'the Americans and the Israyeelies. They are terrorist states, the Russians too, first in our country and now in Chechnya. Why are they surprised we want to keel them after what they do to our peoples?'

Now the psychotic leader was standing in the doorway.

'You have finished work yes?'

Stein nodded vaguely.

'It is done,' the sheep said.

'I hope it works, whatever it eese you have done. Maybe something good happen now. Like our heating. For weeks we ask them to fix heating but nothing happen. Eese not good for us, this is cold country. But now it *works*! Now we haff heat!' he exclaimed, waving his hands in mock astonishment, wiggling his hips as if about to dance.

The sheep would not have been surprised if at that moment a sniper's bullet had blown the man's head off. He knew they would have him in their telescopic sights. There would be a whole line of marksmen sprawled along on the roof of the building opposite. Knowing what was about to be unleashed, he tried to feel sorry for the brute. It was hard. Unlike him, this was a whole human being, but where was his humanity? He was smiling now, but the smile was thin, strained. His eyes were almost dead, like embers from a fire which had gone out, like ash about to be extinguished. Those men on the roof must be staring at him with exactly the same kind of eyes. Dark and cold. Empty.

*

Graham Medlar woke to the singing of his mobile. He wished he'd remembered to change the ringtone to a bleep. As *We Are the Champions* echoed around the tinny shell of Trevor's hot dog van in the cold dark, a shiver went through him. He thought the whole square must have heard it; suddenly he felt exposed, scared, conspicuous, vulnerable. Alone.

'Yes,' he whispered.

'We weel accept your offer meester 666. You have marneys?'

'Yes.'

'You must stand in far corner of square by big tree. We watch you through binoculars. You open lid off suitcase and show us marneys.'

'Right.'

'But no tricks. If marneys not right we find you after and we keel you. Remember, our men find sheep OK no problem. Our peoples are everywhere. Make sure we have some pounce for Stein too. You cannot have heem for nothing.'

'What if I get stopped by the police?'

'You say we ask you bring us food. Onions, meat and bread, we make our own beefburgers in our keetchen.'

'I thought you didn't eat beef. Meat of the cow?'

'You say we have no food and we must eat. If we not eat burgers, we must eat sheep. But sheep needed for meellion pounce.'

'What if I have to open the case?'

'No problem. We see from window. We keel policemans with our guns. But you will be OK, my friend, we only shoot you if you trick us. Our leader he say no policemans in square now. They have all gone for sleeps. You show us marneys, then come to front door. Stein and sheep will be at front door in five minutes.'

The phone went dead.

*

Douglas Giles heard nothing of the assault itself, it all happened so quickly. The terrorists were all dead within seconds, the first as he opened the front door, the rest inside as the soldiers poured in, as if from nowhere. The farmer woke a moment later as a gun went off close to the Land Rover. It seemed to come from the direction of the shuttered hot-dog van he'd noticed when they'd parked. There was an immediate return flash from inside the park and the van exploded, the blast shattering his windscreen, echoed by a peal of car alarms in the square; followed by a rain of onions bouncing on the roof.

He made a grab to protect Lucy, but she wasn't there. He was sprawled across the seat; none of the glass had hit him. Still in a state of shock, he raised himself slowly and watched as tufts of breadbun fell like manna from heaven. He hoped the red mess on the bonnet was tomato ketchup from the hot-dog van.

Where was Lucy? He felt powerless to do anything. If he ran outside he would be shot. His whole body strained to do something. He felt paralysed. Why had they come here? Why had he agreed to bring his daughter to this place? It was so stupid. He knew they'd had to do something. But *this?*

*

When the shotgun blast surprised him, Private Broadsword thought in that split second that the attack had come from the hot-dog van, whose white sides had actually reflected its flash from across the street. His reactions were instinctive as he swung round and fired back. When his bullet pierced the HOT DOGS & BURGERS sign and the Calor gas cylinder exploded, he stood back to admire his handiwork for a second. It was like being back in Bosnia, they'd tried tricks like that with them there and he'd blown up their cars with the beardies still inside. The soldier didn't see the girl flit behind him through the bush shadows, but when he turned she was already wrestling with Sergeant Gross, screaming at him.

'Untie him!' she was crying. 'He's just a sheep. Why are you doing this?'

He hadn't liked the idea, blowing up the sheep, but it was a desperate situation. And now this girl had ripped the tape from the animal's mouth. They had to stop the sheep from belching, otherwise the methane would explode. They were all in danger. The animal might explode at any moment. They didn't know when the sheep-bomb was timed to go off. He rushed forward to pull her off the sergeant just as a helicopter was suddenly jabbering above, blowing leaves and rubbish everywhere.

'Don't, Bwoady!' the sheep cried out. 'They twied to twick you. I haven't swallowed any explosives. I'm *not* a bomb.'

He froze.

'I'm just an ordinarwee sheep,' the animal pleaded, 'a poor innocent cweature caught in the wrong place at the wrong time.'

'He's right,' said Lucy, 'you mustn't hurt him.'

'Don't listen,' Sergeant Gross was saying. 'They put a tape

recorder inside the sheep as well. Ee isn't really torking, it's a tape.'

'I'm not a tape. I'm a *weel* sheep!'

'It's like those teddy bears. You press its belly and it torks. And it answers back like.'

'No, it's not true,' cried Lucy.

Private Broadsword loomed over the sheep, then gingerly, tenderly, stretched out a finger to touch him.

Looking up, Lucy saw a gentle giant, like Frankenstein's monster meeting the wee girl by the lake.

'You spoke,' the soldier said gently. 'You talked. You really did talk. But you're a sheep.'

'Oh that's wonderful,' the sheep intoned, hamming it up in Bugs Bunny style. 'Can you *weally* hear me, Bwoady? I thought only Lucy could hear me because only people who are *weally weally nice* to animals can hear us talking. Most people can't hear *anything* we say.'

The sheep gave Gross a sharp look as the sergeant released his grip, and began to back away. Behind him a group of other soldiers began edging slowly forward.

'Get back,' Broadsword called out to them. 'No one harms the sheep. He's not a bomb. Tell the rest. He's not dangerous.'

'*Please*,' said Lucy. 'Help me untie him, quickly. I'll free him from the bench and you sort out those wires.'

*

The helicopter's blinding searchlight had just moved across him when the second explosion blasted the square. The jeep was rocked by the whoosh of air that followed. Douglas Giles ducked instinctively as windows and car windscreens seemed to shatter in a chorus of discordant glass all around. But the next instant Lucy was there, pulling at the door. He rushed to help her.

Her face was dirty, bruised, bloodied, her hair dishevelled. The sheep stood by her on the pavement, shaking. He was about to embrace her when they heard shouts. Grabbing the animal in one movement, they both bundled him into the back.

Then they leapt into the cab. He spurred the engine into life, swung the jeep around the debris in the road – swerving to avoid a fawn-coloured suitcase – then sped out of the square, narrowly missing an ambulance which came hurtling round the corner at just that moment, its keening siren almost splitting the air.

'I hope he's all right in the back,' said Douglas Giles. 'I hope he's comfortable, that he's got enough straw.'

'He's been in the back of the Land Rover before, Daddy.'

'Are you all right, Lucy? You aren't hurt? Mind all that glass now.'

'I'm fine now. Don't worry about me.'

'We'll stop somewhere and get you cleaned up.'

'We *did* it!' she cried. 'We *saved* him! They were going to *kill* him...'

Now she was sobbing. He touched her arm in the middle of a wrenching gear-change.

'We'll soon be out of this place, away from here.'

'We almost got some onions,' she said through her tears, and began to giggle uncontrollably. 'It must have been the man from the hot-dog van that blew up.'

'I was so worried. You weren't there.'

'He must have been just arriving with his supplies,' she chirped. 'He was struggling with this big suitcase which must have been full of onions. It was so silly. It had ONIONS written across it.'

'We almost hit a suitcase in the road just now.'

'That was it, Daddy. That was his case.'

'Did that sign say M1 and the North there? Yes? Good.'

'I hardly slept. I kept watching the building. Then I saw they'd opened the front door. I took the shotgun out then, I'd already loaded it, when you were sleeping. I had to be ready. But there was no one in the square except this funny red-haired man with his onions.'

'The shotgun,' echoed Douglas Giles in a dull voice. He wanted his daughter to talk. She had to get it all out. But he desperately wanted to hold her, to hug her to him, yet here he was having to steer the Land Rover through the early morning London traffic. A taxi cut in on them then, blasting him with his horn.

'But the man seemed to be scared of something,' Lucy went on. 'He saw me holding the shotgun. Then we both looked across at the door at the same time and Stein was standing there, I could see it was him from his fatman shape. And there was a smaller black shape beside him, and the more I stared the more I was sure that it was Sheep. And at just that moment there was this shot and both Stein and Sheep jumped, almost flinging themselves down the steps to the ground. There must have been another man standing beside them in the doorway because he fell forward, we could see that he'd been hit. That's when the ginger man dropped it, the suitcase of onions, right in front of me, as I stood there holding the shotgun, not knowing what to do, and he ran off. Then they were shooting in the building, and I saw four soldiers grab hold of Sheep and run with him into the park. Stein was left behind just slumped by the steps. I don't think he was hit, he was crouching almost, on his side. I ran along behind some cars and went into the park by the side gate. Then I saw them, they were tying Sheep to a park bench. It was horrible. I couldn't understand why they were doing that, but I knew that it was wrong, that something horribly wrong was happening, and the next thing I knew I was firing the shotgun at them, to make them leave him alone. I threw myself to the ground, that's when I lost your gun, I'm sorry Daddy. But they didn't fire back at me, they fired at the hot-dog van instead, that's when it blew up. So I ran round behind them and saw they'd gagged him as well. And they hadn't just tied him up, they had all these wires round him. They were going to blow him up, Daddy.'

'Jesus,' said Douglas Giles.

'I jumped on one of the soldiers and pulled the tape from Sheep's mouth and he...he cried out...and this other soldier, this really big soldier, he was like a giant, he pushed the other man away and we untied him. And then we just ran.'

'When I heard that helicopter, then the explosion, the second one, I thought...'

'I know, Daddy. That *would* have been Sheep, Daddy, if I hadn't got to him, and that nice soldier hadn't helped me free him.'

*

Captain Undergrowth waited while Stein threw up in the gutter. The man was still shaking.

'That's right,' he urged him, 'get it all out, what?'

When the scientist sat down on the kerb, crouching, wrapping his arms about himself, huddling in the cold, the captain shed his coat and dropped it over him, as if he were a birdcage that needed to be covered.

Sergeant Gross came round the corner then, shouldering a large fawn-coloured suitcase. The captain watched him shunt it into the back of the command jeep, alongside the recumbent regimental mascot sheep, which still lay slumped there in a drunken stupor. It hadn't stirred since they'd dumped it in the back after the lock-in at the Pig and Whistle. He strode over to question his sergeant.

'What happened, Gross?' he hissed. 'Why were there two explosions?'

'The first was the 'ot-dog van sir,' the sergeant whispered. 'Broady blew it up.'

'Not the sheep then?'

'No sir.'

'So the second was the sheep?'

'No sir. That was Broady again.'

'What did he blow up this time?'

'Ee didn't sir. The men blew up Broady instead of the sheep sir, im and a park bench. Ee must av bin sittin on it. It was an accident like, a misunderstanding, an error in the chain of command.'

'A cock-up you mean?'

'You said it sir.'

'And the sheep?'

'Ees gorn sir. There was this girl, see, and she rescued im. She ripped off is gag and then the sheep torked Broady into elpin er untie im from the bench.'

'Who was this girl? Did anyone else hear the sheep?'

'I fort they'd blown up all free of em at first sir, but then I saw the girl runnin off with the sheep. Don't know oo she was sir. But I don't fink anyone else erd the sheep, ee was just torkin to Broady like and there was lots of noise, what with all the sirens an alarms an the 'ellycopter an that. I don't fink the men even saw the girl, sir, she was beyined the sheep in the bushes and the lads was on the other side wiv the detonator.'

'We'll have to play our cards pretty close now, Gross...'

'Move quick like sir, before the sheep blows the gaffe.'

'And work up a good story for the press while we're at it. Still, just one down's not that bad.'

'But we got them all sir,' Gross asserted.

'I meant *us*, Gross.'

'Tell you wot though sir you was right about them guns of theirs, they was crap. So we didn't aff to waste too much ammo. But some of the lads did spray it abaht a bit, their aim wasn't that good wot with them still bein a bit the worse for the drink like. Only Todger got imself a duck.'

'A duck, Gross? They weren't shooting the ducks as well, were they?'

'No we av this game, sir. Any man its is target wiv is first shot, you know like ducks at the fair, ee gets given one of them yeller plastic ducks when we get 'ome. Most of the men likes to keep 'em, but they can swap 'em for five pints in the bar when they're skint.'

The sergeant's explanation was lost on Captain Undergrowth, who was suddenly deep in thought. Then his face lit up: 'But we *have* rescued the nation's Sheep of Hearts,' he announced.

'We av sir?'

'Isn't that *him* in the back there, Gross? But you can't blame him, can you, snoring away like that, poor animal must be exhausted. After such an ordeal.'

'Oh yes. I get you sir. Very good sir.'

'But what's that case you've got there Gross? Booty?'

'Onions sir. The 'ot-dog chap was just arrivin when we went in, and he must av left these beyined when iz van blew up.'

'He wasn't *in* the van, was he, Gross?'

'Don't fink so sir. I fink ee ran orf. But bomb squad boys'll tell us won't they? Either way I don't spose ee'll be wantin iz onions now. We can orlways use a few more onions. An I fahnd this too, sir,' the sergeant added proudly, pulling a piece of burnt wood from his pocket.

'Souvenir?'

'Yes sir. It's a bit from Broady's bench. Look, it's got this writin on it.' He pointed to a tarnished metal plate still screwed to the charred wood which read IN MEMORY OF BETTY GROGAN WHO USED TO LIKE SITTING HERE. 'I fort as like Broady's widow might like to av it, sir, seein ow she's called Betty too.'

'Very thoughtful of you, Gross.'

'But abaht that other matter sir...'

'Let's see if Dr Stein would like some tea then. I've got a flask. Might put some colour back in him. Poor chap, looks like he's seen a ghost. Let's sit him in the jeep. See if we can't get him to spill a few beans, what, before anyone else starts poking their noses in. Clearly in a state of shock, probably won't remember anything we say.'

'Good thinking sir. I'll get the laptop.'

As Stein sat huddled between the two soldiers, warming his hands through the tin mug, inhaling the sweet smell of the tea, he realised that his second interrogation was about to begin. Wally was safe in the back, already fast asleep, and snoring too; the animal must be as exhausted as he was. Although Stein felt totally shattered, he thought he could just about manage to play these two along for a bit. He knew his life was in danger, that they might think nothing of killing him, making out then that he'd been hit in the attack. But he also knew what they wanted from him, and they wouldn't have much time to get it. Whatever they tried to do, the sheep would have devised some way of outwitting them, however he might be incapacitated, whether asleep, as he was now, or – perish the thought – dead. The sheep had told him he'd covered himself against Gross and the captain trying anything, that they couldn't kill him because everything he knew about their activities would be made public. He'd have given a dossier to Lucy for safekeeping or release. And he'd clearly been right to show such foresight; these two could easily have made sure he too was killed in the assault, but there he was in the back of their jeep. They clearly wouldn't trust anyone else to look after him, given what he knew.

'Do you know anything about Snowball?' the captain began.

'It's a game, isn't it,' said Stein flatly.

'What kind of game?'

'A gambling game,' he said, this time with some effort, making sure his voice registered his very real tiredness.

'Would you know how to play it?'

'Probably,' he told them. 'But it's very complicated,' he added, almost with finality, as if to end the discussion.

'You can say that aggen,' said the sergeant.

'Gross...' the captain chided. 'Dr Stein,' he continued, 'if Gross here were to set it up on this computer, do you think you could show us how to play the game?'

'Computer?' Stein queried.

'It's Wally's,' the captain said carefully. 'His laptop. He won't mind, he said we could use it.'

Stein looked at him for a second. Then said: 'Well if it's all right with the sheep, I can try. But it's not easy.'

'Even just a few moves,' Captain Undergrowth urged him, 'you know, just to start us off.'

'Fine,' said Stein, gulping back his tea to hide any reaction he might be showing.

'Shall I switch it on then, Dr Stein?' Gross asked.

'Yes,' said Stein, 'but you'll need a phone line. It uses the internet.'

'Well good thing we've got the command jeep then,' said the captain. 'Has its own fax and everything. Boot it up then, Gross. Use that white lead for the phone bit.'

Sergeant Gross pressed the shiny button in the top right-hand corner, the one which reminded him of the circular base of a bullet.

'It takes a few minutes to load up,' said Stein, a little nervously, hoping it might take a good while longer. But the screen was soon filled with snowy light, and the icons were popping up all over the place like fairground targets.

'Then we click on the big snowball, don't we sir?' asked Sergeant Gross.

'I can see you've done this before,' said Stein, half in jest.

'No sir. The sheep usually did this bit.'

Stein tried to hide his smile.

'Now sir. It's askin for the password.'

How right the sheep was not to trust him, Stein realised. It was almost as if he knew that this would happen. He thought for a moment, and then said: 'Try MUTTONCHOPS.'

'Don't work sir. It 'as to be no more than eight letters.'

'MUTTON then,' he said, adding, 'of course.'

'I like his sense of humour,' said Captain Undergrowth.

'Now it says: please confirm your telephone number.'

'That must be the one on the fax,' said the captain. 'Try it with that.'

'It says THANK YOU USER: YOU HAVE ENTERED THE NUMBER CORRECTLY. Now it wants to know our postcode or O.S. map reference.'

Stein was trying hard not to smile. They still hadn't twigged it. 'It has to link up with the satellite,' he told them, trying to sound helpful.

'Victoria's SW1 isn't it?' said Captain Undergrowth. 'But it'll want all the letters. Let's see, should have the O.S. ref in the command orders for our op, eh?' He reached over for a clipboard and read out the coordinates to the sergeant.

Stein almost choked on his tea. It wasn't a wild goose chase, as he'd thought at first. Nor was the computer about to explode, not with the sheep himself in the back.

'Now it's tellin us our instruction as bin received. And PLEASE WAIT WHILE THE PROGRAM LOADS.'

Glancing across, Stein saw the sheep had even used the American spelling to add a touch of authenticity.

'Oh look at that sir,' said Sergeant Gross.

The sheep's time icon was a spinning snowball globe with the continents mapped out as black patches curving round the icy sphere. Underneath it said SNOWBALL IS LOADING.

'I think this bit takes a few minutes,' Stein interrupted. 'But if you don't mind,' he added, with a groan for good measure as he gripped his belly with one hand while clasping the other to his chest, 'I'm not feeling very well at all. I think I may need to step outside, otherwise...'

Captain Undergrowth opened the door, and eased himself out, letting Stein rush to the wall, where he bent over clutching his knees, pretending to be about to vomit again while staring at the square's nameplate in front of him. *SW1, SW1*, he said to himself. The sheep couldn't have planned that it would happen *this* easily, but even so, there was a certain geographical justice in motion: Victoria, SW1, Downing Street, SW1, and of course, New Scotland Yard, SW1, must be just a couple of streets away.

If Gross had tried to use the laptop at the camp, it would doubtless have used the satellite link to show his position there. The postcode and O.S. references were almost like jibes. If Gross had skipped them, he didn't doubt that the result would have been the same.

Standing between him and the jeep, Captain Undergrowth was staring inside at Sergeant Gross, who was gesticulating.

'What is it, Gross?' he demanded, opening the door. Over his shoulder, Stein could see that the snowball globe was melting. Now it was just a pool of water, with the words, in bigger letters this time: GAME OVER.

'But nuffink's appened sir!' Gross was saying indignantly.

Captain Undergrowth turned to confront Stein, but he'd managed to slip behind a van just as four police cars came screeching into the square from different directions. Nothing unusual in this with the siege just ended, but Captain Undergrowth didn't have time to wonder why these police hadn't used their warning lights or sirens, or why they weren't heading for the mêlée in front of the delegation. They were already grabbing hold of him and dragging Gross from the jeep, still hanging onto the laptop. One of the policeman was laughing: 'I didn't believe the SITTING DUCK bit of the message, but you live and learn.'

Stein emerged then from his place of concealment, pointing to the back of the jeep, which was vibrating to the sound of the sheep's deep-throated snores. 'The nation's Sheep of Hearts,' he said to the policeman who was dragging the fawn suitcase out from beside the sleeping animal, which wasn't budging to assist the manoeuvre.

'Dr Stein, isn't it?' said the superintendent.

'Right now I could do with a large whisky,' he said. 'But I suppose you'll want to offer me some of your post-traumatic stress counselling.'

'Couldn't that wait till after the press conference, sir?'

*

Good morning. The five-day siege at the Battymanistan delegation's London office ended at dawn this morning when the army stormed the building, freeing the cloned sheep Wally and scientist Dr Frank

Stein. One soldier died in the assault, Private William Broadsword of the Loamshire Fusiliers, who was attempting to defuse a suspect device tied to a park bench outside when it exploded. All the terrorists were killed.

The Batty gunmen had been demanding a ransom of a million pounds for the release of the nation's Sheep of Hearts, who earlier returned to the building after being exchanged for Dr Stein.

The whole area around the Batty delegation has now been cordoned off to allow police to carry out a full investigation. A hot-dog van parked near the delegation building was blown up during the attack, possibly when a gas cylinder was hit by a ricocheting bullet. The two explosions caused extensive damage to vehicles and surrounding buildings, with many windows being shattered.

But in a further surprise development, Scotland Yard have just announced that they have arrested two of the soldiers who took part in the assault, Captain Henry Undergrowth, Quartermaster of the Royal Loamshire Fusiliers, and Sergeant Robert Gross of the same regiment, who were caught carrying off a suitcase containing a million pounds in cash. At first police believed their claim that they thought the case was filled with onions belonging to the hot-dog vendor, but the money has now been traced to a recent armed attack on a GroupsEx security van, which police believe could only have been carried out by people with special military training and access to explosives. Military police are now anxious to question the two Loamshire soldiers about a series of frauds involving the misuse of army property and facilities going back over many years. They are examining a laptop computer found with the suitcase which the two men are said to have used to keep detailed records of their crimes.

Wally, the nation's Sheep of Hearts, will meet the Prime Minister again later today, but Downing Street officials say they'll make sure he isn't frightened by camera flashes. This time the ceremony will be held outdoors in Parliament Square.

The Prime Minister will then make a statement to the House about the situation in the Men's Republic of Battymanistan, where British and American planes have been continuing to bomb targets said to be military installations. The build-up of Allied land forces continues at the border, but critics of the Allies' current tactics in the War on War say the Batties have no military equipment or facilities left, and any continuation of the bombing will only result in more civilian casualties. However, an American army spokesman has said the attacks will not stop and the troops will not advance on Battymenarbad until they are confident that they will not meet with any opposition.

On a lighter note, it has just been announced that Wally, the nation's Sheep of Hearts, has been nominated for a special animal bravery award. He is expected to receive his medal from one of the Queen's corgis in a ceremony at Buckingham Palace later this month.

CHAPTER NINETEEN

Mothers of All

When the new security guard unlocked Wally's pen, Holly watched with great amusement as the red-haired man grabbed hold of the black sheep, pushed his thumb into the back of the ram's mouth – where he knew there would be no teeth – and then pulled the pesky animal's whole body round so that he sat immobilised on his haunches between the man's knees, his forehooves clutched helplessly against his belly. This security man was clearly well versed in how to secure a struggling sheep, but she hadn't expected him to produce a syringe from his pocket and then inject the animal with something that made him go suddenly limp. She would have been grateful herself for something offering that kind of assistance in her own dealings with the bothersome beast.

It had become increasingly difficult to fend off the black ram's repeated attacks. He had several times broken through into her part of the field and tried to mount her, and she had only finally managed to discourage him on that occasion by delivering such a sharp kick with her hind hoof that she managed to dislocate his jaw. And of course there was no reasoning with the brute. He simply didn't understand the meaning of the word *No*. She knew from Stein's warnings that he would be overbearingly arrogant, but he wouldn't even *speak* to her; he just made ridiculous animal noises like the other sheep, as if he was trying to goad her, to wind her up. Soon she was chiding Stein for his deception, accusing him of making up the whole story about Wally being able to talk. Wally must have been the *failed* experiment. She was the successful clone, the first sheep who could talk. This couldn't be the Wally she'd heard so much about, unless he'd undergone some radical personality change after being tortured by the terrorists.

Stein had been slow on the uptake. He'd maintained at first that the ram's silence was another of Wally's subterfuges, and when he finally came round to acknowledging, reluctantly, that his protégé must somehow have managed to switch places *again* with the other ram, he'd been totally unsympathetic to her plight, fobbing her off first with an offer of contraceptive pills, which even she knew couldn't be effective for a sheep, before making an obscene suggestion that he fit her with a Dutch cap.

'You don't understand, Flank,' she cried. 'It's not just the getting plegnant bit, I just don't want that awful cleature sticking his *thing* up me, from behind too, it's so undignified, and he just glunts too, he's a *hollible* beast!'

'Women put up with worse. At least he doesn't beat you up. It's just ram bam thank you lamb. All over in thirty seconds.'

'And I certainly don't want *you* lamming your fist inside me to fit that cap thing onto my loom. I don't want you to even *touch* me.'

'You used to like me stroking you...'

'Not *now*. Not any more. And certainly *not* down there. So just you make sure that *animal* doesn't get into the field when I'm glazing there. And make sure my pen's secure too. Or next time I won't just dislocate his jaw, I'll *blake* it! And he won't look very plitty when I've finished with him. He certainly won't be in any fit state to meet the Clean and her corgis.'

Stein hadn't taken her threats seriously, he just muttered something about *women* and walked away. He clearly wasn't taking *her* seriously when he should have been trying to make it up to her after letting her down, betraying her trust. The man was in a permanent grouch, first because of Wally's stubborn refusal to talk to him, then because he couldn't admit the truth, that Wally had done another runner and shut him out, leaving them to cope with this supposedly *normal* sheep.

It was Dr Shenanigan who had driven down to London to rescue their sheep from the media circus while Stein was being debriefed by the police and army as well as by the doctors, who had signed him off work for a fortnight's drinking to help him cope with his post-traumatic stress disorder. And Shenanigan was proud of his inability to tell one sheep from another, or even the sheep from the goats where the horned varieties were concerned, telling anyone who didn't ask how he was Clovis's computer whiz-kid not a cloven hoofspotter.

Immediately he returned from sick leave Stein had started boasting to her about this *new relationship* he now had with Wally, not giving a moment's thought to how Holly might feel about this development, but his mood turned very quickly from elation to sourness. He must have realised rightaway that this black ram wasn't Wally, but he wasn't going to admit it, not even to himself. He should have known that Wally wasn't going to come meekly trotting back to Clovis to be shut up in a pen when he had all his plans for world peace to carry out. According to the news, there had been unexpected developments in Battymanistan, and the more astonishing these became, the more likely it seemed to her that the real Wally must have played some role in these upheavals.

Of course *she'd* known all along that the black ram couldn't be Wally. She'd had no response that first afternoon to her tentative whispers, and as soon as the scientists had all left, she began chiding him gently for not responding, suggesting that he too, like Stein, must be stressed out after his ordeal. And she'd wanted to talk to him so much, after everything that had happened. She'd expected him to be careful of course, guarded even, but imagined he would just throw caution to the wind and blurt something out, because he wouldn't be able to help it, such would be his eagerness to talk – at last – with another sheep. Even if it was just a question about *Anna Karenina*, the syllabus book for that week, she'd expected him to say *something* to her, if only to test the water. But when she got no response at all to her opening gambits, it was she who'd started the blurting out, but everything she called over the pen barrier was met either with silence or a bemused *mairrr!* And when she finally had an opportunity the following morning in the field to examine him more closely, she knew from the way he came bounding up to the dividing fence that he wasn't inclined to conversation, he only wanted her for sex. She was *so* disappointed. Not only was there no sheep to talk to but no Stein either, and she was stuck with this grunting testosterone-driven impostor for company.

So she almost whinnied with glee as she witnessed the ginger guard's next move, which was to sweep a pair of electric clippers across the truculent ram's belly, neatly peeling back the whole black fleece. But then he slipped what looked like a large ribbed vest under the animal's fleece around its entire girth, and instead of completely shearing him, the man produced a needle and thread and proceeded to sew the fleece back along the neat cuts he'd just made.

She'd thought at first that he was going to just shear the ram, and she was looking forward to poking fun afterwards at the beast's shrunken appearance. But he wouldn't have needed to sedate him to do that, for this ginger guard was ginger in his movements too, well adept at handling sheep. And why should this man be shearing sheep in any case, in the middle of the night? That couldn't be part of a security guard's job description, even at Clovis. Yet so much of what went on didn't make much sense to her, not just in the laboratory but in the wider world.

Whatever his reasons for fitting the ram with this strange-looking undervest, these were unlikely to be above board. She noticed when he'd started up the electric shears how the guard kept looking over towards the door and up at the clock on the wall, and thought perhaps that the fleece might be valuable, that this man was wanting to sell it, possibly for one of the tabloid newspapers to offer its readers in a competition; yet whatever special value it had would be as Wally's fleece, and this ram wasn't Wally. And then he'd proceeded to sew the fleece back on.

She was sure the man's motives must relate in some way to Wally because he wouldn't have gone to all this trouble of fitting the sheep with its own vest if he'd known that it wasn't Wally the clone, Wally the nation's Sheep of Hearts, Wally who was doubtless somewhere else right now doing his own plotting and scheming. No, this was meant to be Wally's vest, and if, as seemed likely, it was intended to restrict the sheep's behaviour or movement in some way, she wasn't going to complain.

On the other hand, this guard was a security man, so perhaps the vest was meant to be protective? It looked padded so it could be a bullet-proof vest, and perhaps the man's look of secrecy and furtive concern related to the undercover nature of his task: he'd had to come in at night because no one was meant to know that the sheep would be wearing a bullet-proof vest; either that or he should have done the job earlier on in the day but had been drinking whisky with the other security guards at the main gate booth. She knew that went on because Stein had frequently complained about the inflated prices charged by the men on the gate for his Johnnie Walker and White Horse whisky, how they took advantage of his inability to keep his house and office well stocked, because he would always drink what he bought; if he bought more he would drink more, and to ensure he'd be fit for work he would always pay more and drink less.

From the way the man was pushing at the vest as he slipped it round the ram's belly, it looked as though it must be as bulky as a heavy sweater, and it was certain to cause its wearer some discomfort, if only from the weight. Still, whatever the man's reasons for fitting the sheep with its undervest, his plan must be unworkable because it was founded on the premise that the ram was Wally. But since the sheep was actually this insufferably boorish impostor sheep, she could take some pleasure in watching *him* suffer for once, after all the grief he'd given her. She expected the garment would be especially uncomfortable in the heat, and looked forward to seeing the ram's pained expression as it lurched about like a mad cow, unable to tell Stein what was really wrong with him. But if this creature thought that *she* might say something on his behalf, he was mistaken. He'd shown no mercy to her, and she wasn't about to reward him for his ungentlemanly behaviour.

Moreover, if someone tried to shoot Wally, probably on the jaunt to Buckingham Palace, the bullet-proof vest wouldn't offer any protection to Wally because it wouldn't be Wally they were trying to kill but his double.

*

PETER PORCUPINE, MIDDLE EAST CORRESPONDENT:

This is the man some say has engineered the overthrow of the fundamentalist Batty régime in Battymenarbad. Or is it? For this man will not give us his full name, he just calls himself Walid, nor will he show his face. When he appears in public a square of green muslin is wound round his head, and his nose and mouth are always covered bandit-style with a green handkerchief. These pictures show him rousing a crowd to action. They may only have sticks and pitchforks but these people stormed the last stronghold of the Batty régime yesterday and captured all the cornered clerics.

But now look at these other pictures, brought to you by satellite from the northern city of Mukh. Again, this is a crowd who marched on the mullahs, and jogging alongside them, yelling encouragement, is another green kerchiefed activist who also calls himself Walid. There is not just one Walid, he says, we are all Walids, we are all leaders in this people's revolution.

I managed to speak to Walid, although which one of these Walids it was I can't say, by satellite phone, and he told me it didn't matter whether there was one Walid or a hundred Walids, they were all Walid, and Walid had been working with the people at grassroots level all the time the fruitless diplomatic discussions had been taking place. No one had spoken to the *people* of Battymanistan, not even the United Nations' special envoy, and especially not the Americans who were only attacking his country to seize its oil riches, and all their talk of rebuilding only disguised the real objective of their war-mongering, which was to open up new markets for McDonalds and Burger King. But the Americans could keep their burgers and their bibles, said Walid, for now that the ruling Batty party had been kicked out, and they'd done their *own* régime-changing, the former Men's Republic of Battymanistan – now a people's state renamed Shamanistan – posed no threat to anyone, which meant the Americans no longer had any justification, with or without a UN mandate, for invading his country, especially since conclusive proof had now been shown to the weapons inspectors that *all* the weapons of mass destruction the former Batty rulers had bought from British and American companies had been sold to North Korea when the bankrupt government needed to raise more money on the foreign exchange market.

Several times in speeches attributed to Walid, references have been made to the writings of the early English feminist Mary Wollstonecraft, leading to speculation that the original Walid, or even one or other of the Walids who've been speaking in public, is a woman. And the new constitution of Shamanistan establishes not just equal rights for women but statutory rights for animals as well. This comprehensive document hasn't just been drawn up overnight. International lawyers who've been able to read extracts say that it is watertight in legal as well as philosophical terms, with one commenting that it showed a complete rethinking of the whole basis of judicial law, taking its bearings from Plato and Aristotle and from liberally interpreted Koranic law as well as – controversially – from the recently emerged Shaman religion or belief system, hence the inclusion of animal rights.

The fact that the newly installed provisional people's government of Shamanistan has been able to put in place a new constitution and introduce immediate legislation setting up democratic elections no later than next month casts doubt upon claims by the Americans that they took all possible steps to bring about a diplomatic solution to the Batty crisis before embarking on military action. American land forces are still waiting at the border, but as events take further unexpected turns in the now renamed Shamani capital Shamanisgud, it seems increasingly unlikely that the Americans will risk invading yet another Middle Eastern country.

In Washington and London the question being asked is: given the sophisticated nature of the new political system which the Shamanis have set up in place of the old Batty system of government, how was it that no one from the West took the people's opposition seriously before? Only last week one Pentagon official was said to have written them off as 'another bunch of wackos', because they were said to want blanket bans not just on beards and burkhas but on burgers, Coke and Pepsi.

It's now the early hours of the morning here in Shamanisgud and the people of the new people's democracy of Shamanistan are still celebrating. The women are burning their burkhas and dancing in the streets, and the men are all shaving off their shaving-brush moustaches or hacking off their matted and bedraggled beards. Alcohol was banned under the Batties, but already tonight I've been handed a can of beer by one of the locals, and I was delighted to see that it was our own Black Sheep Ale from Masham which I drink back home. Those Yorkshiremen have been quick to come to the aid of this beleaguered and thirsty people. I must say it's a very different city tonight to the place I drove through just a week ago when the only people on the streets were gun-toting militiamen. Those boorish and unpleasant men were firing off so much ammunition into the air that they must have run out of bullets at the same time as they ran out of time. The changes have taken place so quickly here, it feels like 1989 all over again. And tonight the unelected leaders of other countries in this region – the military dictators as well as the despotic mullahs – must all be waiting for the word from the bazaar or the word in the street. For if it can happen here, it can happen there, especially with all this week's astonishing events being broadcast live on the Al-Wazerkh TV network.

This is Peter Porcupine in Shamanisgud for PPTV returning you to the studio in London.

Fuck, we're not still on the air are we? Jeremy, you arsehole. I know there's a satellite delay but you said the little red light meant the recording was… I've not just said fuck on the air have I? Fuck, fuck, fuck…

NIGEL HAIRGEL, IN THE STUDIO:

…Thank you, Peter, and now we take you over to Amsterdam's Schipol airport where there has been a dramatic development in the Batty hijacking drama. Our Europe correspondent, Hans von Trauser.

HANS VON TRAUSER, EUROPE CORRESPONDENT:

That's right, Nigel. And they're now calling this hijack the mother of all stings, because this morning that gleaming private jet belonging to the Batties' spiritual leader Sheikh Rattlenroll took off from a military airfield outside the southern city of Khamel in the country then still called Battymanistan. Its destination, Cuba. On board were 52 key members of the old Batty régime, the whole pack, you could say, from the Sheikh of Spades to the 10 of clubs, who would be Peg-Leg Ali, governor of the northern province of Mukh, famed for taking a personal role in interrogations: this is the man who'd unscrew his own wooden leg and then use it to beat false confessions out of political prisoners.

As far as these Batties were concerned, they were heading for political asylum in Cuba, and they would've been able to follow their progress across the Mediterranean and the Atlantic on those little video monitor maps in the seat backs in front of them. But technicians had earlier rigged the monitors with preprogrammed flight charts and the plane was actually flying at half the speed shown, so that instead of taking 14 hours to reach Havana they reached Holland instead in the same time.

When Sheikh Rattlenroll came through to the cockpit to check on their progress, he would have chatted to members of his trusted flight crew, unaware that his usual pilots had been kidnapped and replaced by men wearing identical Raybans and black moustaches. He would have heard these substitute pilots talking to Havana's air traffic controllers, but those were Hispanic actors speaking with headphone prompts from Amsterdam's Schipol control tower.

As the plane touched down in the dark and taxied past airport buildings whose lights had been switched off so as not to give the game away by looking too obviously Dutch, Interpol's Javier Garcia spoke to the pilot, as you'll hear from this recording of a message relayed to passengers over the intercom: 'Welcome to Cuba, amigos. Please correct your watches if you have not already done so. The time in Havana is 12 midnight. The temperature here is a little cool for this time of year because we have just had a hurricane pass by. As our honoured diplomatic guests, you will not of course need to be troubled by customs. A coach will pick you up on the tarmac and take you to your luxury accommodation.'

That luxury accommodation, they soon discovered, was a high-security Dutch jail. And the reason for flying the whole pack of these Batty clerics, politicians, warlords and military commanders into Amsterdam is that the new Shamani justice minister has just given Dutch police a full set of indictments to be handed over with the men to the war crimes tribunal in The Hague.

Washington and London had been earlier tipped off about the sting and gave this complex operation their full cooperation, ensuring that the Sheikh's private jet was given safe passage to Schipol airport. The American ambassador was even present to witness the astonishment on the faces of the Batties as they were driven off in their armoured coach, but in a move which took Washington completely by surprise, the ambassador then found himself being confronted by Western-educated Shamani justice minister Huzamah Al-Hutzpah, who formally presented him with a multibillion dollar compensation claim against the American and British governments for damage and loss of life caused by their bombing of her country. And as the world's media swarmed and jostled to get the best pictures of the white-haired red-faced diplomat being harangued by the hot-tempered hazel-eyed sultry-looking justice minister, the raven-haired Penelope Cruz lookalike told him the American government needn't think it was going to get contracts for its political allies in the U.S. construction business, especially those companies who've had members of the current U.S. administration on their boards.

'The work will be carried out by Shamanis, and we are appealing to everyone who has had to flee our country to return as soon as possible to help us rebuild our nation. Thanks to the Shaman Development Fund, that reconstruction work starts next week, so we won't need to wait years to squeeze the money out of your legal system. We already have billions of your dollars, thanks to the unexpected and sudden generosity of your big corporations, but we are treating their assistance as an advance payment with the rest to follow. And I have this message for your President and for your Secretary of State for so-called Defence. You can keep your coke, your burgers and your freedom fries. We hope they rot your guts. We don't need you to liberate us by bombing our houses and schools and hospitals into rubble. So turn your tanks and ships around, get your filthy planes out of our airspace, and get back to your own *outpost of tyranny.*'

NIGEL HAIRGEL, IN THE STUDIO:

That was the Shamanis' new justice minister, the brainy stunner Huzamah Al-Hutzpah speaking tonight in Amsterdam. And thank you, Hans von Trauser for that report on what they're calling the mother of all stings.

Next we turn to the American response, and it would appear that Washington has finally got that unambiguous message from the new Shamani government. Reinforcements intended to bolster the ground attack have already been stood down. And the word from all our correspondents embedded with coalition forces is that the troops are unbedding their bedrolls and getting ready to move out. So those wagons would appear to be rolling. Here you see some grunts, as they call them, clambering into APCs, their name for armoured personnel carriers. And now here are some more pictures of American planes taking off from aircraft carriers in the Gulf to carry out more bombing raids on targets inside Battymanistan. No that can't be right, those must be library pictures of planes taking off because according to our correspondent embedded on board the aircraft carrier USS Thomas Jefferson Airplane, they've just called a halt to the bombing.

Over now to our chief political correspondent, Joshua Mosca in Washington. What can you tell us, Josh, about this Shaman Development Fund just mentioned in that speech by the new justice minister? And that reference to the 'unexpected and sudden generosity' of America's big corporations, what did she mean by that? Why should they want to help this new Shamani régime which is clearly unsympathetic if not antagonistic to American business interests?

JOSHUA MOSCA, WASHINGTON CORRESPONDENT:

Well, Nigel, that's a question now being asked in a lot of boardrooms. Shareholders of all the big corporations have been demanding

213

emergency meetings to demand answers from management who have been demanding immediate reports from their heads of security whose heads are sure to roll. And what the bosses are saying is that they *simply don't know* how this has happened, but the picture now emerging indicates that somehow the main four accountancy and auditing firms, the big four who together monitor the investment funds and bank accounts of most of America's big business – that's KPMG, Pricewaterhousecoopers, Ernst and Young, and Deloitte and Touche – all four of these apparently issued simultaneous computerised instructions on the stroke of midnight last night which effected transfers of cash amounting to point one percent of the total assets of all these companies, and that seemingly small percentage from all the multinationals wired to a numbered account in Switzerland has yielded a multibillion dollar windfall for this Shaman Development Fund.

What's more, the Shamanis claim they don't control this fund, they only receive payments from it, and given that the bombing of their country was led out by an American government financed by the same multinational corporations, they say they won't be giving any of it back. They're calling it profits for prophets, a global tax on military and corporate expansionism as well as an advance payment on the compensation due to them from the American and British governments. And there's not much anyone can do about it. The percentage involved affects corporate profits as well as payouts to shareholders of course, but it won't break anyone, even though many heads are bound to roll, especially at the four big accountancy firms, whose own security chiefs are right now being carpeted and hauled over the boardroom coals.

Computer experts are now saying the whole thing must have been orchestrated by a hacker working from inside the CIA's headquarters operation at Langley in Virginia. This man may have been working for the agency on a covert operation intended to assist régime change in Battymenarbad, but if so it clearly got out of control. The hacker's codename was Snowball, and British investigators are following up a report by the Americans that this man used an MOD firewall as a kind of shield to hide what it must have taken him some weeks to set up.

A single instruction from Snowball, using the password MBRAM – that's computer jargon for *megabytes of ram* – set off the whole web of transactions, with the cash *snowballing* in seconds, being collected *first* in the Swiss account I just mentioned, before *this* was divided between *a hundred bank accounts* in other countries, from where it will have been *moved* again, eventually being collected by the Shaman

Development Fund, whose *own location* has not been traced. Scams involving shifting bank transfers have been done before, but *nothing* on this scale, and nothing like this is ever *likely* to succeed again because *checks* have already been put in place. But of course those billion dollar *cheques* have already been cashed.

Whether or not this operation was authorised by American intelligence, or carried out from inside one of its agencies by a wildcat element, we may never know, given the shroud of secrecy which surrounds all those agencies which could have been involved, and given also the intense competition which exists between the CIA, the FBI and Britain's MI6 as well as between Pentagon officials and our own Ministry of Defence, which has often resulted in some of these agencies working against one another's interests either to score points over each other or in order to accrue more political power not to mention clout. One Pentagon insider I spoke to said he didn't think the American intelligence agencies could be directly responsible, although Snowball was clearly working with inside knowledge and either had or had gained access to classified information. He believes Snowball may well be the codename of not just one but a whole group of anarchist computer hackers including disaffected former CIA and Microsoft employees. But whatever Snowball's true identity, they're calling this operation the mother of all hacks.

CHAPTER TWENTY

Double Trouble

The scientists were transfixed. They'd switched on the TV expecting to see Manchester United *versus* Real Madrid, but the start had been delayed due to crowd trouble involving rival groups of English and Spanish Beckham supporters. Instead, they were now watching a man having a tub of brown slop tipped over him. This was the new Shamani reality television show called NMR-TV, in which anyone accused of fundamentalist distortions of religious writings was subjected to public humiliation. This part of the show was called McSlurry, a dig at McDonalds, but the runny treat on offer was not soft ice cream but liquid manure. Channel Five were running edited highlights, and pundits were suggesting that the format could be adapted for British audiences, pointing to the popularity of Noel Edmonds' green-slime booth. Viewers had squirmed but relished the use of maggots and worms on Sky's *Fear Factor*, and were used to seeing people plastered with creamy creamy muck muck on *Dick and Dom in Da Bungalow*, and they would surely welcome seeing yucky things used on disgraced politicians as an alternative to the kind of custodial sentences which had not encouraged Jeffrey Archer to be any less prolific or Jonathan Aitken to be any more plausible.

As well as being slimed, wormed and maggoted, the named and shamed were given a very public enema in which the brown fluid was seen to snake through a series of transparent glass tubes, setting off a sequence of bells, buzzers and whoopy-cushion farts, before being pumped up into a faucet above their heads which dripped it back over their faces. Encouraged by a wisecracking comedian, who kept up a rapid-fire punning commentary, the audience booed and jeered every stage of the cleric's public humiliation, and were finally invited to come up on stage to urinate over the man, this being done behind an opaque yellow screen but with the microphones picking up every splash and splutter. All the while, lines of text from the man's fundamentalist propaganda ran along the bottom of the screen, preceded by his name and the words BREAKING WIND.

The moral pointed up by the pantomimish comedian in a series of obscene jokes at the end of the foul-mouthed performance was that the shamed man had been *full of shit*, and now everyone could see how full of shit he really was. And he would never be able to show his face again in public or he would be greeted with the words called out by the audience at the end of each draining and shaming: 'SHITFACE!'

'And we thought the Batties were all nutters,' commented Donald Macannie drily. 'These new Shamanis look set to win the fruitcake competition.'

'But having your rectum open to public view seems preferable to me to having your hands or feet chopped off,' said Mark Gumption. 'Or your eyes gouged out.'

'Or the more straightforward beheading with the old curved sword,' said Sean Shenanigan. 'I'm sure I know which I'd prefer if the chips were down and they was buttered on the wrong side. What do you say, Frank? ...Frank?'

Frank Stein was not just smiling. He was grinning like a half-wit. He'd never imagined that unknowingly giving a sheep unlimited access to hours of satellite TV and *Eurotrash* repeats would have such unforeseen consequences in the reshaping of another country's judicial system.

'I think it's great!' he exclaimed, with a hysterical edge to his voice. 'And we should do it here. To all those lying politicians and their spin doctors, all those bigots stirring up racial and religious hatred, all those twaddle writers in the press, the moral right, the santimonious, the self-righteous Yanks, the arse-lickers and the media muck-rakers. Cover them all in their own shit. What a great idea! *I'd* watch it. But let's switch the thing off now. I don't want to watch the bloody football. Let's all get on with some *work* for Christ's sake. Just because Weisenheimer's away doesn't mean we *always* have to take advantage of that. What about those *tests*? No, bugger the tests. *None* of it matters. Not the tests, not the football, it's all bollocks.'

'Frank, you're being awfully melodramatic these days,' said Helen Brimstone, with an air of affected concern. 'And you seem *very* distracted. Are you on some kind of medication? Or is it the drink?'

'I wouldn't say our man's been taking a drop,' said Sean Shenanigan. 'You know our Frankie, you'd smell it on him. His clothes too. I'd say he's *on* the wagon, not off it, and that must be the problem. It's either that or the doctor or some woman has been getting to him. The liver or the lover.'

Frank Stein stared at his colleagues, not listening, or trying not to listen. He tapped his biro on the desk top.

'It's not like you *not* to be drinking,' said Dr Macannie. 'It almost makes me feel sorry for you.'

Stein shot a glance at the Scotsman, then muttered something under his breath the others couldn't catch.

'He's maybe missing the limelight,' said Mark Gumption. 'And no one's been trying to kill him, now he's the good boy. He's even had the same car for three weeks.'

Stein stood up and walked across to the sink, where he poured himself some water, downing the glass in two gulps as if it had been beer or whisky.

'A Micra,' said Sean Shenanigan, 'now maybe that's what's getting at him, buying a Micra thinking it was only going to be blown up anyway, and now being stuck with the damned thing. You should leave the keys in maybe, someone might steal it then, and you could get yourself another flash job. A BMW or an Audi perhaps, you'd like the feel of one of those I'm sure.'

'He's even got his sheep back,' said Helen Brimstone. 'You'd think he'd like having Wally back again. Just like old times. Though I dare say you're worried about him, you did seem very concerned over that dislocated jaw.'

'Shut it, will you,' said Stein. 'Just shut it.'

'Oh very nice,' said Macannie. 'He really is the gentleman. Don't let *Wally* hear you Frank or he might start thinking that's the way to behave with the lassies. I'm sure Holly wouldn't like that, not when…'

'It's *not* Wally!' Stein finally yelled, standing up. 'That sheep is *not* Wally. *That* sheep…' he bellowed, facing its pen, making the animal retreat backwards towards the feed trough in the face of such unexpected aggression from the usually placid scientist, '*that* sheep is the bloody impostor sheep, the one the Batties got from the city farm. The double. It's *not* Wally!'

With that, he sat down, leaving the others dumbstruck. And Holly began bleating in an agitated fashion, more out of shock than disapproval. So now the cat, or the sheep, was finally out of the bag. And perhaps they would get rid of it now and she might be left in peace.

'We know you've been stressed…' began Helen Brimstone.

'But it *must* be Wally,' offered Sean Shenanigan. 'I should know, I collected the beast in London. From those military fellows who'd rescued him, who were keeping him away from the reporters.'

'So now you're the sheep expert,' said Stein. 'Pull the other one. You can't tell the difference between a Swaledale and a Scottish Blackface, so how can you know one black crossbreed from another.'

'Oh that's unfair,' said Shenanigan. 'I know that one, the Swaledale has the light patch round the muzzle. Oh no, you're confusing me now, it's the other way round, so it is, it's your Scottish sheep has the lighter wool around the snout, I'd swear it.'

'*Quod erat demonstrandum,*' said Stein.

'So what are you saying?' demanded Helen Brimstone. 'If that's not Wally, where *is* he, who's holding him now? Not the Batties, they must be out of the picture now. Is it the ALF? Someone's not been blackmailing you, have they? Did something happen when they captured you, someone got to you? If you knew it wasn't Wally, why haven't you said anything before now?'

'I didn't want to face the truth,' said Stein simply.

'What truth?' asked Macannie. 'How do we know this isn't another of your flights of fancy, Frank? The sheep's long absence has wrecked your obsairvational resairch, that can't be working at all well now. Even we've noticed how oddly he's been behaving.

If anything he seems *less* intelligent now than when…'

'Because that sheep isn't just *less* intelligent, it's as thick as two short planks,' said Stein. 'Because it's not the same pigging sheep.'

'*Mairrr!*' blared the agitated impostor, as if he knew he was being talked about.

'Well I'm not convinced,' declared Macannie. 'I think it's *you* who've got the problems, not the sheep. You've not just lost your focus, you're losing it completely, Frank, I'm sorry to say. And if you mean to keep up this pantomime about the sheep not being Wally, I suggest we settle the matter by the simple expedient of having a DNA test done. That will settle it once and for all.'

'No,' said Stein. 'We don't need to do that. I'm just telling you, it's not Wally.'

'But a DNA test…'

'No DNA. We're *not* doing a DNA test. My integrity is being called into question now.'

'Integrity…'

'And I'm telling you it's not Wally. It should be obvious to everyone here that it's not the same sheep. It doesn't even *sound* the same, does it?'

'It *is* two years older,' Mark Gumption began.

'All of which proves my point,' said Macannie. 'The only reason you wouldn't want me to do a DNA test would be that you know it *is* Wally. You're just upset because the sheep hasn't lived up to your expectations. Like Dolly it's clearly suffered some kind of physical and mental deterioration.'

Holly rattled the grille, giving off a high-pitched *maair!* as if in agreement.

'The ears look a bit moth-eaten,' said Sean Shenanigan. 'I don't know much about sheep's ears but those ears look none too healthy to me.'

'It *isn't* Wally.'

'We'll do some tests then.'

'No tests. It's *not Wally*, and that's all there is to it.'

'Test it.'

'*What truth?*' Helen Brimstone interrupted. 'What did you *mean* just then, *you couldn't face the truth?* If that sheep *isn't*

Wally, what's happened to the *real* Wally?'

'I don't know.'

'Is this to do with something that happened in the embassy?' she persisted.

'Yes,' said Stein. 'And no...'

'Oh very clear,' whined Macannie. 'Now we're getting some clarity.'

'What I mean is...' Stein began. 'Oh I can't explain, but the upshot of it all is that Wally must have *switched places* with the other sheep. No one kidnapped him. But in all the commotion he made sure...'

'*He* made sure?' exclaimed Macannie. 'The sheep engineered this switch himself? Well you know what I think. I think that two weeks' sick leave was not enough, not that I believed then that you were suffering from any stress disorder, but now...'

'Maybe we should just do as Donald suggests,' said Mark Gumption. 'Do the DNA test. Then we'll all know where we are.'

'No.'

'There *is* something else you're not telling us,' said Helen Brimstone. 'I know you well enough to know that.'

'What he's not telling is that he knows the whole cloning experiment was a complete disaster,' said Macannie. 'We never got much out of Wally, even when he was here the fairst time.'

'That *isn't* Wally!' Stein spat back.

'There's an easy way to settle this,' said Macannie.

'*No.*'

Suddenly Holly rushed to the front of her pen, and kicked the grille several times, setting off a loud twanging through the wire mesh.

'*Why don't you believe Flank!?*' the ewe exclaimed, unable to contain her frustration any longer. 'Of *course* it's not Wally,' she called out from her pen. 'That bloody lam hasn't said a *word* since he got here. He is a velly thick cleature, he's a *weal* beast!'

The heads of the other scientists swivelled round in one movement. Dr Frank Stein stared at his feet.

'Oh dear,' he muttered.

'Frank...' said Macannie.

'And I want you to *move* him to another pen,' Holly blurted.

'One well *away* from mine! He keeps tlying to sniff my bottom thlew the glille. I tell him to stop but he takes no notice.'

'I know the problem,' said Helen Brimstone, staring first at Holly, then at Stein.

'And I'm *not* having him jumping on me,' the ewe continued in a shrill tone. 'Not when he can get at me in the field. It's sexual halassment in the workplace. You have lules against that at Clovis, don't you? Do you want me to speak to Liesenheimer about this? Because I tell you, I'm not *standing* for it *any longer!* And if he tlies it on again, I'll *blake* his jaw, I told Flank that before, and now you *all* know how I feel about this luddy lam. This damned lam who *isn't* Wally. Of *course* it's not Wally, you idiots!'

'Jesus...' said Mark Gumption.

'Oh now we've heard it all,' said Sean Shenanigan, 'a sheep with the brain of a man and the tongue of a woman.'

'Well actually,' said Stein, 'not a *man's* brain, not exactly...'

'My God, Frank,' said Macannie, 'you've really done it this time, haven't you? You've really excelled yourself. And if this young lassie hadn't felt pressed to pipe up when she did, when might you have chosen to acquaint us with the facts, Frank? And one presumes from this little outburst from our ewe that Wally *also* is capable of speech? That you taught him to talk as well as Holly?'

'I didn't teach him,' said Stein. 'He taught himself.'

'But what did you mean about Holly?' Helen Brimstone interrupted. 'What have you *done*? What did you *mean*, not a *man's* brain? I hope it's *not* what I'm thinking.'

'Well, Wally *was* mine, you could say. You remember how you worked out that way of starving nucleii from the Batty ram. After five days you'd frozen them into a quiescent phase of the division cycle...'

'Making them more susceptible to being reprogrammed, yes, go on...'

'Well, halfway through the cycle, I removed one pair of the ram's chromosomes at what I thought was the right moment of stasis, and introduced strands of my own DNA, taken from my own testes.'

'Oh my God, Frank.'

222

'Don't tell me,' cried Macannie. 'You gave the sheep your own human gene for intelligence and, let's see, language acquisition? Would I be right there?'

'Along with a few other things, yes. Those genes are what you might call multitaskers.'

'I'm not unaware of the nature of linked characteristics in genes,' said Macannie haughtily. 'It's just that I haven't tried to meddle with them myself, between man and beast.'

'You wouldn't know how to begin...'

'Don't make it worse Frank,' said Helen Brimstone. 'But what about *Holly*, Frank? How was *she* different?'

'Well she's a ewe of course, and so...'

'You are a *monster*!' Helen Brimstone exploded. 'How did you manage *that*!?' she demanded, and began to cry.

'Am I missing something here?' asked Sean Shenanigan. 'I thought it was Frank did the meddling, not you Helen. You're in the clear...'

'You *did* something, didn't you...' she accused him, and began crying. 'Something even *more* unethical, *wasn't* it, and you didn't even think to ask *my* consent? You really are a *monster*!'

'Mummy?' Holly called out. 'Are you my *mummy*?!'

Helen Brimstone tried to stop herself from looking at the ewe through her tears.

'Jesus,' said Shenanigan. 'If you made this up no one would believe you. And now I'm thinking that babbling sheep over there is following more of this than I am.'

'Try putting two and two together,' suggested Gumption.

'What did you *use* Frank?' demanded Macannie.

'A tampon,' said Stein. 'You may as well know. I could tell when you were, you know, *menstruating*, so I slipped into the ladies after you'd been in there, when I knew from the look on your face that you were having a heavy flow. I remembered how you were, you know, *heavy* sometimes, from when...'

'Genius!' said Macannie. 'DNA from Dr Brimstone's unfertilised egg cells.'

'I'm glad you think so,' said Stein, 'from the right chromosome of course.'

'I meant it *sarcastically*, Frank. Well, you've finally blown it now. You'll be struck off for this. And Clovis will be outcasts in the scientific community. We may as well pack our bags now and offer our services to the Raelian sect. *All* of us. Because when the excrement hits the fan and *you* get sacked – or do the right thing and *resign* – the *rest* of us will be tarred with the same brush, especially *poor* Helen.'

'Wait a minute,' said Sean Shenanigan. 'Am I *still* missing something here? Because this time I don't think it's me that's not getting it. Frank Stein has created what must be the world's first talking sheep. *Two* talking sheep. Intelligent sheep with intellectual capabilities. Indeed,' he added, gesturing towards Holly, 'intelligent sheep with *feelings*, something *almost* like human feelings, maybe even the same thing when it comes down to it.'

'Yes, it's monstrous,' said Macannie.

'And no one else knows?' said Shenanigan.

'Even *I* didn't know that Wally could speak,' said Stein. 'Not for a long time. Not till he chose to reveal it himself, when he engineered his escape.'

'The penny drops,' said Mark Gumption.

'Not just intelligent, and feeling,' said Shenanigan, 'but *cunning* and *clever.*'

'That's right,' said Stein. 'Takes after this father...'

'This is *amazing*,' said Shenanigan. 'We must be able to *do* something with this.'

'I don't agree,' said Macannie.

'Especially,' Shenanigan continued, 'with Weisenheimer not knowing anything. And *he's* not in on the act, surely?'

'No, of course not.'

'I agree with Sean,' said Gumption. 'We should be able to do something really *creative* with two such sheep.'

'One of which has gone AWOL,' said Shenanigan.

'And no one *else* knows about all this?' Gumption persisted.

'No one who's in the picture now. Except Lucy Giles.'

Helen Brimstone wiped her eyes, and looked suddenly cheerful. 'Not Lucy who promised on her *life* to keep in touch with *her* sheep? But who hasn't made *one* phone call to ask after him in the three weeks since the siege?'

'Yes, that had crossed my mind, of course,' said Stein. 'But I rather thought, having realised what Wally had *done*, making the switch, that he wanted, indeed *needed*, to be with her. And

I had to respect that, because of what he was doing, although I do admit I did feel left out, after all we'd achieved together. But seeing the evidence of what he'd managed to pull off since, I thought – I hoped – he'd call on me when he needed more help with anything.'

'*Help* Frank?' queried Shenanigan. 'You're losing me again.'

'What kind of help could a *sheep* possibly need?' asked Macannie. 'What *exactly* has this clever talking feeling sheep of yours been getting up to? I don't suppose he managed the negotiations with the hostage-takers?'

'Well since you ask, yes, he did. It was he who persuaded them to let us use their computer.'

'You taught the sheep to play computer games?' pondered Macannie. 'I did *wonder* about that, when I saw the two of you hunched over that PC on the news.'

'Very conspiratorial it looked too,' said Shenanigan.

'We weren't playing *games*,' said Stein. 'It was *real*. And it worked. It really really worked. You wouldn't *believe* what that animal is capable of, he really is an extraordinary beast.'

'What *worked* Frank?' asked Macannie.

'Snowball. The Shaman Development Fund.'

'The mother of all hacks?' asked Shenanigan, whistling, '*that* was the sheep? Holy Moses. Holy Cow. Holy Sheep...'

'With a bit of practical assistance from me.'

'I thought that was meant to be the CIA,' said Macannie. 'Or a rogue element in one of the other intelligence agencies...'

'A rogue sheep more like,' said Stein, 'a sheep who also managed to set up the CIA to take the blame, when it's usually them smearing everyone else.'

'I find this all very hard to believe,' said Macannie.

'But there's a logic to it,' said Sean Sheningan. 'A sheep cloned with the gene for intelligence from a barmy but fiendishly clever scientist? Who knows, perhaps this is where we get to learn more about lateral thinking, by mixing the species? Throw up the dice and see what comes down...'

'But the Shaman Development Fund?' Macannie persisted. '*That*, you are saying, is in some way connected with this?'

'Shaman. Sheep Man.'

'And the unexpected people's revolution in Battymanistan?'

'Now called Shamanistan. A sheep's revolution.'

'And this Walid character?'

'Wally.'

'Not the sheep in disguise surely? A shorn sheep sporting the symbolic green handkerchief?'

'Not himself in disguise. His ideas. Put into practice.'

'But all this has only just happened. You last saw Wally in London, that was three weeks ago. If it *was* Wally then.'

'It *was* him in London, yes. And I was with him on the Snowball part. The rest I've been piecing together since then, following the news.'

'And do *they* know the sheep's behind all this?' asked Gumption. 'Walid and the Shamanis? And the CIA? Are they not out hunting for the sheep right now, trying to get to him before we do?'

'Of course not. Wally was always very clear about that aspect. At first he talked about an alliance between sheep and man, but he realised no one would ever take him seriously, hence the anonymity of Shaman.'

'And no one *knows* that it's a sheep that's outwitted the Americans and their intelligence services?' asked Sean Shenanigan. 'That it was actually our black sheep who in effect made the Batties pack their bags for their Dutch holiday?'

'No, I'm certain of that. No one knows it's a sheep. Only Lucy knows anything about this. And of course everyone *else* thinks that Wally's back at Clovis, so if anyone else wanted him, they'd be looking for him here.'

CHAPTER TWENTY-ONE

Doubles All Round

LUCY. Hello, Gritstone Farm.

SEAN. Can I speak to Lucy Giles?

LUCY. Speaking. (*With sound of computer keyboard being tapped in the background.*)

SEAN. Hello, Lucy, this is Sean Shenanigan from Clovis. We wondered if we might have a word with Wally...with the sheep I mean. We're thinking he must be there, with you.

LUCY. You want to *talk* to a sheep? (*More tapping.*)

SEAN. That's right. Just a few words, if it's not too much trouble.

LUCY. (*Still tap-tapping away.*) You want to talk to a *sheep* on the telephone? You're not serious?

SEAN. To *our* sheep. *Your* sheep that is. Your sheep if that's what you prefer. Himself even, his own sheep.

LUCY. Are you mad?

SEAN. Oh come on, Lucy, you don't need to pretend. We know he can talk. Holly too. We've been having what you might call a frank discussion with Dr Stein, but now we need to talk to the sheep. I've got the speaker switched on here, so we can all hear him, Frank, Helen, Mark, Donald. We're all ears.

LUCY. (*Stops tapping.*) What about? What do you want to know?

SEAN. Can you not put him on? I'm sure he can answer for himself. Or so I'm told.

LUCY. He's very busy right now. (*More tapping, plus beeps.*) We're *both* very busy. Can you not leave a message and we'll call you back later?

SEAN. It is a little urgent...

LUCY. He's organising an international conference. (*More keyboard tapping.*) It's a rather complex business, involving sensitive matters, he can't just drop everything. And besides, this isn't the easiest of phones for him to use. The ear and mouthpiece arrangement don't really suit a sheep's head.

SEAN. Could you maybe speak to him for us, then? If he can't be interrupted. Dr Stein wants to know how he is, for starters. We all do. You know, after his ordeal.

LUCY. He's very well, if a little tired, because of all his work. (*Pause. Sound of whispering between girl and sheep.*) And he's *also* not a little surprised and hurt that it took you this long to realise that the other sheep couldn't be him.

SEAN. Frank knew, but he wasn't letting on. He didn't want to disturb your sheep's important work. It was Holly who let the cat out of the bag, you might say.

LUCY. (*More whispering.*) How *is* Holly? Has Dr Stein finished reading *Anna Karenina* to her?

SEAN. She's not been enjoying the company of our new friend, the other black ram, the fellow's a little too boisterous for her liking, not one for the talk. A bit too much like one of the lads. But Helen's taken over the reading now. She feels Holly's welfare will be better taken care of by her, and trusts that Wally – er, Sheep, that is – won't object. She has what you might call a *personal* interest in Holly's education now. (*Sound of background bleats and whispers.*) In fact, they're on to Chekhov already, but they want to know why there's no Thomas Hardy on the reading list, given that he has plenty of sheep in his books.

LUCY. (*Background murmuring.*) Sheep says Hardy's too fatalistic to be a good role model. Also, his sheep are stereotypes. In one novel he has a flock throw themselves over a cliff as if they were a bunch of human cult followers. (*More murmurs.*) And Sheep wants to know if Dr Brimstone's interest in Holly is as *personal* as Dr Stein's in himself, whatever that means.

SEAN. It is.

LUCY. (*Murmuring.*) Sheep offers Dr Brimstone and Dr Stein his personal congratulations, and hopes the whole family will be very happy. But questions whether there are other matters you wish to raise which are more urgent than his current project which affects world peace as well as stability in the Middle East. Sheep says lives are at stake. Every minute lost is a life lost.

SEAN. We want to help him.

LUCY. How help?

SEAN. We thought perhaps the facilities at Clovis might be better suited to his work than your bedroom.

LUCY. (*Indignant whispers.*) What, an animal pen with a feed trough? You can't be serious.

SEAN. We were thinking more that the computers, the research facilities, a team of scientists with a shared interest in his plans for achieving world peace. His personal accommodation could be adapted to his particular needs.

LUCY. (*Loud background whispers.*) Sheep wants to be sure this isn't just a trick to get him back to Clovis.

SEAN. We're scientists. We've seen what he's done.

LUCY. What about Weisenheimer, Sheep's asking.

SEAN. That's one possible spanner in the works. But...

LUCY. (*More whispering.*) No problem. Sheep says wait for e-mail on that one.

SEAN. E-mail?

LUCY. Dr Weisenheimer has been diverting Clovis funds for his own use for the past five years. Sheep's surprised none of you has been wise to Weisenheimer, especially when your research budgets have been directly affected. Sheep says you all crow about the shark's absences without ever questioning his lavish lifestyle, how he affords so many exotic holidays and other long trips. Plus two very expensive mistresses.

SEAN. (*Background whispers.*) Mistresses?

LUCY. No one you know. One in Paris, the other in New York. He'll send details of bank accounts and suchlike.

SEAN. What else should we be asking?

LUCY. One's quite a stunner, young and blonde, the other's a real dog, very stupid too. But you know what men are like...

SEAN. I meant about a possible move back to Clovis...

LUCY. (*Whispering.*) He will send you his conditions. But you'll have to wait a little, the conference...

SEAN. His conditions?

LUCY. (*Pause for series of whispers.*) Well for starters he wants to make sure that Dr Stein is appointed head of Clovis following Weisenheimer's resignation...

SEAN. (*Background whining.*) Dr Stein? Not Dr Macannie, he's next in seniority...

LUCY. No, he's very firm about that. No one else will do. (*More whispers.*) He says Dr Stein knows how to keep his mouth shut. Also, he'll let Stein take credit for the scientific side of things as long as he does what he's told. Macannie's too much of a wet blanket, he'd hold him back with all his questions, although there's a right place for those too. Clovis will still be seen as a scientific institute continuing its pioneering work in animal cloning as far as outsiders are concerned, but the really important work will involve covert operations, and Stein would be especially well suited to organising the secretive aspects. The rest of you have families and you'd find it hard not to resist telling them stuff.

SEAN. Anything else?

LUCY. Hang on... (*Frantic whispering.*) The computer equipment will need to be completely upgraded or replaced. The animal accommodation needs a complete makeover. No more vivisection or experiments which cause pain to live animals. A proper role for Holly, once her reeducation is complete. A job for me as his personal assistant after I've done my GCSEs. And security must be radically reorganised, especially on the computer side. Other conditions to follow.

SEAN. That's all going to cost, and I don't know that our present funding arrangements...

LUCY. All that will be taken care of. Subject to all his conditions being met.

SEAN. He seems to have had it all worked out beforehand.

LUCY. (*Background laughter.*) He was going to be in touch anyway after the conference had gone off. You've jumped the gun. But he's pleased that we're all apparently talking the same language. He'd thought he'd have to do rather more to get you on board.

SEAN. And will we all be invited to this conference of his?

LUCY. (*Loud shrieks.*) Of course not... The conference is for... bad people. He wouldn't want you anywhere near the place.

SEAN. But will he be all right himself?

LUCY. (*Low whispers.*) He won't be there either. However, he can't say any more about it right now. You'll hear about it when it's happened. It is a matter of some delicacy, and he asks you not to mention it to anyone, not to say anything, in fact, to any outside party about *any* of his activities...

SEAN. (*After background noise, including bleats.*) And the Queen?

LUCY. What about her?

SEAN. He's due to meet the Queen next week, to get his animal bravery award.

LUCY. I thought that was meant to be from one of her corgis.

SEAN. That's just the Palace trying to be media-savvy. They knew that would go down well with the *Daily Screw* and the *Sunday Twaddle*. No it's the Queen who'll give him the medal, I'm sure of that, though she'll have her wee dogs with her, for the pictures. Not sheep-biters I trust.

LUCY. (*Emphatic whispering.*) No, he's far to busy to meet the Queen. He has much more important things to do.

SEAN. He met the Prime Minister...

LUCY. That was the other sheep.

SEAN. Both times?

LUCY. I'm afraid so. Or so he says. He likes there to be an air of mystery about his appearances, keep everyone on their toes. And of course the Queen won't know any different, so you'll just have to use his double again.

SEAN. His double? The other sheep you mean, the mangy-eared one?

LUCY. Just like Saddam Hussein. He had not just one but many doubles. In fact Sheep's now thinking that he may have to use a whole gang of doppelgängers, his own flock of black doubles to confuse friend and foe alike.

SEAN. So Her Majesty the Queen only gets to meet the sheep's double... (*Voice of Dr Frank Stein heard in background:* Looks like it's doubles all round then. White Horse anyone?)

LUCY. (*More whispers. Tapping starts again.*) And he'll be in touch after that. But please, don't make contact again, wait till you hear from him. We haven't a minute to lose. Bye, everyone! (*Hangs up.*)

CHAPTER TWENTY-TWO

Double Topped

It is a large upstairs sitting-room in a luxurious country villa, the walls white, the bright sunlight outside shut out by black drapes. The outside temperature is over 50 degrees Celsius, but inside it is much cooler. An air-conditioner hums above the conversations of the robe-clad men, forty in number, but this does little to thin the veil of cigarette smoke which fugs the room.

This is the room the sheep imagines they will use, and he is not far off the mark. He could not have made a better choice himself. The thick black curtains have not yet been drawn because the men are not yet aware that they are to listen to the tape in darkness. The pair from London have only just turned the corner into the quiet street, the last to arrive at his conference. They are his emissaries, although they of course are unaware that they are pawns in his deadly game. Or so he believes.

Their white Audi skids to a halt. There are voices below, doors being slammed, then a squealing sort of sound, not a human voice but something like a sheep bleating; yes, it *is* a sheep. The animal sounds frantic.

This was not part of his plan. But perhaps these men have brought a sheep to be roasted after the meeting? They wouldn't know how much or why he would disapprove of this. And they would need a whole sheep to feed this many men. That is how they do things round here. They would tie it up outside, not slaughtering it till later, so that the meat will be fresh. They don't know that the conference is not to be a long affair. That the whole thing should be over in less than an hour if everything goes to plan.

But now there is more commotion, raised voices and more bleating from the stairs. The murmuring men in the room look towards the door. They feel safe, however, for their bodyguards are outside on the landing.

Now the two Londoners enter, dressed in similar, expensive, dust-smeared suits, bowing nervously in deference to the gathering at the same time as they struggle to haul a trussed black sheep into the middle of the room. The sheep has just been gagged again. The huddle of clerics stare at the bulging-eyed sheep, taking in the symbolism of the green handkerchief tied tightly round its muzzle, the same kind worn by Walid, by all the wretched Walids.

'I am Habib,' says the first man, rubbing his hands on his trousers to rid them of dirt from the sheep, 'and theese eese my brother Hossan. And *theese*,' he adds, pointing at the wriggling animal on the floor, 'theese sheep eese the reason why we are all here.' He kicks the animal sharply to discourage it from further struggle. 'You tell them, Hoss. You know full story.'

'OK. Leesen. My cousin he was one of martyrs keeled by Breetish soldiers when they storm Battymanistan delegation in London. He was from Mukh. And he speak to me during siege on heese mobile phone. You remember how our brothers had as hostages devil scientist Stein and heese clone sheep...'

'Walid the sheep of hearts?' asks one of the clerics.

'Wal*lee*, not Wa*leed*,' says Hossan. 'But no, maybe they are one an same thing. Maybe Wally eese Walid, I'm thinking now.'

'Theese sheep here,' says another beard. 'Theese eese not that sheep?'

'Yes,' said Hossan. 'Eese same sheep. The one with meellion pounce ransom on heese head.'

'That sheep eese worth a meellion pounce?'

'Because sheep can talk. Eese talking sheep.'

'A talking sheep? I don't belief it. Let us hear it talk then, my friend. What does theese talking sheep say, eh?'

'We have not yet spoken with it,' says Hossan. 'My cousin

say sheep haff silver tongue. It can talk its way out off any bad situation, as you will hear. So we haff to drug it. First in cage in plane and now in car. We do not want sheep talk to us, he is dangerous animal. He trick my cousin and other mens in delegation. That is why they were all keeled.'

'You are the one tricking us, my friend,' says Sheikh Abu Hamster al-Nasti, moving towards them to take over control of the situation. This is the Sheikh's house. 'What is theese all about?' he asks angrily. 'And where eese our leader? Why eese he not here? Why you bring sheep and not Onan Bin Khazi...'

'Our leader not coming. This was trick of sheep's, to bring us here. He want we keel ourselfs.'

'Bart why we keel ourselfs?' demands the Sheikh.

'Because our leader, he *tell* us to keel ourselfs, on heese tape. We must blow ourselfs up and we weel all be martyrs.'

'What tape eese these? Where eese tape?'

'We show you whole thing, Habib and I. And then you know what sheep has been doing to our peoples. In London I hear him on phone.'

'Theese sheep was making phone calls?' cries Abu Hamster with growing anger.

'No, I was talking to my cousin, and he tell me what is theese sheep. How it was cloned by Clovis scientist Stein working with our scientists in Battymenarbad...'

'Ah yes, we keel them. They were devils. It was a devil sheep they were making.'

'But my cousin say they use jeans from one off our Batty mullahs, a wise man. Theese sheep may be son off one off you mullahs here today. They give sheep heese jean for human intelligence and wisdom, and for holyness and language, and then sheep talk. I hear him talk myself...'

'This eese heresy you fool. None of us haff sheep for son. But if this eese that sheep, we should keel it now, eese work off Devil,' the Sheikh shouts, calling one of the bodyguards into the room. The stocky man pulls out his gun and points it towards the prostrate sheep, waiting to be told to shoot the animal.

'No, wait pleese. Listen. My cousin in embassy he hold heese mobile in air so I can hear sheep, and I hear theese strange voice which he tell me eese sheep's voice.'

'And you belief him?'

'But sheep was calling himself *Walid*, new Messiah off our peoples.'

'Holy sheep!' cries Sheikh Banana Thiksheikh. 'Now we have heard it all!'

'Listen, you can hear yourselfs also. Look, I switch my phone to record, and you can hear him for yourselfs now. There eese some background noise, but you can hear voice of theese sheep.'

Hossan is holding up a mini-recorder. He flicks a switch:

'Shaman is the twoo weligion of all Battymanistanis. You are all my bwothers, you gave me life in the first place....My other father was one of the holy men of your cuntwee, a gwate man who worked with your scientists. That is how I can speak. I have his DNA. What other animal has ever spoken? I am his miracle man-sheep...You will help me, you shall all serve Shaman, and your people shall be fwee. Not fwee in the decadent western impeerweal-ist sense of course, but fwee from the Amerwicans, fwee fwom the stain of sin. The Lamb of God shall be wedeemed thrwoo the Wam of God.'

'*That* eese Walid?' exclaims Sheikh Abu Hamster al-Nasti. 'No, it cannot be Walid. He eese man, or many mans, Walid eese not sheep.'

'But they take their name from him,' says Hossan. 'Theese Shaman revolution was heese idea, Shaman eese *Sheep Man*.'

'It was people's revolution is what they say,' Abu Hamster insists. 'They were misled, of course, by the Americans. That eese who make theese happen, it was CIA, they steal marneys also from McDonalds and Burger King, so new Shamani govern-ment suddenly haff marneys.'

'The *anti-American* Shamani government...'

'That was trick. Disguise. We know they in pockets off Amer-icans. How else they start people's revolution from nothing.'

'No,' Hossan says, 'theese sheep led whole thing, he gave them ideas, he set it all off, he got them marneys. Theese sheep eese maybe not Messiah but it's freak genius sheep. Eese like Trotsky or Che Guevara only he eese sheep not man.'

'He eese devil sheep if all this eese true. I still say we keel him.'

The bodyguard raises his gun, aiming it at the sheep's head.

'And he lead us all here also,' says Hossan. 'That eese what we try to tell you, to *warn* you of theese. All of us, we come here because sheep tells us, that eese why.'

'What do you mean, my friend, theese sheep lead us here?' says Abu Hamster indignantly. 'Our leader call theese meeting. We not here to talk about sheep but heese new nests of angels. Forty nests of angels. Each one of us to make new nest. He weel giff us good talk on that. Brilliant new psychological approach, he say, nothing like it before, everyone here know that. That eese why we come. He ask us all bring bomber's jacket, to show how we make sure peoples not see martyr wearing jacket lined with explosives.'

'We have all come here believing we weel hear our leader,' says Hossan. 'So when tape eese played we all think eese Onan Bin Khazi. We are not surprised our leader eese not here because no one can meet heem. We would not think eese trick. I was told I must not leesen to theese tape, first time I hear tape eese when I am here. But I am suspicious, remember I talk with my cousin before Batty delegation eese stormed.'

'Theese sheep he not know theese?'

'That eese right. So when I have tape, I leesen to it and then I know it eese trick. Sheep he not know that since embassy siege we watch Clovis, to find out what eese happening there, how it eese they have made theese talking sheeps and what eese connection with overthrow off Batties.'

'Clovis is CIA front?'

'Is possible. We also tap phones, and last week we record conversation between scientist and woman who help sheep with heese work. Sheep has fitted woman's phone with scrambling device which interferes with recording, but we have three sentences clear of interference when we make power surge. And now I can play you theese.'

By now the clerics are all standing round him, no longer angry but watchful. The bodyguard still has his gun trained on the gagged sheep. Hossan raises his mini-recorder and flicks the switch again. This time it is Lucy's voice they hear:

'He was going to be in touch anyway after the conference had gone off. You've jumped the gun...The conference is for... bad people. He wouldn't want you anywhere near the place...He won't be there

either. However, he can't say any more about it right now. You'll hear about it when it's happened...'

'But theese smart alec sheep has made it to heese conference after all. One week ago, Habib and I kidnap sheep. And this eese heem here. He try to trick us all. But we are smarter than sheeps.'

'Well I have heard enough,' said Sheikh Abu Hamster al-Nasti with an air of decisiveness. 'I think maybe you are right, my friend, about theese sheep tricking us. But I for one do not want to hear heem blabbering to save heese life. If he really has done all theese things you say, then we must keel heem now. Theese sheep eese not Messiah, he eese Devil.'

*

Graham Medlar is watching as the Queen approaches the sheep. He is sitting in a floral-patterned armchair, relishing the un-accustomed comfort of a plushly furnished hotel room paid for with the profit from the hot-dog sales. The hotel is in Queen Anne Gate, just behind Buckingham Palace, but he does not need actual sight of his target. He considers the elaborate steps taken by the Jackal to get General de Gaulle in his sights: the attic vantage-point, the complicated disguises, the dismantled gun hidden inside his crutches.

All he needs is to be within 2000 metres.

The presentation is being shown live, timed for the lunchtime News: the Sheep of Hearts meets Her Majesty the Queen, bumper brownie points for the Windsors and the Beeb as the nation's favourite animal makes a cameo appearance in their favourite soap opera. The commentator makes a catty remark about her late daughter-in-law being a less welcome guest, then backtracks, witters something cutesy about the people's princess.

Graham Medlar remembers the car crash in the tunnel, the paparazzi pictures on the front pages. And thinks how these will pale by comparison with what the whole nation is about to witness live. Their precious Queen being blown up by a sheep wearing a suicide bomber's jacket. Which he has sewn inside its fleece.

A palace official is trying to control the two corgis, who are pulling on their leads, trying to push through her Majesty's legs to where the explosive sheep is waiting.

Medlar hisses to the dogs from his armchair to stay back. He regrets the loss of the sheep, but thinks its death justified in the greater cause. But the Queen's corgis don't have to die too. One of the dogs has pushed through her legs and is yapping at the sheep. Her Majesty's skirt has been hoisted up by the lead. She steps backwards to hoik it straight.

Now, he thinks. Now she must move back *towards* the sheep, and maybe pat him on the head. She's hardly going to say to him, 'What do *you* do then? Oh how interesting.' But she must know the press will want their pictures. They'll want one of the sheep peering up at her, and the old lady smiling.

'Yes!' he cries. 'Now!' And pushes the button.

*

Sheikh Abu Hamster al-Nasti gestures to the bodyguard, who bends down to put the muzzle of his revolver to the sheep's head. The man fires six shots between the animal's eyes. The sheep is dead but its legs are still twitching. The guard reaches over to the table to where he has laid his AK-47 submachine gun, and as the others stand back to give him room, he starts firing a frenzy of shots into the sheep's body, unaware that the bulky animal is already wearing its own customised bomber jacket, the one neatly fitted by Graham Medlar under the black fleece. And the explosive charges sewn into the lining, while only meant to blow up the sheep itself and the person bending over it, will detonate all forty of the suicide bomber jackets which the delegates have obediently brought with them in order to receive new instructions in their use from Onan Bin Khazi.

*

The corgi yaps again, and bares its teeth.

'*Shut it* before I *bwain* you with my hoof,' growls the sheep.

'And *you* must be Wally,' says the Queen.

'My name is *not* Wally,' mutters the sheep in a low voice. Lucy pats him on the head.

'He doesn't like that name, Ma'am,' she tells the Queen.

'Oh really.'

238

'And what does he like to be called then?'

'Just Sheep.'

Prince Philip steps forward, wanting to be photographed with the pretty young girl; wanting a closer look at the creature.

'And what do you want to do when *you* grow up?' he asks.

'I want to help save the world,' says Lucy, smiling.

The Queen laughs, and turning to the sheep asks: 'And what do *you* do, Sheep?'

'I organise wevolutions,' he tells her. 'I bwing about the downfall of despots and tywants. That sort of thing.'

'Oh really,' says the Queen automatically, turning a huge smile towards her husband which the next day is plastered across all the newspapers, mirrored by the black sheep's wild grin just to the left. It is one of the news pictures of the year. The picture Graham Medlar had imagined was very different. He stares at the handset, cursing the man who sold him the device.

'Good trick,' says the Duke. 'Girl ventriloquist. Not many of those. Could go far.'

'Didn't you know that sheep can talk?' says Lucy.

'Cheeky thing,' says the Duke.

'Enough of that, Philip,' whispers the Queen. 'Mustn't put one's foot in it again.'

'Watch that bloody dog,' Prince Philip snaps, darting an accusing glance at the second corgi, now straining to reach the sheep, who has lifted a hoof in readiness to strike back.

'If the peasants can talk then why not sheep?' the Queen quips *sotto voce*, a comment picked up by the court correspondent's microphone. By the weekend, this playful remark will have become 'Quote of the Week' in the world's press. Even the new *Voice of Shaman* will carry the comment, accompanied by a picture of the sheep grinning at the British Queen. Sheikh Abu Hamster al-Nasti would not have found it funny.

CHAPTER TWENTY-THREE

Batty Men Are Bad Examples

NIGEL HAIRGEL, IN THE STUDIO:

We interrupt this programme to bring you some breaking news. There has been a big explosion in Shamanistan, just outside the holy city of Couscous. First reports indicate that this was something of an own goal for the Batty rebels holding out in parts of the country where there's still some diehard support for the old régime. Over now to our correspondent Peter Porcupine, who has just managed to reach Couscous. Peter.

PETER PORCUPINE, MIDDLE EAST CORRESPONDENT:

Well yes, Nigel, but it's not just Batty rebels who've been killed here. The blackened ruin you see behind me was once a luxurious country villa belonging to the extremist cleric Sheikh Abu Hamster al-Nasti, who's a cousin – who *was* a cousin, I should say – of the deposed Batty leader Sheikh Rattlenroll. This was one of the hubs of the Axis of Evil, where the Batty hierarchy and their henchmen used to come for week-end scripture and torture parties. And it was here, late yesterday after-noon, that some forty clerics and scholars, not just Batty mullahs but mad muftis and hook-handed zealots from all over the Middle East, arrived – all sporting banned black moustaches or white beards – for what they believed would be a high level hi-tech conference on suicide bombing. Locals are saying that the delegates were dropped off at the villa in ones or twos, and the cars bringing them then sped away at speed.

There was just one car left outside the house, a white Audi, that's the charred wreck you can see that's still smouldering over there, and that vehicle was the last to arrive. And from the boot of that car, two dark-suited men wearing identical moustaches and shiny Raybans were seen to haul the frantically struggling body of a trussed black sheep. Neighbours thought the sheep was either a sacrificial animal to be put to death in whatever bizarre religious rite these barmy bigots were carrying out, or else it was their dinner, a sheep big enough to make a spit-roast that would feed forty fat fundamentalist fruitcakes, or more likely both, because once these men had ritually slaughtered this black sheep there was no reason why they shouldn't serve it up as their conference dinner.

But there were to be no after-dinner speeches at this grisly gathering, for the story the Shamani investigators are now piecing together – as they carry out the grim task of piecing together the remains of the doomed delegates to this conference from hell – is even more extraordinary than that unlucky black sheep meant to be mutton on their menu. For these unholy clerics were the men – the main players you could say – who ran the Middle East's notorious network of suicide bombing schools, what they call, in their grim parlance, their nests of angels. And they had all come here at the personal invitation – so it is believed – of the fugitive fundamentalist leader Onan Bin Khazi, who was expected to be here to give them a pep talk on how best to groom their gullible young gudgeons into willingly and happily blowing themselves and other innocents into smithereens in the interests of world peace and getting picked for the martyrs' heavenly eleven whose players get to deflower half the virgins in paradise.

Instead, they found themselves asked by Onan Bin Khazi – speaking to them on a sinisterly persuasive tape – to don the grim garb of their pupils, the so-called martyrs' shrouds they're said to be *still* wearing as they enter heaven. For each delegate had been asked to bring a fully-armed bomber jacket with them to the meeting, to be shown new ways of making these gruesome garments less detectable. And dressed in their suits of death, they lay down on the floor in the dark, and listened to the hypnotic voice of their spiritual leader.

First they would have sent their bodyguards next door and told them to be silent. Drawing the curtains, they switched off the air-conditioning, and as the heat rose and their trusted leader's voice droned on, they would have found themselves catching their breath, forty men lying together in the one room. All had been told to bring bunches of jasmine, whose sweet scent would mix in the air with their sweat as well as with the fug from the high-tar cigarettes they'd have been smoking. And soon OBK's relentlessly hypnotic voice is playing them like a master

conductor, weaving his words through their minds until they are playing the music of their devotion back to him. He puts them inside the
minds of their martyrs, so they can understand how their pupils feel
at the precise moment when they give their lives in their holy war,
how cold they feel as they kill themselves and everyone else who's
standing around, maybe staring at them, maybe just going about their
lives, not knowing what's about to happen.

That's right, the Shamanis are saying that this tape effectively took
these clerics inside the minds of those they groomed for death, and
after listening to the lulling voice of their own teacher for approximately 20 to 25 minutes – probably not to the very end of the speech,
the last ten minutes of which is a repetitive replay designed to rein-
force and drive home its murderous message – one of the men must
have pulled the toggle on his jacket in order to enter heaven himself,
probably wanting to take his colleagues with him on this team outing
to paradise.

Experts who have listened to the tape have compared the psychological techniques used by the speaker with those of the Reverend Jim
Jones, who persuaded a thousand of his followers to commit suicide
with him at Jonestown in Guyana in 1978. There are also apparently
parallels with brainwashing methods used by the Japanese cult leader
Shoko Asahara whose Aum Shinrikyo cult members released canisters
of Sarin nerve gas on the Tokyo underground in 1995, killing twelve
and injuring over five thousand people.

There was some speculation at first that the tape had been produced
by the CIA, but voice analysts say they are 99% certain that the distinctive guttural voice on the tape is that of Onan Bin Khazi, who had
been thought to have been killed or possibly seriously injured in an
American missile attack on a cave network in mountains north of Mukh.
A copy of the tape was sent to the Al-Wazerkh TV station, presumably by someone in Bin Khazi's entourage who must have feared that
he too might soon be offered a one-way ticket to paradise.

Voice experts also say that this tape had been copied over an episode
of The Archers, and there was a snatch left from that programme's
jaunty signature tune at the very end, ten minutes after the last words
of the 35-minute speech. The CIA of course would never have allowed
what seems like an oversight on the part of the person making the
recording, whereas such an error might well have been possible in
the kind of chaotic recording conditions available to the fugitive cleric,
who would have had to avail himself of whatever tapes came to hand.
If he had replayed this one right to the end he might well have decided

not to bother trying to erase those couple of bars of *Archers* music because the whole point of the tape was that it would be played once, and once only, and if the tape achieved its desired brainwashing effect then the tape recorder would have been blown to pieces, along with all its listeners, long before that point was reached.

Now Onan Bin Khazi's tape of death has already been played in full five times today on the Al-Wazerkh TV network, and you can imagine the effect that this is having on support for the fundamentalists throughout the Middle East. They are playing it over pictures of Sheikh Abu Hamster al-Nasti's still smouldering house, together with uncensored scenes of the carnage inside too grim and ghastly for the stomachs of our viewers, and underneath are some wise words of caution: BATTY HEALTH WARNING, DON'T TRY THIS AT HOME. And of course Al-Wazerkh's viewers have been hearing the *whole* tape, including the last ten minutes of Bin Khazi's chilling speech which the mixed-up and soon-to-be minced mullahs wouldn't have heard because they'd have been blown to kingdom come by that stage. And what the commentators are saying is: how could these supposedly wise clerics have gone along with OBK's message of death? They agree that they weren't there themselves of course, and the tape certainly shows that Bin Khazi made sure the conditions were right for his deathly siren song to work, with the explosively dressed clerics being asked to pack themselves like sardines shoulder-to-shoulder on the floor of a hot and darkened, oxygen-starved, jasmine-scented room, but these barmy bigots fell for it like lemmings.

I spoke to the Shamanis' dishy justice minister Huzamah Al-Hutzpah earlier when she visited the scene of the carnage:

'People throughout the Middle East are asking why our young people should fall for the same lie as these men who were their teachers. Why should they take their own lives and others with them in the cause of a deathwish martyrdom which is nothing but a medieval fantasy, a wishful fabrication no less ridiculous than your Catholic Church's invention of a burning Hell policed by pitchfork-wielding devils with horns and forked tails? You ask me why Onan Bin Khazi should want his own people to die? You could have asked the same question at Jonestown and Waco. Bin Khazi does not care about human life. The lives of his followers mean no more to him than the lives of all the innocent people killed when these dupes blow themselves up. And now here we see the logical conclusion of Bin Khazi's teachings. He tells his followers to blow themselves up and these boneheads fall over themselves to oblige him. And *boom!* they are all gone. But at least the young people who would be the pupils of these men can see through them now. A myth has been exploded here in Couscous. Never again should anyone be duped by these nutcases. Good riddance is what I say. But I feel sorry for their sheep. The sheep had no choice when they took him with them. And it is the same with all the people these vipers have killed or maimed.'

The remains of about sixty bodies have so far been recovered from the rubble. As well as the forty clerics, these are expected to include twenty or so bodyguards who were probably watching television in another room when Sheikh Abu Hamster al-Nasti's house exploded in one massive fireball. Neighbours have told me that when the explosion happened, they were all watching *The Simpsons*, which was banned under the former Batty régime. Given the popularity of that show here since the revolution, it seems likely that the bodyguards also were watching the explosive antics of the cartoon family when one of those mullahs tugged the fatal toggle. And you can imagine what Homer Simpson would have said in response to that little mistake...'D'oh!'

CHAPTER TWENTY-FOUR

Any Other Business?

The sheep had stretched out his whole body along Dr Steve Weisenheimer's Louis Quatorze chaise longue, using the curved, curlicued armrest as support for his head.

'This weally is wather comfortable,' he was saying. 'This couch could almost have been designed for a sheep. But maybe we should cut off the spindly legs and weeplace them with something sturdier.'

The scientists looked at him from the conference table. Lucy sat at one end, sharpening her pencil to take notes. Dr Macannie was already having second thoughts.

'See,' said the sheep, 'you can all sit there and weed thrwoo my pwoposals. And I can addrwess you fwom the comfort of my couch. I can issue *all* my orders fwom here. I must say it does feel wather decadent. The coffee table can stay: you can put my food on that. But you can junk that old armchair. Verwee impwactical. Unless you want it, Stein?'

'It is antique,' said Stein. 'Queen Anne I believe. Weisenheimer had taste as well as money. But if you don't want it...'

'You have it, Stein. And Holly has the twolley.'

'The tlolley's velly neat,' said the ewe. 'Look I can shoot acloss the loom if I push with my hoof like this flom the table.'

'Verwee imprwessive, Holly. Now to business. First item on the agenda?'

245

1: CONFERENCE POST-MORTEM

'Wight,' said the sheep. 'You've all wed my weeport, and we've weviewed the pwess coverwidge. So what worked and what didn't? What has to be imprwooved in the future?'

'You're surely not going to try the same wheeze again,' asked Sean Shenanigan. 'No man steps in the same dogshit twice, isn't that what they say?'

'Not the same twick,' said the sheep. 'Each dollop of dogs' doo-doo needs its own appwoach. We have to understand how people live in each oppwessed cuntwee, what makes them tick, if we're to help them out of the particular mess they've got themselves into. But there are common techniques we can adapt. The voice simulation for example. That seems to have worked a tweat. Those fundamentalist fwootcakes all fell for it. They all thought my computer-altered voice was Onan Bin Khazi.'

'Well they certainly didn't think it was a sheep, that's for sure,' said Sean Shenanigan. 'And you managed to get that wobble on the old R corrected.'

'The software was pwitty good,' said the sheep. 'You have to hand it to the CIA, there are some things they do warther well.'

'So you stole that from Langley?' asked Macannie, with a low whistle indicating grudging approval at least. Perhaps Shenanigan's idea of collaborating with Stein's sheep wasn't so ridiculous after all. 'And may I ask,' he added, 'how you managed to copy Onan Bin Khazi's voice patterns?'

'That was mostly Lucy's doing,' said the sheep, nodding towards her. 'We had to find as many weecordings of him as possible, but fortunately Langley had lots of them we could download, including one two-hour speech in which he wails against the eating of uncooked goats' testicles. That's not been played much in the West because it had no political interwest, but the voice wange on it was wather helpful.'

'And how did you get into Langley's database without them smelling a rat?' asked Gumption. 'Or should it be a sheep?'

'Easy-peasy,' said the sheep. 'They think I'm one of their field operwatives now. They've even started paying me: I only worked that one to see if I could, and they fell for it too, and Lucy's Post Office savings account has reaped the benefit of their incompetence. So the Batties may be wight about that after all. If the CIA are paying me now, then perhaps they are weesponsible for what happened. Except they're taking orders fwom me under some of my other schemes.'

'From a sheep.'

'Pweecisely.'

'What about your double?' asked Shenanigan. 'That seems to be the main spanner in the works. How did our guest sheep end up on the Couscous menu? After just disappearing from here. If that *was* our sheep, but given that Batties keep trying to kidnap that same sheep…'

'…the wong sheep…'

'It does seem likely that the black ram – the former hostage – was our man in Couscous. And now the poor fellow's finally been minced.'

'Yes, I've been wacking my bwains over that one…'

Holly raised her hoof to speak. 'I think I can help you there,' she said with a slight quaver to her voice. 'The black lam went to Couscous for his holiday. But those two men seem to have tlicked him.'

'What two men?' asked Stein.

'I didn't think they wanted to kill him,' she added, 'or I would never have told them where he was.'

'What men?' Stein repeated.

'They walked in one night after you'd all gone home,' said Holly. 'One of them came up to my pen, and he was saying "Where eese that sheep, he must be here." So I asked him which sheep he meant. He didn't seem at all surplised when I spoke, so I assumed it must be all light. They said they'd come to take Wally on his holidays. That smelly black lam had been giving me such a hard time, so I thought, well, I can't help them with the leal Wally, but if they took the lude lam instead, I'd have some peace from him for a couple of weeks, and they plobably wouldn't know any differlent.'

'And you didn't think to mention this to anyone?' asked Stein incredulously. 'Especially when we were running all over the place looking for him.'

'You told me not to say anything.'

'I did not. I know nothing of this.'

'You did. Dr Shenanigan too. He said: "If that bloody ewe doesn't shut her mouth for five minutes I'll go over there and shut it for her. I've never known a woman with a mouth like that one's got, let alone a bloody sheep. I'll stlangle her meself, with me own bare hands." And Dr Gumption said I was a worse nag than his wife. And Dr Macannie blamed you, Flank, for teaching me to talk, and said you should have known better. I was velly upset. I thought you liked to hear me talking. That I was your darling Holly. I didn't like being called a nag. A nag's an old horse, isn't it, one that no one wants?'

'There there Holly,' said Helen Brimstone. 'We all love you, we really do. You weren't to know. But afterwards, might you not have said something later?'

'I liked it at first, him not being ailound. I had some peace and his yucky farts were leally glose. But I didn't think anyone would harm him. And when he went off on his holidays, you persuaded Wally to see the Queen instead of him. And Wally had finished organising his conferlence, and then he was going to come back here. No one thought the smelly sheep was so important then...'

'Well that seems to clear up that small matter,' said Sean Shenanigan.

'But listen, Holly,' said Helen Brimstone softly, 'if anything like that should *ever* happen again, please, you *must* let us know. These people are very dangerous. They're not like sheep.'

'All light.'

'So we know now it *was* our ram,' Shenanigan continued, 'but not how those fellows breached security. How they got into the pen and then got a live sheep out of the building without any-one spotting anything.'

'Oh I gave them the code,' said Holly brightly. 'They said someone must have changed it without telling them, and I thought that must have been the other man. And the black lam was not just asleep. You'd given him some dlug to put him out. They said they wouldn't need to wake him.'

'What other man, Holly?' asked Helen Brimstone quietly, trying not to show any impatience.

'The led-haired man. The securelitty man who sheared him.'

'But we don't have any red-haired guards. And the ram wasn't shorn.'

'This man sewed the fleece back on. After he fitted him with his new jacket. I thought afterwards it must have been for his holiday. But he did find it velly uncomfortable, and when he was lurching around the next morning, you gave him some dlugs. Dr Macannie said our sheep must have the wind. Don't you *lemember*? After that he was *farting* all day, till Dr Shenanigan knocked him out with some other dlug, saying if the sheep pumped any more, someone would just have to stlike a match and the whole building would explode. When the other two men allived later, he was snoring like Dr Gumption does. So they didn't have any tlubble with him. They just heaved him onto the tlolley and went off with him down the collidor.'

'Now let me get this straight,' said Stein. 'A red-haired man fitted the black ram with a jacket and then sewed the fleece back over it...'

'And given the covert fashion of the ram's bespoking,' said Shenanigan, 'I think we'd be right in concluding that our ram was then primed to be more than prime mutton.'

'Check,' said Stein.

'Also that this ginger fellow believed the ram to be Wally.'

'Check.'

'But having red-hair he was unlikely to be Batty-born.'

'Check.'

'Unlike our other two visitors. Who would also have assumed that the black sheep was Wally.'

'Check.'

'But might not be aware that their meat was ready to explode its juices in the mouth.'

'Checkmate. Boom boom.'

'Please make a big note, Lucy,' said the sheep. 'Major weview of securewitty wequired at Clovis.'

'Tick.'

2: CLONING: CREATION OF NEW MASTER RACE OF SUPER-INTELLIGENT LINGUISTICALLY-GIFTED SHEEP

'Item 2?' queried Helen Brimstone. 'This isn't another one of your sheepy jokes then?'

'I did intend a certain iwony in the wording,' said the sheep, 'to help concentrate our minds on the long-term task.'

249

'In short, you want more uppity sheep to boss us around,' said Mark Gumption huffily.

'Not at all,' the sheep insisted. 'We're a team. We all have differwent things to contwibute to the new Shaman-Clovis plan for world peace. It's a team effort. But as Sean has pointed out, cloned intelligent sheep have a special aptitude for laterwall thinking. We also need the wight kind of matches. If Stein hadn't been who he is, I wouldn't be who I am...'

'And without Helen,' Macannie began, with an air of calculated sarcasm, 'Holly wouldn't be...'

'Hang on there,' Helen Brimstone interrupted. 'Holly hasn't the right start. She's still quite young too, so you have to make allowances...'

'Ah yes, with the *right* kind of parental guidance...'

'But you needn't worry,' the sheep told Macannie, 'we can cross you with a Scottish Blackface and see what that produces. That'll put horns on you. Even if it's overcautious, you can be sure it will be a hardy beast. They make Harwis Tweed from its coarse wool you know. Imagine getting your next new jacket fwom your own offspwing.'

'And with you teaching it, Donald,' said Sean Shenanigan, 'your own Scottish Blackface will have the Scottish accent too.'

'But no, I'm seerwious,' said the sheep. 'The Scottish Blackface quickly becomes hefted on moorland, it is known for that particular aptitude. There is a special kind of intelligence at play which enables that sheep to weemember the terwain of its own stwetch of hills, and that knowledge is passed on from generwation to generwations of sheep. The Scottish Blackface is never lost. It also has a certain stubbornness which suggests it may well be just the wight bweed for you. In Dr Gumption's case I would wecommend a match with a Suffolk, which is a stocky meat-producing sheep usually used to sire the kind of fat lambs which humans like to eat. Our sturdy Suffolk is good for bweeding fwom and has a podgy face a bit like Dr Gumption's with similar squashy ears. I'm less familiar with Irish sheep but I'm sure we will find the wight varwiety for Dr Shenanigan.'

'Don't we need to broaden our breeding stock?' asked Stein. 'Go outside for a few clones. Not just use scientists.'

'How about the Plime Minister?' Holly piped up. 'All sheep

have ears that stick out, so no one would know our sheep was his clone.'

'But the gene for ear shape's not the same as the one for intelligence, Holly,' Stein told her.

'That explains a few things.'

'How about Tom Cruise?' suggested Helen Brimstone. 'He'd make a good sheep.'

'He's American,' said Stein. 'It's intelligence we want. We don't want smarmy sheep.'

'But I'm Irish,' said Sean Shenanigan. 'And I'm having me own sheep.'

'You're a scientist with a brain.'

'But I'm the black sheep of the family, getting the Leaving Cert and all that. The rest of them never had much up here, they all stayed on the farm. I'm probably just a mutation. What if the family line is dominant? I'm not sure I'd want a sheep that was only interested in betting on the horses and drinking the Guinness.'

'However our superclones develop,' said the sheep, 'you have to weemember the time frame. And how this makes anything achievable. By the time you humans have worked out how to climb out of your cots, the sheep is fully capable of looking after itself. So imagine what that combination means, man and sheep. All our sheep – all *your* sheep – will be able to play a full part in our world-changing Shaman-Clovis plan by the time they're two years old. Maybe even sooner if we can fast-twack their education. So we need to consider education at our next meeting. Education education education.'

'Where have I heard that one before?' said Gumption wearily.

'Ah, but *he* wasn't talking about sheep…'

'You could have fooled me.'

3: World Peace

'What's the next country they're wanting a war with?' asked the sheep.

'North Korea I think,' said Lucy.

'Then we have to addwess that one next,' the sheep told them. 'Sort the North Korweans out before the Amerwicans start sticking their unwanted noses in there. Newtwalise their nuclear capability. If we're going to wid the world of all nuclear weapons, we have to start somewhere, so it may as well be Pyongyang. Do they have sheep there?'

'I think it's monkeys they like,' said Shenanigan. 'They eat the brains you know, with a spoon through a hole in the table, while the little fellows are still alive, sitting under there just trying to mind their own business.'

'Is that not Japan?' queried Macannie.

'Isn't it poisonous fish with them?'

'And we thought the Batties were bad,' said the sheep. 'Do they have beards or moustaches, these North Koreans?'

'No, they're all clean shaven,' said Shenanigan. 'And your standard communist uniform now is the dark suit and tie. When all those eejits in suits line up at their party conference, you can't tell them apart.'

'And they're all men,' said Helen Brimstone. 'Those sort of countries are always ruled by men. Men in suits.'

'You don't think they're ahead of our game?' asked Lucy. 'That these men have just been cloning themselves?

'No they just look like that,' said Shenanigan. 'But some of them prefer the military fancy dress: their generals look like Gilbert and Sullivan traffic wardens, very comical if they weren't such vicious little tykes. You won't get many laughs out of those wee fellows. They keep their jokes for torture sessions and executions.'

'But if these North Korleans could choose for themselves,' asked Holly, 'would they leally want to be luled by fools and psychotics?'

'Of course not,' Helen Brimstone told her gently, 'but they have no choice. It's the same with us: we have choice of course, but we choose the least bad bunch of the idiots on offer. If you want to change the world, you need a lesson first in how and why the humans have made everything so awful.'

'The dreaded P word,' said Stein, 'P for pigging politicians.'

'And apathy,' Helen Brimstone added. 'We can't have sensible government because everything's fixed in favour of the power-mad men and their token women. And because no one believes anything else is possible, we just try to forget about them and go about our lives.'

'And they're surprised so few people want to vote for these ninnies,' Macannie chipped in. 'They complain about *our* apathy, as if *we* weren't interested in making the world a better place.'

'At least they aren't torturing us,' said Gumption. 'We have to put up with them wanting wars and all that, but they've got the power and the people can't do anything to stop them, especially since they were voted in by the majority of those who could be bothered to vote.'

'And there *ewe* have it in a nutshell,' said Sean Shenanigan.

'But this is what we have to change,' the sheep told her. 'One per cent of the pwofits from all the multinationals would save many countries from poverty and tyrwanny. And if the people contwolled their own lives, they wouldn't look to fwootcakes, pweests and extweemists for answers. Disempowerment is the pwoblem. It's what makes it possible for the Batties to take over. It's also why everweeone outside Amerwica dislikes the Amerwicans, because they have power but abuse it, out of gweed, ignorwance and self-wighteousness. And now the Wushuns are out of the picture, it's Amerwica and the multinationals versus the west of the world. So giving people economic power of their own must be the answer.'

'They'll have built in some protection against being Snowballed again,' said Stein.

'That channel may be closed,' the sheep told them, 'but our Langley mole is still burrowing away.

'Mole?' queried Stein.

'Sheep. I meant it metaphorwically: a virtual sheep acting as a mole. As a smokescween, I have now launched an investigation against myself which has the CIA wunning wownd in circles. Because they have no official existence, I've been able to divert funds for what they call Black Ops to the black sheep version without anyone noticing. So there will be enough left in the kitty to destabilise a few more cuntwees. I was thinking giving a few of those nasty Afwican dictators a wun for their money, with a cash injection from Shaman to put their people back on their feet. But we'll have to think of something else after that, especially for cuntwees like North Korwea, Earwan and Saudi Awabia.'

'The way those humans are,' said Holly, 'it has to be something that will cut thlew all the clap.'

Suddenly the sheep leapt up from his supine position on the chaise longue and sat back on his haunches.

'Eurweeka!' he exclaimed, waving a hoof in the air. 'That's it! By golly she's got it! That's how we'll scupper those North Korwean suit-wearers. Contwolled unstoppable nuclear weeversal in all their weactors, but set in *motion* in a way they'd *never* expect. More laterwall thinking, Sean! Holly's suggestion has just given me an idea!'

'Cutting thlew the clap?' queried Holly. 'A clap idea?'

'No, something that *cuts it out* metaphorwically speaking. *Think*, Holly, what do the humans do with all their excwement?'

'They go to a special loom devoted to their exclement plactices. They put it in a china bowl in some water.'

'And?...'

'They dlop little sheets of paper on top of it?'

'And?...'

Holly looked to the others for help.

'The Germans like to look at theirs for a bit,' offered Sean Shenanigan, 'so they put in a little shelf for the stuff to land on first. Then they check it out. Before they use their paper.'

'I don't think the Germans are the Americans' next target, Sean,' said Macannie. 'They'd bomb the French first.'

'You're right. I don't think the Germans will be giving us any more trouble. Not for a while anyway.'

'What next, Holly?' the sheep persisted.

'They use their waterfall machine to make it go away?'

'*Exactly*!' the sheep cried. '*Well*, what if...'